They'll need love and courage
to see the dawn…

He's a hometown native, returning from the war, determined to change the world he'd fought to protect. She's the girl who's been his secret friend since childhood, now a beautiful woman. Her wartime letters kept him alive. But he's black, and she's white.

In 1946, Gideon, Texas, their undeniable love might get them both killed.

Angel whispered his name and the tilt of events pushed them closer still. He hung in the moment, hearing the heavy, rhythmic pounding of the rain on the roof echoing in his chest, and he thought of a thousand things as his hand moved on her waist. He thought of their forays into the trees and of the letters she'd written to him through the war, letters that had leant courage and comfort and hope.

Wordlessly, she moved a step closer and raised her hand to his face. Lightly, lightly she touched her fingers to his mouth. Isaiah fell forward with a soft groan to press his head against her, his forehead close to her diaphragm, his nose against her stomach, his arms tight around her body. The smell of her filled his mouth, his heart, the world, and he breathed it in as if it would save him. She made a soft noise and bent into him, gathering his head closer, her cheek against his hair.

For a long, long moment, they rested together like that. He no longer felt the ache in his head or ankle. It didn't matter that the world outside this room would curse him, that bloody Texas had hanged men for less.

The Sleeping Night

by

Barbara Samuel

B

Bell Bridge Books

Bell Bridge Books
PO BOX 300921
Memphis, TN 38130
Print ISBN: 978-1-61194-127-2

Bell Bridge Books is an Imprint of BelleBooks, Inc.

We at BelleBooks enjoy hearing from readers.
Visit our websites – www.BelleBooks.com and www.BellBridgeBooks.com.

10 9 8 7 6 5 4 3 2 1
Cover design: Debra Dixon
Interior design: Hank Smith
Photo credits: Sky (manipulated) © David M. Schrader | Dreamstime.com
Girl in window (manipulated) © Yakov Stavchansky | Dreamstime.com

:Lstn:01:

Dedication

There is only one person this book could possibly be dedicated to, and that is Christopher Robin, aka Neal Barlow, who heard the story of a book I had stashed away, made me dig out the manuscript, paid to have it scanned (when such things were quite difficult), visited the British Imperial War Museum and the beaches of Normandy with me, listened to a thousand conversations about all of it. Mainly, it is because he believed and wouldn't let me give up that this book is making its way out into the world. Thank you!

PART ONE: DAWN

An angel, robed in spotless white,
Bent down and kissed the sleeping Night.
Night woke to blush; the sprite was gone.
Men saw the blush and called it Dawn.

—*Paul Laurence Dunbar*

—1—

Gideon, East Texas
2005

On the morning that Angel Corey was arriving back in her home town of Gideon, Kim McCoy buzzed around her bookstore like a mad woman, trying to get things ready. The author was arriving at 11 o'clock to talk to the Black And White Book Club.

Corey had written plenty of books in her eighty years, but mostly they were spiritual in nature—ponderings on the nature of the soul and God. And she was famous for a radio show she'd been hosting for some forty years now.

Her new book was different, written—or rather collected—to commemorate the sixtieth anniversary of the end of the war. In the window were copies of Corey's book, *War Letters (with Recipes)*, which had been deemed frivolous by MariAnna Hayden, who was twenty-four and Very Serious About Books and never liked it when they picked something with even a hint of romance or "traditional" women's work, like recipes.

The older women in the group let MariAnna rage, remembering their own days of drama and agitation, and went ahead and read the book anyway. They read it for the Gideon connection, mainly, and to give themselves a bit of a pat on the back. The book club had been instrumental, after all, in the war memorial that was being christened today.

But the older women cried over Corey's book, too, remembering things in their own lives. Remembering a time when things were harder, when the town wasn't quite as easy in its skin as it was now.

Kim stacked copies of the book, with its cover of handwritten V-Mails, in the front window of her bookstore, Morning Books. She had taken the name from a poem by Paul Lawrence Dunbar. The store, cozy with armchairs and plenty of shelves and corners, sat right on the main drag of Gideon proper, a bookstore that featured African American books mostly, with some local history.

Which was actually another point of contention with MariAnna, that they were bringing a white author to an African American bookstore. MariAnna wasn't black or even biracial, like Kim herself, but she made more noise than anyone. Honestly, she got on Kim's last nerve, but she was grandmothered in since *her* grandmother had been an original member of the Black And Whites.

Kim said it was *her* bookstore and if she wanted purple people in it, she'd invite them. The Black and Whites backed her up.

The book club had been meeting once a month since five young women, three white and two black, had established the reading group in 1972. The South had not been entirely integrated in those days, and they had felt very daring and *avant garde*. Their first book reflected that: *Fear of Flying*, by Erica Jong. It broke the ice and let them read pretty much anything else they wanted after that, including some incendiary things like *The Letters of Angela Davis* and, later, *Helter Skelter*, after which they reckoned they didn't much care for true crime.

They kept the rules loose, and the selection of titles absolutely fair. Each person put her name on a list (there were only women, no matter how often they tried to tempt spouses, sons, fathers, friends into the club) and when a name came up, the book club read whatever book she chose. Period. Each reader had one veto she could utilize once every two years (which was so strict because of Betty Michelin, who didn't like anything but mysteries and killed pretty much everything else that came up; Betty quit the club the very next month and everyone breathed a sigh of relief).

The Black And Whites had struggled a time or two. Once was when they decided to brave themselves and public opinion and go see a Spike Lee movie. It ended up hurting just about every single person's feelings on some level, requiring Augusta Younger, then president, to call a halt to the evening discussion and send everybody home to cool off. The subject of the film was forbidden for one year, and at that time they all had cooler heads and could talk about it a little more calmly.

The club now had twelve members, five white and seven black. They tried to keep it more or less half and half, to preserve the spirit of the founders, but the truth was, they hadn't lost a member or picked up a new one in nearly three years, since MariAnna joined, taking her grandmother's spot. One year before that, Johniqua Younger, just turned nineteen, had joined, taking the spot left vacant by Tillie High, who had finally died of the lung cancer that nagged her for years.

The whole group had said, *too bad Tillie wasn't alive* for this day. *Too bad she couldn't be here for this.*

Kim stepped back to look at the store through narrowed eyes. Would it pass muster? This was the most important guest they'd ever had.

If not for the book club, Kim would not own the bookstore that was her pride and joy, complete with two cats—one white, one black, naturally—who chased the mice away and kept customers company when they curled up in an easy chair. If not for the bookstore, she would not had the courage to leave her husband, who was not abusive, not evil, just completely and utterly wrong for her.

The Black And Whites were all aflutter about Angel Corey coming to town. Years ago, everybody in Gideon had thought she died, of course. That was the funny part of the title of one of her books, *The Resurrection of Angel Corey*. This morning the first thing Angel was going to do in Gideon was visit her grave and put some flowers down on it. Kim thought it was morbid, but what did she know? She was only thirty-six. Graves seemed a long way out.

At ten, Kim did a walk-through. They'd agreed to a morning meeting since the ceremony for the Medal of Honor winners and the unveiling of the Gideon WWII memorial was at two pm. They'd all want to be there for that, too, of course, especially Angel.

The book club, along with one guest each, strictly enforced, started gathering by 10:20. All women, because Angel's brand of spirituality had been directed at women all along, all ages, from old to young. They brought mock apple pie made with Ritz crackers, and Spam with beans, and somebody even tracked down some Postum, which Kim thought was just about the nastiest thing she'd ever tasted.

At 11 o'clock on the dot, a black car drove up with proper pomp. A beautiful young man got out of the driver's seat, tall and caramel skinned, with a glaze of black hair smooth against his head.

"Hel-*lo!*" said Johniqua Younger.

They *all* swooned over the way he opened the door and helped the woman within to her feet, but then she brushed his hand away and he laughed, making it plain they knew each other.

And Kim had to touch her tummy to rub at the butterflies, because there was Angel Corey herself, her hair snow white and clipped short. She was a little stooped, but otherwise looked spry in a chic dress, belted at the waist. Her arms were full of bracelets, and she strode into the store with an air of happy expectancy.

"Hello," she said. "I reckon you're all waiting for me." She smiled, looking at each one of them in turn. "Now, which one of you is Paul's granddaughter?"

Kim stepped forward, and lifted a hand shyly. "Here," she said with a little squeak.

And Angel Corey, who was famous in sixteen countries, and had written twelve books, and had established a foundation named after her own father, Parker Corey, came forward and kissed her on the cheek. "I am so happy to meet you, sweetheart." She squeezed Kim's arm. "Thank you for giving me a reason to come back to Gideon."

"Thank you for coming," Kim managed. She gestured toward the food. "We made . . . um . . . lots of things. From the war."

Angel smiled, her pale green eyes as beautiful as they were in her pictures, and took Kim's hand. "How about if I read a little first? You want to come sit beside me? I think," she said, taking what the Black And White's called The Queen's Chair, because it was the chair the book club leader always sat in, "that there's only one thing I can read from."

Sunny Walker, as pretty as her name, edged forward, holding the book out. "*The War Letters?*"

Angel nodded and took the book. Only then did Kim see that the old woman was struggling with high emotion. "Can I get you something? Water, coffee?"

"No, sweetheart." She squeezed Kim's hand. "An old woman is allowed to be emotional." A glaze of tears brightened the green eyes even more, and she paused for a long moment, taking in the group seated in a circle around her. "I'm looking at all of you and thinking how happy my father would be to see your book club. This is a fine, fine day, and I'm so proud to be with you."

The young man at the back of the room edged forward, grabbing a bite off the table before he sat down nearby Johniqua, who straightened and pretended to ignore him. He smiled, and scooted over one more chair so he was sitting beside her.

Angel composed herself, opened her book, and began to read.

"*It began with a letter from Isaiah High, who had been my friend when we were children, but not for a very long time.*

"*November 25, 1942*

"*Dear Angel,*

"*I heard from my mama about Solomon and I'm just writing to tell you how sorry I am . . .*

PART TWO: DUSK

And who shall separate the dust
What later we shall be?

—*Georgia Douglas Johnson*

— 2 —

Gideon, Texas
1926

Everybody always said too bad about Angel Corey, living out there on the edge of Lower Gideon with only her crazy daddy Parker and no mama to put her straight.

The word in town was that Parker had seen a vision in the trenches of France in the Great War, just before they shipped him home for the gangrene in his feet. Parker never spoke about it, but it was clear he took seriously the notion of Jesus being "the least of these," because from that day forward he treated every rag-tag stranger and down-and-out colored like the good Lord himself.

Had it just been Parker by himself, living like some crazy preacher out there in his store, folks might have turned a blind eye. A Corey had run the store since the War Between the States, after all, and he wasn't much trouble, miles down the road from Gideon proper. A man had a right to make a profit and, though the coloreds had little enough, they spent most of what they had right there in Parker's store.

But his little girl was the kind of child people never can leave alone. No accident she was called Angel. Gobs of spun-sugar hair the color of morning and great green eyes as strange as her mama's, who appeared in Gideon out of nowhere one hot summer day and died one quick year later when her baby came into the world. Women were always sending Angel clothes they'd cut down from something of their own, and *tsking* over her hair when they saw her at church. More tongues wagged over the lack of a woman to put pin curls in those tresses than over Parker's lack of inclination to marry again, though both received considerable discussion.

Among the men in town, another subject took precedence over her curls or lack of them. They worried about what kind of ideas she was picking up down there. Only decent people she ever saw was the ones at church and the odd farmer stopping in at Corey's if he didn't want to go all the way to town. Parker had even taught her to call colored people by their last names—Mrs. this and Mr. that. More than one person had tried to talk her out of that habit, including her aunt Georgia, Parker's own sister. Georgia told Angel it was plain silly, that habit of hers—she wouldn't call a dog Mr. Spot, now would she?

But typical for Angel, that's just what she started doing. Every dog and every cat, Mr. Rover and Mrs. Puffy.

Lotta people decided right then she was lost.

Tsk as they might, Angel never felt overlooked or unloved. She had her daddy, who told her stories at bedtime—stories about faraway places, about the chateaus and vineyards he'd seen in France, about brave soldiers and pretty dancing girls in cafés in Paris. In his voice, even the stories about Noah and Abraham took on a special sense of excitement. He read to her about King Arthur and Merlin; about elves and leprechauns; about all kinds of places and people and things nobody but her daddy seemed to know.

She also never missed her mother, seeing as she'd never had one to miss. Anyway, if she needed a mama, there was always Geraldine High, who scooped Angel up in her lap on the warm Texas nights, singing to her on the porch of the store while her husband Jordan—who was the only other man in the whole county who'd gone to Europe for the Great War—and Parker talked late in the night.

Angel often shared Mrs. High's cushiony bosom with Isaiah, both of them falling asleep as she sang lullabies. Isaiah, two years older, was sometimes her best friend, sometimes her brother. It was Isaiah who listened with her to the stories her daddy read, Isaiah who brought her bluebonnets and wild daisies, Isaiah who colored church pictures with her late at night.

It seemed to her that a child could not have a better life than she did. She would sit on a corner of the porch on Saturday nights, her legs tucked up under her dress, and listen to the voices swirling around and into her bones, a quick-slow rhythm in the black voices that was unlike the voices of the white folks in church. Sometimes, with the indigo summer sky stretched overhead, she would listen to Jordan High laughing and think of God: God in a good mood, like he never was in church; God like he must have been when he made the sky. It was a luxurious sound, rich with knowledge and awareness and love. She'd close her eyes and let that laughing flow through her, thinking of God with a black face and strong black hands, and all the children of the world gathered into his lap.

She had enough sense to know that she couldn't tell her Sunday school teacher that she thought God must be black. The God in church wore long robes and a long beard and he was always mad about the sinners. But in church on Sunday mornings, she never felt God spinning around in her heart and head, so big, like he did on Saturday nights when Jordan High laughed.

One August night, Angel sat on the front porch of the store in her bare feet, waving away mosquitoes with a cardboard fan. They ate her like she was lunch, and her ankles were already spotted with bites she couldn't resist scratching.

A slow stream of customers came in, as they did every Saturday. Laughter spilled out of the screen door behind her, and the radio was playing and, nearby the window, two men swapped friendly insults about something that happened that afternoon in a cotton field. Over all the voices, her daddy's, deep and full, boomed out greetings to his customers.

From down the road, on foot, came a pair of travelers, one tall, one small. Angel straightened expectantly and waved. Isaiah dashed ahead of his father and ran to the porch.

"Hey, Angel," he said. "Look what I found down by the river." He held up the papery skin of a snake, almost whole.

"Can I see it?" Angel asked.

"You *lookin'* at it now, girl," he said. "You can hold it, too, if you want. Careful though. I ain't never found one like this before."

As Angel held out her hands, palms up so as not to wound it, the boy's father gained the small pool of yellow light cast through the windows of the store. "Evening, Miss Angel," he said in his deep voice. "How you doin' tonight?"

"Just fine, Mr. High." She displayed the skin. "You see what Isaiah found?"

"That's quite a prize," he agreed and touched his son's shoulder before going up the steps to the store.

Isaiah sank down next to her. Bony knees stuck out from below his cut-off pants. His ankles were streaked, his shoes muddy, and he smelled like sunshine and dust and river water. "How come you don't get scared like other girls?"

"What's to be scared of? I think it's pretty."

"Me, too, but Florence Younger screeched like she seen a ghost when I showed it to her."

Angel shrugged and handed it back to him. "You wanna do somethin'?"

"Yeah." He grinned, his wide mouth a mix of half-grown teeth and baby teeth and two that had almost reached full size. "Go on and get your daddy's book. The big one."

Angel looked at him for a moment.

"Go on," he said, nudging her, a secret in his dancing dark eyes.

Suspecting a trick, she nevertheless did as he said, finding the book on the table in the living room where it always sat. As she hurried back through the thinning collection of customers in the aisles, her daddy caught her arm. "Where you think you going with that book, gal?"

"Just to the porch, Daddy. Isaiah said to get it."

Parker pursed his lips, then let her go. "Be careful with it, hear?"

Angel drew herself up to her full height, the heavy book clasped against her chest. "Have you ever known me or Isaiah either one to be uncareful with a book?"

Behind her, a man chuckled; Parker, meeting the man's eye, grinned, too. As she hurried on her way, she heard somebody say, "You got your hands full with that 'un. Smart as a whip, she is."

But Angel paid it little attention. Grown folks always talked like that about her, and about Isaiah, too. Which was why she imagined they had become friends. Somebody was always shaking their heads about one or the other of them, or making a little sound in their mouths like the food was good, "Mmn-mm-mm." Only in this case it was a "what are you ever gonna do with that child?" noise.

Once, some grown-up had looked at Parker and Jordan, talking quietly by themselves and said (like Angel and Isaiah were deaf) "What are you gonna do about those children?" Straight out.

Parker had looked at the woman through the smoke of his cigarette and said, "I don't aim to do nothing. They're children."

The woman had made that sound in her throat, then gone on with her shopping. Isaiah and Angel had talked about it and decided the difference they felt in themselves was the fact that both their daddies had gone to France for the war. They came back different, so naturally their children were different, too.

Parker often read to them on these soft Saturday nights after all the customers went home. He read a lot of books. But this one, both agreed, was the best. *Fairy Tales from Around the World.*

Angel carried the book outside to Isaiah.

"Sit down," he said, the secret spreading now to his face, where a dimple winked in his cheek. He opened the book with ceremony. "Which one you want?" he said.

Still puzzled, she shrugged. "I don't care."

"Come on, Angel. You always pick one."

"Okay. *Hansel and Gretel.*" She giggled, because he hated it. It scared him.

But without a single protest, he opened the book to the story and began to read, *"Once upon a time . . ."*

Angel listened, her mouth hanging open for a long, long moment, staring at him as he bent his head over the open pages. He didn't read it as good as her daddy did, but it was a whole lot better than what Angel could have done.

"You can *read?*"

"You hear me, don't you?" But a grin betrayed his belligerent tone, and he softened. "Pretty good, huh? I been practicin' all summer. Your daddy gave me a book of my very own."

"Oh, you're doin' real good." She tucked her dress over her knees. "Read me some more."

And he did.

Much later, Parker and Jordan came out on the porch, where the children had moved to drawing with pencils on flat sheets of butcher paper. The men's voices drifted over Angel, making her sleepy, and she laid her head down on her hands to rest for just a minute. Their words were indistinct, only their voices plain, and she waited for the laughing that would come.

But tonight their voices were serious. Isaiah's great dark eyes focused on the men, the crayon in his hand forgotten.

"What's wrong?" Angel asked him.

He frowned in a puzzled way, his gaze fixed on his father. "I ain't too sure," he said in a soft voice. "Somethin'."

Parker glanced at the children. "Little pitchers have big ears," he said, pursing his lips.

"Well," said Jordan, a gentle smile replacing the worry in his face, "so they do. You children done already?"

Isaiah glanced at Angel quickly. If they said yes, then Jordan would stand up and hold out his hand for Isaiah. The evening would be over. "No, sir," he said.

"Whyn't you come on over here, anyway. Let me tell you a story tonight." He settled back in the chair to make room on his long legs for both children. They scrambled up and he looped an arm around each, slowly beginning to rock back and forth in the still night. Parker turned off the porch light, then lit a cigarette, ice clinking in his tea as he lifted the glass to his lips.

Angel settled her cheek against Jordan's shirt. Isaiah rested his head on his daddy's shoulder. The gentle rocking made Angel sleepy and she yawned, closing her eyes as Jordan's deep voice rumbled through his chest into her ear. "A long, long time ago . . ." he began.

Long as she could hear that velvety rich voice in her mind as she drifted off to sleep, Angel didn't even care about the story. Isaiah shifted, his knee bumping hers, and she drew her legs a little closer to give him more room. She heard him take in a shuddery, long breath that turned into a hard yawn. Without opening her eyes, she smiled.

Much later, she stirred, and found herself in her own bed. Foggily, she turned over. She listened for a minute, and sure enough, the sound of her daddy and Jordan talking came in through her window. She drifted away again.

The next Saturday was the last of the month. Things had gone pretty much like always all day. Angel ran errands for her daddy, fetching lengths of cloth and keeping tea brewed to cool the lips of the customers. As she worked, she kept looking for Isaiah, who was always first through the door.

The night grew later; the customers drifted away. Angel's daddy told her to get the broom and start sweeping up.

She was angling the old broom under the lip of a set of shelves when Isaiah burst through the screen door, letting it slam hard behind him. His face was dirty, his clothes askew, and his chest heaved like he'd been running a long way.

An immediate hush fell over the voices of the remaining customers, voices that had, until that minute, been rolling easily about the long front room of the store. All eyes fell on the boy, including Angel's. They knew, looking at that face, that whatever they heard wasn't going to be good. Angel felt her stomach fall to her feet and she clenched the handle of the broom with fingers that would be full of splinters the next day. Isaiah's eyes swiveled around the room, lit on Angel, and passed to her father, who broke the silence.

"What is it, Isaiah? Speak up, child, speak up."

"Mama said come get you." His voice was thin with horror. "They killed my daddy." His lip trembled, his eyes wide and shimmering with terror. "They killed him—"

At the remembered ugliness, Isaiah fell straight to the floor in a dead faint. Later, Angel didn't remember doing it, but she ran to Isaiah, washed his face with a cloth she had wet with cool water, then helped him out to the porch to get some air when he came around with a jerk. By then there was hardly anybody else around; only a few women with a keening sound to their voices and a worry in their whispers.

It didn't make sense to Angel right away, about Jordan High being dead because it was the first time in her life (unless you counted her mama—and she didn't remember *her*) anybody she knew died. As she sat holding Isaiah's hand in the darkness of the porch, she heard the rich sound of Jordan High laughing in her mind. She looked at the stars and Isaiah wept. Angel held his hand in the darkness, feeling something big and sad move inside of her. But instead of tears, she held on to the thought of Jordan High in heaven, laughing with God.

After a time, there came the flicker of torches and flashlights through the trees, winking in the darkness of thick pines. Isaiah dried his eyes and let go of Angel's hand. He stared at the silent crowd. A hardness drew up his face as he watched the pinpoints of light weave toward them, and Angel had enough sense to know not to say a word.

PART THREE: DARK

How arrives it joy lies slain
And why unblooms the best hope ever sown?

—Thomas Hardy "Hap"

When I was a child, I spake as a child, I understood as a child, I thought as child: but when I became a man I put away childish things.

—I Corinthians 13:11

— 3 —

Mrs. *Rachel Pierson*
#2 Old Farm Road
Gideon, Texas

June 29, 1945

Dear Isaiah High,

    I went yesterday to Corey's store, for Parker is not well. There I saw your mother and, when I asked after your health, she shared the news that you have decided to stay in Europe for a time. She gave me your address when I said I might have a job for you to do, if you are interested.

    It has been a long, difficult war and you must be very tired (I remember well the exhaustion of the soldiers in our last war) so, if you cannot do this thing for me, I will understand.

    My wish is this: that you would see for me if there are any of my sister's family remaining alive. They were Jews from Holland, and I had hopes I might hear from them when the war ended, but I have not. There was my sister, her husband, and their daughter, who will now be in her middle twenties. I will be happy to pay you what ever you wish. I want only to know if any of them are still alive so that I do not have to spend the rest of my life worrying if one of them is starving. If you find any of them alive, I will take them in here.

    Please let me know at your earliest convenience if this is a task you wish to undertake.

Sincerely,

Mrs. Rachel Pierson

— 4 —

Gideon, Texas
May, 1946

By the time the train reached Texas, Isaiah felt like he'd been traveling a thousand years. He was weary of sitting and wanted a meal that filled him even more than he wanted a night's sleep. His temper had been boiling for thirty-six hours and, if he'd had any doubts that he could return home for any length of time, riding Jim Crow through the South, where his uniform with its bars meant nothing at all, had disabused him of that notion.

He had been in Europe for more than four years, first in England, then across France and into Germany. He'd understood that his service had changed him. Until he'd been forced to board the colored car at the Mason Dixon line, he had not realized that it might be impossible to return to the Jim Crow South, to fit himself back into the rigors of a system that now seemed antiquated and peculiar.

However much he and his fellow soldiers had changed, it was clear the South had not. Companions warned him with stories of the beatings that soldiers received when, after long years away, they forgot themselves and tipped counter girls or filled paper cups with water from white water fountains.

Some of them, naturally, were young men who wanted to test the walls upon their return, soldiers full of themselves and the guns they'd held and the freedom they'd discovered on foreign shores.

Most had just forgotten. A grandmother in a blue calico dress warned Isaiah that there were always those willing to remind a colored man of his place.

"Yes, ma'am," he said. "Thank you kindly."

Isaiah worried over Gudren, up front in the white cars—worried about her being alone in her frail state, with her accented English. He'd found her in a refugee camp, half-dead, and it had taken several months before she'd been well enough to travel. Those months had given her some dignity, giving her time to flesh her emaciated frame, grow some hair, lose a little of her refugee look. She would still be plainly a stranger. He didn't like to think of anyone being rude to her.

Though, considering all, a little rudeness wouldn't be anything much to a woman who'd survived the camps.

At last they made it to Gideon. Isaiah and Gudren were the only passengers to get off the train.

"This is Texas?" she asked in wonder. "I thought it would be a desert. This is beautiful."

"I reckon it can be." He picked up her bag. "Let's look for Miz Pierson."

The car, a long fat Chrysler, waited near the door of the station. An old white man had evidently driven the car, for he still sat behind the wheel. Standing outside it was blind Mrs. Pierson, her chin jutting out. Only her hands, restlessly wringing themselves, gave her away. Her face had aged thirty years since he had left just before the war. It made him sad.

"Miz Pierson," Isaiah said, "I brought you your niece, just like I promised. This here's Gudren Stroo."

The two women met with outstretched hands. Each waited a little shyly, until Gudren said quietly, "My mother talked about you so much."

Tears, unmistakable in the late afternoon sunlight slanting through the pines around the station, glittered in Mrs. Pierson's sightless eyes. "I only wish it could have been sooner," she whispered.

Gudren bent to hug her aunt and Isaiah stepped back, his throat closed. It was worth coming back to Texas, worth Jim Crow a hundred times, to deliver this single life into the keeping of one who knew and cared.

As he slung his duffel bag over his shoulder, Mrs. Pierson's voice halted him. "Isaiah High," she said.

He turned. "Come see me in the morning. We have things to settle between us."

"No, Miz Pierson. We're square."

"Perhaps," she replied. "Nonetheless, I wish you would take the time. You must allow me to thank you for this precious work you've done."

Isaiah hesitated, knowing she would press more money on him. He didn't aim to accept it, but there was no harm in stopping by anyway. He nodded. "All right, then. I'll be there."

Gudren stepped up to him and held out her hand. "Thank you."

Isaiah, conscious of the curious faces of the onlookers, ignored her hand and kept his head angled low. "You're welcome. You get well, now."

He left them, setting out toward home. As he passed through

Gideon proper, he kept his gaze fixed firmly on his path so that he wouldn't be required to speak to anyone, wouldn't accidently meet the eyes of anyone who'd take offense. It shamed him to do it, after so long walking like a man in the world.

Even with his lowered eyes, it was apparent nothing in Gideon had changed in his absence. Women still shopped in flowered cotton dresses, men still gathered in little knots by their cars to talk cotton. He felt their eyes following him.

What had he expected? He shook his head. Something. The entire world had turned itself inside out, spilling intestines from one corner of the globe to the other. Fifty million people were dead, Europe was almost destroyed, and horrors he could barely comprehend had been unleashed.

But here, white folks lived in Gideon proper, black folks across the river and down the road in lower Gideon. The library wouldn't give him a book and he better not try stopping for a beer until he crossed that bridge.

His walk carried him through a path in the woods by the Coreys' store, but he didn't stop. He glimpsed the worn roof through the trees, and the sight brought a surprising clutch of sorrow and... what? Nostalgia, maybe. A time lost to him.

Parker and Angel. Before he left, he would have to stop to see them. On his way out.

He crossed the bridge into Lower Gideon, black Gideon. Here the houses sat a little bit farther apart, leaving room for chickens and hogs and the occasional cow. Almost every yard boasted the flat of a newly planted garden.

Nothing had changed here, either. Houses still had need of a good coat of paint. Rickety rockers sat on rickety porches. He took a breath against the pang it gave him, seeing the truth. They were so damned poor. He'd forgotten—poor and proud, or poor and tired, or poor and defeated, but poor. Here and there, fresh whitewash had been applied to a fence or a new screen door hung. Here and there, holes in windows had been patched with cardboard, or pigs had ruined a yard.

In the middle of the afternoon, there was no one much about. Field workers were planting cotton for the farmers who spread for twenty miles in either direction. Domestics were busy cooking and cleaning in genteel Upper Gideon. Those unlucky or unmotivated enough to have no work at all slept or gathered in the back rooms of the juke joint further down river. Isaiah saw only Mrs. Cane, hoeing in her garden, an apron tied around her dress. She didn't see him and Isaiah didn't holler.

His mama's house sat as close to the river as the Corey store on the other side, and Isaiah knew if he jumped in and swam across, he'd be able to jog through the woods in a nearly straight line to the tree house he and Solomon and Angel had built. Not that he would, not with copperheads and water moccasins lurking in those sleepy depths, but once he had. He shook his head at the memory. A wonder he hadn't been bit to death.

It was plain no one was home in the High house. If his sister had been there, she would have had the radio on, and his mother never worked without singing something. A gentle quiet surrounded the simple house with its polished windows and swept walk. Someone had recently built a new set of steps up to the porch. The new wood gleamed in contrast to the old pine boards above it.

Inside, Isaiah took off his hat and hung it automatically on the coat tree, pausing at the scent of home hanging so richly in the room, a combination of cooking fat and lemon oil and a hint of his mother's talcum, an unexpectedly powerful mix, like the sight of the roof of the Coreys' store.

Then the nostalgic mood broke with a vicious growl from his belly and he headed for the kitchen, finding two leftover chops, gravy and three biscuits from breakfast. There was even, to Isaiah's deep delight, half a pecan pie. He wolfed all of it down. Finding himself still longing for more, he scrounged around in a closet for a fishing pole. Time of day wasn't the best, but he figured he might catch a catfish for supper. Surprise his mama when she got home.

Geraldine High walked slowly up the road toward home. Her right knee ached with a vengeance, which told her there would be rain in a day or two. It was swollen twice its normal size, and she'd be lucky to sleep tonight with the pain of it. In her shoulders was a weariness born of lifting and folding and scrubbing. With one palm, she rubbed the tight spot.

The earthy scent of frying catfish drifted out into the early evening air as she walked up the porch steps. Geraldine thought gratefully that her daughter Tillie must have gotten home from the cotton fields early. Maybe a neighbor had dropped by the fish after a good catch. Whatever it was, she was thankful that for once she didn't have to cook it.

She headed straight for her bedroom when she came in, unbuttoning her blouse as she went, thinking about the day. Mrs. Hayden's grandchildren had been underfoot since they'd tumbled out of bed at breakfast.

"Never met such a pack of undisciplined children in my life," she muttered, shedding her skirt. They'd run through the kitchen, trompled up and down the stairs and slammed out the back door, scattering their things all over the place. Mrs. Hayden had told Geraldine not to worry herself about the children, to let them pick up their own things. Easier said than done when their toys were on the counters where Geraldine cooked, when their squabbling spilled into the kitchen. Once, she thought, pulling a loose cotton housedress from her closet, once she would have scolded any child in her kitchen, given them an ear boxing they wouldn't forget and sent them firmly outside with their games. Now . . .

She sighed. Both she and Mrs. Hayden were too old for all those children.

In her loose, comfortable dress, she went toward the kitchen, giving her scalp a good scratching. "I tell you, Tillie, I'm going to get after those children tomorrow. Can't be letting them run all over like that. I'm so tired tonight I can't even see straight." She breathed deep. "That cat sure smells good, honey."

It was only then that she looked up. And it wasn't Tillie home from the fields at all. It was her son Isaiah, grown as broad and sturdy as his daddy, looking so such like him (*except for his eyes*, she thought proudly, *those eyes are mine*) that it nearly gave her turn. With a little cry of joy, she moved forward, lifting her hands to cup his face. "Isaiah! What are you doing here? Why didn't you tell me?"

"It was a surprise." A full, rich chuckle rumbled up in his throat and he scooped her into his arms. "I sure missed you, Mama."

His arms were like blocks of wood, his shoulders broad as oak trees. "Put me down!" she protested, laughing. But she gripped him back, relief flooding her. It was good, so good to have her child in her kitchen, lifting her clear off the floor and laughing in her ear. Tears stung her eyes for a minute. They were blinked away by the time he let her gently down.

He kissed her head. "I figured you might be hungry."

Looking at all the food piled up on the counter, she said, "You didn't have to go all through this, son. I'd have fed you."

Isaiah bent to check the cornbread browning in the oven. "Naw, Mama. I ate everything you had in this kitchen when I got home. Had to make up for that." He pushed her toward the table. "You set down and put up your feet. We'll eat in a minute. What time Tillie get home?"

Geraldine waved a hand. "No telling. She may not *be* home. Girl's gone wild, Isaiah. Spends most her time over to Harry's, raisin' Cain." She sighed. Her youngest had always been in trouble. She needed a daddy, that's what ailed her. Now she spent all her time looking for somebody to fill up that empty spot and, when nobody could, drank it away. In one way, Geraldine understood it. In another, Tillie had been better taught than that. She'd come to a bad end one day.

But that was her second child. This one standing before her, her eldest and her son, was something else again. Not that he wasn't no trouble, because he sure had been in his turn. Too proud and too smart for his own good and, as she eyed him now, she didn't see that had changed much.

Maybe war had taught him prudence.

Guiltily she thought about Parker Corey. She oughta tell him. But later. Right now, she was going to keep him all to herself and eat the meal he'd cooked for her and drink in the wonder of his presence right here in her kitchen. After supper. There would be time enough then to tell him.

She stopped for one minute behind him, putting her head against his back. "Boy, I missed you more than I can even tell you."

"I know, Mama," he rumbled. "Me, too."

They talked all through supper, and he told her stories—safe stories, funny stories, not the dark or ugly ones—then Isaiah cleaned up the supper dishes. Now, his ribs straining after the huge meal, he squatted against the south wall of the house, smoking a Chesterfield. The sound of the river swishing and splashing mixed with the copper-edged notes of a steel guitar in the juke joint—Harry's—not far away.

Texas weighed in the air like blood. Isaiah smelled the faint rot of growth on the riverbank, smelled cornbread and bacon fat and somebody baking a chocolate cake. All of it was familiar, the signposts of his childhood. Once, he had taken pleasure in the view of the sky through the branches of cottonwoods that lined the river and clogged the sewers around lower Gideon, had felt his heart pumping in joy at the sound of the music playing down yonder.

Tonight, he could barely breathe. His nose had learned other scents—lavender and heather and death. Gideon had become like one of the places he'd read about as a child. Real, surely, but without meaning.

The man he had become could not bow under the weight of this old Gideon. One way or the other, it would kill him if he stayed. His plan had been to see his mother and sister tonight, then head out tomorrow, maybe west to Colorado or California. He meant to pause at the Corey store only long enough to tip his hat before he jumped back on that train and took himself out of Texas. He wasn't a man that needed lessons taught more than one time.

But now he'd learned that Parker Corey was dead, had been buried only a few days before. Whatever he said to himself, he knew he'd pay his respects, both to Parker and to his daughter, widowed by the same war that had spared Isaiah.

Flicking away the butt, he straightened—and started as a figure appeared in the trees beyond the house. He frowned, trying to make out who it was.

His sister strolled into the light—but not the child he'd left. "Lord have mercy," he said, shaking his head, for she was six feet tall and broad shouldered, with a ripe, lush figure beneath her worn dress. He whistled, low and long, in admiration. "Honey, you did some growing while I was gone."

She whooped and ran toward him, up the steps to throw herself into a back breaking hug, bringing with her a scent of whiskey. "So did you," she said, and broke away from him saucily. "But while I got better, you just got uglier."

A little bit tight, Isaiah thought as she flung herself upon the porch rail. Something tense and wound and hard inside of her. He propped a foot up on the rail and shook a cigarette out of the pack toward her. "That's all right, honey," he said with a lift of his eyebrows. "I got all I need."

"Little easier to find it someplace else," she said, dipping her head to the match he held. "Men get to run away. A woman's always stuck behind."

"You wanted to go fight Germans, Tillie?"

"Bet I'm as strong as most the men you fought with, bigger than most." She spit a bit of tobacco from her tongue. "Don't see why I couldn't have learned to fire a rifle."

"Yeah, well, it wasn't no adventure."

She jumped off the rail restlessly, and moved a few feet to stare into the dark. "Maybe. Maybe not. All over now, anyway."

He thought of the rubble in the cities, the empty, blasted fields. It would be a long time before Europe forgot. But he didn't want to talk about the war. "I hear you broke my record for picking cotton."

"I sure did." She grinned, showing straight white teeth and the same dimple Isaiah had. "Mama tell you?"

"Angel wrote me about it."

Tillie stared at him for a minute, smoking, her long, exotic eyes unreadable. "She wrote you letters?"

He nodded. "I think she wrote every soldier in town."

"I don't know about all that," she said quietly. Then, "You heard Parker died, I guess."

"Mama said it wasn't but a few days ago. Can't believe I missed him by so little."

"It was a blessing, Isaiah. You better off remembering him the way he used to be. It's a wonder he lived as long as he did." She shifted and smiled in memory. "*He* didn't think it was so silly I wanted to be a soldier.

Told me I'd be a good one—and I would've been, too."

Isaiah smiled back. "I reckon you would have. Probably better than me—I didn't like it."

"Someday," she said wistfully. "Maybe I'll have a granddaughter goes to war someday."

He touched her shoulder. "Maybe it'd be better if we didn't have no more wars instead."

"Yeah." She snorted, then ground her cigarette beneath her heel. "Give me a hug. I gotta get me some sleep before I fall over. I'm glad you're home, 'Saiah," she said, hugging him tight. "I really missed you."

In the morning, Isaiah went by Mrs. Pierson's as he'd promised. She tried pressing money on him, and he refused—she'd already sent him a bundle, and he had money saved from his pay through the war. He didn't need it.

She offered him a job, rearranging her considerable yard. He gently turned that down, too. "I'm not staying, Miz Pierson. I'll spend a few days with my mama, then I'm on the next train out."

"I reckon you'll want to pay your respects to Angel Corey at least."

He bowed his head. He'd been thinking maybe he could skip out. What difference would it make?

As if she sensed his hesitation, Mrs. Pierson said, "Her father—"

"I know," he said curtly, hands laced together. "He saved my life. I owe him."

"I was going to say her father loved you like a son."

Which just shamed him that much more.

After leaving her big house, he cut toward the river where it ran through town and followed it north to the cemetery where Parker had been laid four days before.

It was an old, old graveyard, the ground uneven with the roots of trees buckling the earth, knocking headstones a kilter in the oldest areas. In the midday sunlight, the air was still and green and quiet, broken only by the twitter of finches fluttering in the branches. He paused, feeling the peace of it ease down his neck.

As he stood there, wondering if he really wanted to visit a grave or just go on home, Angel Corey came from the town end of the graveyard by herself.

Isaiah stepped backward, hiding himself beneath the low hanging arms of a pine tree. She came slowly, weaving through the headstones in her ambling way, wearing a simple white dress with a wide collar, legs bare, feet stuck into a pair of slides. She was slight beneath the vastness of the Texas sky, and the pale, fine hair just skimmed her narrow shoulders, straight as if she'd used a ruler to cut it.

She was older, too. Skinnier. Not a beauty, never that, but still pretty as she'd ever been.

At Parker's grave, she knelt, brushing that hair out of her face with an impatient hand, and placed a handful of flowers on the freshly turned earth. Then she stood and let her hands hang at her sides. Isaiah thought she might be talking, but he was too far away to tell for sure.

She looked so damned alone. Lonely. And it was no illusion. Her husband had been torpedoed in the Pacific three years before and, with her daddy gone, there wasn't going to be anybody else in Angel's corner.

Sure as hell couldn't be Isaiah.

What he should do was go on and get it over with, he thought, give her his condolences and get himself on out of Gideon. But he couldn't seem to make himself move forward. Or away.

As he watched, she lifted her face to the sunshine and closed her eyes. Little as she was, he thought she looked strong. He swallowed the thickness in his throat, then turned away and walked back toward home the way he'd come, a thousand memories of her presenting themselves to him. Angel as a little girl, and a teenager, as a widow writing him letter after letter, keeping his spirits up. He hadn't told her he was coming back, either. He'd stopped writing to her once the war was over. It had been time to create some distance again.

Along the way through the woods, he found himself plucking wildflowers. When the worn roof of the Corey store came in view, he left the dimness of the forest to put the flowers on the step, where she'd be sure to find them when she came back home. For a long conflicted minute, he wondered if he ought to just wait for her.

Tomorrow, he thought, crossing the bridge to lower Gideon, maybe tomorrow he'd be ready to talk to Angel Corey. Face to face, without thousands and thousands miles between them.

And then, he'd just go on to California, far away from Gideon and Angel and the whole sorry mess that began when he started writing those damned letters.

— 5 —

November 25, 1942

Dear Angel,

    I heard from my mama about Solomon and I'm just writing to tell you how sorry I am. He was a good man, and I can say that in spite of everything that happened between him and me. I've been wishing I could have told him I understood why he had to do things the way he did.

    He loved you better than anything on earth, which I think you knew. When my mama wrote me about y'all getting married, I knew Solomon had to be crowing from the rooftops, even if he did have to go to war so soon after. He's wanted to marry you since you were twelve. So I'm glad (and you should be, too) that he got what he most wanted out of life, even as young as he was when he died.

    Knowing you, you're trying to think of ways you could have done better with him, married him sooner or worn your shoes like he wanted, or maybe had some children to remember him by. Don't think of the sad things, Angel. Think of the good ones.

Sincerely,

Isaiah High

— 6 —

"You just aren't thinking with your right mind, Angel," her aunt Georgia said. "Now your daddy's gone, you can't stay down here by yourself like this."

Angel slid down on the worn chair, smelling the night air. Beyond the porch, pines bristled up against the east Texas sky, trees that stretched clear into Louisiana from this little store. A three-quarter moon washed out the light of the stars and she could smell the river. "Listen to all those creatures out there, would you?" she said, ignoring her aunt. "You always forget how noisy the summer is until it comes again.

Georgia sighed. If there had been a table to clean, she would have done it. As it was, she had to content herself with straightening the lavender-sprigged skirt of her dress. "You never have listened to a word anybody said. Just like your mama."

Angel thought longingly of the cigarettes hidden away in her bedroom. "I wish," she said quietly, "you'd just let it alone, Georgia."

"How can I? You've got every tongue in town waggin'. How do you think that makes me feel?"

"It isn't everybody in town, first of all. It's the Walkers and a few others." A lot of others, probably, if she was honest with herself. "I need the work. You'd think some those women would be standing up for me, anyway, instead of gossiping behind their hands about me all the time."

"Oh, no one's gossiping. It's just natural conversation. Your daddy's gone, Angel. It's natural people will talk about what'll happen to you now."

"I'm not a child. I'm a full grown woman, a war widow. I've earned the right to make a living for myself." She crossed her legs and wiggled a foot impatiently. "And I know it's not like up North, but a lot of these women worked hard during the war."

"That's different, Angel, and you know it."

"It isn't different—I've run this store almost by myself for last two years. Why is it that I'm supposed to be helpless now?"

"The men need the work."

"So does a woman alone," she returned wearily.

"You're alone by choice."

Angel laughed bitterly. "No, I'm a widow."

"Well, it's been over three years. How long you gonna keep everybody at arm's length?"

"Maybe always." She shot a sharp glance at her aunt. "You can't honestly expect me to even consider Edwin Walker."

"I don't see why not."

"I've never even *liked* him, for one thing. That seems reason enough to me."

"You set your standards too high. Edwin Walker's got medals and money, and you can't tell me he's not a good-looking man."

"He's also been crazy as a mad dog as long as I can remember." Angel crossed her arms. "And I frankly don't see that war did him a whole lot of good."

"You're strong. You could turn him around."

"Aunt Georgia, stop it. I don't want to. No."

"Well, you could probably catch the preacher if you had a mind to. He's a good man."

"Yes, he is. And I like him. I don't want to be the preacher's wife, either. I'm not interested in having some man tell me what do all the rest of my life." All she really wanted right this minute was a little peace and quiet, some time to have a wailing good cry and maybe start thinking about what was next in her life. "I just want to be alone for a while."

"That's unnatural, child. People are meant to be in families, in pairs. Don't you want to be a mama?"

Angel stretched her neck back and closed her eyes. The night swirled over her face like a lover, bath-water warm and soft as talcum. "I've lived in this house since I was born—it's all I know. I really can't believe you want me to sell out and give up everything, just like that." She snapped her fingers for emphasis. "My daddy hasn't even been gone a week."

"Oh, honey. It isn't the store." Now Georgia had something to do. She reached over to hold Angel's hand. "I'm just worried about you living here without a man in the house."

"What you're afraid of," Angel said distinctly, yanking her hand away, "is that some colored man is gonna come in here and ravish me."

"Angel!" The retort was sharp and shocked and scolding all at once.

"Well, it's true. That's what you're all afraid of." Angel sighed. "Georgia, do you think you could listen to me for just a minute? One minute?"

"If you're gonna talk like that, I don't want to hear it. Makes me sick."

"I'm not going to talk like that. That's just the point." Angel pulled her aunt's hand to her face. "I want you to really hear what I'm saying.

Please?"

Georgia relented, smoothing the fine pale hair from her niece's face. "Go ahead, baby, speak your mind."

"I know every single person that comes in this store, and their mamas and sisters and brothers. They're as familiar to me as you are. Nobody's gonna hurt me."

"You never had to be out here all alone." Her voice dropped. "You can't trust these people, no matter what your daddy told you."

Angel felt a thick stirring in her middle and she pushed Georgia away. "He was your brother. Doesn't that mean anything?"

"Don't start throwing that in my face, Angel. Of course it does."

"He wanted me to stay here."

"Angel, honey, you're just grieving. Maybe you'll be able to think a little better when you've had some time—"

She jumped up. "I'm not giving up this store. Do you hear me?"

"Your daddy ruined you, Angel Corey." Georgia rose, patrician in her tidy cotton dress. Her silver-streaked chestnut hair shimmered in the moonlight, and the little buttons on the front of her dress winked furiously as her considerable bosom heaved. "If you had *any* sense at all you'd marry Edwin Walker and have yourself some children, try to make yourself a normal life, instead of livin' out here like some crazy spinster." She moved toward the steps, but Angel knew there was more. "You know where to find me. I hope to God I don't see you at my door in the middle of some night."

Angel rolled her eyes, but she stayed right where she was as her aunt walked to the car. The ignition grated, then the engine caught and with a thunk of gears the car pulled out with a little spit of gravel.

Leaving her alone. Which was what she thought she wanted, but now the darkness moved close, pressing in with loneliness. Georgia, bossy and prim, was her only family, and Parker had always been there to intercede. "You gonna have to take care of things now, Angel," he said when he got to the end. "Just remember you're not ever really alone."

But she felt alone, even in the coffee-rich Texas night—her life summed up in a long line of "withouts." Without her daddy, a mama, a husband, children.

That was one thing Georgia had right. Angel mourned her lack of children. She had imagined she would have several by now. And tonight, in the gulf left by her daddy's death, a child would have helped heal this emptiness, a child warm in her lap on this lonely night.

With a flap of wings and a strident squawk, a blue jay landed on the porch railing. He rattled off a series of whistles and chirps and screeches in a dizzying whirl.

Angel laughed. "Well, I didn't mean I was totally alone," she said to the bird. Ebenezer, mollified, meowed. Angel held out her hand and he flew to her, blinking. She stroked his neck. "You're such a pretty baby. My sweet little companion." He preened, his crest high, his feathers catching shimmers of moonlight.

"I reckon I could just go read," she said. Ebenezer chirped and leapt to her shoulder. She gathered the ice tea glasses and carried them inside, her feet bare on the wooden slats of the store. She walked through the aisles and through a door to the living quarters. Five rooms, if she counted the bathroom; kitchen, living room with a radio, two small bedrooms. The kitchen table groaned with cakes and tiny white rolls curled in baskets. In the icebox was enough ham for an army, and big pans full of fried chicken and potato casseroles, all gestures of condolence from lower Gideon, who had loved her father.

In the very center of the dazzling array of food rested a crystal vase full of wildflowers, left this afternoon on her doorstep. She touched the petals with the tips of her fingers, then turned off the light and went to bed.

The rain started the next morning, early. Started slow, a soft gray rain pattering on the trees and the gravel road in front of the store. Likely no one would arrive in such weather, so Angel turned on the radio for company and set about putting things in order.

She'd been nagging Parker for months to change things around. The bolts of cloth oughtn't sit where the sun could get to them, and the cosmetics were scattered so hurry-scurry you couldn't find a blasted thing. She lined up bottles of Breck and tubs of Dixie Peach pomade, ribbons and barrettes and combs. Toothpowder and brushes went with deodorants, cough drops and headache powders nearby. There were a few bottles of perfume in dusty boxes and some lipsticks in colors nobody would ever buy, even if they had the money. But she polished them up and left them, just in case. Some young girl might get a yen.

The bolts of fabric took longer, mainly because Angel couldn't resist fingering them, imagining how this one would fall in a skirt, that one in a blouse. There was a long piece of gauzy green muslin that wanted somebody to do something. Be a pretty summer church dress, good for her eyes.

The rain started pounding hard by noon and the road out front puddled up. The leak in her bedroom at the back of the house dripped into a pot that she left in there for rainy days, and another leak in the bathroom dripped right into the bathtub. It turned into a waterfall before two. A spot in her daddy's room started dripping like it did in the heaviest rain, so she carried a bowl in there, too.

Ebenezer flew from the store in the front to the rooms of the house in back, heading straight for the waterfall in the bathroom. Even over the pounding of the rain and the drops thunking into metal pans, Angel heard him fluttering and flapping under his shower. She peeked into the room. "Havin' a good time, baby?"

He whistled.

By three, the rain had not let up and new leaks were springing open in the roof almost faster than Angel could find them. She moved her bed over and put another pot in the bathroom.

In the store, it was harder. A bad place opened up too close to the stock along the east wall, and then three spots dripped through the ceiling over the counter.

Laboriously, she moved the magazines to the kitchen table, then piled sacks of flour and sugar and beans into a pile in the middle of the kitchen floor, which by some miracle stayed dry. No miracle, she thought, glancing out the window. A tree, planted to shade the kitchen from the hard west sun in the late afternoons, had protected the roof as well.

At five, she ran out of containers to catch the water. She dumped all of them, then rearranged them so that the largest pots were placed below the worst leaks. Then she put on a sweater and escaped to the front porch.

Where, naturally, it was dry as a bone. Figured. Just beyond the protection of the shallow porch roof, the rain fell in torrents—a sheet of impenetrable gray. A fine spray of it touched her face and hands. The road had begun to run like the river that coursed past the back of the house. In the field east of the house, Angel could tell the garden she had planted a month ago had turned into a lake.

She sank into the familiar rocker and huddled into her sweater feeling like an island cut off from all humanity. The roof had been bad for a couple of years, but there'd been no materials to fix it.

How in the world would she fix it now? All her money had gone to the doctors and to medicines and to various and sundry other needs. Exhausted, she slumped forward on to her arms, crossed over her knees, and let go of a heavy breath. There were no tears, much as she would have welcomed the relief, only an engulfing, crushing loneliness.

"Now what, God?" she said aloud. "I'm worn out. You're going to have to be very plain."

The answer could not be Edwin Walker. She didn't believe God wanted her to be miserable the rest of her natural life.

A dozen yards from her back steps, the river rushed by in swollen thunder. She wondered how her neighbors in Lower Gideon were faring. It looked like the river might flood.

All through the night, she stood sentry, wearily empting pots and mopping up the overflow as often as necessary. Her shoulders burned, and her eyes grew gritty, but finally the rain stopped just before dawn. Most of the stock was safe, and the furniture. The living room couch would have to be scrapped, but nobody ever sat in there anyway. Life had always been lived between the kitchen, the porch and the store. With grunts and heavings, she shoved the sofa onto to the back porch to dry, where at least the smell of the old stuffing wouldn't stink up the rest of the place.

The river roared through the trees, white tipped and rough, a normally sleepy ribbon of gray where mosquitoes bred and catfish slept. Today it had edged over its banks a bit and branches floated on the current that hurried it to the Gulf, but the worst had passed. A weak morning sun pushed at the clouds, sparkling on the wet leaves of cottonwood and willow trees.

Angel breathed deep of the washed air. She stretched her fingers up toward the sky and felt her tired muscles ease all along her spine. She spoke again, "Thank you, God, for stopping the rain in time."

She picked up a handful of branches thrown down by the storm and tossed them off the porch. Taking a last, long sniff of the heavy air, she went back inside to get coffee started and put things back where they belonged. There was no guarantee anybody would be able to get over the river or up the road, wet as everything was, but anybody who could, would.

Turned out to be a slow morning, for which Angel, exhausted by the long night, was grateful. Old man Younger passed on his mule, waving as he went by. His place was nearly five miles away, the farthest farm out in a string of cotton lands, most of it parceled out too small to make a decent living on nowadays.

When ten o'clock came and went, Angel knew the bridge to Lower Gideon was bound to be submerged. By nightfall, somebody would have rigged a way across so folks could get to their jobs tomorrow. Again she peered at the river, wondering what the rain had done to the homes across the stretch of water. She could hear shouts and saw a flash of red at the bend near Renden's place. Hard to tell.

Her garden was ruined. The little seedlings, her pride the week before, were buried now under six inches of muddy water. With a sigh, she took off her shoes and splashed barefooted through the yard for a better look, keeping her eyes open for snakes.

The water was cool, the mud gritty on her feet, and Angel smiled, hearing Georgia's howl should she drive up now. She glanced over her shoulder guiltily, then laughed out loud. "Look at me, Daddy. Scared already without you here to chase her off.

Shaking her head at her foolishness, she peered down at the seedlings—drowned corn and flattened tomatoes and demolished collards. Plant again as soon as it was dry, she thought, scanning the sky, which showed clear and blue now, not a hint of the storm left. But that meant another month till harvest, too.

No help for it. Wading into the mess, she began plucking out the obviously dead, measuring the possibility of recovery in others. She was no stranger to hardship, after all. A body did whatever was next. Today, this was it.

— 7 —

January 1, 1943

Dear Isaiah,

It has taken me much longer than it should have to get this letter written back to you, what with Christmas and all, but it's quiet today and I ought to have enough time to get it done now.

Your letter about Solomon came just in time, because I really was feeling regretful about things I could have done better—like marrying him sooner. I don't know why I didn't, seemed like we drifted that way for years and years and years. I guess I thought I might really get out of Gideon, and Solomon didn't want to leave. But then when the war started, I knew I was stuck here, so I married him when he got drafted.

Now that sounds awful. But you know what I mean. You're right. He was a good man, as patient and kind as anybody I ever met. And I know he understood about the two of you, that you knew, I mean, why he had to be like he was. Hard enough for him to hold up his head in town with that family of his (they all went north, by the way, to work in some airplane factory or something) without having to explain why his best friend was a colored boy. So, anyway, thank you for thinking of me. It's sad to think of his body deep in the water somewhere halfway around the world. But my daddy said that war just goes like that.

He's pretty worried about this war. Seems like it's been going on forever, and now it's getting harder and harder to get supplies of all kinds. Folks get mad when we don't have this thing or that one in the store, but a lot of times there's just none to be had. Coffee is hardest to get and keep right now, since you only get a pound every five weeks, but sugar's been a problem for months. Don't really think about how much you use until you have to be careful—iced tea and all my cakes take a lot more sugar than I thought. Guess I'll bake bread more when I feel the yen to get fancy in the kitchen. But we hear it's much worse over there. Do people have enough to eat? Can we send you anything?

How do you like England? (I have always, always wanted to go there, you know.) I would like to hear about it if you ever have time to write.

Was it hard to be so far from home at Christmas? Things went pretty much like always here. My Sunday school class did a good job on their part of the pageant and I knitted my daddy a sweater. I don't know how he did it, but he got me a whole stack of books from Dallas and a silk scarf painted with bright birds.

He's not well this winter. Coughing a lot and, though he doesn't complain, I think he's hurting. Lost some weight, too, though he swears it's my imagination. But you know he'll never go to the doctor. Worries me. Can't be good for him living by this mucky old river, either, and it seems like things never get dry lately.

Anyway, I didn't mean to run on so long. If you ever wanted to tell me about England, I sure wouldn't mind hearing. Must keep you busy, though, I know that. Be careful out there.

Angel

PS I am not just speaking idly in asking if you need something. We'd be happy to send things we can get hold of, so don't hesitate to ask, all right?

A.

— 8 —

When Angel, breathless from the walk to church Sunday morning, entered the room where her Sunday school class met, the children had a surprise for her. The motley collection of nine-, ten- and eleven-year-olds each pressed a rose into her hand and gave her a hug, then stepped back to let Jimmy Hemit present a huge card they had made for her.

Each child had printed and illustrated some verse of comfort from the Bible, and as Angel looked at the laboriously printed words, she clenched the flowers until rose thorns pressed into her thumbs. Tears welled up in her eyes. The children waited, arranged awkwardly around the low table in the room.

Without trying to hide her tears, she slowly met the eyes of each child. "This is so very special. Thank you." She spread her arms. "Let me hug all of you."

Her arms overflowed with thin and round and sturdy bodies. Elbows poked her, giggles wiggled into her ears, hair brushed her mouth and ears and cheeks. She smelled sunshine and starch and soap on their flesh. "Bless these children all of their lives, Dear Lord," she prayed aloud, kissing a head and an arm and a nose. "Bless them for being so filled with Your loving kindness."

Unfortunately, she thought later, that same spirit seemed to have deserted Georgia. Instead of taking her usual seat next to Angel in the pews, she barely glanced at her niece and passed by to sit with her friend Margaret. For a time, it seemed no one at all would sit with Angel, and she sat in one of the front pews, her face burning.

So this is how it would be—they'd just freeze her out until she did what they wanted.

She clutched her fingers together in her lap, sat straighter. She had nothing to be ashamed of, nothing to apologize for. If she let them get to her that easily, her daddy's entire life would practically be a waste. *Ain't always easy to stand up for what's right, Angel,* he always told her, *but God needs our hands to do his work.*

Finally, just before services began, Edwin Walker slid in next to her. A wash of cologne came with him. "Hey, Angel," he said.

She licked her lips, coughing discreetly at the overpowering scent of him. "Morning, Edwin." She didn't look at him, speaking instead to the hymnals in front of her. "How are you?"

"Fine." His voice carried a raspy edge that seemed to add to his appeal as far as the women in Gideon were concerned. To Angel, it sounded liked he'd thrown one too many temper tantrums. "I'm just fine," he repeated. "How are you?"

"Considering everything, I'm all right." She could feel his gaze licking at her face, but she kept her attention fixed on the pulpit, where the now preacher was standing, getting ready for services to begin.

Edwin leaned a hair closer, though even he wouldn't act in an unseemly way in church, particularly since he'd just been named a deacon. But the truth was, more than one older member of the congregation would be pleased to see Edwin win his long suit of Angel Corey. If she looked around, there would no doubt be gentle little smiles directed their way. Taking a long breath, she steeled herself not to move away and give them even more to discuss in their tittering little voices.

"I hear your roof got torn up in that storm," Edwin said quietly. "I'd be happy to fix it for you if you'll let me have first option on buying the store."

"No, thank you," she said. "I've already hired somebody to do it for me." It was a lie, but nothing on earth would induce her to let Edwin Walker come down that road every single day and hang around her store with his crazy eyes. And if she even *thought* of selling it to him, her daddy would flat turn over in his grave. Probably cause an earthquake, she thought with a private smile.

"I see," Edwin said. "Must be somebody you like, the way you're smiling."

Annoyed, Angel looked at him. "It's none of your business, Edwin Walker—and that's not what I was smiling about, anyway."

The pianist struck the chords of the first song and, grateful for the distraction, Angel grabbed the hymnal and stood up. For the rest of the service, she ignored Edwin no matter what he did to get her attention—bumping her ankle, brushing her elbow, coughing. Subtle enough to ignore. She was relieved when it came time for the offering and Edwin stood up with the other deacons to collect it.

As services ended, she made her way through the milling, visiting groups of parishioners. No one spoke to her. Shoulders squared, she passed Georgia without looking at her and made for the door.

The preacher stopped her. A thin young man with a high-bridged nose and earnest dark eyes, Reverend Adams had only been pastoring the First Southern Baptist church for a few months. "Good morning, Angel."

"Morning, Reverend." She smiled. "Good sermon."

"Thank you." He took her hand gently. "How are you doing?"

"Well enough, I reckon. I miss him, but he was ready to go."

"It's never easy, but he was the most honestly Christian man I've ever had the pleasure of knowing. I like to think of him telling jokes to Jesus."

Angel laughed. "That's a fine picture. Thank you."

He didn't release her hand. His brown eyes sharpened. "I'm sorry the church family hasn't been kinder to you this morning."

She looked away. Last Sunday, with her daddy two days gone, the church had swarmed around her in comfort. She supposed she had expected some chilling, that she'd understood the town would not take her keeping the store lightly.

What was alarming was to find out that she cared. It was a lot harder to stand up for herself knowing that she had to do it alone. She shrugged off the unkind comments rising to her lips. "They'll get used to my having that store by myself in time. I'll be all right."

"I know you will." His fingers tightened gently and released her. He stepped back a notch, hands folded properly over his belt buckle. "You let me know if you need anything." His eyes warmed. "If it helps at all, I think you're doing the right thing. God bless you."

Angel felt her heart lighten for the first time since her Sunday school class. "Thank you, Reverend."

She stepped away as other members of the congregation pressed forward to their pastor and, heart lighter, she stepped outside into the bright sunshine. A soft breeze blew away some of the worry of the past few days.

Somehow, things always worked out. She ought to remember that. The store had been busier than ever last night, the customers' pockets fuller than they'd been all winter now they had field work.

She kicked a rock with her toe. Even those receipts wouldn't buy a new roof, though, and it wouldn't make it through another rain.

Maybe that was the big plan. The roof would go and she would be forced to find another life for herself. Maybe God had something planned for her that she didn't know anything about and he was just using this whole trouble to get her to see it.

A crow sailed overhead, cawing noisily at a hapless cat whose ears flattened immediately. Angel grinned to herself, thinking that she'd been looking a lot like that cat these days, almost certain the sky was falling. "Is that it?" she asked, continuing her conversational prayer. "If so, I wouldn't mind a little hint of the direction we're going."

It occurred to her that she almost never spoke to God in church. She prayed, if a body could call it that, in bed and while she did dishes, while she served customers in the store and while she embroidered and tended her garden, but almost never in church. Maybe it had something to do with the Southern Baptist's stormy, angry God. Maybe she didn't think that one would listen.

She grinned to herself and took a long deep breath, letting it go as the store came into view. As she neared the porch, a laugh rolled out into the high noon sunlight. It was a luxurious sound, rich with patience and pleasure.

Angel froze. For a moment, she thought it was God laughing, just the way she always heard him in her mind, and had since she was a little bitty girl.

But God didn't laugh out loud, not that Angel had ever heard, anyway. As she stood there frowning, she placed the familiar notes. Twenty years and she could still remember it—Jordan High laughed that way.

But ghosts, so far as she knew, didn't laugh either.

Realization washed over her, and she pressed a hand to a place in her ribs that suddenly pinched. Sudden, emotional tears clogged her throat.

Isaiah. Only a year had passed since his last letter to her, but five or six had gone by since she'd last seen him. Somehow, she'd imagined that she would have some time to prepare.

And yet, there he was, coming around the corner of the store. Isaiah, grown into a man. He'd been a thin and leggy boy, with hands too big for his wrists and feet like flippers. Now he was a tall man, long-limbed and lean, with skin the color of oiled pecans.

As he noticed Angel, staring like she'd been shot, he halted. The small boy walking with him stopped, too.

She swallowed. "Hello, Isaiah."

"Angel," he said with a nod. His eyes, luminous and grave at once, took her measure as surely as she took his.

She found it hard to keep looking at him, harder still to stop. "Your mama didn't mention you were home when I saw her last night."

"I asked her not to."

"Oh." The word came out a little airless and she tried to think of normal things you might ask some returned soldier, a person who was essentially a stranger. Except that he wasn't, not really. She cleared her throat. "How long you been back?"

"Got home the day after they buried your daddy." His voice had grown deep on his travels, and some of Texas was gone from it, replaced with a hint of places Angel had never seen. "I'm real sorry."

She shifted under the warming sun, trying to swallow the quick grief swelling in her throat. Waving toward the porch, she asked, "Y'all want some tea? I have some made."

"No, thank you." Isaiah glanced up the road. "We just stopped for a minute."

Angel shaded her eyes to look up at him. The sun haloed his proud, well-shaped head and tipped the edges of his ears, throwing his face into shadow. "You look well, Isaiah. The Army must have done you some good."

He shrugged. "Some good, some bad."

"I sure didn't expect to ever see you in Gideon again."

"Brought Mrs. Pierson's niece home to her. I don't aim to stay. "The thought seemed to give him some pause, for his eyes narrowed briefly before they fixed on Angel again. His mouth moved, pursed and relaxed. "I hear your roof is ruined."

"Been going a long time," Angel agreed. "This last rain did it in."

"I come to say I'll fix it for you."

Angel made a dismissive noise, halfway between a laugh and a snort. "I don't have any money." She shook her head. "And I won't have any. Cost me everything I had to bury my daddy."

He measured the roof with his eyes for a minute. "That man got me out of here when there were folks who would have gladly seen me go straight to hell." He looked at her. "I'll take care of it."

She hesitated. It gave her a worrisome ache in her shoulders to think of him here, after all this time, working so close by.

"What else you gonna do?" he prodded.

"I don't know." She looked at the roof. Even at this distance, it was plainly shredded. "I just can't let you do it all for nothing."

"You been doing for people your whole life," he said quietly. "Let somebody do something for you."

Biting her lip in indecision, she made herself look at his face. His dark eyes, above the high slant of broad cheekbones, glowed briefly with a pale white light. His square, smooth chin lifted. She remembered there was a dimple deep on one side of his mouth, but it didn't flash now.

"All right," she said suddenly. "Thank you."

He nodded, glancing at the boy. "I reckon we better get back before they eat without us."

Angel wiped a palm on the skirt of her dress. "Well."

"I'll come by to look at that roof tomorrow sometime."

"Fine." Feeling paper crackle in the pocket of her skirt, she shook off her surprise at Isaiah's sudden appearance. "Oh, Paul, wait a minute." She smiled at the boy, the ginger-haired grandchild of Maylene McCoy, a four-year-old with a crooked smile and mischievous eyes. His mother had gone north a few months before to find work. "I saved this for you, and was going to give it to your grandmamma tomorrow, but you can have it now." She reached into the pocket of her skirt for an assortment of cut-outs of disciples, left over from Sunday school.

At the sight of the sheet, he looked puzzled. "What is it?"

"Just paper dolls. Look, here's Paul."

The child flashed his impish grin. "Thank you, Miss Angel."

"You are so welcome."

"See you."

As they turned to go, Isaiah paused. "Miz Pierson asked me to tell you to come see her when you have a spare minute." He cleared his throat. "Said this afternoon might suit her well, since the store's closed."

"Thank you."

Isaiah nodded and walked away, the boy in his stead. Angel went inside to pour herself a glass of iced tea from the pitcher, and drank it with a deep thirst, hoping the cold would wash away the discomfort laying heavy in her chest. She stared out the kitchen window, watching sunlight play over the shiny leaves of a cottonwood, trying to tie the man Isaiah with the child she had grown up with.

Isaiah. She closed her eyes, pressed her hands to her cheeks.

Even without speaking a word, he bristled with presence. That wasn't new. At sixteen, seventeen, the bristling had been anger, and had scared Parker half to death. Grumbling that history would not repeat itself, not as long as he had two legs, Parker had talked himself blue until Isaiah reluctantly joined the Army, one step ahead of the war.

She poured another glass of tea. As a boy, he'd always been quiet. Saw everything with those big dark eyes and showed nothing. That was after his daddy died. Before—Angel reached back, back to evenings on the porch of the store, when she and Isaiah had played hide and seek or tag while the grownups traded stories and took some time off from their hard weeks to chat. In those days, Isaiah had been sunny and laughing, full of riddles and jokes and surprises.

She smiled suddenly, remembering the mysterious gift of wildflowers. Isaiah must have left them. Some of the small boy was mixed in there, then. And some of that bristling older boy, too. And something else, found in battlefields and faraway lands.

A flat red tin in her bedroom held the dozens of letters that chronicled his war days, some quick little notes, written hastily as he waited for duty, others long, pages and pages and pages of people and thoughts and comments on the lands he visited.

Real, she thought now. In his letters, he'd been himself. Outside a few minutes ago, she hadn't been able to find a cornerstone upon which they could meet. Not in childhood or in the letters they'd traded. Now he was like the seventeen-year-old Isaiah who had avoided the store at all costs unless his mama forced him to come help her carry purchases of one kind or another. On those rare occasions, Isaiah mumbled replies to Parker's questions with his eyes lowered, his mouth sullen.

One afternoon when they were teenagers, Angel had been hanging out the laundry and had come around the side of the house to rinse her washtub at the pump in the garden. She'd surprised Isaiah sulking against a tree and she'd been pleased, so *pleased* to see him, out away from people where they could talk. But his only response to her cheerful hello had been a single, searing glance of purest hatred.

Angel had backed away, wounded but wiser. To make matters worse, her daddy had yelled at her from the back porch with a hard note in his voice, like she was five years old and poking holes in flour sacks to watch the white stuff flow out in a tiny stream.

"Get your bottom in here, girl," he'd hollered, words rough with fury.

Now, so many years later, Angel knew it had been Isaiah her daddy had been worried over, worried sick that he'd get himself killed somehow. On that sunny afternoon, all she'd felt was a vague, thudding guilt.

A vestige of it lingered. For as she'd heard Isaiah offer to answer her prayers for a new roof, her first thought had been that her daddy wouldn't be there, that there were times no customer would be shopping and Isaiah would be up on her roof, bristly and grown into his anger, and there was no place, no way for them to meet as friends.

— 9 —

March 10, 1943

Dear Angel,

I see you all over the place here—in the rain and the castles and the fog, in the girls who look like you with their soft complexions. If somebody asked me what place was made for Angel Corey, I'd have to say England.

It was real good to get your letter. Sometimes, even with all that I hated about it, I miss home, miss seeing all the people that know me without me having to say a word. I miss playing chess with Mr. Parker and visiting with the preacher and hearing the music from the juke joint come up river on the night wind. Funny. Big ole Isaiah High, homesick as a little boy.

[Never mailed.]

March 12, 1943,

Dear Angel,

It was good to get your letter. Thank you for all the news. Sometimes, a body does get homesick.

You asked me to tell you about England. It's different. The weather, the people, the way things look and feel—all of it. I expected it to be like the States, but it ain't.

I remember how bad you wanted to come to London. Well, that place sure isn't the same place it was, I can tell you that. There's big holes everywhere from the bombing, and all kind of buildings looking like they might fall down any minute. You probably seen the newsreels, but it's something to see it in person.

There's a lot of shortages of everything here, too, but you said you heard it was worse, and you were right.

There's just nothing, but people just go on and do what they usually do, only in smaller ways. They invite you to tea and go dancing and try to pretend nothing is different, much as they can.

Here's something you'll like—people have yards around their houses, but they call it a garden. I kept looking for some vegetables, but it's just the yard. There's a lot of flowers (not this time of year, naturally) and you'd like how people take it seriously, the flowers around their places. Course now everybody is growing vegetables, too, even right in the city. On my days off, I've been helping some folks in one neighborhood get the soil tilled and ready to plant. Most of them are old, cheery, and all they young people are soldiers and nurses and suchlike.

The people themselves are kind of funny. Like they have this thing about never being surprised, but I know I run into people who never saw a man as black as me in their lives, but they act like it's natural. And they seem to like Yanks, as long as the soldiers (white or colored) don't mess too much with their girls. Course, no Yank's ever quite as good as a Brit. Funny.

I've made friends with an old lady who shares her tea with me when I can get there. I felt bad at first, cause she don't have a lot and I didn't want to take her share, but one time I said no and you could see she was crushed. So I go. What she wants is somebody to talk to and tell her stories to. Her husband was in the Foreign Service and they traveled all over "The Colonies" (that's how she say it, like it's in capital letters). He died a few years back. She's old, but she's sharp and I figure there isn't too much she ain't seen or heard. We have a good time. I take her cigarettes when I can, and my mama sent a batch of brownies a while back, so I took those, too. (Don't tell Mama.) She brings me books and I been reading a lot. Just finished A Farewell to Arms, and it was a good book, though I still don't like him much. What have you been reading these days? Anything good?

*You asked if it was hard to be so far from home. No. I miss people, but I don't miss Texas. It's okay here. We work hard (just finished a **CENSORED**), but I'm used to that.*

There's been terrible stories in the paper about the rest of Europe, things I don't know if I can believe. Rumors about what Hitler's doing to the Jews, mainly, but they're so bad—I just don't know. There's sick people on this earth, that's for sure.

I gotta get to work now and mail this. Tell your daddy I said hey. You take good care of him now. Drag him to the doctor if you have to. Write and tell me what happens. I think about y'all a lot, specially since I knew without you telling me how bad you always wanted to go to England. I never did. Funny.

Your friend, Isaiah

PS If you wanted to send things, I'd take them to Mrs. Wentworth. Food of any kind, of course, anything you can ship. Tea if you can get it. These folks are living on little enough. Thank you.

— 10 —

Angel made her way to Mrs. Pierson's house that afternoon. It was one of her favorite places on earth—gentility embroidered in every detail. The house burrowed near a grove of pines just past the southern edge of Gideon proper, a rambling, two-story clapboard painted white. Around the wide, low porch were planted roses in a dozen colors, yellow and red and white and combinations of all three. The blooms stained the air with a heady fragrance that mixed with the melon scent of grass from the lawns that spread luxuriously beneath the shade of pecan and sycamore trees. As if in anticipation of the coming heat, a handful of chairs were gathered in a cove beneath the thickest branches.

The house had been built at the turn of the century with invention money. That's how people always said it: "invention money." Nobody seemed to know exactly what had been invented, patented and sold for resultant fortunes, only that it had something to do with electrics and kitchens. Having made his fortune, the first Donald Pierson had settled his wife and son in the big white house and proceeded to write scholarly pieces for magazines nobody in Gideon ever read.

His son had traveled east for his education just before the Great War and turned to war reporting as soon as he finished his degree, hoping to make a name for himself. Instead, he'd been shot in France and returned to New York.

There, recovering, he'd met and married the present Mrs. Pierson, a refugee from somewhere in Eastern Europe. They traveled back to the family home in the midst of the influenza epidemic of 1918. The younger Mr. Pierson, weakened by his wounds, succumbed to the virus shortly thereafter, leaving his worldly possessions to his lovely, young and frightened wife. The elder Mrs. Pierson, bereaved beyond comfort at the loss of her only son, died shortly thereafter.

Gideon's citizens, suspicious of strangers to begin with, certainly weren't crazy about a foreigner in their midst, no matter how pretty she was. They clucked over her accent, speculated over the scandal of that young woman living in that big house with the odd inventor and circulated rumors of all sorts to explain her blindness.

Just as matters had nearly driven Mrs. Pierson insane, Angel's mother had arrived, been wooed and married by Parker in less than three weeks. And the gossip machine whirred violently, changing direction.

Because of their outcast status, the two women had naturally become friends, and Mrs. Pierson had extended her friendship to Angel as well, providing odd extras in Angel's life—books and magazines no one else read, stories of Europe before the wars, a sense of elegance that would otherwise have been missing.

On this deep spring afternoon, Angel knocked on the door and was admitted by a slim, dark woman. "Hello, Miss Angel," she said. "Hear your roof got right tore up in that storm."

"Well, it was going long before the storm, but that was the nail in the coffin." She stepped inside and blotted her forehead with a handkerchief. "I just saw Isaiah High and he offered to fix it, praise God."

"That so?" Angel caught a flicker of surprise in her face before the ubiquitous smile returned. "Go on in the parlor. Mrs. Pierson was hoping you'd come."

Angel made her way through the polished hall and into a sunny, airy room. Lace curtains hung at long windows, and ferns in big pots thrived in corners and nooks throughout the room.

Mrs. Pierson, slim and tidy in a tailored dark blue dress, rose at the sound of Angel's feet at the door. With her was a painfully thin young woman whose white-blond hair was cropped short, curling slightly around her ears. Angel caught a quick impression of enormous dark eyes before Mrs. Pierson's hands caught hers.

"Angel!" she exclaimed and kissed her cheek. "I am so pleased you could come. My rheumatism has been snapping at me with all this wet weather, and I have worried about you. Come, sit."

With her customary ease, she led Angel to the couch. "This is my niece, Gudren—you remember I talked about her? Showed you the photographs of my sister's daughter? Here she is!"

Angel couldn't hide her shock. *This* was the fat little girl, the rosy cheeked, black-eyed niece from Holland? "I remember well," she said, quietly meeting her eyes. "I'm Angel."

A smile broke the pale face. "Yes. My aunt and Isaiah have spoken well of you." Her English was heavily accented but very clear. "I am happy to meet you."

"Likewise," Angel said. Yes, those were the snapping black eyes of the little girl, housed in a face whittled clean of any excess flesh. Her cheekbones arched over deep hollows and skin stretched tight over the bridge of her nose. "I just saw Isaiah a little while ago. He said he came back with you."

"A kind man," Gudren said with an inclination of her head. "I was not well and he waited for me to be well enough to travel. It was—"

Angel waited for the rest, but Gudren simply shook her head.

Mrs. Pierson spoke instead. "My niece was disturbed by our railway system." She took a minute sip from her china cup.

"Ah." There wasn't much to say about that: *Yes, we should change that. Yes, it's an ugly rule, Yes, there are other things, too* . . .

In truth, though, Texas without segregation struck her as unlikely as a civilization on the moon. No matter how often her daddy had talked about it changing, she didn't see that it ever would. "I reckon that was a shock," she said finally, thinking of the Europe Isaiah had illuminated in his letters.

"A shock," Gudren agreed. "Coffee?"

"Please."

Gudren leaned forward to pour. On the tender white flesh of her inner arm, Angel saw a series of blue numbers tattooed. She lowered her eyes, as embarrassed as if she'd seen the accidental exposure of a naked breast.

After a moment, she raised her chin, fully aware that her cheeks must be the color of cherries. Gudren had folded her hands in her lap, and looked at Angel with a steady and somehow patient gaze.

With a gesture Angel knew she would not forget, Gudren held out her arm and brushed graceful fingers over the tattoo. "It must not be hidden."

"No," Angel whispered. "I'm so sorry."

"I am alive." She poured tea. "Here I sit, with my aunt, and her guest." She handed Angel the cup and saucer, and smiled. One day, she would be beautiful again. "Here we are."

Angel raised her cup. "To life."

Gudren laughed. "Yes. L'chaim!"

After that, the conversation turned to lighter subjects, to what was planned for vegetable and flower gardens, to the weather; to movies and books. As the afternoon deepened, they played parlor games and Angel joined them for a quiet supper of beef noodle soup and pie.

For Angel, the evening was restorative. She'd spent a lot of time with Mrs. Pierson through the war, visiting for an afternoon or evening, sharing books and ideas and conversations. Especially now, she was glad to have the refuge.

It wasn't until nearly sunset that Angel took her leave, walking through the woods in a silvered dusk populated with the whistles and chirps of birds who were capturing the last of the day's food. She loved these woods, the smell of needles and river, the peacefulness and, tonight, the weight of her grief and loneliness was easier to carry.

At home, she changed into a house dress, and walked barefooted to the front porch to call Ebenezer, imitating his strident squawk as well as she could. He hopped up to the porch railing and answered her with his series of gurglings and meowings. Angel held out her finger. "How are you, baby? Full day?"

A movement in the edge of the woods across the road caught her eye and she peered into the deepening evening. Edwin Walker stepped into the road. "Evenin', Angel."

"Evenin'," Angel answered warily. "What brings you out so far tonight?"

"You do."

She put Ebenezer down on the chair. He leapt with a flash of blue wings to the top of it and fixed tiny black eyes on Edwin's approach. Angel squared her shoulders. "Is that right?"

Edwin climbed the steps and leaned lazily on the railing. He said nothing for a minute, fixing his neon blue eyes on the road before he swiveled them to her face. He smiled softly, showing no teeth. "You looked so pretty in church today that I've been thinking about you all afternoon."

"Thank you."

He cleared his throat and extracted a pack of cigarettes from his pocket. "Mind if I smoke?"

"Not if you'll offer me one."

He relaxed and extended the package. When Angel pulled one out, he lit it. "You never did make it easy for a man," he said after a moment.

She exhaled gladly, watching the smoke weave through a bar of light coming from the window. "Easy how?"

"You know what I mean. Even in school, nobody could sweet talk you, not even me."

"And I imagine that was a rarity, Edwin."

"Oh, don't make it sound like I'm conceited, now. I can't help it if women like me."

Angel looked at him.

"Everybody but you, that is," he said.

"No use throwing myself in there in the competition."

"Wouldn't've been no competition for you." Smoke circled his head, pale against the darkness of his Black Irish face. It was said the Walkers had Indian blood, too, and she could believe it of Edwin with his hawkish nose and fine lips. Too handsome for his own good. The eyes seemed almost to carry their own light, an eerie glowing where there should be nothing but reflection.

"And, you know, that's the trouble." She inclined her head. "It's people's nature to want what they can't have, Edwin. I'm no more your kind of woman than you are my kind of man."

"What do you know about men, Angel Corey?" He smiled, glancing over her figure lazily. "Solomon?" He raised his eyebrows. "You were married, what? A week, maybe two?"

"We went through this in high school," she said with a sigh. "I'm not interested, Edwin. I like you fine, but I'm not going to be your girlfriend. I don't want to be *anyone's* wife."

"School," he said, lifting his cigarette, eyes fixed on her through the smoke. "A woman needs things a girl never thought about, and I reckon there's a lot you still haven't learned."

She narrowed her eyes. "And you figure you're the one to teach me?" she said, shaking her head. "Thank you for the offer, but just because you went off to war and won you some medals doesn't mean I changed my mind."

His nostrils flared as he exhaled and Angel watched a string of muscle draw tight from his jaw to his temple as he stared out at the creeping darkness. "All right, then, Angel," he said in his rough voice. "I got time." He flipped his cigarette butt away. "Take care now, hear?"

"Night, Edwin." She watched his broad back disappear into the night.

Rubbing a foot over the other arch lazily, she smoked and considered the problem of Edwin Walker. "What am I gonna do about that man, Ebenezer?" Nothing she said seemed to make the slightest difference to him. He just kept coming back, like a boomerang.

And whatever he said about changing, those eyes had grown worse, not better, while he'd been gone. She didn't care if he was a deacon at church—wouldn't care if he was the preacher himself. Something had always been off-kilter with Edwin Walker and it was tipped clear sideways now.

Ebenezer whistled sharply and she held her hand out for him to perch on her fingers. "What do you think, baby? Maybe I oughta get me a guard dog or something." He answered with a soft purring. She stroked the downy feathers of his breast. Edwin's unearthly eyes burned into her mind.

— 11 —

May 6, 1943

Dear Miss Corey,

I cannot even express my delight over the package that Isaiah has just brought to my door. So much bounty! The nuts and candy will be a lovely addition, but I am most delighted by the tea. It is my great weakness, you see, and it pains me to parcel it out so.

While I have nothing of great value to send you in return, I hope you will enjoy the enclosed book of Emily Dickinson's poems. Poetry is my other great passion. Isaiah and I have been enjoying great discussions when he is able to come to town. He is a very great help to me.

Please write again, and when this war is over, I hope you will come to see me. I will show you the land as I know it, an insider's view.

Again, my deepest thanks, Miss Corey.

Most sincerely,

Mrs. Angela Wentworth

— 12 —

Isaiah rocked on his mama's porch in the mild evening. His mother and sister had learned to let him be in the late evenings, when things he couldn't speak of crowded into his mind. Things no one should see. Things that could not be unseen.

And yet, through it all there had been a measure of freedom. Now it was seeped away, drop by drop, changing the tilt of his head, the angle of his shoulders.

A fat woman wanting a piggy back ride, that was Texas, and no matter how he fought to keep her off, she still climbed on and insisted he walk upright and bear her weight.

It wasn't that she struggled to jump up on him again that surprised him. He had expected that. The thing that amazed him was that he had not ever really understood her obesity until she had been flung off.

Not all at once. The Army, at first, had been no different than home—colored soldiers were colored first. Crow was part of training and the Army. Just like home.

But Isaiah had been lucky. As the States had been drawn into the war, he had been among the first troops assigned to Britain. There the class structure had been intimidatingly different. Its subtle complexities had been so confounding that he was afraid to do much of anything at all for the first few weeks.

Slowly, though, he began to enjoy the first real freedom he'd ever tasted. The English, wary of colored troops to begin with, had finally decided the American color problem was none of their concern. They flung open the doors of their pubs and dance halls and homes to colored soldiers as well as white.

When the trouble came, later on, it wasn't the Brits that caused it. The murders and stabbings and fights stemmed from the fury of the Americans. Eventually, out of self-defense, the Brits had been forced to hold dances on alternate nights, arrange lodgings in separate areas and give pubs over to one race or the other. White Southerners had forced it.

In spite of all that, Isaiah had liked the Army. He didn't complain about the building they did, because building had always been his dream. Building roads and runways might not be glamorous work, but he gained valuable education doing it.

And in England, he had met Sergeant Owens, a black man with a big mind and a need to talk. It had been Owens who had given Isaiah the books he now held in his hands.

He looked down at the volumes of poetry and novels, all of them written by black men.

Black men.

His initial reaction upon reading the words of black poets had been fury—how had he lived to the age of twenty without ever knowing there were poets of his own color?

Why had no one ever *told* him?

But the fury was replaced with excitement. If those men could write and publish their words, it was possible that he could fulfill his own dreams.

The covers were worn now, the pages soiled with repeated readings in battlefields and ditches and farmhouses. They'd kept him company through the worst of everything, when it seemed he'd spent a whole year in the same smelly uniform. There was never a chance to bathe or change and, like the other soldiers around him, he trudged along doing his job as bombs and mortar exploded and bullets flew.

Not his own bullets, naturally. White soldiers were the infantry, gaining glory. Colored mainly did the dirty work. They were mine sweeps and grave diggers, called by every name but soldier. Later, as the mortality counts rose, colored soldiers had got their guns, all right, been pressed into service in the desperate need for cannon fodder, Isaiah among them.

During those long, grim days the poetry had become to him like the Bible others toted with them, the only comfort he could find, outside Angel's letters.

"*I'm so tired and weary, so tired of the endless fight,*" he read now. "*So weary of waiting the dawn and finding endless night.*"

The words had been penned by Joseph Seamon Cotter, Jr., but they echoed Isaiah's thoughts this night, seemed to embody the fat woman on his shoulders, seemed to echo in the blues floating on the mild night air and the hush of endlessly waiting lower Gideon. The people waited here in this little town like they'd waited in the villages in Europe.

But no army was marching to free Gideon. There would be no liberation, no dawn to break the endless night. For the first time, he understood what had driven his father to protest so loudly, so long—until he'd protested right into his grave. Parker and Jordan had seen things in the first war that had triggered the same restlessness in them that Isaiah felt now.

Isaiah had seen the futility of Jordan's fight, and Parker's. If he were to make use of this life, it wouldn't be in Gideon.

Tossing away his cigarette, he went inside to the comfort of his family. Perhaps the chatter of voices he knew and understood could drown his sorrow for one more night.

Monday, Angel rose at five to prepare the morning offerings before the sun rose. In addition to dry goods and the sundry items any five and dime would carry, the store sold soda pop and doughnuts and pie, coffee or iced tea for a nickel. A sprinkling of colored women had made it a habit to stop by with dawn's light to have a bit of the richly brewed coffee before heading off to other women's homes to make breakfast and scour floors. There were five with positions in the homes of upper Gideon, and they were highly prized situations—long term and good pay.

But the moments at Corey's store were often the only moments of silence they found in a day, the companionable silence of women united by the tasks ahead. Here, for a moment or two, they were free of husbands and children and employers, could speak their minds in some semblance of truth.

It had always been Angel's project to open the store early. As long as she could remember, she'd awakened to the twitterings of blackbirds in the cottonwoods. Alone in the deep quiet of morning, she'd dress and slip outside to the front porch, waving to those first early travelers on the road to town. It had only seemed natural to go ahead and open up the store. And sometimes, someone would buy thread or a length of cotton or some such thing for the day ahead, but mostly they stopped for the comfort of friendly faces.

The first customer this Monday morning was Clara Jackson. She came in just as the coffee was finishing, a short, rotund woman with shiny black skin. "Mornin', Angel," she called in a high, sweet voice.

"Good morning, Mrs. Jackson." She poured a thick ceramic mug full of coffee. "Let me run and get the milk out."

"Take your time, honey. I'm in no hurry."

Angel filled the pitcher and returned, putting spoons on the counter. Mrs. Jackson took one to stir sugar into her cup. "Hear the rain put some new holes in your roof."

"I had buckets all over the place," she commented, pouring herself a cup of coffee. "How'd you do?"

"Well, it ruined my garden, of course, but we sit up kinda high. Nothin' else was hurt."

"It drowned my garden, too. I'm thinking I might try planting again this afternoon." She stirred milk into her cup. "I never liked growing vegetables, but it got to be such a habit during the war that I can't imagine a summer without it now."

Two other women came in, Geraldine High, Isaiah's mother, and Maylene McCoy, Paul's grandmother, with Paul in tow.

"Good morning, Clara," said Mrs. High. "Mornin', Angel."

"Mornin'." Angel poured two more mugs of coffee and looked at Paul. "What'll you have, sir?"

The boy beamed, crawling up on a stool. "Coffee."

Angel glanced at Mrs. McCoy, who nodded. "He drinks half coffee, half milk. Can you do that? I'll pay for the extra."

"Oh, don't be silly. I can spare a little milk."

Maylene looked tired, Angel thought, her beautiful walnut skin pulled taut around the eyes, her mouth drawn. "Are you feeling ill this morning, Mrs. McCoy?"

The older woman shook her head and sipped her coffee.

Geraldine High spoke. "She's had to take Paul with her to work for a week now." Isaiah's mother met Angel's eyes. She was nearing sixty but it didn't show. Her bearing was straight, and behind her spectacles, her deep brown eyes were clear and sharp. Not a single wrinkle marred the skin, a fact that Angel marveled over again and again—especially since she had begun to notice a few on her own face.

"Last Friday," Geraldine continued, "Paul accidentally broke a crystal vase and there was considerable fuss."

"Why do you have to take him?" Angel asked.

"Anybody that might keep him is in the fields for the planting right now. They was about to get done, but now with that rain . . ." she trailed off.

While they talked, Paul had leaned over the counter to grab a handful of straws kept in a tall glass. Angel shook her head, holding out her hand for the straws. He placed them in her palm with a sheepish grin. She winked. "Why don't you let me keep him here?"

"Oh, that's kind, but I can't impose like that."

"In case you never noticed, I really like children, and I like this one here in particular. He won't be any trouble." When she saw Maylene still hesitated, she added, "You don't have to pay me anything, if that's your worry. It's been lonely around here and I'd like the company."

Maylene's face softened. "We all miss your daddy, honey. No doubt about it." She frowned at her grandson. "If I let you stay here, are you gonna mind Miss Angel and stay out of her way?"

"Oh, yes, ma'am. I'm always good for Miss Angel."

Clara nudged Maylene. "Go on. Ain't no sense in you losing your place."

"All right then. You know," she said to Angel, "that I sometimes don't get done till after dark."

"That's fine. I'll feed him."

Geraldine lifted her chin. "Isaiah told me he'd be stopping by here on his way home from Miz Pierson's this afternoon."

Angel waited.

There was an odd expression in Geraldine's eyes—a combination of worry and pride, and something Angel didn't quite understand. "Why don't you send Paul home with Isaiah? He surely can't work in the dark."

"I'll do that."

Clara stood up. "I guess we better get moving. It's almost six-thirty."

Geraldine let the other women go ahead of her. "God keep you, Angel."

"Always has." She turned to Paul as the screen door swished shut. "Well, sweetie, are you gonna help me out around here today?"

"Yes, ma'am.

"I have to plant my garden. You can help me put the seeds in."

"I know how to do that."

"You have any breakfast yet? Let's start there."

"Can we have pancakes?"

"Why not?"

And he might only have been four, but he brought a lot of energy into the day. She really had been painfully lonely, first through Parker's decline, and then his death. Unless she was at church or made the effort to walk up to Mrs. Pierson's, she didn't have a lot of contact outside the store, and that was casual. A friendly wave, an exchange of funds. Done.

Today, a handful of customers drifted through, but most everyone was busy in the fields or in town. Angel straightened the house and the store, then took a hoe and a rake and packets of seed to the garden.

"What are we gonna plant?" Paul asked.

"Carrots and radishes, first of all," she replied. "The corn looks like it came through all right, some of the collards are okay, too." She tucked her hair under her hat. "And what do you say to sunflowers and pumpkins and watermelons?"

"Okay!"

She paced off the plot, counting under her breath. "Tell you what. If you work hard, I'll give you a watermelon vine and some sunflowers of your own to take care of, how 'bout that?"

"Can I have a pumpkin, too?"

She grinned. "You betcha."

As Angel squatted in the cool earth, digging and planting, she sang. Paul bent with fierce intent, meticulous about even the tiniest seed placement. He was born tidy, his mother said, with a powerful sense of how things were meant to be.

He also had a chatty, silly personality, the side effect of being an only child, a situation she understood completely. Angel laughed at a joke he told, and when they made hills for the watermelon vines, she said, "When I was a little girl, my daddy let me have a whole patch of corn and sunflowers and pumpkins and melons. I just couldn't wait for it all. Every single day, I asked him to check them for me. Seemed like it took forever."

"Is it gonna take forever for mine?'

She laughed. "Probably will seem like it. But you know, at the end of the summer, you'll have eaten the melons, and you'll still have sunflowers, and then you'll pick your pumpkin. It's nice like that. You can roast the seeds and then, all winter long you can nibble on them and remind yourself of summer."

After a lunch of peanut butter sandwiches and sweet tea, they settled on the back porch. Angel left the doors between front and back open to hear the bell if it rang, then slumped in her rocking chair. Paul climbed in her lap. Ebenezer roosted on the railing, his mellow song underscoring the peacefulness of the day.

She rocked slowly, arms filled with small boy, his legs draped over the arms of the chair, his head nestled into the hollow of her shoulder. He smelled of sunshine and a clean wind and good, rich dirt, that smell of boys fresh from outside. His skin beneath her fingers was a little dusty. She hummed as she rocked, a nameless lullaby someone must have sung to her when she was tiny.

When she imagined herself with children, it was always with sons. She liked little girls, liked their seemingly innate sense of propriety and the natural order of things, liked their self-conscious hair-flinging and play cosmetics. But it was boys she imagined herself bearing and raising. Boys like Paul who smelled of sunshine, boys like Solomon and Isaiah who fished and climbed.

She loved the feel of this one settling sleepily into her, his weight and size as comforting as an answered prayer. On that warm thought, she dozed and dreamed the child was her own.

Isaiah found them there, napping in the warm afternoon. Angel's cheek had fallen against the ginger hair of the boy, who snoozed slack-mouthed and utterly secure. Such unconcerned slumber had become rare to Isaiah in wartime, where sleep came to a man in uneasy bits, and often not at all. He was loath to disturb them.

Silently, he let his unobserved eye wander over the curve of Angel's cheek, where a spray of almost silver-pale hair drifted on a current of wind over her poreless complexion. Her reddened hands, clasped around Paul's slim body, were fine of bone and raw with work. His gaze wandered down the cotton-draped thighs and lingered at her fragile ankles and bare, dusty feet. He smiled. A grown woman and still didn't put on her shoes. Calluses showed on the heels and along her cracking big toe. Solomon had hated her barefootedness; had muttered and bullied her about it constantly. Angel had listened in her patient way and worn shoes whenever she thought Solomon might be coming around.

In some way, Isaiah must have made his presence known, for her eyelids lifted suddenly. For a long moment she regarded him sleepily, openly, in the way she had when they were children. She smiled, then pressed a finger to the oddly voluptuous lips. She rose, cradling Paul gently, and carried him inside.

She returned without him, shoes on her feet, careful politeness not quite able to erase the soft friendliness of her waking. Her cheek showed the mark of Paul's hair, and she rubbed it self-consciously. "He'll have a nice nap," she said. "He worked hard in the garden this morning."

Isaiah nodded, vaguely unsettled and at a loss for words. Angel, too, seemed nervous. She pressed a hand against her stomach.

He glanced at her feet. "You didn't have to put on shoes for me," he said without knowing he would. "I ain't gonna tell nobody there's a crazy woman down here."

She let go of a small laugh. "Oh, well. I try to behave myself." She stepped off the porch. When she stood next to him, her head rose no higher than his shoulder. "You seem so much taller now," she said looking up to him.

Impossible, he thought, to keep himself aloof from her easy observations, from her long, clear knowledge of him, even though he had intended to. "You just shrunk."

"I'm sure that's it."

It felt good to just look at her up close, in real time. So familiar, every detail remembered and imagined and re-imagined when she wrote to him through the war. Heavy-lidded, big eyes with such a softness of color, a mouth too big for the rest of her face. With a little more color to her skin or hair, she might have been a beauty, but she was as pale as the moon.

When she put on her lipstick, bold as a honk, that was a whole 'nother story. He'd forgotten that until right now, what lipstick did for that mouth.

A flush crept up her face and her eyes dropped. Isaiah shifted, realizing with discomfort that he'd been staring. Gruffly, he said, "Why don't you show me where that ladder's at, and I'll take a look up there?"

She led him around the side of the house, pointing at the ladder beneath the old cottonwood. Stepping aside to let him pass, she said quietly, "Thank you, Isaiah."

He forced himself to walk to the ladder and pick it up. "It ain't nothin'."

A pick-up truck pulled up in front of the store and Angel backed away. "Holler if you need anything."

As she hurried around the house, he let go of the ladder, bracing himself against it for an instant, eyes closed.

He had missed her like an eye, like a thumb.

And standing here now in the hot sun, he had to tell himself the truth or be damned. He hadn't come home to see his mama or deliver Gudren or any of the other things he'd told himself he had to do. He had come home because Angel was here. Every road always led back to her somehow.

But time hadn't changed a goddamned thing, and he was much a fool as he ever had been. Didn't matter if the world was shaking, if his life had shifted. No matter what he'd seen or learned or become in his years away, not one damned thing in Gideon had changed with him.

Want had no place here. Wishes were for children.

Arms heavy with anger and a very real fear, he lugged the ladder around the house and climbed the roof with purpose. The sooner the roof was done, the better. Quicker he was gone, the more likely he'd live to tell the tale.

Hank Crockett, a white farmer from down the road, needed a handful of things that Angel rang up for him at the counter. "Shame your daddy ain't here to see the crop this year," Hank commented. "He's the one been talkin' up rotation. I only got a little bit of cotton this year."

"I'm sure he knew you'd change your mind eventually," Angel said, smiling. "Wasn't a more stubborn man in all of Texas."

Crockett cackled, his face breaking into a wreath of wrinkles. The deep blue eyes sparkled. "And his little girl's cut from the same cloth, ain't she?"

Angel lifted her eyebrows quickly and let them go.

Paul ambled out then, rubbing his eyes.

"Hello there, young fella!" Crockett boomed. "You sleeping on the job?"

"Isaiah's outside, sugar," Angel said.

"'Saiah?" Paul smiled eagerly and ran outside.

"Major case of hero worship there," she commented, watching Paul leap from the porch.

"Good-looking little boy." Crockett held out his charge slip, at the very end of his arm. "You're gonna have to read that for me, darlin'. My arms just don't stretch far enough these days."

"Pair of glasses might do the trick."

"Ah, hell no. Somebody might think I'm an old man." He winked and gathered his purchases. "You're getting your roof fixed, are ye?"

"Hope so. 'Bout time, I'd say."

"Yep." He patted his hat down firmly on his head. "Well, I better get this stuff on back to the wife. I am real sorry about your daddy, Angel. You need anything, you just let us know, hear?"

"I will. Thank you." She lifted a hand in farewell, reassured somehow. Not everyone would shut her out, after all. Crockett wouldn't. He was grizzled and set in his ways sometimes, but he was fair, always honest with his help.

She cut up a chicken and threw it in a pot for supper, then wandered outside. Led by Paul's laughter, she rounded the house to the east, eyeing the smooth flat of her garden plot for a moment. Briefly, she imagined the plants that would sprout from the smooth earth in a week or two, pleased by the hidden life gestating there in the flat earth.

The sound of Isaiah's laughter drew her around the side of the house.

He had climbed down the ladder and stood by it, his feet clad today in the heavy boots that had probably seen him through the war. With them he wore pressed, faded khakis and a soft work shirt that buttoned up the front.

He was laughing, standing just beyond the ribbon of deep shade that clung to the side of the house. Perched on his finger was Ebenezer, chattering in an almost earnest attempt to communicate. "This your bird?" Isaiah called, holding up his hand.

As she approached, his smile didn't fade. It showed his white teeth and the dimple in the side of his face, and her skin rustled in a forgotten way, making her shy.

Ebenezer spread his jeweled wings, preening, and she focused on the flash of blue in his fathers. "He fell out of a tree and ruined one of his wings, so I kept him."

"I never knew they could be friendly. He kept me company up there, chattering away."

"He can't fly very far, but he likes to be up high."

"He sat on my shoulder," Isaiah said in some wonderment, then extended his arm to give him to Angel. Ebenezer skittered up Isaiah's arm to his shoulder, where he made soft, cooing sounds into Isaiah's ear.

"Why, Ebenezer," Angel said with her hands on her hips, "you traitor! See if you get the chicken scraps tonight."

Isaiah laughed again and the sound moved through her very bones, settling in elbows and knees. She wrapped her arms around herself, cradling joints in the palms of her hands.

As Ebenezer cooed close to Isaiah's ear, he ducked away. "Figures a woods gal like you would tame a bird."

"Always wanted a squirrel. Never thought about a jay really."

"You tamed enough critters for a zoo."

"And my daddy always made me take them back." She found she could meet his eyes when they were smiling. The unease in her chest softened although it didn't fade entirely. For a minute, everything was normal, as it had been in their letters.

Before he abruptly stopped writing. She wanted to ask him why, but of course she would not.

He cleared his throat, looking back to the roof. "It's going to take me a couple weeks to do this properly, but I can get it fixed up for you."

"It doesn't matter how long it takes."

"I'll get some paper and tools tomorrow."

"Fine, Isaiah. That's just fine. Thank you so much."

"I'll take Paul home with me now, then, and see you sometime tomorrow afternoon." He didn't meet her eyes again as he gently took hold of Ebenezer and set him on the ground.

"Tell Mrs. McCoy she can leave Paul tomorrow, too, if she needs to."

"I'll tell her." He took Paul's hand and led him away.

Angel whistled at her bird, forcing herself not to look after them.

— 13 —

May 16, 1943

Dear Isaiah,

I'm writing this from my favorite place, the tree house you built. Stands just as strong as it did the day you hammered in the last nail—how long ago now? Must be ten or twelve years. Seems more like a million sometimes.

Anyway, it shows what a builder you are, this little tree house in the woods. I hope when this war's all through you'll think about that again. God gives a man a talent for a reason, and if I ever saw a man who could build things, you're him.

From up here in the trees, everything looks so peaceful. It's just past suppertime and I can hear the river. Some birds in a tree next door keep looking at me suspicious-like, but I think they finally figured out I'm not gonna bother them. They're singing a little. I worry sometimes about the birds over there, in the war. It must scare them when the bombs come.

From where I'm sitting, all there is to see is tree branches and sunshine coming low through the leaves. The cottonwoods are glittering like Mrs. Pierson's gold-button earrings. It's a little hazy because it's been raining. It's so beautiful it makes you imagine those trees could be hiding a magic kingdom or a deserted isle, just like we used to pretend. (Poor Solomon—he never did have an inkling of our games. Nobody ever read to him. We were lucky in that way, at least. Or maybe not—I don't know, maybe it's easier not to know anything).

Yes, it shimmers out there and I wish I could still play pretend.

Because under those trees is only Gideon. Three telegrams in the last week about boys killed. I go see their mamas and wives because I was the first one to lose anybody, and I probably know a little something about how they feel. It doesn't help very much. Mrs. Allen said yesterday that she just can't stop thinking about her Jim's bottom when he was a baby—a little soft bottom, pink and white. I don't know what that's like. How can I say anything?

And without war, there's the mean little uglies nobody likes to talk about. Somebody probably told you about Mabel Younger. Nothing but a child, beaten and God knows what else. Course no one is saying who did it, but I reckon it was the same one that's been beating and hurting people in these woods as long as I remember.

Of course, no one tells me these things. Not any of them.

Even my daddy treats me like I'm simple. Gotta protect Angel. Keep her sweet. She might end up like her mama.

Like I can't see what's under my nose. Like I can't hear. Like he hasn't been after me since I was twelve. Like I don't know he nearly killed you. I saw you that night. Bleeding all over. I stood in the doorway to my room and watched you and my daddy in the kitchen. Saw you shaking mad and hurt. Heard my daddy talking, talking, talking. Knew enough to stay where I was.

But you saw me. Looked right at me. Like it was me that had done something, had hurt you. Then joined the Army and went away and have the nerve to write me a letter like we're friends. I wish we were, Isaiah.

Because you were always the only one that didn't ask me to be somebody else, who looked into my eyes and saw me, who listened when I talked.

I hate Gideon Texas. I hate it. And I know I'm not ever going to get out of here. Not ever. It's just gonna strangle me and bury me. At least you got out. At least one of us got a chance.

[Never mailed.]

May 17, 1943

Dear Isaiah,

Flowers are in bloom by now, I bet. Tell me, what kinds? Have you got to go to a play or anything? Tell me more about your older lady. Where did she go in the service? What's it like to have tea? I know you're there to fight a war, but I'm just so jealous I could spit.

I've sent along some cigarettes and other stuff we thought you could use. Wish it could be more.

Heard Edwin Walker (your old friend, ha ha) is going to England soon. Saw his mama at church and as usual she talked my ear off about him. I never saw a woman as blind about her child as that one is. She flat spoiled him rotten.

Daddy is doing a lot better now the weather's turned warm. He's still awful thin, but he works every day and I think he's getting better. You know he won't go to any doctor.

Have to go wash clothes, now. I'm enjoying your letters a lot. It's like a serial in the newspaper or something. I feel like I have some inside information.

Angel

— 14 —

By Friday, the days settled into a comfortable pattern. Isaiah worked mornings for Mrs. Pierson, tearing up her former yard and putting in a new one, a whim she could well afford and he suspected she had invented to give him work. He took it in the spirit it was intended.

When he finished around two or three, he walked back to the store, eating a sandwich or some cold chicken. At Corey's, he climbed the ladder and got to work on the roof, working straight through until about suppertime, when he would climb down, refuse Angel's offers of tea or cake, and take Paul home. He ate with his mother and sister, then went out to read and think on the porch.

His strategy was to keep to himself, only speak when spoken too, avoid contact with everybody as much as possible. His mama dragged him to visit with neighbors now and again, but he avoided them the rest of the time. Women came, one pretty, one smart, one both, all three angling for his attentions. He gently deflected them. Friends from childhood stopped by, eager to hear his stories of the war, of the world beyond East Texas. He ducked them, too, unwilling to find attachments that would snare him into staying in Texas.

The results were that nobody in upper Gideon much noticed Isaiah High was back home. In lower Gideon, he gained an unpopular reputation. He was satisfied with both.

The only time keeping his distance was hard was with Angel Corey. On Tuesday afternoon, when he climbed down from ladder, she had called to him. "Isaiah, you about finished up there today?"

He wandered to the back door where she stood with Paul. Her dress was the pale green of new leaves, touching the color of her eyes, and she smiled at him in her open way. "Why don't you sit and have some chocolate cake before you go?"

"I reckon not. Thank you."

"You can't have grown up out of chocolate cake, Isaiah High. I remember when you could eat a whole one by yourself."

"That was a long time ago."

"You gonna tell me you don't like it anymore?"

"No." He didn't smile. "We ain't children no more, Angel, and I don't want to sit on your back porch and eat chocolate cake." He set his jaw. "Wouldn't be seemly."

"I see." There was an airy breathlessness to her words. "You can have Isaiah's piece, Paul. Come on inside. I'll get you some milk with it."

Now, on Friday afternoon, he ripped shingles from the roof with vigor and he could smell cake baking again. She was famous in three counties for her cakes, which she baked for church socials and potlucks and just on general principles. The smell of this one was making his stomach grumble.

Parker Corey had been a good man, but he hadn't done right by Angel. She was as likely to get killed as Isaiah was, unable to shake the Biblical injunctions her daddy had given her.

Parker had taken "Feed the hungry" literally, had greeted every man, woman, and child as Jesus incarnate, white or black, rich or poor. Never had gone to any church, though he had a good reputation among the preachers on both sides of the river, had just read the Bible and done his own interpretation. He said he'd had a vision in the war, his feet half-gone with gangrene. Jesus had come to his bedside in the hospital in France, and put his hands on the putrefying wounds. "Go among them," Jesus said, "for these, too, are my children." There had been no doubt in Parker's mind about just exactly who Jesus meant.

Isaiah had heard the story from his father, who had heard it told in town while he worked. And Jordan had thought all the more highly of Parker for his silence.

Thinking of the old man, Isaiah felt a prick of sadness. He'd really wanted to see Parker again. Seemed a crying shame that he'd missed him only by a few days.

Below him, he could, hear Angel humming as she waited on customers, swept the porch, rattled around doing something.

That cake.

This time the sweet hot smell might be pineapple upside down cake. Damn. And as if he was in a battlefield, thinking about food to distract himself from the harsh reality of life, he found himself imagining it in detail—steaming yellow cake and hot, juicy pineapple, the edges crisp with sugar.

He ripped a nail free. Food was his weakest spot, always had been, and after six years of Army food, he didn't know how he could turn down a slice of cake again.

Not likely she'd offer, he thought, thinking of Tuesday. Could be the cake was for a church supper or for a sickly neighbor.

But once the thought of it was in his mind, Isaiah had trouble loosening it. He cursed himself all the way down the ladder. When his feet were planted on the ground, he glanced at the sky, figuring the time until supper. Seemed like all he could smell was that sweet cake, heavy in the air. He walked around back, intending to ask for a glass of water.

Angel met him at the door, a curious expression on her face.

"You done already?"

He cleared his throat. "Just hot. Can I trouble you for a glass of water?"

"I'll be right back."

When she returned, Paul tagged behind her. They came through the screen door together, Paul carrying two plates of cake, Angel with glasses of tea. Ebenezer appeared as well, squawking a welcome to Isaiah as though he hadn't seen him in a year. He flew right to his shoulder and perched there.

Isaiah couldn't help himself. He laughed, shaking his head. "Crazy bird."

Angel extended the glass and looked at Paul. "You give it to him."

Isaiah looked the plate. His mouth watered. He thought of her letter about cake, and shot a glance at her. She remembered, too.

"I knew you couldn't stand to smell it cooking and still say no," Angel said.

He said nothing, holding the cake in his hands, his appetite gone to dust. He glanced up at Angel. She met his eyes steadily, and for the first time he saw that she was no longer a girl, any more than he was a boy. The weariness of time showed in her eyes, and at the corners of her mouth were the slightest lines.

She met his eyes steadily, soberly, and tucked a lock of hair round one ear. "Your letters where so full of food I'd have to go have a snack when I finished one."

Letters. He still had all of them, every one she'd written, stuffed in a canvas bag tucked in the bottom of his duffle. Sometimes those letters were the only reason he could think of to keep going.

"Go on and eat, Isaiah," she said. "I'm gonna go get me some."

Hell. The porch was shaded and cool. Isaiah sat down and measured the cake, savoring the scent of it, then took a bite. It was exactly what he had imagined, warm and syrupy and spongy all at once, melting on his tongue before he could taste enough of it. He ladled up another forkful and glanced at Paul, who was watching him as if he were the end product of some experiment. "What you lookin' at, boy?"

"You like cake?"

"Course."

"How come you didn't want no chocolate?"

Isaiah took another slow bite. "Just partial to pineapple, I guess."

"Not me."

Angel stepped onto the porch, letting the door slam in place behind her. "That's what makes horse races, my daddy always said." She sat in the rocking chair. Isaiah could feel her motions behind him as she shifted, and now he could smell her over the scent of the cake, a simple flowery smell he remembered from childhood. He didn't turn.

No one spoke for a minute. They sat in silence, eating. Then Angel said, "You know, I've won prizes for my baking. I wonder if I could write a cookbook."

Isaiah laughed. Her voice was the same as the younger Angel's, huskier than it should be, slow enough it hid her sharp mind, and he found himself responded to the memory of her. "You been saying you were going to for a hundred years."

"I never had a typewriter."

"You could've found somebody to loan you one."

"I reckon I still could. And I bet people would *buy* it, too. Everybody likes my cakes."

He swallowed a mouthful, able to smile freely as long as his back was turned. He pressed crumbs into his fork. "That's why you had to make this one, cuz you couldn't stand to have somebody turn you down."

"You're eatin' it, aren't you?"

He stood and turned to look at her, curled on the couch with her feet tucked up under her. "Ate it," he corrected. "And it was exactly what I thought it would be. Thank you." She made him think of a cat, curled so luxuriously and comfortably—a silky cat with long eyes and graceful limbs. His eyes lingered a moment on her mouth with its strange, ripe lips, plump as late grapes. Thought again of waxy red lipstick.

Swallowing, annoyed with himself, he put his plate carefully on the step and backed away, eyes on the ground. "I'm gonna go finish up now."

The legacies Angel's mother had left her were few. No grandparents; no uncles or aunts or cousins, no stories of her girlhood. Wraith-like, Lona Corey had just appeared one day in Gideon. She had been a fragile, breathtakingly beautiful woman, and some said she had come from the brothels in New Orleans. Not even Parker had been able to extract her story, one that had died with her when Angel came into the world after three days of screaming labor. She left behind a green velvet dress, a pearl necklace, a box of cake recipes, and a single photograph. Nothing else. Lona was formless in Angel's mind, a vague personage as ethereal as the soft white heads of dandelions gone to seed.

On Saturday morning, Angel baked another chocolate cake, this one taken from her mother's box of recipes, for a potluck at the church the following day. It was flavored with the bushels of mint coming up around the house. In a burst of creativity, she topped it with swirls of thick chocolate frosting and pretty clusters of leaves.

Once it was tucked away in a cake safe, Angel mopped the wood floors of the store and straightened the stock, making notes for her orders Monday morning. Then she went through the outstanding customer charges likely to be paid that evening, swept the front porch, watered the garden and the flowers. Meantime, customers drifted in and out, and Angel attended to them, glad for the hard work.

When business lulled, she slipped outside to do some gardening. Morning glories sprang up on the east side of the porch, vines that would creep over the railings and wind up strings Angel tied to the roof. In front of the porch were snapdragons and chrysanthemums; around the side grew holly hocks and chives and mint. There were even rosebushes, sheltered from the heat of the Texas sun by the slanting shade of the back porch. All of them had been planted, in a frenzy of digging, the only summer Lona lived in the house.

The photo Angel had of her mother was taken in late summer in front of the morning glory vines. Her pale hair was swept back into a ponytail and she wore a pair of Parker's trousers. The expression on her face was distant but pleased, an expression that embodied for Angel the mystery of her mother.

As a little girl, Angel had prodded Parker over and over again about some hint of where Lona had come from, or who she was before she appeared in Gideon. He had nothing to give her but the same stories he'd repeated a dozen times—the meeting in front of the feed store, the first date they had (at a dance sponsored by the First Methodist Church), the whirlwind courtship that made Lona his bride in three weeks' time. And then her death a scant year later, her serene baby daughter in her arms. "Parker," Lona had said, stroking the headful of cotton candy hair, "she looks like an angel, don't she? Like she come to tell me God's waitin'." In two hours, bled pale, Lona died.

On this sunny afternoon so many years after her mother had planted the flowers, Angel pulled stubborn weeds between the vines and wished she had known her. Or maybe that was just loneliness talking.

Because if she told herself the truth, there it was. She was desperately, painfully lonely out here by herself. Nobody to talk to. No one to share her days with. Everything just blended together in a blur of not talking to anybody much.

Maybe Georgia was right and she ought to just throw in the towel, give up the store and go live in town. But that idea made her feel so claustrophobic she'd rather drown herself in the river.

The river. She looked toward it, thinking of Isaiah. Or rather, *deliberately* thinking of him, because she hadn't really had more than five minutes go by that hadn't had some hint of Isaiah in them since he got home.

Isaiah. She rocked back on her heels and closed her eyes to relish the lowering sunshine, thinking of his sheepish wish for that pineapple-upside-down cake yesterday. The look on his face as he ate it. *The way to a man's heart*—

She conjured him up in memory. Standing there with a plate of cake in his big hands, sun glittering on the curve of his head. She called up the moment he met her eyes and she glimpsed him, *her* Isaiah, behind the guard he kept up. For one second, they had been real.

It nearly stopped her heart.

She knew it was wrong. She knew it was dangerous and foolish and impossible. Foolish. She knew, she knew, she knew. She'd always known.

But knowing didn't change what she felt. Knowing didn't stop the rush of heat and dizziness she felt thinking about him. Her limbs were weak with it, and a prickly circle of restlessness lived on the back of her neck.

Craziness.

She had to stop it, stop making small talk with him, trying to get his attention. It wouldn't take that much longer to get the roof done, and Isaiah could be safely on his way.

She wished her father was still alive. She would never have dared such boldness if he were still around.

Maybe that's all this was, loneliness and grief and fear. A breeze carrying the scent of the river brushed the small plants around her ankles, and she looked up at the sky, wondering if her daddy could hear her thoughts now. "Are you ashamed of me?" she asked.

His death, for all that he had been sick for nearly three years, had been sudden. One day he was working, talking to his friends as they stopped in. The next day he couldn't get out of bed. One week later he was gone.

In the nights since the funeral, she'd lain awake in her bed, night after night, the silence around her as thick as the grave itself. It was silence that carried both heft and emptiness, and for the first time in her life, her faith wavered cruelly. It seemed, suddenly, that she had been a fool about everything, that God existed but obviously did not care about any one person. If he did, how did he let all those soldiers die, all those children, all those tigers, minding their own business in a cage in a zoo.

Worse, it suddenly seemed plain that she had missed the obvious: no matter how big he was, there was hardly any time for him to worry about one single human being, what with wars and starving children and all the rest.

Each morning, when the sun rose, Angel felt ashamed of her night thoughts and asked forgiveness in her morning prayers. Break her daddy's heart for her to doubt God, for one thing.

Not to mention her own. Faith had woven the spine of her life. If it disappeared, what would she have?

One flower bed was cleared of weeds and, regretfully, Angel straightened, easing the clutch of muscles in her lower back with one hand. As much as she would have liked to stay outside in the soft light, there were linens to be washed, shelves to be stocked. Saturday nights were usually the busiest night of the week, and she had to get ready.

Going inside, she frowned to herself. Last Saturday had been a little strange. The customers were there, but the men were quieter, quicker than when her daddy had been around. The women, led by Mrs. High and the others who stopped on weekday mornings for that cup of coffee, chatted and gossiped with one another the same as always, or almost. Angel couldn't put her finger on what the difference was.

Seemed like the women came first, came in pairs with children. And the store felt like it always had on Saturday nights, cheerful and full of jokes and *tsks* and mockery. The children tried getting into things and women scolded them, Angel among them.

Then the men drifted in, mainly from the fields, and instead of coming right in, they gathered on the porch with lowered voices. As soon as there was a weight of the men on the porch, the women's voices lost a little of their banter, and eyes were cast at the shoulders and heads visible through the window in deepening twilight. Men came in two or three at a time, picked their supplies and paid up their bills. Then they exited, taking their wives and children with them like magnets taking iron shavings, until the store was cleared and silent.

Angel couldn't complain about the money, for the receipts had been even a little better than usual. Just that something had shifted with her daddy's leavetaking.

She was foolish to think she could stay. Keep the store. Live her life just the way she had been for her entire life.

Terror shimmered along her throat, dove into her belly: if not this, then what?

To stave off the worry, she bustled around, sweeping the floor, picking things up. Humming a tune from the pageant her Sunday school children would present in the morning—Shadrach, Meshach and Abednego—she plunged her hands into the soapy water in the kitchen sink. The cracked places on her fingers stung. She'd have to take care with her single, precious pair of stockings or they'd be torn to bits by those dry places. Maybe tomorrow she'd wear her green dress. The thought of the dress and the children cheered her. At least that was something she could count on—her children.

As the afternoon waned, she took a few minutes to change into a clean dress for the evening. She bent over the vanity in her bedroom to make sure her face was clean while she fastened the buttons of her dress and brushed her hair. Her cheeks were sunburned and in the pale red, Angel could see a handful of dry skin lines.

"Good grief," she said, "look at this. Got wrinkles and no children. Next I'll be getting gray hair." She shook her head. No help for it. On her dresser lay a stack of library books she needed to return and she took them with her, putting them next to the cash register where she would remember them tomorrow morning.

From there, the evening went much like it had the week before. A gaggle of women and children filled the store and made it merry with voices and laughter until the men came a little later. They stood outside a bit, talking quietly among themselves, then in twos and threes bought their supplies and faded into the darkness until the store was empty.

The clock read eight o'clock. The night stretched ahead as empty as a pocket. She turned on the radio for company and stepped out back for a cigarette.

Was this it? The moon was absent and, beyond the small circle of light thrown by the windows, an inky darkness surrounded the store. A breeze rustled the trees. From across the river sailed the muted music of the juke joint, joined in chorus by crickets and other night insects.

The despair she'd been fighting all day pressed in hard. She saw her life stretching forward decade after decade with nothing changing except the wrinkles on her face and the looseness of her flesh. She saw herself as one of those strange old women children fear and make up stories about. Saw them throwing tomatoes and eggs at her windows in the night, running away in fear of her witch's powers.

She closed her eyes against the vision, panic pressing into her chest. "Oh, God," she breathed. "Please don't let that happen!"

Out of the shadows on the road from town a figure emerged. Angel straightened sharply. Desperate as she was, there wasn't a force on earth that could make her consider Edwin Walker seriously, no matter what happened. And there was no one else who would be coming from that direction this time of night.

She squared her shoulders, her fingers tightening on the glass of tea she held. But it was Isaiah, not Edwin, who stepped into the circle of light, still dressed in work clothes dusty with the day. One hand was bandaged. "Evenin'" he said.

She let go of a breath. "You scared me."

"My mama gone already?"

Angel nodded. "Nobody stayed long." The pinch in her chest appeared suddenly, giving a vague trembling to her hands. She sipped her tea but, unable to hold it steady, put it down beside her on the porch. "You worked late tonight."

"Yeah. Gudren was feeling poorly. I stayed to talk to her awhile—" There was a hard sheen in his eyes. "She could use some company, I reckon."

"I'll see what I can do. It's been hard to get away, now it's only me."

"Ain't trying to tell you your business, but she'd come here. I could bring her in Miz Pierson's car when I come."

"That'd be fine, Isaiah. You know better than to even ask."

"Good." He nodded. "Store still open?"

"Of course. What do you need?"

"Peroxide." He lifted his bandaged hand. "Tangled with a rose bush."

"Come on in. I'll get it for you."

While Angel found the peroxide, Isaiah paused at the counter and touched her library books. From the corner of her eye, Angel watched him lift one, then another, pausing at the third one down, *The Robe*. As she came back up the aisle, she said, "You read that yet?"

He shook his head and put the books down, stepping back from the counter. From his pocket, he took a quarter to pay for the peroxide. Angel waved it away. "Just take it."

"No way to run a business."

"I reckon it's my store."

"I reckon it is." He eyed the stack of books, and looked up at her, as if he would say something. Angel stayed right where she was, telling herself to pretend her daddy was in the other room, but she couldn't make herself believe it. Her hands wound around themselves.

Isaiah lifted his chin toward the gesture. "Am I making you nervous, Miss Angel?"

She stopped. "No."

It seemed the air was heavier, that his eyes were saying something partly hostile and partly not, but Angel stayed right where she was.

Finally he moved to take his medicine from the counter. Angel picked up the book he'd fingered and pushed it toward him. "Go on and take this, too." It was an old custom, one born in childhood.

He picked up the book and stuck it beneath his overalls. "Much obliged."

— 15 —

October 24, 1943

Dear Angel,

Don't have a lot of time, but thought I'd scribble out a little note. Keep hearing the King on the radio and it makes me think about you every time.

You remember how you wouldn't let either me or Solomon be king when we played pretend? I been wondering lately how you knew at such a young age that a queen didn't have any power if there was a king.

Thanks for the warning, about Edwin, that is. Go halfway around the world and still run into your worst enemy—that's just my kind of luck. I did run into him, down to one of the canteens. Figures. Couldn't even be stationed a long way from me. Got to be right here under my nose. They'll be some trouble, I reckon, but this ain't Texas and I'm a grown man now, not a boy he can set to with his hounds.

Maybe it's just time old Edwin had a taste of his own medicine.

Anyway, I got to go to work now. Meant to tell you about the old man I met in a pub last week. Remind me. He was really something.

Your friend, Isaiah.

PS Sent you a newspaper clipping. Show it to your daddy, see what he thinks.

Hitler Murdered Three Million Jews in Europe

Hitler has murdered or destroyed by planned starvation, pogroms, forced labor and deportations, more than 3,000,000 of Europe's Jews, according to a statement of the Institute of Jewish affairs, published in the United

States.

Russia and other countries have given asylum to 2,000,000 exiles, says the report, leaving only 3,300,000 of Europe's pre-war Jewish population of 8,300,000 unaccounted for.—B.U.P

(THE PEOPLE, 17 October 1943)

— 16 —

Sunday morning dawned sloppy, wet and cold, a fact Angel noted with more than a little dismay. Mornings like this in the past, Georgia had always driven out from town to take her to church. If she'd only had to carry herself and the cake in the sunshine, it wouldn't have been a problem, but she'd show up for the pageant looking like a drowned cat.

Swallowing her pride, she called Georgia. "Morning, Aunt Georgia," she said. "I know you're mad at me, but I really a need a ride to church this morning. I have a cake and the children are giving a program."

"I fully intended to come down there for you, Angel. I'm not heartless, you know."

"Thank you."

A half hour later, Georgia showed up in her big black car. She carried the cake to the car and Angel carried the materials for the pageant. When Georgia put the cake down next her on the seat, she peeked inside the safe. "Oh, honey, you outdid yourself this time. That's the prettiest cake I've ever seen."

"Been thinking about it a long time," Angel answered. "There was just never the right occasion."

"Be sure you hide a piece for me, all right?"

"I will." Angel peered out at the drizzle. "Thanks for coming out here this morning, Aunt Georgia. I really didn't know how I was going to get there in this mess."

"I may not approve of everything you do, baby, but you're my dead brother's only child. I owe him at least seeing you to church where the Lord might change your mind."

In the interest of peace, Angel simply nodded.

"You hear about Mrs. Pierson's niece yet?" Georgia asked.

"I met her last Sunday."

"Pretty thing, if she gained some weight, don't you think?"

"I'm sure she will," Angel said mildly. "Takes time."

"So it's true, then?"

"What?" Angel felt a stirring of disappointment, seeing the point to this ride to church.

"That she spent the war in a concentration camp."

"I don't know."

"Oh, you do, too. I heard that nigra your daddy was so fond of is fixing your roof. He's the one brought her back. Didn't he tell you?"

"I didn't ask." Angel sighed. "You just do that to bother me."

"Do what?" Georgia waved her hand. "That's polite! You're too sensitive." Too enmeshed in her story to fully register Angel's disapproval, she continued, leaning forward over the steering wheel as if the story were rolling out on the dashboard. "When I saw her yesterday, I thought to myself it was just like when your mama showed up here, out of the blue." She cocked her head, sending the feather on her hat dancing. "Wonder what it is about Gideon that would attract pretty women?"

"How is Gudren like my mama?"

"Oh, she isn't not really. Just that suddenness and the prettiness."

"I've never once heard you say my mama was pretty. You said a whole lot of other things—none of them particularly nice."

"You're right, Angel. And I'm sorry about that. The truth is, nobody knew where she came from till the day she died. But young women don't usually come from nowhere unless they got something to hide and I speculated like everybody else."

"Wasn't it enough she was a good wife to my daddy?"

"Your daddy never had a lick a sense about women. He always liked the sexy ones."

"Was Mama sexy?"

"Law, yes!" Georgia rolled her eyes. "About lit the street afire. I was so jealous of her I could spit." She chuckled, mellow and expansive since her place of importance was guaranteed by Angel's known relationship with Mrs. Pierson—and therefore the beautiful stranger. "And you look just like her, honey, but you're sweeter. You don't sizzle like she did. Just as well."

She swung her big car into the lot behind the church, waving to various members as she took her place. As Angel got out, she said, "Thank you, Aunt Georgia. I appreciate the ride."

"You're welcome, honey," She lifted the cake almost reverently. "I'll take this in for you. You go on and get those children ready."

The small room where her Sunday school class met could hardly contain the feverish mood of the children. They fidgeted and jabbed each other with elbows in nervous stage fright. Angel managed to get them dressed, and then ran through a quick rehearsal before regular services started.

As the pianist struck up the prelude to services, she herded the children toward the sanctuary. The miniature villagers squirmed in agitation as the pastor announced the special play Angel had written for their study of the Old Testament. She'd chosen the story of Shadrach, Meshach and Abednego, who defied Nebuchadnezzar, mainly because she loved the names of the principles, although she kept that fact to herself.

The pianist took up the music Angel had found to complement their story as the narrator, a mature girl from town, began to read. Among the nervous children only Shadrach was calm, his dark curls cascading over his ears, dark eyes clear and untroubled. Angel was touched, looking at him, pleased at the dignity he lent his simple role. She would have to remember to tell him he was a natural actor.

After the pageant, the church applauded, the hymns were sung and the pastor delivered his message. As Angel listened, she was puzzled at the anger that edged his words, surprised that he chose "Love thy neighbor" as his subject when the pageant would have given him such a perfect opening for any number of other things.

Still, it wasn't her place to question his direction from God. A warmth spread through her as she listened. Whatever the end result might be, she was serving her neighbors to the best of her ability. Perhaps time would mellow the rigidity of the townspeople. Hadn't Georgia come around?

When the congregation stood to sing the Doxology, Angel's voice rose sweet and clear. "Praise God from whom all blessings flow, praise him all creatures here below . . ."

Her neighbor in the pew glanced at her and Angel smiled around her singing mouth.

Because of the weather, the potluck had been transferred to the basement, a damp but serviceable room below the sanctuary where long tables had been set up with folding chairs. Along one wall, tables groaned with the best the women had to offer—a huge, shining barbequed brisket with slices of orange and lemon peel clinging to the meat, a ham slick with brown sugar and studded with pineapple, heaps of fried chicken and potato salad and deviled eggs, a fruit salad swimming with cream, cakes and pies and gallons of sweet tea. Freshly brewed coffee sent up its fragrant steam from a fifty-cup container.

Flanked by her Sunday school class, Angel made her way down the line, filling her plate with a little of everything until it nearly collapsed under the weight.

"Are you gonna *eat* all that?" asked Harold, the boy who had played Shadrach.

"You betcha," Angel answered. "I'm hungry enough to eat a hog."

"Me, too," piped Margaret, the child on Angel's other side. "I'm specially gonna have some of them debiled eggs."

"You're gonna have some of those deviled eggs," Angel corrected gently.

"Right. Those."

Edwin Walker eased up behind Angel. In his suit and tie, his hair combed neatly from his face, it was hard to think of him as a threat. "Which one of them cakes is yours, Angel? I know you had to bring a cake and I want me a piece."

He leaned a hair too close, until her vision was filled with his neon eyes and full lips. She turned her head. "The chocolate with mint leaves on top."

"I've been waiting all morning for this." He handed his plate to the matron behind the table. "Miz Hayden, would you be so kind as to cut me a slice of that chocolate cake there?"

"Certainly, Edwin. How's your mama?"

"Oh, she's fine. Doc says she'll have that cast off in a week. I know she'll be glad to be up and around again."

"You tell her I said hello, won't you?"

Edwin smiled, his mesmerizing eyes fixed directly on Mrs. Hayden. "I'll do that."

He'd managed not to dump a whole bottle of cologne upon himself this morning, Angel thought with a smile. A wisp of the exotic aftershave he wore drifted toward her, making her think of seaports and sailors.

"You gonna let me sit with you today, Angel?"

"I don't think there's room, Edwin. My class already asked and I told them they could." She pointed to a chess pie. "I'd have a piece of that one, Miz Hayden. And cut a piece of the chocolate for my aunt Georgia. I promised I'd save her a piece."

In spite of her indication that the children would leave him no room, Edwin followed Angel to one of the long tables, her Sunday school class trailing her like a hive of bees, bees that settled around the table. Edwin squeezed between two of them cheerfully, right across the table from Angel.

She didn't speak much to him, listening to the children instead, but his gaze, bright and unnerving, was fixed upon her face as he ate. As she finished her meal and the bees began to buzz away, he spoke.

"How's life down in nigger-town, baby?"

She winced. "You've got the manners of a mongrel dog, Edwin Walker."

"Aw, honey, I didn't mean no disrespect."

Angel looked at him.

"You Coreys are just touchy, that's all. No white person in this county gets upset about niggers 'cept y'all. And your daddy was crazy, Angel. Everybody knew it. Why don't you just realize your natural place and forget about them poor colored folks?"

She folded her hands on the table. "And do what, exactly?"

"Get outta that store and find yourself a husband, have some babies or something."

For a brief second, Angel wished for the clarity of his clear-cut world. If she had been raised like Edwin, she'd never think about her deepest heart being afraid of standing alone in the presence of Isaiah High and what that meant. She'd be afraid for a simple reason then, because any decent white woman was afraid of being alone with any colored man. Not this complex thing she felt constantly with Isaiah, that pinching in her chest she couldn't shake. She'd never have to despair over the business in her store falling off. She would go to town and see silly movies instead of working herself half to death.

Then she thought of Paul's grandmother, dragging the child with her to work until she no longer had a place. And thought of the women who stopped in the store early, because she'd decided to give them a place to have a cup of coffee. She thought of the Walker brothers cheating their colored customers, thought of the rhythms of black laughter and black voices lost to her.

She shook her head. "I don't think that's what God has planned for me, Edwin."

He laughed and tipped back his chair, folding his hands over his tie. "We'll see about that, honey."

Angel stood. "Excuse me. I've got to take this cake to my aunt."

"Nice talking with you."

"The pleasure was all yours."

His laughter followed her as she walked quickly away.

Georgia was sitting with her friends Margaret and June Green.

"Here's your cake, Aunt Georgia."

"Now, isn't that beautiful?" Georgia patted the place next to her. "Have a seat, sugar."

Just then, the pastor touched her shoulder. "Morning, y'all," he said to the older women. "Angel, can I talk to you for a minute, please? In private, if you would."

"Of course," Angel said. "Excuse me."

He led her to an empty corner of the room, past the full tables and animated conversation of the diners. His steps were filled with a stony heaviness rare to him and a clutch of worry rippled through her stomach—had there been some violence or a death she would mourn? When they reached the corner, he turned, a frown creasing the pale flesh between his clear, intelligent eyes. He licked his lips.

"You're scaring me to death. Whatever it is, just spit it out."

"Angel, I have to tell you that you won't be teaching your Sunday School class anymore."

"What?"

"The board voted last night to find another teacher for the six to nines. There some feeling that you might be . . . morally delinquent." His nostrils flared. "I fought it, Angel, but I'm a new preacher and ain't got a lot of political influence around here."

Dumbstruck, Angel stared at him. "I can't believe it. I've been teaching Sunday school since I was seventeen years old. And I'm a good teacher! The children like me!"

"I know." He squeezed her arm. "I'm so sorry, Angel."

A red fury surged up through her throat, blurring her vision with a bloody cloud. "Lord knows I'll certainly corrupt those children," she said bitterly.

Tears of anger pricked her eyes as she whirled away from him. As she marched back up the aisle between the tables with their folding chairs, the murmuring voices quieted. Angel ignored them and headed straight for Georgia.

At the table's edge, she quivered uncontrollably for a long moment before she could speak, fighting the tears, fighting to hold control of her voice so that it would not quaver.

When she managed her words, they were low and flat and cold. "You knew," she said. "And you had the gall to come down there and get me this morning like you loved me."

Georgia tugged her sweater over her bosom, her mouth pinched closed.

Angel leaned over the table. "You knew that class was the most important thing in my life right now and you didn't even try to stop them, did you?"

Georgia, lips grey around the edges, tried to argue. "Honey, I thought maybe it would bring you to your senses."

"Don't even talk to me anymore. And as far as I'm concerned, you're dead from this moment on." She spun away, holding her head up as she made her way to the door.

"Suit yourself, girl," Georgia called behind her. "You gonna die crazy Just like your daddy."

Angel left the church in the pouring rain. No one followed her and she didn't look back.

Isaiah had read long into the night, and picked up the book Angel had loaned him in the silence of Sunday morning at home, his mother and sister out to church no matter what the weather. He never went, figuring God knew where he was and how he felt.

Around one, he finished reading and set the book aside, feeling restless, and paced out to the porch to stare at the rain. In the back of his mind was the long, long winter crossing France and into Germany. The cold. The damp. The endless gray skies.

Truth be told, he was bored.

It would be hours before anybody got out of church and he'd been warned to keep his hands off the roast his mama had put in the pot before she left. He wondered how the roof of the Corey store was holding up against the rain and played with the notion of going over to check. He could take back the library book while he was at it, so it wouldn't be late.

Exhaling, he shook his head. Excuses. Every bit of it.

He'd known it would be hard to put up the walls between them again after the long exchange of letters. It was one of the reasons he hadn't planned on coming home at all. No point to it.

This morning, he'd awakened with the sense of her folded into the crooks of his elbows and the palms of his hands. For fifteen years, maybe twenty, he'd kept himself in check, building between them a wall of books and plans and women who eased his physical hungers.

At sixteen, now, he'd believed it might be possible to die of love. Every glimpse of her, every word she spoke to him, was a torture, pleasure and agony. His crazed longing gave him vivid dreams, even more vividly detailed daydreams.

He hadn't died. But his friendship with Solomon deteriorated and fell away, a childhood fruit gone to rot. He avoided the store, kept to himself and lower Gideon where Angel would not venture. And when the Germans invaded Poland, he escaped into the Army.

At seven, Isaiah had told his father he intended to marry Angel Corey. Jordan had stopped dead in the middle of the bridge and knelt down to stare in his son's eyes. He gripped Isaiah's arms so hard there had been bruises the next day. "No, you ain't, boy. Don't you ever say it again. *Ever.* Hear?"

Terrified, Isaiah had nodded. For two weeks, he was forbidden to go to the store. But he'd never gained a lick of sense where Angel was concerned. Didn't have any now. Fact was, he couldn't let her drown in that store all by herself the way she had last time.

He found an umbrella and stuck her library book under his shirt, then gave himself over to the simple pleasure of walking in the rain on the deserted road. Down the road to the bridge, over the rushing water, back up toward Gideon proper.

As he came up the road toward the store, he saw Angel. Never had she looked more pitiful. He paused, marshaling himself. She stood in front of the store, muddy to her knees. Her Sunday dress was stuck to her legs and her shoes were in her hand, saved from the mud but ruined from the rain all the same. Rain dripped in rivulets from the ends of her hair and ran down her nose.

Something terrible had happened, he thought. "Angel," he said gently, holding the umbrella over her. "What are you doing, girl?"

She swiveled her face around to him and the stillness he had thought to be some kind of pitiable defeat showed instead to be a clear and burning fury. With an expression of great disdain, she lifted her chin at the porch.

Isaiah looked. In red paint on the floor of the porch, someone had scrawled "Nigger lover" in letters two feet high. A chill touched him.

With an animal cry of rage, Angel threw her ruined shoes down the road toward town. In stocking feet she climbed the steps and carefully leapt over the letters to go inside.

In a moment, she reappeared with a bucket and a scrub brush, then fell to her knees to scrub the N away.

Isaiah climbed up beside her. Taking a second rag, he began at the opposite end to wash the letters away. The paint had not dried except in spots, but in the weathered floorboards it left behind a ghost image, pale but discernible.

Angel didn't speak until she had washed the first three letters off as well as she could. By then, her hands and arms were stained with the red paint, but her fury seemed to have vented itself somewhat in the scrubbing. When she spoke, her tone was almost conversational.

"They took my Sunday School class away from me this morning."

He rocked back up on his heels. Waited.

She dipped her brush and started on the second G. "I've had that class for six years. Before that, I taught the fours and fives."

"I'm sorry."

"So am I." She bent her head over the next letter. "But I'll be damned if they'll beat me. They've underestimated me all of my life. They won't anymore."

Underestimated. Isaiah thought about that as she put her weight behind the cloth in her hand, rubbing with her soap-reddened hands. It stung a little, that word. He remembered the letters he'd written and never sent.

"Damn them! I'm good with those children. They deserve to have me!" She stood and kicked the bucket hard with the side of her foot, sending water spewing out into the grayness beyond the porch.

She slammed inside. Isaiah glanced at the spilled bucket. He dropped his cloth and followed her. "You swore," he said. "Twice. I've never heard you swear in my life."

Slumping forward on the counter, she said, "I never had so much call to swear before this."

There was sound of weeping in her voice and he crossed the room to stand beside the counter. Her wet hair fell over her hands and face, and her shoulder blades stuck up in sharp relief on her back. "Don't cry," he said, helplessly.

"I'm not crying." She straightened and faced him, pushing tendrils of wet hair from her face. "I'm just tired. Disappointed in everybody. They're treating me like a harlot."

Her face was washed clean by the rain, and age showed a little at the corners of her eyes. A lock of wet hair stuck up over her forehead, and he wanted to push it down, but instead he said, "They just wish you were a harlot, Angel. Make it easier for their consciences. If you're a good woman, they'd have to think about what that means."

She looked at him for a long moment. "Thank you." She shivered suddenly. "I'm going to put on some dry clothes and then make some coffee. You want a dry shirt?"

"No, uh, I . . . just came to check on the roof and bring you back your book." He put it on the counter and backed away. "I guess I better be getting back."

"No sense going in the pouring rain." She bustled out from behind the counter as if it didn't matter, but he knew she was lonely. Lonelier than he was by far. "Might as well stay and have a cup of coffee since you're here. Store is closed today, and nobody is going to be out in this rain, anyhow."

He frowned briefly, glanced over his shoulder as if someone was looking. Gave a nod. "I'll wait in the kitchen."

"Fine. Won't take me but a minute."

— 17 —

Happy Howllllaween! 1943

Dear Isaiah,

 We're right in the midst of the big rush of Christmas mailings, but hopefully you'll get this in time for Christmas. My daddy says a soldier always needs more socks, but I say you might need fudge more. I knitted most of these things myself and hope they fit both of you—and don't you dare laugh at my knitting Isaiah High, until you take a look. I've made a lot of progress the last few years.

 I had a letter from Mrs. Wentworth. What a nice lady! I've sent along some more pecans for her. All the magazines are for you, of course. They're out of date, but we'd just be throwing them away, so you might as well have them.

 As for the book, I'm sure you can get plenty now, all the same, I can't think of a better present for a man who likes to read as much as you do.

Your friend,

Angel

PS I just read The Yearling. Cried and cried and cried. Not your kinda book, probably, but I liked it a lot. Nature and families and animals.

V-Mail
December 2, 1943

Dear Isaiah,

 Merry Christmas, and Happy New Year! I suddenly thought this afternoon that you might be somewhere that it snows at Christmas-time this year. I was going to send a snow-glitter card to you, but they're saying V-Mail gets to y'all in a couple of weeks, so I'm going this route. They sure don't give you a lot of room, do they? I'm trying to write small.

By the way, when we were children, playing in that tree house, I knew the king had to be dead for a woman to be queen. I'm no dummy! All you have to do is read to see that the only time a queen got to be boss was when her husband died or she never got married.

Maybe this will be the year the war ends, finally. It seems like it's been going on forever.

Be careful, Isaiah.

Your friend (too),

Angel

— 18 —

Shivering in her wet dress, Angel headed for Parker's room. In the closet, she found a green flannel shirt and tugged it off the hanger for Isaiah. The jostled clothes sent out a concentrated essence of her father, so tangible it was as if he had stepped into the room with her—his face, long and dark beneath its wreath of black curls, his sharp blue eyes dancing with Irish humor.

She grasped the shirt to her breast, breathless, and bent nearly double at the sudden surge of pain. It was sorrow that grew up from her intestines, filling every cavity within her until it reached her throat, where it threatened to choke her.

The red-painted words on the porch floated in her imagination, and she felt weak, unable to meet the long fight she saw yawning ahead of her.

Then, as clearly as if a movie was rolling out on the wall, she saw his face again, laughing with Jordan High late into the night, without whiskey or gin, laughing with the pure delight of the other's company. Angel remembered, too, the weight of grief her father had carried when Jordan was killed for trying to organize farm workers. Parker's faith had been tested then. As hers was being tested now.

Parker's faith had returned, by degrees. Jordan had died for his beliefs, Parker figured aloud to his daughter. If Parker didn't keep that dream of a better world alive on Jordan's behalf, there'd be no good at all in his dying. Angel had been too young to grasp the violence, much less the complex circumstances that had led to it, but she listened quietly because she knew he needed to talk to somebody.

Now Jordan's son waited in the kitchen for one of Parker's shirts. Angel looked at the emerald cloth, thought of the red words on the porch, of the loss of the children in her class. She closed her eyes. *I'm not that strong!*

Almost as if he were standing there with her, Parker's voice said, "Oh, but you are, girl. You are."

Maybe she was. At the moment, she was also freezing. Shivering, she took the shirt back to the kitchen, where Isaiah was measuring coffee. "Figured I could be of some practical help here."

"Thank you." She draped the shirt on the chair. "I'll be back in a flash."

In her room, she quickly shed her wet dress and the ruined stockings and donned an ordinary shirt dress, and pulled a sweater over her arms. For a moment, she dithered over her shoes, finally deciding Isaiah wasn't going to care one way or another. She pulled on a pair of socks and combed her hair, laughing when she saw the big loop over her forehead.

"You must have been about to split a gut laughing over my hair," she said, coming back to the kitchen. The heady scent of coffee oozed into the damp air. She inhaled it and remembered her cake. "You know what else? I made the most beautiful cake I have ever made this morning. Been waiting to bake it for ages! I could have made it for myself and Paul, and maybe even you would have had some of it." She sighed, leaning on the counter, crossing her arms. "That'll be the last one they ever get, I can tell you that."

He held a fist in the air. "You tell it, sister!"

Angel laughed. He had changed into her daddy's shirt, and it showed off how much he'd filled out during the war. The jeweled green pointed up the deep reddish tones of his skin. "That shirt looks right nice on you, Isaiah. I didn't realize you and my daddy were of a size at all."

He looked away, fiddled with the pot percolating on the stove. "It hurt my heart when I missed him by such a short time."

"He wanted to see you." She took cups from the cupboard, put the sugar on the table and fished milk from the icebox. "A minute ago, I was remembering how he and your daddy used to laugh on the porch. Remember?" She propped one foot over the other. Rain came down in buckets, sheeting over the window so hard she could barely see the cottonwood. "Talk about a broken heart. His was busted good when your daddy died."

"Mine, too."

She straightened and took the coffee from the stove. "I always thought he sounded like God."

"Like God?"

"When he laughed. I thought God laughed like that." She thought, *and you sound just like him.*

"You ever tell the church folks that?"

"Lord, no. Even at five I had some sense. I don't imagine they ever thought of God laughing."

"That ain't exactly what I was thinking of."

"No, I guess not."

"He didn't do you any favors, Angel. Your daddy."

She pulled mugs out of the cupboard. "Maybe not. But maybe that's how the world changes, Isaiah. One father, one child, at a time."

"Mmm-hmm."

There was a thickness in the kitchen that had nothing to do with the rain-wet air. She couldn't seem to look directly in his face, only along the edges of his jaw and the tip of his ear; skim the hard square of his chin and follow the length of his arm to where flannel met the sleek rise of muscle on his forearm.

With an odd sense of panic, she realized how wrong it was for them to be standing together in a house with no one but them in it. He was not Isaiah the child, or Jordan the father, but Isaiah the man, grown to a sturdy height and girth. There was something alarming in that, and in the anger she sensed in him.

Carefully, he picked up his discarded shirt. "I really ought to get back."

Crossing her arms tightly, she nodded, poked at a mark on the floor with one toe. "Well, thanks for checking on me."

He nodded. "It's just so—"

She looked up at him. "I'm not stupid."

"I didn't say you were." He made no move to go quite yet. "I'll bring you bring a book tomorrow. Poems."

"I'd like that."

He cleared his throat, looked out the window. "I don't guess your daddy had a hat in there."

"Only a dozen or so." She headed for the back bedroom and rummaged up a wide brimmed hat.

Isaiah plunked it down. "That'll do."

"Keep it. The shirt, too. He'd be glad to know you had something of his, Isaiah. He loved you like you were his own son."

"Thank you." He tipped his hat and left through the back door.

After he'd gone, Angel was left again with herself. With her disquiet and loneliness. With her exhaustion.

She had so wanted Isaiah to stay, and she was so relieved when he left. Sitting in the kitchen with the coffee he had made, she realized what she needed. Out of the drawer, she took sheets of plain light blue stationary and a pen, and sat back down at the table, leaving the back door open so she could hear the roar of the rain. She began to write.

May 16, 1946

Dear Isaiah,

   It's raining cats and dogs here, so much rain you

can't even see across the road. It's a lonesome sound, but I love the smell.

I've missed your letters like crazy. They connected me to the bigger world out there, and I liked knowing that one of us got outta here, got to see London and Paris, even if it wasn't the most ideal conditions. I loved having a bigger world to think about. The minute you stopped writing, it disappeared, and I felt like somebody turned the lights off, and there I was, sitting in the dark again.

And listen to me, feeling sorry for myself when so many people in the world have lost everything. I have a roof over my head (well, sorta, thanks to you) and my good health and . . . I'm having trouble thinking of more things to be thankful for. I had a Sunday school class that gave me a lot o joy, but that's gone. No family left, to speak of. Looks like this whole store business is not going to work out. So what do I have?

I'm smart, that's one thing. Very smart. I don't even think you really know that, but I am. And that's something nobody can take from you. It's time, I reckon, to put on my thinking cap and figure out what I can really do to get out of Gideon, and find some other life.

You really didn't have to quit writing with no explanation or anything. That was mean, and I'm mad at you for it.

Your friend,

Angel

She folded it and put it in her drawer with other letters she hadn't had the nerve to mail. Like the others, it drained away some of her tension, gave her space to breathe.

She stretched out on her bed and fell into a half-doze, thinking of the tree house she, Isaiah, and Solomon had built when she was six, the boys eight. They assembled it form spare lumber they hunted up along the road to town and at the edges of the river, using a hammer and nails Parker gave them. It took two weeks to put it together according to Isaiah's standards, who insisted the boards had to meet smoothly, had to be braced in a certain way against the tree. When it was finished, it was sturdy and strong, a wide platform high in the spreading boughs of a live oak, deep in the pine forest. From the ground, it couldn't be seen, even at the beginning. As time passed, the natural growth of leaves and branches completely obscured it.

They had played there year round, bringing paper bags full of food to picnic, and pillows and books and toys of all kinds. They pretended, at Angel's insistence, that the tree house was a ship, sailing to far ports. Isaiah liked to pretend the forest was a tropical island, as in Robinson Crusoe, and imagined the pines around them to be banana trees full of monkeys, or palms bearing hard knobs of coconuts.

Solomon, deprived in his early life of books and their wonder, didn't read the stories that inflamed both Angel and Isaiah, and so was relegated to a secondary position. He steered the pirate ship while Angel and Isaiah sighted magnificent coasts, peopling them with flowers and trees of every description. They challenged one another on the grandest descriptions of coasts they could find. When they played the island game, Angel was a princess gone to visit a colony recently acquired, and Isaiah was her trusted earl. Solomon was the poor knave marooned with the royalty.

As a smaller boy, and entirely too aware of his status as the seventh child of his unmarried mother, Solomon didn't complain. He was simply thankful to have friends of any kind. By the age of ten, he had grown secure in his place—even poor white trash had something on the colored. He wouldn't allow Isaiah to hold a position higher than his own, and Angel was relegated to fetching and carrying. It was a slow, subtle shift, but the games had lost their glory after that. Solomon was autocrat and king, boss and master. If Isaiah had work to do and she and Solomon were there alone, she ended up feeling like Cinderella under the supervision of the evil stepsisters. She quit going with him if Isaiah was busy.

When Angel reached eleven, her father no longer let her go with the thirteen-year-old boys into the woods. Nor could she go with Isaiah anywhere. They visited in the backyard or on the front porch, trading stories of books they had read.

One afternoon, just past her thirteenth birthday, she had gone to the tree house to read. It was August. Heat circled the woods and clung to her neck. Even her feet were hot. She was too lazy to read and it was too hot to sleep, so she lay on the boards of the tree house, utterly still, waiting for stray breezes. She stared at the green and gold leaves above her. The sky was pale, as if the color had been sucked out by the heat. Within her chest, her heart beat lazily, even the effort of pumping blood almost too much.

Below her, she heard the feet of an intruder on the tree. Thinking it Solomon and too lazy to move, she frowned.

Isaiah's voice surprised her. "I thought you might be here."

"I was here first," she said without opening her eyes. "You know I can't be here if y'all show up. And I'm too hot to go anywhere else."

"Don't go, then." Cold drops of water fell on her face and she gasped, looking at him. A single ray of sun angled down to set his wet head ablaze. His hair in summer bleached to a glittery auburn around the temples, and this year it was even more pronounced. He was soaked. "I ain't gonna tell, are you?"

He sat down next her, cross-legged. At nearly fifteen, he was mostly arms and legs and feet. The arms were gaining shape, taking on the long ropy muscles they would carry as a man. His brow was high and wide, ending in an even line of hair that fell, when wet, into a natural arrangement of precise, tight rows. Above the high cheekbones that gave his face an exotic look, his polished dark eyes measured her steadily.

"I don't want to get in trouble, Isaiah," she said and covered her eyes with an arm.

"Only person would tell is Solomon and he's in the fields with his mama." He nudged her knee with his big toe. "Ain't you bored this afternoon? Like some company?"

In truth, it was good to have him there, like old times. She felt her mouth curling into a smile, heard his answering laugh, changing now from the boy's piping to the man's boom. Halfway through, it slid up the register and ended on a hoot.

Angel opened her eyes. "That's horrible, Isaiah. You gotta promise not to laugh anymore today."

He laughed again. "Cain't promise. You'll get used to it. I did." He fell down beside her, stretching out his legs to stare overhead. "Pretty. Looks like gold coins."

"Mmm-hmm." She relaxed, lifting a knee. A soft wind swept the platform, rustling the leaves. "That feels good."

"Does," he agreed.

There was no need for conversation. They simply rested side by side in the oven of the afternoon, waiting together for breezes.

A long time later, Isaiah touched her hand with the back of his. She turned her head to look at him.

"I miss you, Angel."

It almost made her cry, and she rubbed her knuckles against his. "I miss you, too. Nobody else thinks like I do."

"Me, either." His expression was solemn. "I wish we didn't have to grow up."

"I know."

Together, they looked again at the roof of branches, letting the back of their hands touch. There they stayed, mostly silent, until the afternoon was late and both heard the call of supper in their bellies. They climbed down together. Angel headed for the path that led to her back yard through the forest, Isaiah for the river, to swim home over the low shallows of August.

It was the last afternoon but one that they had together. Except for that one other time, she never got to even *talk* to him again. She would see him on the road going into town to work and, when forced, he came to the store with his mama. That was all.

Long ago, Angel thought drowsily. In spite of the time that had passed, she could still remember the feel of his knuckles against hers—the satiny smoothness of the skin there, where hands were usually rough. She fell from the doze into sleep, remembering the comfortable quiet they had shared waiting for breezes, side by side, high above the earth and its trials.

— 19 —

V-Mail
January 10, 1944

Dear Angel,

Bless your sweet little heart, girl. I been half-froze since I got here. Thanks to you, I'm finally warm. Everything fits just fine. I'm wearing a pair of socks right now, and the other is hidden good because I'm not gonna take no chance some other soldier's gonna take advantage of my carelessness. They're warm, Angel, So warm. The sweater fits good, too. I wear it under everything else.

The gloves and scarf for Mrs. Wentworth were good, too. She asked me to tell you thank you very much for all of it. I guess you got her letter, too, though? I helped her write it because she got arthritis so bad in her hands in the winter.

You have a good heart, Angel. Thanks for all you've been doing. I'm gonna keep my eyes open for something that you'll like, a souvenir from England just for you.

Tell your daddy hey for me.

Isaiah

V-Mail #1
January 12, 1944

It's a cold, wet day here and I'm about fed up with cold and wet. Feels like my toes is wrinkled all the time, and you just can't get warm. I'll never complain about being hot again as long as I live.

Not far from where our barracks are is a ruined castle, and last night I went over there with a local person. The walls are all tumbled down, with holes for where the windows used to be and a tower with stairs inside leading up to nowhere. Somebody told me it was built in 1285. Think of that, Angel! I thought of you the whole time I was in there, seeing how you loved castles so much when we were children, so I made some little drawings for you.

And I made a point of paying attention like you was with me, so I'd remember lots of things to tell you. Some of the walls are fallen all the way down, but in other places, they're fine, sticking right up in the sky, even with a turret on the top. You can walk around on the inside, and mostly, it's all grown over with grass, and there are clumps of moss and flowers on the walls. You can see where the rooms were, like the kitchen with a hole in the wall where they used to bake bread, still all perfect, and a giant fireplace which must have been the main area, and a little bitty church, which was cold, cold, cold, but you can sit there and know it's holy. Or maybe that's just ghosts, whispering around. In any account, I knew you'd have liked it, would have been cooing like a little pigeon.

The whole country is old. Old, old, old. There's this place on the side of a mountain where there's a great big old horse drawn right on it,

V-Mail #2

and it's been there for two thousand years or something. I kinda get all quiet inside when I think of it, some folks all those years ago drawing that horse, and all the people since then making sure it stays up there, all tidy and nice.

It changes your thinking a little to consider all that time, all those centuries. Did you know the Romans were in Britain? Mrs. Wentworth loaned me a book about it, and she said if I can get there, there's some ruins down south. Imagine that! In Texas, the oldest thing I know about is the Indian fort, and it was what, a hundred years old or something. Nothing. No time at all, considering.

And that makes everything that's happening now both better and worse. Better because no war lasts forever, does it? Someday, this one will be over, too.

But worse, too, because all these modern bombs and planes are doing a whole lot more damage than the old warfare could do. England is wrecked in a lot of places—old churches and things knocked down so bad you know they won't be there in 800 years like those castle walls. Whole streets just a big mess. It makes me sad to walk through and see it. Lot is still here, naturally, but a lot is gone, and it's gone forever. Nobody much remembers what war was going on when that old castle was built, but I can still walk around in it, get a feeling for the way things were, and tell you about it, a half a world away.

I'm running out of room again. Better go. Hope you enjoyed this little "travelogue." Ha ha.

Your friend Isaiah

V-Mail #3

[Sketches of interior of castle ruins]

— 20 —

In the humid stillness of Monday afternoon, Isaiah worked in Mrs. Pierson's backyard, a place that reminded him of the gardens he'd seen in London. Here, as in England, masses of flowers of every description grew and thrived, nourished by the moisture in the air.

The flowers were neatly placed, but the effect was far from fussy. Flowers tumbled from the rows in exuberant falls of purple and red, yellow and white. Some of them he knew by name—alyssum and chives, roses and cornflowers. Others he labeled by their shape or scent. He called the heavy purple ones trumpets, the tiny white ones lace.

The gardens he had planted and tended as a child were practical things, full of greens and squash and tomatoes, vegetables that could be put up in the fall for winter eating. The very notion of flowers had once seemed frivolous.

But Mrs. Wentworth's garden in England had taught him there was joy to be found in the simple beauty flowers provided. He found himself eased when he'd spent an afternoon weeding. It seemed he could smell the flowers long after he quit. Now he loved the idea of something just living because it was beautiful, could understand why somebody might grow something they wouldn't ever eat.

Once Mrs. Pierson had done this work herself, making of herself a legend. Folks couldn't understand how she made those flowers grow like they did, nor why, blind as she was, she would want to. Now, though she'd hired Isaiah to build a flagstone pathway through the garden, she really needed his quiet help weeding and fertilizing and tying up the climbers. He found her an agreeable employer, mainly because he worked *with* her, never *for* her. She accorded him a rare dignity.

This afternoon, Gudren sat on a little stone bench in the yard. Her thin body was covered with an airy kind of dress with flowers all over it, the sleeves short. She had the knack of sitting so still he forgot about her, a contented expression never quite chasing away the shadows around her eyes.

He had believed, before he went to war, that he'd seen human cruelty at its worst. But even his own childhood had not prepared him for the work he'd had to do in the camps or the walking skeletons with their hollow eyes, or the bodies they had buried.

As he weeded, the sun hot on his back, even the simple beauty of a single, heavy blossom couldn't quell the anguish that rose within him. It was an ache so deep and wide he could barely put a name to it.

The graves. He had wanted to see each wasted body buried in a place of its own, so there would be at last, dignity. But there had been too many to dig by hand. In the end, bull-dozers had done the work, scooting limp skeletons over the dirt into their resting place.

He tore out a handful of some creeping weed and cut his hand. He grunted softly in pain.

"Gloves," came a voice behind him. Mrs. Pierson. "Gloves will stop that."

"Yes, ma'am." Eerie how she knew things she shouldn't. The flowers, he understood them. They had scent and shape and texture a blind woman could love. But sometimes, it was like she had another kind of eyes.

He reached for another clump of weeds, waiting. She never just talked for nothing.

"You are blue today, Isaiah?"

He glanced at her. "I reckon I am, a bit."

"Is it the war?"

Isaiah paused. She said nothing, so he finally answered in a low voice, "Yes, ma'am."

"It is not new, Isaiah." Her head lifted a fraction. "When I was four years old, soldiers found my mother and I in a field. They blinded me and raped her." The voice was calm, without rancor. "My mother died. That's when we left Poland."

Isaiah lowered his head.

"The point is, Isaiah, we go on. As your mother has, as you have. God has given you a great gift by showing you the power to be had in one life. One man, Isaiah, can change the world forever."

His jaw burned with holding it closed. The fat lady on his back jumped with glee, her heels thudding hard into his spine. In his mind's eye, brutal images whirled; fleshless arms and legs tumbling into holes in the ground; his daddy's feet swinging; this tiny, strong woman . . .

"It wasn't God led Hitler, Miz Pierson."

"I am aware of that, Isaiah," she said briskly and stood up. "Now, I want you to quit pretending to pull weeds and drive Gudren out for a visit with Angel."

Isaiah smiled in spite of himself as he caught the glitter of humor on Gudren's face. "That all right with you?"

"Of course."

"All right then." He stood up, brushing the dust from his hands and pants. "Let me wash my hands and I'll get the car."

Angel was sweeping the porch when Isaiah came, not on foot as he usually did, but driving Mrs. Pierson's big car. With him was Gudren. She stepped out of the car a bit shyly. "Hello, Angel. I hope you are not too busy for a visit?"

"Heavens, no!" Angel exclaimed, setting the broom aside. "I'm so bored, I'm about to explode."

"I'll drive you back whenever you get ready," Isaiah interjected. "Meantime, I'm'na go ahead and get some work done."

"Did you remember to bring the book you told me about?" Angel asked, shading her eyes.

"I forgot," he said, but the way he shifted and didn't look at her made Angel think it was deliberate forgetting.

At that moment, Paul slammed outside and with the pure trust of a child hurled himself from the top step into Isaiah's arms.

Isaiah laughed as he caught the boy and hugged him tight before setting him down. "You gonna help me today, little buddy?"

"Yes, sir."

"Well, come on then, 'fore the sun sets and leaves us in the dark." He held out his hand for Paul's and they rounded the house.

"How sweet," Gudren commented. "Is he Isaiah's relative?"

Angel frowned. "I'm not sure, exactly. They're related somehow. Both Isaiah's mother and Paul's grandmother come from the same little town in Louisiana. They might be kin."

"Kin?"

Angel laughed. "Related. But it wouldn't matter if they weren't kin at all. Children love that man." She tipped her head toward the store. "Let's go get a glass of tea. I have some cookies I made for Paul."

"Wonderful." Gudren had lost her shyness and now smiled. Her teeth had suffered some, but even so, it was a transforming expression. Easy to glimpse the beauty she had been before the war.

In the sunny kitchen, Angel waved Gudren into a chair. "I hope you like your tea real sweet," she said, chipping ice into glasses. "I managed to do without sugar during the war, but I gotta admit I missed it."

"Sweet tea is fine." She glanced around her with curiosity. "This is a beautiful room," she commented. "You must like blue."

Angel looked at the dotted Swiss curtains and ceramic canisters and cup towels. All of them were in one shade of blue or another. She smiled. "I guess I must, although I never noticed before." She put the tea in front of Gudren and uncovered a plate of cookies before settling across the table. "What's your favorite color?"

Gudren lifted her eyes to the ceiling, considering. Then she looked at Angel. "Red," she said firmly, "It is the color of roses and sunsets and rubies." She laughed.

"My husband loved red. He had a bright red corduroy shirt that he about wore to death."

"Were you married, Angel?" Gudren sounded surprised, and Angel realized that, unlike everyone in town, this woman didn't know her entire history from before birth. There was something curiously pleasurable in that fact.

"Yes," she said. "He was killed in the Pacific."

"I'm sorry."

"Thank you." Angel shook her head. "We were only married two weeks before he left, but we were friends our whole lives."

"Tell me about him," Gudren said, a curious hunger in her voice.

Angel thought for a minute. "He was real fair, and had blue blue eyes. That red shirt used to make his eyes look real pretty."

"Was he handsome?"

Angel picked a cookie from the plate and pushed it toward Gudren. "I don't know," she said. "Not really. He was always kinda skinny and he had a lot of freckles. His nose used to be sunburned right here," she indicated the bridge of her own nose.

Gudren inclined her head. "You did not marry for love?"

"He was my husband."

"Yes." She smiled. "But people marry for many reasons other than love, and much more so during wartime, no?"

Angel brushed a scattering of sugar from the oilcloth. "I always thought I loved him," she said finally, lifting her eyebrows. "But you know what? Mostly Solomon just drove me crazy. He wouldn't stand up straight and always tried to boss me around and he never once, in his whole life, thought of doing anything but get himself his own farm—" She broke off. "I think it was a shock to Solomon to find out there were other countries."

"What led you to marry?"

Angel shook her head slowly. Lifted a shoulder. "I don't know. I reckon I felt sorry for him. Wanted him to have something of his own before he shipped out." A pang of guilt touched her. "I shouldn't talk about him like this. He was a good man."

"Yes." Gudren ate a cookie with surprising gusto. "Perhaps," she said when she could speak, "one day you will marry again. A more suitable husband."

"I don't think I really care to," Angel said. "I'm too independent to make a good wife."

She chuckled.

"Did you have a husband, a sweetheart, before the war, Gudren?"

"Yes. My fiancé. He was lost to the camps. I don't know what happened to him."

"I'm so sorry." And now she understood Gudren's need. "Won't you tell me about him?"

"His name was Daniel," Gudren began, and, once in motion, she talked for nearly an hour, beginning with Daniel and moving on to her mother, her father, her girlfriends. All of them lost to the camps or the war. Angel listened, prompted, refilled her glass, brought out more food. She pulled out a bowl and began to make some dough for supper, and still Gudren told stories of her lost companions.

Finally she stopped abruptly, mid-sentence, and laughed, putting her hands to her cheeks. "I am so sorry, Angel!" she cried. "I haven't talked like this for years."

Angel reached for her, pulling a hand free and pressing it between her own. "I have been unbearably lonely," she said. "I love listening to your stories."

Gudren swallowed. "Thank you."

"Have another cookie," Angel said with a wink to break the tension.

"I have already eaten a hundred! What are they?"

"We always called them River Cookies," Angel said with a grin, "because the pecans look like rocks and they feel kind of sandy, but that's not the real name, I'm sure."

Gudren nodded seriously, eating another. "They are very good."

"These are the things I missed," Gudren said. "My mother was a fine cook, and her best dishes were little flaky pastries, filled with fruits, and nuts. She scolded me. Told me I would become very fat."

Angel glanced at her and was surprised to see tears on Gudren's face. "You must miss her something terrible."

"Yes." She brushed the tears from her cheeks. "It has been a long time since I last saw her, but there has been no time to grieve for her or my father." She sipped her tea and took in a long breath. "I know I am fortunate in having my aunt to take me in. There are so many who have no one alive anymore."

Angel stirred salt and sugar into the flour. "Where do they go?"

"Camps, I think. Perhaps Isaiah knows more than I."

Angel nodded.

"May I ask another question?" Gudren said.

"Of course."

"How did you come to be friends with Isaiah? It seems . . . uncommon."

"Not if you knew my daddy." Angel put a cake of yeast in a little warm water, then leaned on her elbows on the counter. "See, Isaiah's daddy and mine were the only men from around here who went to the First World War. And evidently, Jordan—Isaiah's father—ended up being a hero. Saved all kinds of people." She turned her lips down. "'Course he didn't get a medal cuz they don't give medals to colored soldiers much, but my daddy knew about him. They got to be real close."

"As you and Isaiah became friends." Gudren inclined her head, putting her collarbones in sharp relief. "He is your good friend?"

"Not now. Not really. It's too hard."

"I see." Gudren traced a pattern on the oilcloth with her fingernail. "Perhaps you will be again."

Angel straightened. "Maybe." But privately, she doubted it. Briskly, she turned toward the bowl of yeast and found it dissolved. Pouring it into the bowl of flour, she said, "You know what I'm tired of?"

"What?"

"Being so sad and serious all the time. When I get this bread going, you want to play some cards?" Angel gave her a wicked grin. "I'm not, strictly speaking, supposed to play the Devil's games, but if my daddy could, I reckon I can, too."

"Yes," Gudren said, smiling. "I wish to be young again, if only for a day."

Angel nodded. "Yeah. Young."

Geraldine High blinked against the headache in her temples, blowing a pesky fly away from her nose. In the front room, Denise chatted with her friend Florence Younger, who had brought along her two children. The older one wasn't so bad—almost three and cute as a bug—but the baby had been fussing for thirty minutes. Geraldine knew it was likely a little heat rash or something, and the baby sure couldn't help it, but she just had no patience with babies anymore. Not any of them, especially not after all day with the Hayden children.

Deftly, she chopped strawberries for the jam she'd been canning this afternoon. She had never seen such a rich crop. It was also hot for so early; naturally, since she had a mountain of fruit to put up. At home, and at work, too. In the other room, the girls were slicing strawberries while they talked, which was the main reason Geraldine pushed the baby's noise out of her mind.

Strawberry pie, strawberry jam, strawberries in Jell-O, strawberries in cake. Strawberries everywhere. She'd give them away, but everybody else had the same problem. Strawberries, tomatoes and squash, she thought with a grimace, then shook her head. Shameful to complain about any kind of bounty.

A blue jay quarreled with its mate in the tree just beyond the window, and Geraldine thought of Angel. Maybe she could use a few strawberries—seemed like that was an item the Corey gardens had never boasted. She'd send some with Isaiah in the morning.

As if her thinking had conjured him, her son came in the back door carrying a thick bunch of flowers. "Hey, Mama," he said, and kissed her cheek. "Miz Pearson let me cut these just for you."

"Ain't you sweet! Put them in water for me, will you?"

He fished a tall green vase out of the cupboard, filled it with water and shook the flowers gently until they fell in a manner he was satisfied with. "What else you need, Mama?"

The baby wailed in the other room and Geraldine blinked against the sound. "Will you see if you can soothe that child?"

He gave her a wink and left the kitchen. She heard his big voice rumbling through the door, murmuring something to the baby. The fussing slowed.

After a minute, Isaiah returned to the kitchen, holding the baby, talking softly. "You tell them, hear?" he said, rustling through the cupboard. "Tell them you hungry. A boy gots to chew on something just about all the time."

For an instant, Geraldine was transported back, way back in time, to her husband Jordan holding the baby Isaiah while she cooked, murmuring almost the same phrases. She paused to look at her son, a genuine smile easing the tense muscles in her face. The baby took the cracker in one fist and tasted it, his luminous eyes fixed intently upon Isaiah's face. Somberly, he sucked the cracker.

Isaiah grinned, his dimple flashing. "That's it, huh?" He kissed the baby's smooth brown cheek. "Just hungry, ain't you? These women don't know a man's got to have his food."

The baby gurgled seriously in answer. With one tiny hand, he reached out to touch Isaiah's mouth. Isaiah pretended to gulp it.

The baby laughed.

"C'mon," Isaiah rumbled in a mock whisper, "let's go outside and I'll tell you some more things about being a man."

As they left the kitchen, Geraldine shook her head. He needed a wife, and a half dozen children making a ton of noise. A family would ease the restlessness that sent him pacing like a housecat in the evenings.

But he wasn't going to take a wife. Wouldn't even let a woman close.

She thought, after the long years away, years in which adulthood had claimed him and women found him and taught him the power of his natural way with them, he would understand the uselessness of loving Angel Corey.

Pure waste of a good father and husband. Geraldine could look out the door and pick out six women for him right now, good women. Good looking women to give him good looking children.

But there he was, stuck on some foolishness. He thought she didn't know that he'd written to Angel all through the war, that he wasn't still crazy for her after all these years. It made her stomach burn.

She cut the last strawberry in the pile with a sigh. Damn Parker Corey, anyhow. She wanted to damn Angel, too, but had no heart for it. God had laid his hand upon that child from the beginning, had given her some special task.

The worrying burn worked into her chest. Not for her to know God's way. It was for her to accept it in all its wisdom. What made her fret was the simple truth that God sometimes didn't see things the way folks did. His reward had nothing to do with life on the planet He had created, beyond doing his work, but everything to do with the right work that had to be done.

She could pray for mercy, she thought, and did. But she couldn't stop herself from adding a prayer that Isaiah would never see what Geraldine saw in Angel's clear green eyes, something even Angel herself had probably hidden and no longer knew.

Please, Lord.

— 21 —

V-Mail
February 6, 1944

Dear Isaiah,

I just read your letter about your trip to the castle, and I <u>loved</u> it! Please, please send me more of your travelogues! You have such a good eye for detail and you may not realize it, but your writing is getting better and better. It makes me want to work harder on writing good letters back.

Mainly, I ache to see what you're seeing. I know it's not all roses and we're at war and all of that, but while you're walking around that ruined castle with a new friend, I'm scrubbing the floors or stocking the shelves or figuring out the new ration books and how to make the whole thing work out properly. Not exactly the most exciting thing in the world.

I can hear that you're changing with all these things you're seeing and thinking about. You're getting an "education abroad," aren't you? After you told me about the Romans in Britain, I went and looked it up at the library, and learned all kinds of new things! There are ruins of villas all through the country, and they built many of the original roads. Amazing to think about, isn't it? Romans in togas and sandals building villas in England, so long ago.

V-Mail #2

(you're so clever—I kept thinking I had to limit myself to one page. I'm still worried it might get lost, but today, I'm all fired up and don't want to stop writing yet)

Sometimes, I wish I had a time machine, like HG Wells, and I could jump in it and go visit whatever time I wanted. I'd go to the time of that castle (I believe it was King Edward the first who built those castles, but don't quote me) and see what it looked like when it was new. I'd love to hear it and smell it and taste it. Eat roast pig at a big table and drink mead, like Guinevere. Then I'd hop back in it and go to the time of Ancient Egypt and watch them build the pyramids. Maybe I'd go to England at the time of the Romans.

I'm reading science fiction lately. You never liked it, but I do. It's fun. A person has to get adventures somehow! (wink!)

Take care, and tell Mrs. Wentworth I'm finishing up a long letter to her, too. (She thinks Texas is interesting! I also think she might imagine that I'm colored. Imagine that. haha.)

Your friend,

Angel

V-Mail
February 22, 1944

Dear Angel,

If I had a time machine, I would go back to being six years old and reading books on the porch of the store with one father or the other rocking us to sleep. Or maybe to that one day in the tree house, remember? Or . . .

[Never mailed]

February 20, 1944

Dear Angel,

I'm so glad you enjoyed the tour around the castle. Wish I could give you another one, but we've been [censored]. So tired I can't hardly stand up some nights, but the boys in the RAF are making some real headway. Maybe this war will be over before much longer.

Though not, of course, before the big fight, whatever it is, whenever it comes. You can feel the anticipation in the air, the sense of planning, but all I can figure is [censored] and [censored]. Not a lot I can say, anyhow, because they're getting so careful about every little thing we say. I reckon I understand it.

If I had a time machine, I would go to a Sunday morning breakfast my mama made, and I'd eat 12 eggs, a pound of ham, fried up in grease, and bacon, too, and then 16 biscuits with fresh cold butter and apple butter left kinda chunky with a bunch of cinnamon. Then I'd wash it all down with a gallon of milk and 7 cups of coffee, every last one with 3 spoons of sugar. Then I'd lay down on the floor and die happy.

You should write me a story about one o' your cakes.

Your friend,

Isaiah

V-Mail
March 6, 1944

Dear Isaiah, Pls. disregard my cake story, which I mailed regular, not V-Mail. I got carried away. Angel

V-Mail
March 17, 1944

Dear Angel,

You got me so curious now! Can't wait for the cake story.

Working hard here. Rumors afoot.

Isaiah

March 3, 1944

Dear Isaiah,

A Cake Story
First, I have to put on an apron. It's my favorite, white with a bib to keep my top from getting all splattered, and little cherries embroidered all over it. I tie it and turn on the radio because I like to dance along as I measure things. I'm flipping through my best recipes, trying to decide what you'd like best. I consider chocolate, but as I

recall, you're a pineapple upside down cake man, so that's the recipe I pull out. They just had some fresh pineapples at the market downtown, and I picked up a beauty—I can smell it right now, all sweet and juicy. When I slice off the outside, juice pools on the counter, and I've just got to have a little slice to test it, so I cut off a nice juicy sliver, all yellow and glistening, and pop it in my mouth, and it's like an explosion of sunshine, all over my tongue and down my throat. It's going to make a very good cake. I slice off rounds of it and put them in the bottom of a big cast iron skillet. I sprinkle it with brown sugar, which sticks to my fingers, and I lick that off, too, and the flavor of brown sugar with slightly tart pineapple makes the saliva glands in my mouth pinch just a tiny bit. Over the sugar and fruit goes a layer of butter. It's my special trick that butter—I slice it real, real thin and lay it down like leaves over the sugar.

Then I make the cake, which is a simple thing, just flour and sugar and eggs and baking powder and a tiny bit of vanilla all blending together to make a golden batter. I beat into a nice airy froth, and then pour it over the pineapple, and pop it in the oven. Of course, then I have to lick the spoon, which has sweet, sloppy batter all over it. Some gets on my chin, but I don't care. It's delicious. If you were here, I'd let you have the bowl, but since you're not, I scoop the batter out with the spoon until there's nothing left.

Meanwhile, that cake is baking, filling the air with that sugar scent, and I know the pineapple is getting all caramelized, the juice from the pineapple mixing with the sugar and the butter to make a hard, sweet crust. When the cake is baked, I take it out and let it cool just a little bit, then I put a plate on top of the pan, and flip it. This takes some doing, because that pan is pretty heavy, and I want it to land on the plate just right. So I wrap the handle up with a dishtowel and pick it up and turn it over and feel the cake settle. This is the test. Ever so easy, I pull on the pan, and there, on that crystal plate, is the pineapple upside down cake. I slice a piece for you, a <u>big</u> ole piece, with rings of pineapple soaking into the cake, and dark brown sugar caramelized on the edges, and the smell of heaven in

every single molecule.
  Enjoy it.

Angel

April 14

Dear Angel,

  Your letter took a long time, but it was worth the wait.
  I'm taking that plate from you, and for one long, long minute, I'm just looking at it, smelling it. My mouth is watering, but the anticipation is worth it. The smell is like a summer afternoon, and I can almost hear cicadas whirring in the branches, feel the humidity making my skin sticky. It's a beauty, this cake. The pineapple is juicy, and the cake has those tiny, tiny holes in it that means it's gonna be light and heavy all at once. I break off a piece of the sugar and the taste fills up my whole mouth, and I make myself take one small, small bite—cake and pineapple and sugar and summer and Texas and home— and put it in my mouth and close my eyes. The pineapple is still kinda hot against the roof of my mouth, and the cake is falling apart against my tongue, and then they all blend together sugarfruitflourheatbutter. And then, I just can't help myself—I gobble it down, that whole piece, and then another, and another, until the whole cake is gone and I'm full. For once. For now.
  <u>Mighty</u> good cake. I knew it would be, from you.
  Thank you very much, my friend.

Isaiah

— 22 —

In the warm Texas evening, Angel read a novel, fanning herself lazily with a pasteboard fan somebody had left on the counter a few days before. The mosquitoes had gnawed her ankles so bad outside she'd had to move into the store, to sit by the big front window where a breeze might catch her if she was lucky.

It was a Heyer, a good romance, set in Regency England, comedy of manners, with clever women and droll men. She'd been reading *Forever Amber*, but it made her restless and hungry and there was just no point, was there? Reading Heyer made her laugh.

She paused to light a cigarette, blew the smoke through the screen and watched it float in a pale blue stream into the darkness beyond her little pool of orange light.

A vague, dreamy restlessness stirred in her middle, the same restlessness that had dogged her through her life. If not for books, she might have been perfectly happy with her life but, early on, she'd been infected by stories. At eight, reading about Anna Pavlova and Isadora Duncan, she'd wanted to be a dancer, had spun in circles around the kitchen floor while her daddy cooked supper, dreaming she was on stage in filmy costumes, admired by all.

Then it had been Robinson Crusoe and the Swiss Family Robinson. By twelve, she had grown drunk on Shakespeare and King Arthur and Dickens, reading constantly, voraciously, insatiably, and English history captured her. England, with its moors and castles and fogs, its cliffs and seasides and chivalry; its customs and words and spirit. Never had she been more jealous of a human being as when Isaiah had been stationed there.

His letters, filled with details of the faraway, had given her new things to think about, dream about. She read *The Berlin Diaries* and all the war news in the magazines, and grieved for losing a world she would never see.

Lazily she smoked, her bare feet propped up on the ledge, and thought of Gudren, with her strange, huge eyes, who'd seen all of Europe, but didn't speak of it. Isaiah either. It sometimes made her tremble with longing, to know what they wouldn't say, to know what they couldn't share. She wanted to ask Gudren about Europe before the war, about the old world before it had been broken, irretrievably. Had she ever gone to a ball, worn a long satin gown and long white gloves'? Her father, from what Angel could gather, had been an important man. Surely there had to have been balls?

It was self-centered of her to think that way, she knew that, but she couldn't seem to help it.

Faintly, music poured down the river from the juke joint across the way. It was jazzy and upbeat and she imagined a crowded dance all with people laughing and drinking whiskey and dancing until they sweated. She thought of London and distant island paradises and Africa and New York City, and she was suddenly so sharply aware of all the things she would never see or know that she wanted to weep.

Considering everything that happened, what point was there in ballets or swimming faraway seas or seeing Big Ben with her own eyes? She felt vaguely ashamed at her longings, but it seemed there was, somehow, a point. A point to afternoon tea with cucumber sandwiches and white lawn curtains and waltzes, even if she would personally never see any of them.

She took a last sip of the cigarette and stubbed it out, folding her hands across her belly.

Why not?

The thought was unexpectedly mature, and she recognized that it had been brewing there in her mind for who knows how long. She would die if she had to stay in Gideon. Die of boredom and longing.

Perhaps she would never attend a ball or sit in a gondola in Venice. But there was larger world outside Gideon that she could explore if she had courage enough. In the movie magazines, there was always a story of some plucky young actress who'd arrived in Hollywood penniless and friendless to make her way to stardom.

Angel had no interest in Hollywood, but surely there was somewhere she could go, a place she would be happy. Obviously, she wasn't going to be able to hang onto the store, and that had only been a fleeting loyalty to her father, born from grief. She wanted to honor his memory, but it was one thing for her father to buck the system. Quite another for Angel to do it.

In a sudden flash of inspiration, she realized there might be another buyer—that if she found the right person to take the store, there would be no betrayal of her father. Then she could leave.

But go *where?* And do *what?*

She jumped up and paced up and down the aisle between hair supplies and Big Chief tablets. Go anywhere, she thought. Do anything.

Well, anything within reason. She could work in stores, be a waitress, clean houses. Did it matter, as long as it wasn't in Gideon, Texas?

Filled with a ripe sense of excitement, went to stand outside in the humid night, and leaned on the porch post, idly rubbing a mosquito bite with one foot. Could she do it?

It scared her to think of it. Going by herself out of Texas, when she'd only been as far as Dallas only once in her life? Where would she go, logically? California? New York? New York was closer to Europe, but maybe there were still too many refugees. Maybe she'd starve in New York.

But maybe she wouldn't.

A crunch of footsteps on the road caught her attention and she found herself poised, nervous, afraid to see Edwin Walker emerging from the deep blackness. It was the heavy gait of a man; no woman would be out so close to ten on the road alone.

Stubbornly, she stayed where she was.

When Isaiah's face emerged from the gloom, a wash of relief flooded through her. She smiled as she felt it settle in her knees, thinking this was the second time she had anticipated Edwin and found Isaiah instead. Funny that the one who should scare her made her feel secure and vice versa.

"Hey, stranger," she said.

"Hey." He paused at the foot of the steps.

"Miz Pierson must be keeping you pretty busy."

He nodded, his face impassive as he looked off down the road toward something unseeable. "You shouldn't be out here all alone, Angel."

"I live here," she said. "I'm bored. And it's hot. I don't remember a spring as hot as this in a long time."

"And there's folks in this town who are not taking lightly you keeping this store. You're also a woman alone."

"All true," she said with a nod, then took in a long deep breath through her nose and let it out in a sigh. "Bet you got used to cooler weather while you were away."

"I liked the summers all right," he said, and propped one leg comfortably on the stair. "Winters were something else again."

"I remember you wrote about the snow," she said. That had been the last letter but one, the long, long letter about the snow and the cold and the forest as they pressed into Germany.

"It always looked so pretty in pictures." He shook his head ruefully. "Had no idea what it would feel like, not really."

"Is it pretty, though, anyway?" Somehow, tonight, he was different, not so hard, more like the Isaiah in his letters than the man who'd come back. Still, she tried to keep her voice calm, empty of the hunger she had to just talk with someone for a little while.

"Like sugar, like those little houses you and your daddy used to make at Christmas—remember'?"

"Gingerbread houses." Angel smiled. "I haven't been able to make one since before the war."

"Maybe this year."

She sighed, thinking of her lost Sunday school class and her departed daddy. "I really doubt it."

Isaiah said nothing for a moment, but Angel felt him looking at her with pity. "Why don't you let the store go, live with your aunt Georgia or something?"

She laughed without humor. "Not Georgia. But I have just been thinking that I'm going to die of pure boredom if I don't get out of this town. If I have to think about chopping tomatoes and listening to gossip and going to the movies on Saturday afternoon all the rest of my life—" She restlessly moved her shoulders. "It makes my skin feel like it's too tight."

"Ah-huh." He pursed his lips. "And where you headed, girl? Gonna go to California and be in the movies? Or maybe you thought you'd go straight to Paris? Or you got some other place picked out from those books of yours?"

"Stop it," she said, stung to tears. She blinked hard, glad for the cover of night. "You're as bad as the rest of them. Not a single one of you sees *me* when you look at me!" She shook her head, clearing it. "It doesn't bother me from them, though. It hurts me from you. In your letters you *talked* to me. You listened. Nobody ever listened to me like that in my life. Then you just quit all of a sudden and now you're acting like I'm about as smart as a turkey." She looked away. "It isn't fair."

He bowed his head. A whir of cicadas flicked on suddenly, as if to fill the silence, their song a roar in the quiet night. The whirring pulsed and pulsed and pulsed, then just as suddenly cut off. "I quit writing to you, Angel," he said quietly, "because the war was going to be over and we—" He cleared his throat. "The end was bad, Angel. I didn't have any words to tell you about it. I didn't want to put those things in your head." He looked at her gravely. "I still don't."

Angel moved toward him, wanting to take his hand. Instead she nudged his boot with her bare toes. "I know the end, Isaiah. It's different, knowing and seeing, I know that, too. But you don't have to make words for things there are no words for."

"I also knew," he said and looked at her toes, resting against his boot, "that I'd come home and we'd have to learn how to be right again." His jaw tightened. "We can't be friends, Angel. We aren't children and it ain't worth dying for." He straightened. "You go on inside, lock up."

Angel met his gaze for a long, long moment, then she turned and went inside, feeling his presence as she closed the door and bolted it. There she leaned on the door frame and let the hot tears spill out. Stupid girl tears over stupid lost things, but they burned in her throat and filled her mouth and she just wanted to open the door and ask him to sit down and just talk to her.

She missed his letters, missed them still. He could say whatever he wanted to the contrary, but Isaiah knew her as well or better than anyone in the world, and she had a feeling the same was true in reverse. He was one of the most constant people in her life, as far back as she could remember. There were gaps, naturally, but none that mattered as far as the person inside was concerned. Just now, when he'd talked about the end of the war, she'd known that what he wanted to do was cry. How could you carry the inside of a person with you and not call them a friend, no matter what the rules said?

Stop it, she told herself. She looked through the window, but he was gone.

It's not worth dying for. In the bathroom, she washed her face with cold water, then went to her bedroom. Unbuttoning her dress, she wondered. Friendship seemed a better cause than what a lot of wars were fought about.

The next day, the sense of other places dogged Angel as she did her chores. When the magazine man came, bringing his weekly load of periodicals, they seemed to all be filled with things Angel had never seen, lifestyles she'd never know. All the restless straightening in the world wouldn't change that.

As the afternoon grew hot, she had her brainstorm. "Come on, Paul," she said to her small charge, "let's go inside. I have a great idea."

Always game, he trailed her into the kitchen, watching soundlessly as she pulled a stoneware teapot from a high shelf in the pantry and washed it off. She set water on the stove to boil, then opened a loaf of bread and had Paul trim the crusts off with a butter knife. There was no watercress, of course, and she wasn't entirely certain what a scone was, but she made tiny sandwiches with pimento cheese, and peanut butter and jelly, then put them on a pretty platter. In a basket lined with cloth, she placed a handful of cookies, then put Paul to work setting the table neatly. When the water had boiled, she dropped tea bags and mint in the tea pot and set out her prettiest cups. When it was finished, she grinned at Paul, waving him into his chair grandly. His eyes glittered.

"A long, long way away from here," she said, putting her napkin on her lap, "there's a place called England. It's a very, very old country—people have lived there for thousands of years."

His eyes widened appreciatively, and he draped his own napkin over his slim legs in imitation of Angel.

"Well, if you lived in England, every afternoon, you would have a snack like this." She waved a hand at the offerings. "If you were rich, servants would bring it to you in the drawing room."

"What's that?"

"Oh, it's like a really fancy living room. You'd put your piano in there, maybe, and there's probably a big fireplace."

"For Santa Claus to come down?"

Angel smiled. "You bet. And to keep you warm on cold days, because it's a lot colder in England than it is in Texas." She put several of the tiny, crustless sandwiches on his plate and poured the tea. "If you weren't rich, you'd do like we're doing right now, you'd put what you had on a plate and have it with a pot of tea. "

"Can I eat now?"

"Go right ahead. Sandwich, first though."

"I know." After a minute, he said, "My mama said we's from Africa."

"Some people think—and my daddy was one of them—that Africa's had people living there longer than anyplace else. Not thousands of years—millions."

"How much is a million?"

Angel laughed, "I don't really know, to tell you the truth. If you started counting right now, and counted every minute, you probably couldn't count to a million before you were ten at least."

"Ten?"

The bell attached to the front screen door signaled the entrance of a customer. "Angel Corey," bawled a familiar voice, "I need some help out here."

Edwin. Angel glanced at Paul. "You stay in the kitchen 'til I get back, you hear?"

He nodded. "Bad things happen when you're disobedient."

She touched his nose with a finger, "That's right." Smoothing her dress, she left the kitchen and went down the hall to the store. Edwin's big dark head showed above the shelves. "What can I help you with?"

He smiled as she joined him near the cash register, a smile that made her feel nervous. "I just wanted you, honey." His breath carried a hint of liquor.

Angel rounded the counter, putting it safely between the two of them. "That so?"

Undeterred, he leaned over, settling his elbows on the wide flat wood. "Yeah, I'm sorry about your Sunday school class."

"I'll bet."

"I am, Angel. I know how you like them kids." He lifted neon eyes. "All you have to do is sell this damn store and you can have it back."

"Well, I guess I won't be teaching Sunday school anytime soon, then."

"Damn. You're as stubborn as your daddy, ain't you?"

She crossed her arms. "Worse."

"Oh, now, don't take it out on me. I didn't have nothing to do with it. I sure as hell don't care if you teach those kids. I don't have any." He stood up, touching his chest. "Don't blame me." Casually, he strolled toward the end of the counter, toward the wooden magazine rack that stood against the wall there. Picking up an *Ebony*, he chuckled. "And if you didn't have this store, where'd these folks find their nigger magazines?"

"Edwin, what do you want?"

He put the magazine back, straightening it ostentatiously, then gave her a lazy once-over, his eerie gaze lingering over her breasts and belly and legs." I already told you." He slowly walked toward her, trapping her behind the counter. "You."

"And Edwin always gets what Edwin wants?" She folded her arms more securely against her. Stupid, she thought, stupid to get herself stuck back here. He kept advancing until he was right up on her. She could feel the window sill against the back of her knees. But she didn't move, not even when he lifted one hand to her arm—if you let a dog see you get scared, he'll bite you. Likewise staring in their eyes—it was a challenge.

So she looked toward the cash register stonily, as if she didn't care, as if his hand on her arm didn't make her skin crawl, as if she didn't have to swallow so her voice wouldn't croak. "Leave me alone."

"Angel, you know it ain't like that. I ain't some monster." His was voice low and raspy. "I've wanted you for years and years and years and I ain't got you yet, have I? I'm just getting so tired of waitin', Angel. The least you could do is give me a little kiss."

"No." She put a hand between them, close to her face. "I want you to get out from behind my counter and out of my store."

He laughed. "Or what?" He pushed his body against hers, rubbing his sex on her hip bones so she'd feel it. A bleep of alarm sounded deep in the back of her brain, sending alerts down her spine and into her limbs.

Think.

He was drunk, or on the way there by the smell of the liquor. But not crazy drunk. Drunk like he'd been sipping at something all day long, just a little bit. She softened her body language deliberately and looked at him under her lashes. "Please, Edwin. My daddy's only been buried two weeks. I'm just not in the mood for kissing and all the rest right now."

"It'll help," he said, and grabbed her chin, hauling her face up to face him. She smashed her mouth as tight as she could, keeping one arm between them, but it wasn't enough. He pinched her mouth open and thrust his tongue in her mouth, groping her right breast painfully. He tasted of sour whisky.

Angel cried out, pushing against him with one arm and struggling to shift her head. His thumbs dug into her cheeks and he shoved his erection against her pelvis and squeezed her breast so hard she wanted to cry out in pain. Finally she bit his lip as hard as she could, tasting blood before he yelped and pulled away.

She had one instant of relief before his fist caught her on the cheek with a jarring smash. "Don't you ever do that again. I'll—"

Diving through the window of opportunity, Angel scrambled up and over the counter, landing hard on one knee. Scrambling to her feet, she thought of Paul in the kitchen and ran the other way, toward the front door of the store, thinking of the open road. Surely he'd leave her alone out there?

But he was faster than she expected, and came around the end of the counter, grabbing her arm. Angel jerked free. "Leave me alone!" she shouted, backing away. "This isn't a war. You can't do whatever you want! Get out of my store." She glared at him. "And don't you come back here."

For an instant, he stared at her, breathing hard. Then he smiled slowly, licking the blood off his lip. "I'm going," he said, and lifted an eyebrow. "You'll come around. I can wait."

He walked out.

Angel stared at the retreating back in disbelief and shock. Reaction slammed her legs and she sank against the counter, shaking. She pressed three fingers to her cheek. "Lord have mercy," she said aloud. "What will it take to get through to him?"

A small voice sounded behind her. "Miss Angel?"

She whirled. Paul stood at the end of one of the aisles, looking small and vulnerable and afraid. He wasn't crying, but he was very close. "Oh, sugar," she said, moving toward him. "It's okay."

She kneeled and gathered him into her arms. "It's okay," she repeated. "I'm all right."

Paul said nothing, but he nestled his head in the hollow of her shoulder, his hands around her ribs, and let himself be held very tightly. Angel hugged him as much for herself as for him. She held his head, kissed his forehead. "It's okay, honey, it's okay."

When she felt steadier, she said, "Let's finish up our tea, shall we? Isaiah will be here pretty soon."

"You don't have to carry me," Paul's voice, oddly deep for a child, was tight, but sturdy. "I can walk."

"Of course you can." Angel put him down. They walked through the store and in to the short hallway to the kitchen. As if the mention of his name had summoned him, Isaiah appeared at the back screen.

"See, what did I tell you?" Angel said. "Speak of the devil."

But the last thing he looked like was a devil. His big frame filled the space of the screen door, looking like a wall of protection. But of course that was illusion. Everything was dangerous. Everything she did. Everything she thought. Everything, everything, everything.

Struggling to keep an even tone, she waved a hand. "Come on in. We're having English tea, aren't we, Paul?"

"Is that right?" He opened the door, and Angel saw that he carried something in his left hand. Lifting the case, he smiled. "Brought you something."

"Bring it on in here. " She pointed to the kitchen. Her eyes were fixed to the case, black and bulky, and by the way the tendons in his arm were straining, heavy. A light sparked in her mind. "Isaiah High, is that a *typewriter?*"

"Bout broke my arm, carrying it down here," he said, lifting it with a thud to the kitchen table. "What this?" he asked Paul, gesturing to the spread on the table.

"We had tea." He still held Angel's hand. "Like Mrs. Wentworth used to talk about."

"We haven't finished," she said. "Haven't even touched the cookies yet."

"I ain't hungry no more." He pulled his hand out of Angel's. " I'm'onna go pull weeds."

Angel swallowed, feeling Isaiah's eyes hard upon her. "Okay, sugar. Put on your hat. It's hot out there." As he left the kitchen, she smoothed her skirt, resisting the urge to pat the seared spots on her face. In a bright, brittle voice, "So, did Mrs. Pierson lend you the typewriter?"

"Yeah." Curt and cold. "That Edwin Walker I saw on the road?"

"I don't know who you saw."

He narrowed his eyes. "Are you aware that you're bleeding?" His tone was disgusted rather than sympathetic, and it took every shred of control to keep from crying.

"Just go, will you. I've had enough today."

His hand slammed down, jingling her good china teacups in their saucers, "Look at this—this—*make-believe* world you live in! That world you keep dreamin' about don't exist! And the longer you dream, the worse it's gonna be when you wake up." He leaned forward over the table. "That man is gonna kill you before he's through, you don't wake up." He flung himself upright. "You need to doctor up that cut. I'm gonna take Paul home."

Angel forced herself to be very, very still, not looking at him until he was gone. Then, feeling as brittle as candy cooked too long, she cleared the table, washed the cups and saucers, put the teapot away. The place where Edwin had back-handed her ached with a low, steady throbbing and her tongue found a tooth that had been knocked loose. When she finally went to the bathroom to rub salve on the spot, she sighed. No black eye—that would have been hard to explain—but a greenish purple mark showed dark against her fair skin, right along the cheekbone. And on the arm Edwin had wrenched, just above the elbow, were the fingerprints he'd left in reminder. She opened her dress and looked at her breast, small and white, and saw bruises there, too, purplish smears on her tenderest skin.

It made her feel a little ill, that he'd managed to leave marks. She knew he'd like seeing them. Seemed almost as shameful as a hickey and, finally, she let the humiliation and fear out of their hiding places, sinking down on the side of the tub, its narrow ridge cold on her legs. It had been the accusation in Isaiah's eyes that had shut her up. As if she'd done something wrong, or at least something not right.

She didn't know where to go or what to do. "God, if you're listening to me, I could really use some help," she said, and covered her eyes with her forearm, cradling her bruised breast with the other.

But she had no feeling of God hearing. Not even Ebenezer, sleeping in the branches of the cottonwood, answered.

— 23 —

V-Mail
April 3, 1944

Dear Isaiah,

It's late, and my daddy's gone to bed. I'm sitting on the back porch, listening to the radio play quiet while I write this letter by the porchlight. Air's nice and smooth, the way it is sometimes in the spring. Something sweet is blooming in the forest, but I couldn't tell you what it is.

All day, I've been working on my garden. Victory garden! That's what all the posters say. Plant a Victory Garden! I'm missing my flowers to tell you the truth, but if I spent all my time on dahlias, I'd be shamed right out of the county. Daddy's been helping some, though he tires real quick. We planted tomatoes and beans and corn, which has already sprouted up to my ankle! Collards and potatoes and watermelons. Pumpkins just for fun. My Sunday school children will like that, come fall. We'll roast the seeds and make pumpkin pies. I'm learning to can, but you can't make me like it! What a big chore! I'druther buy pumpkin in a tin can like always.

Course the garden means I haven't had as much time to read as I'd like, but I did check out Brave New World from the library, like you told me. I'm only about halfway through, but by the time you write back, I'll get it finished, so go ahead and tell me what you thought of it. I'm not sure, yet. Sometimes you like books that are much darker than the ones I like. I still haven't forgiven you for <u>Down and Out in Paris and London</u>! Nasty, sad people.

What else you been reading lately? Did you get the peanuts and hard candies I sent yet?

Saw your mama yesterday and she's doing fine, don't worry. It was just a spring cold, nothing serious, not like the pneumonia she had last winter. I promised I'd keep an eye on her and I am. Cross my heart and hope to die, stick a needle in my eye. (ha ha)

Well, I reckon I better hurry up and close. Running out of space, even writing this tiny. Your friend, Angel.

V-Mail
April 12, 1944

Dear Isaiah,

I finished Brave New World last night, and I will be thinking about it for a long time, and I think he's right— that people would do more for pleasure than anything else. Think there's any chance we can ever get that far, to create a world where people are mainly happy? Not that it was all good in Huxley's book, naturally (mainly because you can't take a drug and expect to be happy), but when I look at the world at this very moment, we're a long way from peace, joy, and happiness.

You know what I'll say, that it's God who needs to be our soma. That's the real peace and joy, and there's a direction that comes from God, too. We all have something to do, some work, some task, and it makes us happy to do it. What if everybody did that? Did their work, found the thing that gave them joy? What if you got to build things every day for the rest of your life, plan them and build them and admire them when you were done? I bet you'd be happy as a pig in slop.

Out of room. Angel

V-Mail #1
May 4, 1944

Dear Angel,

We are so bored here you can't even imagine. I wish we could plant a garden, do something besides sit around getting on each other's nerves, playing cards and dice and getting into fights. Seems like it's been gray or raining for about 10,000 years and my blood is too thin for the damp cold we've been having. Everything's always just a little bit damp—clothes, socks, books, even this here paper. So believe me when I say I am so grateful for the magazines and books you been sending. I'd go plumb crazy without them, and I pass them around to the other guys. Everybody likes Detective Stories best, and Amazing Stories, next. Me, I like the books. Double Indemnity is my favorite, though I bet you didn't read that one. I'm sure it was Parker's book.

Sorry he's not doing well. My mama would say he should have cod liver oil. Have you tried it? (I'm chuckling to imagine him actually swallowing it!)

Mrs. Wentworth sent some books, too. More poetry, of course, this time some old guys they call the Cavalier poets, (I recommend you read them. Robert Herrick.) and all the Shakespeare sonnets. I imagine you've already studied the sonnets in school or something. You were always the big English girl, but I never had read them and specially now, when everything is gearing up, they're rich, rich. I walk off by myself to read them so I can read them aloud, like Mrs. Wentworth showed me, and the words are powerful, powerful things.

V-Mail #2

The guys already call me The Professor, so I don't care if they hear me, or if they catch me reading poems or Detective Stories. They don't have much schooling—not much value in it in they worlds, anyhow. Book smarts might take your mind somewhere, but street smarts are what keep you alive.

Thing is, though, books can teach a body to think for himself. That's what I think will make the world peaceful and full of joy, like you said God will do. Education! That's what takes you somewhere. God might plant the seed, but education is what takes you there. Till everybody has a chance to learn to think for himself (and I'm thinking about womens, too), they ain't gonna be able to do whatever they called to do. You got to be able to think.

This whole war is about people not thinking. That's what Shirer said in Berlin Dairies, remember, that it was too hard for the Germans to think after all they'd been through, so it was a relief to let the government tell them what to think. That's what Huxley's saying, too—think,

think, think. Think for yourself. Think about everything, even when it's hard.

Sometimes, I reckon I'm thinking too much, to tell you the truth. But still, what if

V-Mail #3

more folks had been thinking anywhere, when all this was rolling into power? Could we have stopped it before it came down to practically every man on the earth in one uniform or another, killing each other? Makes no sense atall.

Anyhow, I got up on my soapbox, and that's what I mean, thinking too much. Let me ask you, though, Miss God Is Everything, if you weren't a girl and there wasn't a war and you had all the chances anybody could have to go to school or whatever, what would you do with it?

Your friend,

Isaiah

V-Mail
May 16

Dear Angel,

Collards! Damn, I'd give my little finger for a big plate of greens and ham. Big greasy pork chops, and some pineapple upside down cake for desert. Have mercy.

Thank you for the candy and peanuts. You are the #1 favorite in my unit today. Gotta go now. Big craps game. (Which you needn't mention to my mama or Parker either one.)

Isaiah

V-Mail
May 14, 1944

Dear Isaiah

I'm hurrying this morning—like a crazy person, I've up and lost my ration book, and I have to find it—but I wanted to let you know. Your letters got here so fast! And there's so much to think about. I did get to the library and checked out a book of Cavalier poets, and . . . well! I'd say I'm blushing, and I reckon I should be, but I'm not. They made me laugh. That's all I'm saying about that, except my favorite was Robert Herrick.

My daddy's sending you some fresh socks, so look out for those.

More later,

Your friend,

Angel

V-Mail
May 15, 1944

Dear Isaiah,

I found my ration book under my pillow for no reason I can fathom, but I was all a-flutter with reading the other night and must have just got distracted. It happens. Between the store, the garden, and taking care of my daddy, plus my Sunday school class, sometimes it seems like I'm a chicken with no head! Bawk bawk bawk!

What a big question you asked! I wish I had an answer, Isaiah, about what I'd to if I had all the opportunities you listed, but it's almost impossible to even imagine. A man, and any college in the world, and enough money to get through—! I don't even know where I'd start.

Well, maybe I do. I'd just start by studying, and I write that and think, "Study what?" and that's a little harder to pinpoint. I feel like I need some grounding in thinking, in the ways humans have thought about God and themselves all these centuries. Is that philosophy? Theology? More philosophy, I suspect. The rules and regulations never have been as interesting to me as the place of connection between a person's spirit and God. That individual connection. I've been reading a lot of New Thought publications, from the Divine Scientists and their ilk. Edgar Cayce caught my attention and I just can't get over it, how he does all those things, so I'm reading and digesting things he's written, which led to some other reading. (All this much to my daddy's amusement, I must say—but he says himself he taught me to ask questions, so he can't be too upset when that's exactly what I do.)

—more next page—

V-Mail #2

It makes me think more about God, and connection, and I guess, as boring as it must sound to you, that's what I'd like to spend my life thinking about. If I were a man, maybe I'd be a preacher, but not a Baptist or a Methodist. Something . . . oh, I don't know . . . .kinder than that, you know? Seems to me people are mean or evil because they're scared, mostly, or in pain, or afraid they're going to lose something. I'd like to be in a position to help them heal so they didn't have to be mean. What's Hitler so afraid of that he had to make all this craziness? He must have been really, really afraid.

Anyway, that might be more than you asked for, but I've also been reading Vita Sackville-West, <u>All Passion Spent</u>, and it's about women who need work, a career, something besides just a man and a bunch of kids. We have work to do, too, and I like that idea. You see it all over the country now, women working the same jobs men always did, and doing just fine.

You're right about one thing, and that's education. Everybody should have the freedom to learn as much as they can, and it does make you think, think for yourself. What a world it would be if we did that! What if it didn't matter if you were a female or colored or an Okie, you could just go to school and drink up as much as you wanted, be a doctor or a preacher or whatever. How about that?

Stay safe, my friend. Thanks for so many things to think about all the time. I'll ship out some more Detective Magazines and all real soon. I like being #1! (ha ha!)

Angel

— 24 —

No one was home, of course, when Isaiah got to his mama's house. Maylene McCoy, Paul's grandmother, would still be working, too. Isaiah found the fishing poles in the closet and gave one to the boy. "You old enough to be quiet?"

"Yes, sir. But I ain't allowed to go to the river, on account of the snakes."

"Well, there's snakes, all right, but we'll be careful and I'll explain to your grandmama it was time to teach you to get catfish."

They walked through thick cottonwoods and shrubs, through clouds of lazy gnats, to a semi-circular clearing near a curve in the river. Isaiah sat on the hump of a boulder. "The trick to fishing for cat," he said to Paul, "is knowing the river you're fishing. This one here, it's slow, but it's got a lot of little pools. See where that big rock is out there? Next to it the water gets darker. That's a big pool and those cats love it, because all kinds of things get swept up in there."

His fishing line was weighted about ten inches above the hook, which Isaiah filled with soured cereal mash, automatically holding his nose. Paul coughed at the smell and Isaiah grinned. "Stink bait. Horrible stuff, ain't it? But they like it." He cast the line into the water, long practice landing it in the pool. "Here, boy, you take this. Hang on to it, now. You feel a tug, let me know."

Paul nodded solemnly, big dark eyes full of the ominous responsibility of feeling a fish on the hook. His plump lips turned downward in concentration. It made Isaiah think of Parker, who'd been unable to turn a screwdriver, shovel dirt or ring up cash without some corresponding twitch of the lips. He thought of a day when he'd been no older than Paul, watching Parker dig earth with a small spade. Every time he'd poke the spade down, his lips would thrust out. When he paused to drop a seed in to the ground, his mouth would fall lax. Isaiah hadn't quite dared to laugh out loud.

Just now, the thought of Parker made him furious, and he focused on fixing his own line, casting it into the water easily. They sat quietly in the long, gold sunlight that fell in bars through the trees, and listened to the swooshing and gurgling of the river. The sound reached under Isaiah's skin and untied the knots gathered in his shoulders, and the spring sunshine eased away the other tensions in his body.

When he knew he could speak without scaring Paul even more, he said, "That man you saw in the store today."

Paul looked up. "Yes, sir?"

"You stay away from him. Far away. He comes to the store again, you get out of there, fast as you can. Understand?"

Paul stared out at the water, chewing the inside of his lips "But what about Miss Angel?"

"Miss Angel is grown and big enough to take care of herself." It was plain Paul didn't buy it. Isaiah *tsked.* "I'll see that Miss Angel can take care herself, okay? Now what you gonna do you see that man coming?"

"Run." He smiled, showing his tiny white baby teeth. "Run all the way home."

"That's it."

Quietly, Paul added, "Bad things happen when you're disobedient."

And even when you ain't, Isaiah thought.

After supper, as the sky turned pale gray with twilight, Angel went to her garden. Ebenezer rode on her shoulder, his claws gentle against her flesh. When she turned the water on, he sailed from his perch to joyfully flitter and prance in the stream, little noises of satisfaction warbling from his cream-colored throat. He spread his wings. The blue of his feathers was deepened and intensified in the gray light.

Angel smiled. "You're so pretty, Ebenezer."

He cocked his head to level one black eye on her, then squawked once loudly in agreement. She laughed and moved the sprinkler back and forth over him to give the impression of rain, "The way you act, you'd think you'd been born a duck, silly bird."

Ebenezer meant "stone of help," and he was aptly named. Whenever she was tempted to think God was too far away to care much about little Angel Corey, all she had to do was remember Ebenezer and she knew it wasn't true.

Almost four years ago now, a man in uniform had delivered and read a telegram to her. Solomon, barely six months into the war, had been killed when a Japanese torpedo hit his ship. *He died in the service of his country, ma'am.*

Her first, bitter thought had been, *What did his country ever do to serve him?* Only the shock had kept her from saying it out loud.

The days following had been a dark blur. Nothing Parker, the preacher, or Georgia said helped at all, helped make any sense of that sweet, bright face being blown to bits. The only company Angel could bear was that of Mrs. Pierson, who offered no platitudes or false bits of patriotic cheer. She seemed to know how bitter and hateful Angel felt, and didn't blame her for it.

One day about a week after the telegram, Angel had been sitting on the back steps at home. In spite of the beautiful day, her thoughts were grim, and she felt as if her nerves were wide open, as if she could hear the bombs exploding a half a world away in both directions, hear the screams of babies terrified by the noise, feel the dying agony of soldiers, like Solomon, who'd had their whole lives ahead of them.

A screech sounded from the wild grass near the river , eerily echoing her thoughts. Heart pounding, Angel went to investigate. At the foot of a tall cottonwood, cushioned by a pile of leaves, was a baby blue jay. His feathers weren't quite in, and there was a gray fluff around his neck, but the black bands had come in on his bright blue tail and wings.

"Oh, you're a beauty," Angel said. She glanced around apprehensively. Any minute now, some parent would come screeching out of the sky to dive-bomb her head—she'd had that experience when she'd happened upon some baby jays just learning to fly.

This one was a tad younger, she thought. And mad. He looked directly at Angel and shrieked bloody murder. "Are you hungry, little one?" She glanced around for something to feed it and saw a shiny beetle crawling out of the leaves. Using a twig to pick it up, she tossed it to the baby bird. He pounced greedily, his beak crunching the beetle's back. Angel backed away, still wary about the mother jay, "That'll keep you until she finds you're missing," Angel said. She went back to her post on the steps. Blue jays had a special significance to her, or at least their feathers did. Parker said her need to find talismans was the Irish in her. Maybe. Whatever it was, she had a huge collection of blue jay feathers in a jar, tokens of answered prayers.

On that evening four years ago, she had waited for a mother bird to claim her lost offspring, hearing the tiny bird screech and call and beg for assistance. When full dark had fallen, Angel slipped on her gardening gloves and crossed the yard. "Guess your mama is lost," she said to the baby jay and picked him up. He trembled in her palms, but he stopped squawking. She took him inside to show Parker and they fed him some bacon. It was obvious one wing was damaged, but Angel had no doubt that he would live.

That now-grown bird whistled in merry greeting at a figure on the road, indistinct in the twilight. But Angel didn't need to see his face to know it was Isaiah, partly because Ebenezer wasn't friendly with that many humans, but mostly because she recognized his rolling, graceful walk.

She looked back at her garden, her mouth setting. He joined her without a word, standing a few feet away. Angel moved the sprinkler slowly, back and forth, back and forth. Neither of them said a word for long moments.

Finally Angel said, "If you came to yell at me some more, you can just turn around and go home."

"I didn't come to yell at you," There was apology in his tone, and from the corner of her eye, she saw him shift. "Came to make sure you're all right."

"You know," she said, "this has always been my favorite time of day. I love to come out here and water and weed. You ever notice how bright the colors are at evenin'-time? Makes me feel calm."

"Angel," he said, "I'm sorry about this afternoon. "

She lifted one shoulder in a shrug.

"Paul's worried you might be in trouble."

"I wish he hadn't been here. Maybe I ought to tell Maylene he should stay somewhere else."

"No. He loves to be here and you like having him. Somewhere else it might not be so good." His voice deepened. "I told him if he sees Edwin, he's supposed to run home right away."

Angel nodded. She gave one last swoop of water to the garden, then turned around and walked over to the pump to turn it off and shook drops of water from her hand. "Edwin Walker has chased me since I was thirteen years old. I'm not being vain—he only wants me because I never liked him, but there's something weird about his eyes, especially since he came back . . ."

"I know."

Even though she was angry with him, his presence gave her a sense of safety. She had never seen a man as strong—long muscles ran down his arms and over his chest under the light cotton shirt he wore. It wasn't difficult to imagine him in combat, with a gun in his hand. But she also knew he hadn't liked it, the business of killing. "You know, Isaiah, I don't have a lot allies. I'm stuck and I'm lost and I really don't need you to be so . . . mean to me. Do you understand? I can't take it."

"You're right," he said. "I just didn't . . . it was such a bad situation . . ." He halted. Met her gaze. "I'm sorry. I should've at least made sure he didn't hurt you. Bad, I mean."

A tinge of humiliation burned along her jaw, up to her ears as she thought of the bruises. "I'm fine."

"After a fashion."

She laughed quietly. "After a fashion," she agreed, and let herself look up at him. They stood several feet apart. Ebenezer whistled between them on the ground as he pecked at worms soaked out of the wet earth. Isaiah's eyes were grave and kind and steady, and there was suddenly between them a sense of knowing and history; all the Isaiahs she'd known melded into this one man, with his elegant bearing and rich laugh and troubled heart.

He shifted abruptly. "I brought you something." His voice was gruff. "Let's go inside."

"All right. I made some coffee just a little bit ago," she said, and led the way to the back door. "You're welcome to some."

As they entered the kitchen, he said, "I saw Edwin on the road and it scared me, thinking of you in here alone, and no telling what he'll do, and then I came in here and you had that whole tea party going, and I just wanted to smash something. Didn't really mean for it to be you."

She listened and nodded. "Apology accepted."

He reached under his shirt in the back and brought out a revolver. He put it on the table, "You know how to use this?"

She paused in the act of pouring a mugful of coffee. "A gun?"

"I believe I could use a cup myself," he said.

Automatically, she took a mug off a hook and filled it for him. "I've never fired a gun in my life." She carried the cups to the table and put them down. "They look so evil."

"No good for anything except killing," he agreed. "But I ain't gonna have a four-year-old out here trying to defend you. You gonna learn to do that yourself."

She stared at the gun for a long moment, then recognized the truth in his words. "All right. What do I do?"

"First, you always figure a gun is loaded." He flipped open the chamber and took the bullets out, piling them carefully on the oilcloth, then held the gun out toward her. "Go on. Get the feel of it.

It was a lot heavier than it looked, and it took both hands to hold it steady, but once she had it straight, she squared her shoulders. Isaiah showed her the mechanics, how to line up a shot, how to fire. His arm brushed her shoulder, his chest was warm behind her, and she knew she would think about it later. For now, she listened, practiced with the empty gun, tried to get the feeling of it.

"When there's bullets in there, it'll kick," he said, "and there's no way to show you how to make up for that. You'll just have to practice. Take it outside and use a tin can or something when you got time."

"All right. Show me how to put the bullets in."

He loaded the first, then let her do the rest. "Go right now and put it someplace safe, high enough it's out of reach of Paul. "

She picked it up, testing the heft, and looked at him dead on. "I will use it, Isaiah, if I have to. God helps those who help themselves."

There was tenderness in his eyes as he looked at her, and she knew that the bruises were visible here, in this light.

"You and your God." He gestured with one hand toward the front room. "Go on and put it up."

While she was gone, Isaiah picked up the typewriter and settled it on the table, lifting off the heavy square lid. When she came back, her skirt swishing against her legs, he said, "You pour me another cup of coffee, I reckon I could show you how this works, too."

She lifted her chin, one hand on her hip. "Conscience bothering you, Isaiah?"

He glanced at the typewriter. "I reckon it is."

"About time," she scooped his mug from the table, refilled both cups, and sat down. "Okay, now show me. Whole lot better than a gun."

"You got that right." He illustrated the carriage return and the shift key. Angel slipped a piece of paper into the carriage and sat down in front of him to try typing a line. He stood behind her, smelling the mix of sweat and oranges that came off her skin, noticing her small, well-formed head and the fine wispy hair. He thought of moving her hair off her neck, putting his nose to the damp place at her nape. He knew she would not turn away.

And then they'd both end up dead, or worse. "You gettin' the idea," he said, and moved toward the sink, drinking his coffee.

"I know there's a way to type with all your fingers. Do you know how?" She pursed her fat little lips. The bruise on her cheek made his head ache.

"You can probably get a book at the library." He put his cup in the sink. "I have to get back. "

"Oh." She stood up, catching her hands behind her back. "Thank you, Isaiah."

For one last, long minute, he indulged his long loneliness and told himself to remember how those wide green eyes looked, right now, with their flecks of yellow and blue. Then he swallowed and backed away. "You're welcome."

Even to his own ears, his voice was gruff.

On the back porch, she stopped him. "Isaiah, I'm not a fool, you know."

"I know that."

"It's just all so . . . overwhelming. My daddy. The store." She shrugged. "You."

He only listened.

"I'm trying to figure out what my life should look like, but I don't know right now." She held out a folded piece of paper. "I wrote you a letter the other day."

He half-smiled. "You couldn't just talk?"

"No. You won't let me."

"We're talking now."

"You know what I mean." She wiggled the paper at him. "Take it."

"We can't be buddies, Angel, and you know it." But he came close enough to take the paper.

She lifted a shoulder. "That's why I wrote."

He was reminded suddenly of her stubborn, almost unshakable will. Sometimes as children they had clashed, but Angel never got angry and shouted. Instead, her voice would drop and steady, and his argument or wishes would melt under her relentless reasoning. He quelled an amused quirk of his lips, because even anticipating it would have fueled the fire. He propped a leg on the stair near her foot and said nothing, knowing she'd talk.

"I've lived my entire life in this little one horse town. I'm sure not sophisticated or world traveled, like you are." Her chin lifted mulishly. "But do you know that I was the number one student in school the whole time I was there? Nobody beat me, ever. And I've read books that took me someplace else, a lot of other places—I've seen other people and other times. I know about history and religion and all kinds of things that nobody in Gideon sure ever thinks to talk about."

She looked at him, suddenly very sober. "I've also always lived right here in these woods. I've been watching the hatred since before I was old enough to understand it, watched my daddy just get eaten up by it. I used to want to leave here, because I thought it was just Texas, you know? That maybe in other places, people didn't have to live like we do, all separated and scared of each other. But then the war made me see that it really doesn't get any better anywhere. It's just another kind of hate, another kind of rules."

A very deep stillness washed through him at her words, a perfect quiet. "It is better some places, Angel. Not perfect, of course. But at least sometimes the hate isn't something folks make laws about." He moved his foot closer to hers. "You'd like England. It would make you laugh, the way everybody seems to know there's a way to do everything. Been doing it five hundred years."

He wanted to take her hand or sit close in the darkness, the way you should to talk about far things, and powerful ones, and terrifying ones.

Instead he had to content himself with leaning on his knee, as close to her as he dared. "Your little tea party made me think of Mrs. Wentworth, how she'd sit in her open air parlor, three walls half-standing, ceiling gone, and have tea anyhow."

Angel laughed. "What did she do when it rained?"

"Have it in the kitchen." He twitched his mouth. "That's where she was when the V-6 got her. I stopped by to see her before I came on back home, and some of the neighbors told me. Those bombs take out everything in their path. There wasn't nothing but a pile of rocks where her house used to be. Didn't have the heart to go look around."

She was quiet for a minute. "Do you think Europe will ever be the same, Isaiah?"

He thought of the wasted landscapes he'd seen as he searched for Gudren, thought of the bombed churches and endless rubble that tanks and mortar fire and bombs had left behind, thought of entire miles of scorched trees. He thought of the hungry, aimless children, hordes of them orphaned by war, and the camp refugees traveling in small knots, fleeing the broken spine of Europe. He thought of Berlin and Paris and London, the legendary cities of their childhood, all of them tattered and stomped and littered with the refuse of battles, like the souls and hearts of the people who remained.

"No. Whatever it was before is gone," he said at last. "They'll fix the streets and replow the fields and build up the churches. Twenty years from now, there'll be children who don't remember. But as long as people live who saw it . . ." He halted, the words crowded from his throat as he thought of the children. The widows. The dead animals in zoos and along the road—lions and bears, spaniels and tabbies. The walking skeletons, the bare heads of refugees.

"It really was like some terrible fairy tale." Isaiah looked away, trying to focus on the sibilant whisper of wind rustling through the leaves, and Texas, which he had once believed to be the most twisted and evil place in the world. In comparison to what he'd seen, it seemed a petty evil in ways. "You know, I don't even believe in God no more, that's an honest fact."

Her dry hand touched his under cover of night, her paper-dry fingers covering his knuckles. Without looking at her, he turned his hand over and met her, palm to palm.

"I imagine God won't mind if you can't believe in him for a while," she said quietly.

He squeezed her fingers in appreciation, but didn't speak. A long time passed just like that, Isaiah standing there with her hand clasped on his knee, Angel sitting on the step.

When she broke the silence, it was hesitant, as if she were afraid of censure. "Do you think there might be somebody in Lower Gideon who'd be interested in buying this store?"

"Could be," he said. "Depends on how you plan to sell it."

"I need enough money to leave here. That's all. But a colored store ought be run by a colored family, don't you think?"

"Yeah," he said, and inexplicably, everything in him lightened. "I do. I'll talk to some folks. I reckon there'll be some interest."

"Thank you," she said.

Before he could be further tempted, he lightly pinched the fingernail of her index finger. "Good night, Angel."

"I'll say a prayer for your soul."

He shook his head, unable to prevent his answering smile. "Do that."

"Good night, Isaiah."

— 25 —

V-Mail
May 20, 1944

Dear Angel,

*You won't be getting this letter till after everything
happens, so I can talk, I guess. Talk as much as I know,
anyway, which ain't much. Time is almost here. You can
feel it in the air, the way the officers walk around, looking
at the soldiers with this look in their eye that shows they
know how many won't be here a month or two down the
line. Soldiers play cards and make sick jokes and eat the
same old food one more time. Yes, sir, war is real exciting
stuff.*

*I'm thinking of you back at home hanging out the
laundry, making a cake, listening to the radio. Thinking of
my mama, singing while she washes dishes, and
remembering that tree house we built, high up in the trees.
Lot a happy days there.*

*Everybody's all jumpy, and I guess I am, too. It all
comes down to this, to what will happen next.*

Say your prayers, Angel.

Your friend, Isaiah

June 8, 1944

Dear Isaiah ,

*It's the middle of the night and I can't sleep even
though we been up all day, listening to the radio and all
the reports of the invasion. Finally, everybody's saying.
Finally. Now we can win this war.*

*All I can think about his how you probably aren't in
England anymore, or maybe you are. I don't know. I'm so
tired and wish I could just stop thinking. Daddy says*

you're an engineer and won't be scrambling on any beach on your belly. But he didn't know what you'd be doing, either. I don't know what an engineer does. Maybe I don't want to know.

I just want it all to be over. Hitler dead and all the boys home. Sugar for my cakes and nylons and cigarettes whenever you want them.

And no more wars. No more. There's got to be, with all our advances, another way to solve problems rather than sending out men with guns on two sides of a line to kill each other. I just don't see the point in it. Whoever kills the most people wins? How does that even make any kind of sense?

Sometimes, it seems like I can hear it all. The explosions and the screaming and the guns, all the shouting and I don't know what all.

I don't know, and maybe I ought to just quit now and go to bed.

Be safe, will you please?

Angel

July 6, 1944

Dear Angel,

Don't worry, I'm not infantry, which is where the heavy losses are right now. I build roads and bring in heavy equipment. We got to Omaha three days after the first wave, and by then, they'd cleared out most of the Germans. Took a lot of men to do it, though. That's not something I'll forget easy. Thank you for worrying about me, and you keep up them prayers, all right? Can't never have too many.

Your friend,

Isaiah

July 16, 1944

Dear Isaiah ,

Thank goodness we got your letter! (I doubt you got my other one yet, but just ignore it. I was plumb worn out and too emotional.) My daddy and I were both so glad to hear you were all right. I know he's not telling the whole truth about what an engineer does exactly, because you wouldn't be in France if you weren't fighting Germans somehow or another, which means you are out there and (scribbled out) just take care.

You'll be glad to know that everybody in America is cheering you on. Me included. Maybe it won't be much longer now before it's all over. Wouldn't that be nice?

I saw your sister Tillie the other day. Isaiah, you would just not believe how grown up she is, or how beautiful! She told my daddy she thought the Army should take women to be soldiers, that she wished she was at Normandy, killing her some Krauts. My daddy gave her a cigarette and said, "I reckon you'd be a hell of a soldier, just like your daddy."

She says, all surprised, "My daddy was a soldier?"

Turns out Tillie'd never heard any of those war stories of your daddy's. I'd forgotten, but not Parker. He told them with as much detail as he ever did—the tiny village and the French forces and Mr. Jordan saving all those people. Tillie sat there like we used to, listening with wide open eyes and a smile around her mouth. For the first time, I realized she was too little when your daddy died to remember him at all. It doesn't seem fair, particularly since I remember him so well.

So Daddy asked her, after telling her about Mr. Jordan, why doesn't she go on and join the Red Cross or the WACS. She gave him the most pained look I've ever seen and said if she couldn't be a soldier with a gun in her hand, there wasn't no point. Daddy cackled so hard he had a coughing fit.

I should have done it myself, but there was Solomon. My daddy, too.

I almost forgot to tell you—I cut my hair. Always thought I'd leave it long forever, but I just got to looking at that silly braid one day and picked up the scissors and went chop, chop. Daddy screamed bloody murder, but it feels so much better. Some days it liked to strangle me, 'specially when it was hot.

Well, I reckon I better get this to the post office. Take

care, my friend,
Angel

— 26 —

The following afternoon, Angel swept up the dust the wind blew through the screen door, a chore she'd done every day since she'd been old enough to hold a broom. Something about the light angling through the trees to fall on the wide wooden planks of the floor transported her to childhood, and she was again a little girl sweeping this very spot as she waited for Isaiah to come in with his mother and daddy. In those days, he had been her best friend.

Lost for a moment in childhood, she remembered the dream. It was one she'd had many times over the years. Usually it came to her just before she awakened, so that it lingered with sweetness as she opened her eyes, leaving her warm and sleepy with thoughts of Isaiah. In the soft dream, she was high in the trees with him, talking and laughing as the gold-washed leaves around them shimmered with summer heat. Safe and high, they sometimes held hands or hugged each other as they had long ago.

Last night, she had dreamed it again, and it surfaced now with curious force. Holding the broom in one hand, she stared at a row of combs on the shelf, seeing instead the dream, feeling it, the warmth of the day, the scent of the air, Isaiah's eyes shining as he smiled at her. But this time—her stomach tightened painfully as she remembered—this time he had leaned over to press his mouth against hers.

Complete invention.

She closed her eyes, awash with it. Isaiah, Isaiah, Isaiah. It was pure torture having him here again. A hundred times harder than she would have imagined.

Suddenly she felt foolish and vulnerable, as if anyone who looked at her would know that she had dreamed a sinful and forbidden thing, as if her expression might show that calculating hardness she had seen sometimes on the faces of women who lived alone for one reason or another, women known to seduce travelers and boys a shade younger than they ought to be; sometimes even a colored man from Lower Gideon, but not too often anymore, not since Maude Sweeney had been killed right alongside the man she'd tried to blame her seduction on.

A car outside the store brought her thoughts back to earth. Smearing tears off her face, she saw Mrs. Pierson's big black car had stopped in front. She could see Isaiah's strong brown hands on the wheel, and something trembly moved along her arms, the back of her neck. She thought of him, last night, standing behind her as she typed, and all the things—

A flush crept hot over her cheeks. How could she even look at him? How could she possibly meet his eyes?

Thankfully, someone else was climbing out of the back seat, laughing—Gudren, with her smooth cap of gilt hair. She smiled at Isaiah as she shook her skirt free, making a joke Angel couldn't hear, one Isaiah appreciated. His loose chuckle rang into the still day.

Angel propped the broom against the door as she headed outside, hiding her trembling hands in the skirt of her dress. The two of them didn't see her. They were still chuckling together, a fact that made Angel want to cry all over again. She glanced off toward the tendrils of morning glories beginning to crawl around the porch railings. Taking a deep breath, she looked back to them, "Hi, y'all."

Gudren came forward cheerfully, "Angel! What a beautiful dress!" She took both of Angel's hands and kissed her on the cheek, and Angel immediately felt ashamed of her jealous thoughts.

"Thank you. I just made it. It's such a treat to get some different kinds of fabric in. Still not much but it's sure better than it was." She paused. "But I reckon you . . ." She shook her head.

"Yes, I know how you feel," Gudren said smoothly. "I am happy every day to put on a real dress, with flowers and lacy collars." She grinned, a strangely impish expression. "The men, they never understand about these things."

Angel laughed, and it untied her strung-tight nerves. "Have you come to shop or visit?"

"I'm visiting today, until Isaiah finishes with his work. My aunt asked me to bring you back for dinner. Will you come?"

"You betcha." She tugged open the screen door and waved Gudren in ahead of her. "Come on in. Let's have a glass of tea." At the door, she paused, not able to quite look at Isaiah's face. "You need anything, Isaiah?"

"No, ma'am." His voice was low.

She looked at him, sure he was making a joke, but his eyes were trained studiously upon the dirt beneath his feet, and his jaw was hard. After a long moment, he looked up and there was fury in his dark eyes. Stung, embarrassed, Angel swallowed and followed Gudren inside. "What's the matter with him, I wonder?" she said as they reached the kitchen.

Gudren shook her head, a curious smile playing around her lips. "He will be better when he works hard, I think. Many times, he arrives at my aunt's house with a big frown, but after he works, he-" She whistled, illustrating, moving her head back and forth in an uncanny imitation of a much bigger person. "You know?"

Paul burst into the kitchen. "Can I go outside and watch 'Saiah?"

"Sure, baby. Just stay out of his way."

As the child ran out of the kitchen, Gudren lifted a thin, worn volume from out of her bag. "Isaiah asked me to give you this." She put it on the table.

"Why didn't he bring it in himself?" She crossed the linoleum to pick it up. The lettering was nearly worn away, the binding frayed along the edges, the pages gone soft with many readings. *The Complete Poems of Paul Lawrence Dunbar.*

She opened it at random, reading a line here and there, and a sense of excitement whispered through her chest. She put it down next to the typewriter, knowing she would read it later, when she was alone. "Thank you."

"He said there is another book, but first you must read this one."

Angel frowned a little, but nodded. Who ever knew why Isaiah did things? That she would learn something she had no doubt, but would she read what Isaiah had meant? "We've traded books for a long time," she said. "Don't always agree on what's good and what's not, but it's nice to trade anyway. Do you like to read?"

Gudren settled at the table. "Oh, yes. Very much."

Angel poured tea into glasses, puzzling over the contradictory anger and offer of the book. Last night, it had been the same—his anger, then his return to apologize and give her a gun and teach her to use the typewriter. Blowing a wisp of hair out of her eyes, she put the tea back in the icebox and turned to serve the cold glasses of tea to her friend and herself. She had to stop spending so much of her time thinking of Isaiah. It wasn't getting her anywhere except in a muddle.

"Tell me what you like to read," she said to Gudren, and the two whiled away the afternoon in that way. Angel hardly thought of Isaiah at all except when his hammer fell on the roof, bang bang bang, bang bang bang, all afternoon.

Isaiah drove Angel and Gudren back to Mrs. Pierson's house. It was odd for Angel to sit in the back and look at his head while he drove, staring straight ahead, bristling with the same hatefulness she'd seen at the store. No one said a word as the car bumped over the road to town, then

Isaiah smoothly pulled the car into the half-circle drive in front of the house.

Angel got out without looking at him. As the two women walked toward the house, Gudren took Angel's arm in hers. "My aunt misses your father very much. She will be happy you have come."

"She does?" Angel asked, puzzled.

"Of course," Gudren replied. "It is to be expected, is it not? He was her husband in all but name."

For an instant, Angel was thunderstruck. Her feet froze on the grass and she literally gaped at Gudren, who finally seemed to sense the bomb she had dropped.

"You did not know." She pressed fingers to her lips. "Oh, Angel, I am sorry."

She shook her head, clearing it. "I don't mind or anything. It's just a surprise." But all the signs had been there, if Angel had just opened her eyes. The nights Parker wandered off on his own, not coming back until very late. The mid-week visits from Mrs. Pierson, the dinners the old woman had cooked for them.

Behind them, Isaiah closed the doors on the car, and Mrs. Pierson stuck her head out. "Isaiah, when you've put the car away, will you come inside for a moment, please?"

"Yes, ma' am." The engine roared to life, purred around the back of the house.

"Ah, my girls," Mrs. Pierson said, holding open the screen door. She kissed Angel's cheek. "I am so glad you could join us, my dear."

Inside the parlor, the radio played softly. Angel sat on the small settee near a bay window and looked out to the vast expanse of trimmed lawn and carefully tended flowers. "Your garden is coming right along," she said, thinking of her father, of Mrs. Pierson. When had it begun? Five years ago? Fifteen? "The honeysuckle's blooming like the devil."

"Is it beautiful? I am grateful that Isaiah is tending it so well." Mrs. Pierson answered from the dining room, divided by an arch from the parlor. Opening a heavy walnut sideboard, she began to take out plates and silver. "Will you help me set the table, my dear? I have already sent Fern home for the day."

"Of course."

"Do I have all the same napkins here?"

Angel plucked a floral print from the midst of the plaids, and took the correct one from a starched set of freshly laundered napkins on the shelf.

"Water glasses, will you, Angel?" Mrs. Pierson said, putting the plates down. She turned her face toward the sound of Isaiah's footsteps in the kitchen. "In here, please, Isaiah."

He pushed through the swinging door between the dining room and kitchen. "Yes, ma'am."

Catching his servile tone, one he'd never used in the presence of this woman, Angel looked at him with narrowed eyes. He stood in the doorway, bristling like a porcupine, all needles and annoyance.

"Isaiah," Mrs. Pierson said. "Will you stay and have supper with us?"

"That's kind of you, ma'am, but I'm going to have to be getting home now, if you don't need anything else."

Mrs. Pierson turned regally, leveling her sightless eyes directly on his face. "Isaiah High, whatever in the world is wrong with you today? You are among friends here and you know that. If you choose to go home, I will understand your wishes, but I would very much like to have your company at my table."

For one long moment Angel held her breath. Holding water glasses in her hand, she waited for his response, and was surprised to see a wry smile ease the tense look of his face.

"I'll stay," he said finally in his deep, rumbling voice. "Thank you."

"Good, then," Mrs. Pierson said briskly, brushing a stray wisp of hair from her face. With one hand, she reached around to find the forks. "You may help Angel with the table, then, while Gudren and I see about the food."

Angel smiled to herself. Of course her father had loved this woman. Of course they had loved each other—two outcast and honorable souls marooned in a place that didn't understand them. How could they have avoided it? Rounding the table, setting glasses out, she felt a settling pleasure in understanding that neither of them had been as alone as she'd imagined them to be.

She gathered cups and saucers from the sideboard as Isaiah laid the silver. "Better turn the knife blades toward the plates or she'll have your head."

"Don't correct me, Angel."

"You got a bug in your ear? What is wrong with you today?"

He didn't even look at her.

She lifted a shoulder. "Do it your way then. You'll see. I've set this table a hundred times, and she's a stickler for details. Seems to me you've been scolded once already this afternoon and you don't need another."

He suddenly and completely softened, giving Angel a single, amused shake of his head. "She can do it, can't she? Don't yell, don't curse, don't even try to make you feel bad."

"Like your mama."

"Mama?"

"She used to scold me to a puddle in about three seconds flat and hardly even say a word."

He laughed.

Mrs. Pierson came back, carrying a bowl of fruit salad she placed on the table, Gudren following with a straining platter of fried chicken.

"Is there more?" Angel asked, and, without waiting for an answer, headed back through the door. She fetched a stack of white bread and a bowl of home-fried potatoes. When the food was all arranged, they sat down, Mrs. Pierson and Gudren at either end, with Angel and Isaiah between.

Mrs. Pierson reached out for the hands on either side of her. "Isaiah, will you bless the table?"

Angel glanced up in time to catch his eye over the platter of golden chicken. He grimaced and then dutifully bowed head. His prayer was perfunctory, muttered, and short, but Mrs. Pierson simply said, "Thank you, young man," and began to pass around the food.

For a few moments, Angel found it odd to be eating at the same table with Isaiah, and from the way he kept his head bent, it was a little strange for him, too. She was pleased to see he had good manners—manners she had not expected of him. He held his fork properly and didn't lean on his elbows or shovel his food in. Gentlemanly, and not like he was trying to remember how you did it, but like it was natural.

Thinking these things, she was ashamed. Why should she expect less? Disturbed, she frowned and concentrated on the food in front of her. Why should she have worried about his being on the roof, now that she thought about it? Or afraid when she was alone with him in her kitchen, or even—and this last was the most disturbing of all—ashamed when she imagined kissing him?

Covertly, she glanced at him over the table, seeing his familiar dimple as he smiled at something Mrs. Pierson said. He passed a bowl of potatoes with his graceful hands, and looked up, catching Angel staring. For an instant, he held her gaze, his smile fading slowly. Then his expression hardened and he picked up his fork, shutting Angel out.

She bowed her head, flushing without knowing why. When had life grown so complicated? Everything, everything, was turned upside down lately. She felt like somebody had thrown her into an unfamiliar room, given her single glance of the furniture, then turned off the lights. All she was left with was a general idea of where she might bump her shins, but who could tell in the dark?

One thing she did know, and that was how little time she ever got to socialize. It would be a shame to waste the evening brooding about Isaiah. Lifting her chin, she joined the conversation.

The four of them talked about things that didn't matter very much—the gossip from town, the weather, crop rotations that some of the farmers were trying this year. Things in Gideon were better than they had been for a long time and it showed. People were building and planting and whistling in the streets. No more telegrams were being delivered, bringing news of husbands or sons or brothers killed in action. No letters with reports of cousins or uncles or friends wounded. The war shortages had begun to ease, though it was still impossible to get stockings.

After dinner, Angel helped carry dishes into the kitchen and brought out the coffee. Now it was Gudren who seemed filled with nervous energy and tension. She paced the edges of the room restlessly, pausing briefly to look out the window to the darkened garden before she paced on. She held her arms wrapped around her, as if she were cold.

Isaiah, perched on the edge of the sofa, spoke quietly. "Why don't you play something for us, Gudren?"

His voice carried tenderness, and Angel looked at him, wondering again at the relationship between these two. Had Isaiah grown to love Gudren as he had waited for her to heal, as they had traveled the long miles between Europe and Texas? She was beautiful and warm and articulate, the kind of woman Isaiah would like. The thought gave her such a pang it was like something nicked one of her lungs, making her feel breathless.

Gudren paused in her restless circling for a moment. "Oh, I am sorry," she said, distractedly smoothing a palm over her short hair. She eyed the piano and, without flourish, sat down and opened the cover, resting her fingers lightly on the keys.

Suddenly her hands crashed down and the dark heavy cords of a classical piece flooded the room. Angel found herself sitting up to listen. The music was powerful and sad, filled with the sounds of storms and war and death, much too large to be played by such a small, slender woman. Angel stared at Gudren's hands as she played, amazed at the agility in the delicate white fingers. Her whole body joined in the playing—her head adding emphasis to hard crashes of notes, her shoulders lifting through more gentle passages.

It seemed to ease something within her, for after a little while her pinched look faded, to be replaced with a winsome smile. Ending the piece with a crash of power and sound, she leaned back, her hands falling to her lap. To Isaiah, she said, "Thank you for reminding me. " She turned toward Angel. "I sometimes remember at dusk—how things were. The music helps."

"I'm glad," Angel replied. "You play so well."

"Gudren was trained as a concert pianist, "Mrs. Pierson said proudly.

"I keep telling her it is not too late to find that dream again."

"And I thank you, Aunt." She ran her fingers over the keys playfully. "But tonight, I think we will do other things, yes? Do you sing Angel?"

"Sure she sing," Isaiah said, grinning. "Loud, too."

"At least I can carry a tune!"

Mrs. Pierson stood. "There is a hymnal under the seat, Gudren. If you will play from that, I would much enjoy it."

Angel looked at the old woman, remembering her father's love of singing, and the way he had whistled hymns at all times. Impulsively, she began to sing one of his favorites:

> *"Open my eyes, that I may see*
> *Glimpses of truth Thou hast for me,*
> *Place in my hands the wonderful key . . ."*

She had never been shy about singing. It felt too fine and sweet to worry about what other people might think of her voice. As she reached the second verse, Gudren had managed to pick out the tune on the piano. Isaiah sang fumblingly at first, more surely as the words of the old hymn came back to him. His voice had richened and ripened over the years and, even to her own ears, their voices were beautiful in combination—her airy lightness dancing through the lower booming of his. He sang like a gospel singer on the radio.

> *"Silently now I wait for Thee*
> *Ready my God, Thy will to see,*
> *Open my eyes, illumine me, Spirit divine!"*

They finished on a flourish, with Gudren playing behind. Mrs. Pierson clapped enthusiastically at the end. "Oh, please! Sing some more."

"What was that one you used to sing all the time, Angel?" Isaiah asked.

"Which one?"

"You know," Isaiah pressed his lips together in concentration, bending his head to hum it quietly. "Can't remember it all. Something about 'all creatures.'" He frowned. "You know?"

Angel grinned and sang the Doxology from church. "That one?"

"Yeah. Can you play that, Gudren?"

"Oh, yes." She did so, smiling. When they began to sing it, she joined in.

Mrs. Pierson moved in closer. "Page 254," she said. When Gudren turned the pages and began to play, Mrs. Pierson began to sing quietly in her accented voice, *Just as I Am.* Angel and Isaiah joined her, but Gudren laughed, calling above their song, "What would the rabbi say, Auntie?"

Mrs. Pierson waved her hand, singing happily, her sightless eyes focused far away.

"That was another one your daddy used to sing all the time," Isaiah said to Angel as they finished.

"Or whistle it."

Isaiah nodded. "You know what I was thinking about yesterday? How he couldn't do nothing without using his mouth."

He pursed his lips and frowned in an exaggerated imitation of Parker, and Angel gave a delight hoot of laughter.

"He was a character," Angel said.

"He was a good man."

The now familiar sorrow plucked her belly. "Wish I could have got him to the doctor sooner."

"It would not have mattered." Mrs. Pierson patted her hand. "After your mother died, he used to come here and sit in this parlor, holding you in his lap. Many times he said that he wished he would have called the doctor, because then she mightn't have died." She paused. "I told him that there is no way of knowing our day or way of dying. God decides."

Before he even spoke, Angel felt Isaiah's instant and rippling anger. "God decides," he repeated in a harsh, old voice. He seemed as if he meant to say more, but halted, swallowing as if to gulp the acid he wished to spit into their midst. His hand curled into fists.

From the bench, Gudren said lightly, "Would you like to learn to play piano, Isaiah?"

For a brief, startled instant, Isaiah stared at her. Then he laughed, opened his mouth and let it roll out, showing his beautiful strong teeth and the dimple in his cheek that he hated.

Angel forgot everything in her wonder at the sound of him laughing at himself, closing her eyes to listen, remembering Jordan High laughing on her daddy's porch in the warm darkness of Texas nights. She remembered the feeling of God the sound gave her, a God with big black hands that held the world. Now, hearing Isaiah laugh, she felt the vast, infinite wisdom of God within her, spilling, filling, overwhelming. It seemed to last forever.

When she opened her eyes again, Mrs. Pierson was excusing herself. "I am very tired. I do not wish to be rude, but an old woman needs her beauty rest. Thank you for coming," she said, bending to kiss Angel's cheek. "And for singing."

Still tingling with the moment before, Angel stood up and hugged the old woman. "My pleasure. Thank you for supper."

"Isaiah, you may use my car to take Angel home, if you like. Just bring it back to me when you come tomorrow."

"Oh, don't be silly. I'll walk, just like always," Angel protested. She couldn't bear the thought of the drive home with Isaiah brooding in the front seat while she rode in the back. "It's a pretty night. I'd like to walk."

"It is not safe for you, Angel," Mrs. Pierson said. "Not anymore."

Isaiah stood, "I'll see she gets home."

"Thank you," Mrs. Pierson said. Her face was drawn and tired. "Gudren will see you out."

After she left the room, Angel waved Gudren back to the bench. "I can find my way to the door," she said. Looking to Isaiah, she added, "And find my way home."

"I know you can."

She had somehow expected an argument, perhaps had even anticipated it. Since it didn't come, she smiled at Gudren. "Thanks for coming to visit. I'll see you soon. Good night, Isaiah."

Humming beneath her breath, she let herself out and headed through the woods, as she had a hundred times over the years. The starry dark stretched over the trees and well-worth path. Something rustled beneath her skin, buzzed at the nape of her neck and down her spine. It hummed with the sound of Isaiah's laughter. What would he and Gudren talk about, alone in Mrs. Pierson's living room. Or would they talk at all?

A ragged bolt of jealousy shot through her belly. Fierce, painful, and not unfamiliar.

As a teenager, she had seen Isaiah more than once on the road to town with a girl, going to town for a soda or just walking on warm summer days. Women liked his big hands and good humor, his royal bearing and beautiful mouth. Walking through the dark, she thought of them, his girlfriends. There had been Vivian Peters, who left Gideon during the war to find a better place. Grapevine said she taught school someplace in New York and had married a doctor. There had also been for a time, Anna Hyde, who eventually married a preacher from near Fort Worth. But the worst had been Sally Reese, busty and smart and saucy. Isaiah had been with her for a long time, up until the time he had gone off to the Army, just after Christmas in 1940, well before the draft would have whisked him off.

Of course, Angel had always had Solomon. Steady, sweet Solomon who never had a new thought in his mind. Solomon who had doggedly loved her and courted her over ten years until she had finally caved in and married him when he joined the Army.

Always before, she'd blamed her jealousy of the women Isaiah had been with on the fact that those other women could spend time with her best friend. Could listen to his big dreams, while she was stuck with Solomon's mild plans for a cotton farm. Those other girls got to listen to Isaiah talk about ideas, about the places he wanted to visit and the education he dreamed of achieving, while Angel yawned through conversations about insect prevention and the best way to plow.

Last night, she had dreamed of kissing Isaiah, and even the memory sent such a raft of emotion through her that she could barely sort it. Yearning and shame and embarrassment that he might guess what she was thinking. In the forest, alone, after an ordinary evening in his company, she halted and closed her eyes and let the kiss rise up through her bones. Isaiah's mouth on her own. His hands on her arms. His breath on her face.

She touched her mouth, traced the shape of her lips, rubbing the pads of her fingers against her own flesh. Overhead, a moon shone down, dappling the ground with pale light. It was very quiet. She walked as if in her dream, imagining Isaiah in a way she had never before dared.

— 27 —

July 30, 1944

Dear Angel,

Here I am, touring a new country on my round the world journey. <smile>

Never worked so hard in my life, nor felt so lucky to do it. We could use whatever you can send, dry socks and the like especially. We just got our first shower in five days and a hot meal that's not out of a tin and enough coffee to fill a belly for the first time. I will have a lot of stories to tell you when I get home. Censors aren't going to let it by. Gotta go, sorry to be so quick. Keep writing, will you? Just cuz I don't have much time doesn't mean I don't enjoy your letters.

Your friend,

Isaiah

— 28 —

Isaiah let Angel get a head start before he took his leave. Pausing at the door, he said to Gudren. "Better now?"

"Yes, thank you. Mostly, I am always better now, but there are times . . ."

He nodded, willing to listen if she needed to share her demons, but also anxious to follow Angel. She wasn't safe out there in that forest. "I understand," he said.

Gudren smiled. "Good night."

Her eyes were full of knowing, the same knowing that had made her offer to teach him to play piano. In this instance, the knowing disturbed him a little. She saw too much.

Now, he simply hurried into the night, nearly running until he caught sight of Angel in her pretty blue dress, ambling like Snow White or somebody through the trees, some fairy tale girl without a lick of sense. As he watched, she reached out to caress the leaves on a cottonwood, ran her fingers over the deeply grooved bark. He shook his head, swearing under his breath. Couldn't she feel the weight of evil in these dark woods? Didn't she know how death hung in the branches of these trees? Couldn't she hear the echo of screams and grunts here? It was a haunted wood, so haunted that he never walked through here at night, only in the full light of day.

He pressed his mouth together, feeling the gulf between them as he had all those years ago when she approached him in the side yard of Corey's store. Her face had been open, guileless, her pale eyes filled with happiness at seeing him. Without even pausing to put down her washtub, she'd come across the yard, calling his name.

Isaiah had still been aching with the beating he'd taken in these very woods. His eye had not yet healed, and his ribs hurt when he breathed. And here came Angel, sweet as a clover flower, untouched and innocent as ever.

It had made him furious, and only Parker hollering at her at her from the back door had saved her from the tongue lashing that had been gathering in Isaiah's mouth.

He was mad that she wanted to be friends, wanted to smile at him like they were still children reading storybooks. He'd glared his hardest stare that afternoon so long ago, and in the brief instant before she turned away, he had seen how he'd wounded her. It satisfied something in him, evened things out.

The same fury boiled in him now, had boiled this afternoon. She didn't walk carefully in these woods and couldn't hear the ghosts wandering through the trees because it wasn't her people crying and dying here.

Damn her. She had no right to look at him like . . . that. With all that softness on her mouth, all trembling surprise. Had no right to still be writing him a letter like she gave him last night, every word slicing his belly a little bit and a little bit more.

He had half a mind to teach her a lesson about these woods, teach her to fear them. But as he tried to form a plan, the sound of several voices came through the shadows. He froze, trying to pinpoint the direction. In front of him, Angel did the same thing, her head cocked to listen. A high, whinnying laugh floated through the stillness.

Edwin.

Angel knew it, too. Soundlessly, she melted in to the shadows, leaving the path for the darker shelter of the trees. But even there, moonlight fingered her pale hair as she moved. The idiot-sounding laughter rang out again, closer this time, and Isaiah reacted like the soldier he had so recently been. Moving as silently as possible, he dashed toward her, seeing her freeze at the sound of his steps just before her reached her.

In a single move, he leapt, capturing her from behind and covering her mouth with his hand before she could scream and alert Edwin and his wolves to their presence. She flung herself against him violently, stabbing his gut with her elbows, twisting fiercely. Terror gave her movements ferocious strength. Finally he snagged her arms against her body. "It's Isaiah," he said almost soundlessly in her ear. "Be still a minute."

Her struggles ceased and he let her go, expecting her to sag in relief. Instead, she looked toward the sound of the voices and pointed toward the left, waving for him to follow. Isaiah caught her hand, frowning, and in that instant, a gunshot exploded into the quiet, followed by the hooting calls of drunks. Angel tugged Isaiah's hand urgently, mouthing *now*. She turned, yanked him behind her, and let go, melting into the darkness.

It was not difficult to keep her in sight, even though she was darting through the forest like a fox, her white collar and pale hair gleaming in the faint light.

When she paused at the foot of a huge, old oak with gnarled branches, she spared an instant to look back to make sure he had followed, then scrambled up the branches as nimbly as a child. He looked up, but all that could be seen was a drape of leaves and branches. The tree house was as invisible as ever. As he had designed it to be.

Isaiah climbed up behind her, conscious of the voices behind him, the laughter and hooting. By the time he reached the railed platform high in the old tree, Angel had already fallen to her belly to peer over the edge. Isaiah fell flat beside her, and she pointed to a small clearing to their left. Fifteen yards away or so, a fire burned, the orange light showing the figures of six or seven men. They were passing around a bottle. Isaiah saw no evidence of the gun they'd heard.

"Drunk as skunks," Angel said in n a voice so quiet he had to strain to hear it. "All of them. I hear them sometimes late at night. I think they're hunting possum or something."

"Why the *hell* you come through the trees then?" His voice was as quiet as hers. "Ain't you got one brain in that head of yours?"

"No place to hide on the road."

He looked away. She was right, but it didn't shake the knot of fury in his belly. The last thing in the world he wanted was to be up here in the dark alone with Angel Corey, but he couldn't exactly leave her to wait out Edwin's crew on her own. Easing away from the edge of the platform, he sat down with his back against the trunk of the tree, and rested his forearms on his upraised knees.

Angel scooted over to him. "How long since you been up here?"

He patted his pocket for cigarettes and took one out, bending his head as if in combat to hide the flame of the match. Cupping the cigarette in his palm to shield the tip from sight, he exhaled. "I followed that collar of yours all the way through the woods. Anybody look up, they'd see it too."

"They're drunk, Isaiah. Can't see two feet in front of them. I'd go now, except I feel safer here than home sometimes." Still, she turned the collar inside her neckline and spread her hands as if to say, *happy now?* She still spoke in a soft voice, inaudible two feet away. "Somebody's always doing their business in the trees, too, and I don't want to get peed on by accident." She tucked her feet under her skirt as it to protect them, and he grinned.

It broke some of the tension. He was a grown man; he'd wanted women before and hadn't died of it. Angel wasn't some witch armed with magic spells to seduce him against his will or make him do something he didn't want to. He knew all the folklore, the stories men told each other about women who put menstrual blood in a man's food, or put their hair in his clothes, but the fact was, resistance was just a matter of mind over flesh.

As if settling in, Angel shifted, crossing her legs Indian-style under her dress, her eyes trained on the flickering fire in the clearing. She seemed content to just sit quietly, so he smoked in silence, admiring his boyhood handiwork. It was still nice, this little tree house. Solid. He'd spent hundreds of afternoons here, winter and summer, sometimes alone, sometimes with Angel and Solomon or even, when they were younger, Angel alone.

The last time had been with Angel. He remembered it very clearly, much more clearly than he thought she would. She'd been in love with Solomon by then, going to church suppers with him, holding hands on the road to town. It had only been by chance that Isaiah had found her in the tree house that day. He sucked on his cigarette, blew out the smoke. "Last time I was here was the day I had to quit school."

"I remember," Angel said. Her hands were motionless in her lap. "You gotta admit it's held up. Can't believe you built it so well when you were only ten years old."

"Come on, now. We all built it."

"Me and Solomon did some nailing and things like that, but you were the one giving orders."

"Y'all were gonna just put up a little shack in this beautiful tree. I couldn't let you do that, not when we could make it solid."

"You always were a bossy child."

He flashed a grin. "Look who's talkin'."

"I never had a chance between you and Solomon. You'd holler about one thing, he'd holler about something else." She shook her head and rubbed a palm over the floor of the platform. "Have you thought about going on with your education now, Isaiah?"

"I know how to build things. Don't need schooling for that."

"I don't mean nailing and hammering—you can do more, and you know it."

He shook his head. "You never stop dreamin', do you?"

"You have a gift, Isaiah, as much as a singer or a painter. God gives you something like that for a reason."

"Girl, I ain't gonna be no architect. If that's what God wanted, he oughta have given a little more thought to the external difficulties." He stubbed the cigarette out on the floorboards. "Just a childish dream."

"That wasn't a dream," she said, leaning forward earnestly. "It was an ambition. There's a difference."

He sighed, looking away from her to the sky overhead. As far as he was concerned, those childhood hungers were about as attainable as the starlight glittering up there—he'd just been too dumb to see it then. He was so intent on his thoughts that he missed the warning signs until she leaned forward and started talking in a quiet, fierce sing-song.

"Poor Isaiah. Poor poor boy. Born poor—" She drew the word out like a song, and he glanced at her sharply, realizing too late that she was mad. "—and colored and all alone."

"C'mon, Angel," he said. "Don't start."

"You think you're the only one ever had to put something on hold? To suffer or do without?"

"I didn't say that."

"You might as well have. What's wrong with you, anyway?" she asked, but didn't give him a chance to answer. "That day up here, when you told me you had to quit school, I remember thinking we were both fools forever believing we could be anything but exactly what the world said we were." She narrowed her eyes. "I remember thinking that I wasn't ever gonna get out of here, that I'd end up being buried in the same little cemetery that I pass every Sunday on my way to church."

He shifted uncomfortably, and she whispered furiously, "Look at me, Isaiah High."

When he did, she said , "You know what changed it? You did. You left here. You got out." She was still whispering. Fiercely, quietly. "And my daddy—God rest his soul—helped you do it, but he never would do one damned thing to let me go. Help me get somewhere, do something."

"Angel—"

She held up a hand. "When he died, I realized I don't have to stay here anymore. That if he pushed you out of here, he knew it wasn't a good place to be, and I can go, too."

"Amen, sister," he said, inclining his head. "Maybe you ought be a preacher."

He'd meant to goad her, and almost succeeded—she opened her mouth, then clamped it tight again. He'd never seen a woman preacher any more than he'd seen a black architect.

She lifted her chin. "Maybe I will be, yet. 'Bout time a woman talked about some other God that wasn't always so interested in wars and such things."

From the corner of his eye, Isaiah caught movement from the clearing and he held up a hand to still her. The figures were dousing the fire, moving away, the whole wild tone of their party turning to something quiet and purposeful. One of them carried a torch in his hand, making their progress easy to trace.

"That's trouble if I ever saw it." Isaiah shifted forward on his knees and swore. He looked back at Angel without speaking.

She stood up, watching the torch flicker through the trees, eerie and evil. When the sound of shattering glass carried on the air, she folded her arms over her chest. There was no question at all of exactly what was being broken.

— 29 —

V-Mail
September something, 1944

Dear Angel,

I really don't know where I am—somewhere in France is as close as I can get. It's rough out here, I can tell you that. Brutal. Used to be pretty, but not so much now with all the bombing and troops and tanks running things over.

The people are tough and damned glad to see L'Americans! Break your heart to see how little they got, and want to share it anyway. I been seeing some of those buildings from that book you got me from the library that one time, remember? Gothic Architecture. Only problem is, most these churches already been bombed by the time we get here, so you come up on this big church with one wall left, and all the rest fallen down in piles of stones around the altar. Maybe one pretty window in place, the rest all over the ground like a bag of spilled marbles.

Tired now. Stink, too, and I'm so hungry for pie and cake and baby limas. Collard greens with plenty of bacon. Like a big glass of real sweet tea, too. I caught me a right fine pile of fish a little while back and fried it up in some bad grease they got around here. I know what it supposed to taste like when you fry it right in cornmeal and bacon grease, but them soldiers I fed it to practically cried, even the white boys.

We been going for days and days now. First rest we really had. Thank you for all your letters, Angel. You just don't know how much they help. War ain't like it is in the movies. Not a bunch of big strong guys standing up to the guns, while all the womens and children are safe in the house, peeking through the windows. Movies never show all the children get killed by the bombs. Or the old ladies. Everybody knows, all the French, too, that we got to drop the bombs, but I ain't the only soldier sick about seen the babies and old folks dead by they house. And I know you're tenderhearted and I ought not to say but I need to tell somebody—I never thought about all the animals. Cows and horses and mules swelling up in a field where they were just minding they own business when the guns and battles and bombs reached them. A shot dog lying in the road. Cat squashed by a piece of house, lions and bears in the zoo, dead in they cages, caught by the war.

You just don't think. It ain't about the soldiers.

I probably shouldn't even write about it all to you, because I know you'll cry, but I don't know who else to tell, Angel, and I gotta tell somebody or I'm gonna bust. Pray. And write me some more letters.

That's all,

Isaiah

V-Mail
August 8, 1944

Dear Isaiah,

I've just been outside boxing mosquitoes for the pleasure of picking the 900th zucchini of the season. I'm going to turn into a zucchini, I swear. Next time you see me, I'll be green-skinned with seed-teeth. (haha) I'm sending socks in a package, not with the letter, and some little food stuffs we thought you could use. Mr. Hayden said his son wrote that they can't carry that much with 'em, but I figure you'd find a way.

Been going to the movies just about every week. Saw Gaslight last week with my daddy. We both liked it a lot. Couldn't believe he wandered downtown with me. We even had a chocolate soda!

Tonight I'm making tuna fish salad sandwiches since we're so hot and not very hungry.

You take care,

Angel

August 11, 1944

Dear Isaiah,

    In my Sunday school class, we've been studying on the loaves and fishes story. One of my favorites. I like the happy Jesus stories for the children.

    I have been on a big reading kick! A man named Edgar Cayce has come to my attention. He's a country man who heals people by going into a trance. They don't even have to be in the same room with him! Somebody just reads him a letter about the problem and he can figure out what's wrong by talking to angels or something. He also tells people about their former lives, which is a very interesting thing to think about, even if my daddy says it's sinful! I wonder what other lives I might have lived. What do you think?

    Best go get the laundry on the line.

Your friend,

Angel

— 30 —

"That bastard," Angel said.

She felt Isaiah look over in shock, but she didn't care. She moved toward the railing, with some idea of going to the store and getting the gun there and shooting Edwin Walker dead on the spot for vandalizing her store. He had no right! She touched her throat, where anger beat so hard she thought blood might explode right through her skin.

As she turned to go, Isaiah grabbed her arm just above the elbow. "You ain't going anywhere right now."

Furiously, she jerked her arm from his grip. "You want me to just sit here?"

"You on a suicide mission tonight?"

She swallowed and looked in the direction of the store, where a whoop of laughter sounded in the dark night. "No." The lunacy of her thoughts sank in. She might, if she was mad enough, be able to take on Edwin by himself. Maybe. Not all of them. She blew out a hot breath. "I'm going to the sheriff tomorrow."

"Uh huh. You think that'll help? That he'll get locked up or something?"

"I saw him with my own eyes. It's Edwin Walker breaking my windows right now, and that's against the law no matter who your daddy is."

"How you gonna tell him you saw Edwin out there? You want to tell him about this here tree house? Saved your behind tonight."

She lowered her eyes sullenly, hearing the truth of his words but unwilling to passively accept Edwin's violence. Again. "He just doesn't have any right to keep doing these things."

"He never did," Isaiah said harshly and tapped a cigarette out of his pack of Chesterfields. He gave it to Angel and lit one for himself, holding his match for her. "Believe me, baby, I plotted some ugly things for that son of a bitch."

Baby. Angel dipped her head to smoke, feeling a curious flutter in her belly, an ache. He was close enough that she could feel his warmth along her arm. His scent drifted toward her on the sleepy breeze—no longer the coppery river-water, dusty, sunshine smell of the little boy that she remembered, but something richer, now, muskier. A man's smell. The dream she'd been fighting came back. Almost without thinking, she looked directly at his mouth. It was wide and well cut, unadorned with facial hair.

How many years had she wanted to kiss him? How many times had she imagined it? She wanted to feel the thudding of his heart through his chest and touch his hair and hold his big hands between her own, feeling him against her breasts and ribs, her belly. The hunger was so sudden and physical and real that it made her hands shake.

She moved away abruptly, taking smoke into her lungs, deep, and blowing it out into the treetops, pressing her palm to the point between her ribs that ached so, turning her back so that her face and all that raw emotion would be hidden from him. When she could speak, she asked, "What did you plot?"

"Chinese water torture when I read about it," he said matter of factly. "And the stretcher machines they used in the Inquisition." He glanced over his shoulder, "But my favorite was that thing the Indians used to do—you know cut off a person's eyelids and tie 'em to the ground in the sun, maybe over a red ant hill. That seemed like fittin' punishment."

Angel laughed. The sound was too loud in the stillness of the forest, and she crouched down to cover her mouth with her hand. The laughing soothed her aching middle and, when she quit, she could look at him again. "I missed you, Isaiah," she said impulsively.

"I missed you, too, Angel," he said and paused. "I tried so long to hate you—" He shook his head. "You just can't hate your best friend."

For a long moment, he looked at her, his eyes shining gently in the darkness, and it was like the day before when he brought her the gun, as if a vine were springing up between them, weaving them together. Yesterday, it had been as fleeting as twilight. Tonight it felt stronger.

She smiled. "Chinese water torture?"

But he seemed not to hear. "They going now." His expression was grim. "Let's give 'em a few minutes to get on back to town, and then we'll go see what kind of damage they've done."

The sound of a truck, and then another roared into the quiet, and then there were lights making their way back toward Upper Gideon, one truck, two, one car, low to the ground. Angel gripped the wooden railing until she had splinters. Behind her, Isaiah said, "They're gone."

Not every single window was gone. The one in the kitchen was high enough off the ground that they hadn't been able to reach it properly, and they hadn't bothered the one in her daddy's bedroom. A couple were only cracked.

The rest were shattered, the glass hanging in the frames like triangular teeth. Angel surveyed the damage silently, no thoughts at all in her mind as she rounded the building. But as she moved, her throat closed, and heat swept over her neck and into her face. Her legs were clumsy.

"I'll never be able to fix all these windows," she said, and then whirled around, thinking of Ebenezer. She whistled for him, knowing how terrified he would have been by the torches and noise.

No response. She whistled again.

Silence. Forgetting Isaiah, she hurried up the front steps. "Ebenezer," she called, and whistled again. And again. She went through the house and came out the back door, calling and whistling repeatedly, her worry growing. Had he just run away in terror?

So focused was she upon the absence of Ebenezer that she didn't realize how uneven the ground beneath her feet was, or how odd it seemed until she heard Isaiah utter and earthy curse. She turned. "What now?"

With a sharp gesture, he bent and picked up a black square. "The roof." He flung it across the yard. "Where's your God now, Angel, huh? When's he gonna send an army to keep your house safe?" He stepped toward her, his eyes narrowed, his voice low. "How come God can't keep you safe from one crazy man? How come, if God is so damned good, he hasn't done something about Edwin Walker?"

For one long moment, Angel didn't know how to answer him. The question went far, far deeper than tonight. It had to do with the evil things he'd seen in war. It had to do with the widows and starving children and dead animals.

God, she prayed silently. *Now what?*

The answer was so simple it made her smile. "He didn't have to send in an army, Isaiah," she said quietly. "He sent you."

He looked at her for a long time, then shook his head. "You'll be safe enough tonight, I reckon." All the fight was bled out of his voice. "I'll come on back early and help you pick it all up."

As he turned to go, a squawk sounded in the quiet night, and Ebenezer flitted down from a hiding place under the roof. He fluttered up to Angel's shoulder, purring, and a sense of relief flooded her. "I thought they got you, too, baby. Who cares about a house, long as you're safe."

"Go on inside now, Angel. Get some sleep."

"Good night, Isaiah. You, too."

It wasn't until she got inside to the light she realized Ebenezer had blood on his beak and claws. She checked him over carefully, but found no wounds.

With satisfaction, Angel knew she had a solid clue to take to the sheriff in the morning.

Isaiah walked home, disturbed by Angel's words. Combined with the gentle chiding Mrs. Pierson had delivered in her garden about the power of one person for good or evil, there was a weight of weary consideration in him. He had been taught that God had reasons for things, that he could turn even the most base of evils into a force for good.

And Isaiah had believed it for most of his life. Believed in spite of his father's murder. Believed in spite of having to quit school to help put bread on the table, in spite of getting half his life beat from him by the same posse that destroyed Angel's windows and roof tonight.

In spite of segregation and bloody Texas, Isaiah had believed God would transform good into evil. His mama preached patience, said God did things in God's time.

Even amid the grisly thicket of war, Isaiah had believed in good, in the power of God, had believed in the nobility of giving his earthly life for the greater good of mankind, had walked proudly with men who had been called to make that sacrifice, and had done it gladly.

Sitting in the dark of his mama's front porch, he lit another cigarette and blew a stream of smoke into the night.

Dachau.

Two years since they had walked down the road toward Dachau, not really sure of what they would find. Two years and still Isaiah remembered every step. For miles, the sweet, rotten odor of death hung in the air, growing thicker and more suffocating until even such seasoned soldiers had been forced to tie handkerchiefs over their faces. Everyone had heard tales about the death camps, but who could believe that they were not some ridiculous exaggeration? Who could believe such things were true?

Even with the stench warning them, the railroad cars were incomprehensible. At first, Isaiah didn't even know what was in them. His mind offered pictures it remembered: firewood, rolled up rugs, even newspapers.

But a hand dangled here, a foot there. Bodies, even as skinny as these, didn't stack as neatly as firewood or rolls of carpet. They were piled all the way to the top of the boxcars, person upon person upon person, car upon car upon car.

Isaiah vomited. He wasn't alone.

A few days later, standing by the ovens, he thought of Hansel and Gretel and how the story had terrified him as a child. Something inside of him had always been sure that no pair of children could outsmart a witch.

Staring at those ovens, Isaiah had felt God die. No god would allow his beloved people to suffer such indignities, such tremendous evil. Any god worthy of the name would have stepped in, sent an army of angels to cut down the enemy like a scythe. Any god that could open up a sea to let his people pass through it could have done something to stop this slaughter.

There was no good possible from this devastating evil. Standing there, his mind reeled back to his daddy's murder, to his own beating in the woods, to all the things he'd been able to make right by believing God had a plan.

God didn't have no plan.

For two years, he'd been living with the knowledge. His mother would cry a river if she knew. Now Angel wanted to cast him in the light of God's hero. Mrs. Pierson, too, would lead him back to God if she could. Parker, had he lived, would have joined the fight to win Isaiah's soul for Jesus.

He cursed.

And yet, as he climbed the steps to his mama's porch, an odd thought struck him. He was mad. Furious. If there had been any way at all he could have understood what God had allowed to happen, Isaiah would have tried. He didn't want to give up all those old dreams. He wanted back the God he loved as a child, wanted to believe God really was all-powerful, all good.

The loss ached in his chest. Another man might have wept, but Isaiah lifted his head toward the dark, silent sky and issued a challenge. "You show me," he said aloud. There was no need to elaborate. If God existed, he'd know what Isaiah meant.

Angel awakened to pre-dawn twilight. It was very, very early, even for her. Ebenezer still had his head tucked up under his wing, and the only sound was a pair of blackbirds whistling outside. As she lay there, waking up, a cool breeze washed over her face and she turned toward the window.

The shattered window, with shards still sticking in the frame. The night came back to her, and with it, a sense of pure exhaustion. Every bone, every muscle, every organ within her felt empty, as limp as unwatered grass. Her lungs felt squashed and her eyes were grainy. For one long, long moment, she stared at the deep lavender sky framed by jagged glass, and thought of all that had happened since her daddy died— Isaiah coming home, Gudren, the store's business falling off, the loss of her Sunday school class, and the trouble with Edwin.

And last night.

Not just the broken windows and torn up roof. A part of her had been expecting something like that. But finding out that Mrs. Pierson and her father had been companions (for how long? how many years?) and sitting in the tree house with Isaiah, swamped with yearning (heat, lust, fear), hearing his laughter, hearing his pain.

A wisp of a dream passed over her mind, thin as a chiffon scarf. Isaiah. She pushed it away, not wanting to know what her dream had been, not when she knew she had to face him in the early morning with none of her defenses in place.

Wearily, she rose and donned a long flannel robe and a pair of slides to protect her feet. She put the coffee on the stove to simmer, then wandered out to the back porch and sank down on the step. She folded her hands loosely in front of her, then closed her eyes and bent her head, reaching for the quiet and swirl of God within her. She had no words for any kind of official prayer; she was just too exhausted.

But this morning, she waited in vain for the weariness to ease, for the worry to fall away. She rested her forehead on her arms, and just let go.

Into the unguarded bleakness of her mind slipped her dream. A memory, really. In it, she stood against the tree house railing in the cold of a late fall afternoon when she was fifteen. Below, she could see Isaiah coming through the trees. At seventeen, he was nearly his full height, with long limbs and a velvety complexion. His hair in the misty day was dotted with tiny diamond beads of water, and he already moved with the strong, sure grace he would carry as a man.

Angel stayed where she was, didn't leave like she knew she ought to, because it had been too long since she'd really seen him, been able to talk to him without somebody listening in. He stopped at the foot of the tree and looked up, meeting her eyes, then climbed up through the branches. Looking around at the top, he said with no small satisfaction, "It's holding up pretty well, ain't it?"

She nodded. "I still come here a lot."

"I know. I see you up here sometimes."

There was nothing to say to that. Angel bent her head and traced the edge of a piece of wood with her toe. She felt him next to her, boiling with something hot and restless. She waited.

"I have to quit school," he said finally, his voice thick with bitterness. "Mama's sick, and I gotta make more than a little part time job can give me." The words were sharp, but his eyes filled with his broken heart as he looked down at her.

"I'm sorry," she said quietly.

"I really thought maybe I could be somebody one of these days, you know?" He shook his head. "And all I am is just another goddamned field hand."

As Angel looked up at him, seeing despair in the hard lines of his face, in the rigid set of his mouth, she saw her own future with perfect bitterness. Saw herself trudging back and forth to town on Sunday mornings until all the life was strangled right out of her, until they put her in a box and laid her to rest in the little graveyard on the outskirts of Gideon. Letting go of a pained sigh, she leaned her head on his arm.

"We ain't even gonna have each other," he said softly, "so we could remember what we used to think. Maybe I could stand it if we could laugh someday about what we thought we was gonna do. But we won't. Time'll come you won't even wave when you pass me in the street. You'll be ashamed when you think of this place."

"No," she said, and raised her head. "Never."

For a long time, he looked down at her, his dark eyes luminous and full of unspoken things. Angel lifted a hand and touched his jaw, hesitantly. He put his hand over hers, holding her palm against his face, and closed his eyes.

She had told herself that a girl got over things, that young love evaporated in the full sun of adulthood. She would get over her crush on Isaiah High and take on her real life. But now he pulled her close and hugged her, bodies crushed together, arms tight around each other. A hundred things moved in her. She moved her face against his chest, smelling the sunlight-scorched heat of his cotton shirt, the heady notes of his faint sweat, a fresh green note that was Isaiah himself, a scent she could pick out of a thousand. A million. His chest was strong from hard work.

Half of her wanted to faint, half wanted to cry, and all of her wanted to stay right there for the rest of her natural life and more, feeling his breath on her hair. When he pressed his lips against her temple, she grasped him tighter still.

They stayed there like that for a long, long time, their bodies rocking and swaying with the breeze in the branches. She pressed every tiny curve, every angle, every scent and pressure and every everything into her memory so she would never forget.

Remembering it now, in the still, pre-dawn quiet of her back porch, she really did cry. Wept for the loss of the simplicity of childhood and the dreams she'd cherished then; wept in vast loneliness and despair. She had no idea what to do, where to go, what was the next step in her life.

A footstep alerted her, and of course it was Isaiah, because she had not brushed her hair, and her robe, which she'd worn since before the war, had holes in the elbows, and she never had cried like a lady, but like a little kid, all snot and red eyes. She made a mournful, embarrassed sound, and waved him away, covering her face with her arm. "Go away."

But he simply bent and gathered her up, sitting down in the shadows of the porch with Angel curled in his lap. He pressed her head into his shoulder. "Go ahead, baby," he said, stroking her hair. "Cry it all out."

In her sorrow and exhaustion, she did. She gave herself up to it, resting her face on his shoulder, clutching his back fiercely. It had been so long, she thought, so long since she'd been enveloped like this, given leave to set down her burdens and admit she was completely lost.

He murmured against her hair as he rocked her back and forth, gently, "It's gonna be all right, baby, you'll see. " He smoothed her hair, her back, with his big hand. "You'll see."

They were no longer children, however, and the sky was growing light. The back porch was private, facing the river, but still.

Angel forced herself to take a deep breath and push away. "I'm sorry," she said, feeling weak in her arms and legs. He let her go easily, one hand on her elbow to steady her. "I'm just so tired today."

His voice was gravelly. "I know. " He touched her arm. "You go on take a cool bath and then you can get some breakfast." He winked. "Once you get some breakfast, things always look a little better."

It was something Parker had always said and Angel managed a smile. Then, conscious of her unbrushed hair and teary face and worn-out robe, she headed up the steps. "There's coffee on the stove. Help yourself."

Things always looked fine in the morning, Geraldine High thought as she walked toward the Corey store. Birds singing, cats chasing moths in the grass, things quiet and cool and easy. She'd heard Isaiah come home late and let him sleep, making her breakfast as quiet as she could in the kitchen so close to his room. She crossed the bridge over the river, humming to herself, anticipating the bits of small talk she'd find among the women at the store in these early hours.

Bless Angel Corey, anyway, for making a place where the women could stop for a minute, just be themselves. Be a shame if she had to let the store go. Better a colored man than any of the Walkers, surely, but no man of any color would be getting up to make coffee for the women like Angel had since she was just a girl. It was her own special thing, something Parker had encouraged but would never have come up with on his own.

Catching sight of the store now, she quickened her steps, taking pleasure in the fact that her legs could carry her so well so late in her life, in spite of working as hard as she had, in spite of arthritic knees and tired feet. She even, in her ignorance, sent up a heartfelt prayer of thanksgiving.

As she rounded the last tall cottonwood by the store, she caught sight of the windows, morning sun catching on jagged edges, making the dark between more threatening. The roof, too, the roof Isaiah had been working so hard to replace, was torn to bits, black shingles littering the ground. Some of them were caught in the morning glories climbing up the porch. Tender trumpets of pink and blue were just now opening under the gentle proddings of the early sun.

Nearby, not sleeping as she had thought, but up much much earlier than Geraldine, was Isaiah, working alongside Angel to pick up the torn asphalt shingles. Geraldine slowed, knowledge burning her esophagus like acid.

It was plain they were unaware of her. There was nothing so obvious as touching, not with hands or lips, or any of the things lovers might display under normal circumstances, but that didn't matter. As Angel bent to pick something up, Isaiah paused. He looked at her, his face and body so full of yearning that Geraldine felt an intruder. It was a yearning that needed no physical touch to complete it, for she could almost see his spirit reach out to circle Angel, saw the exact instant Angel felt it. Geraldine halted, watching as Isaiah turned away, busying himself as Angel lifted her head.

None of that was new. Isaiah had told when he was child that he intended to marry Angel Corey. Geraldine had punished him, made him stay away from the store for two weeks to get the lesson through his head. Nobody would laugh that away, not even from a boy.

But this, now, was new. Angel had grown into her own passion. In the big green eyes was the knowledge Geraldine had always feared. It wasn't lust or a foolish curiosity shining there; Geraldine might have borne that, knowing Isaiah to be a man wise to the ways and guiles of woman.

This was not lust. It was wonder, a recognition of something long held, steady and fierce as a calling. No false shame or fear, not even when Isaiah felt her gaze and turned to meet it. Angel simply lowered her head, letting her hair fall forward to hide the flush on her cheeks.

Geraldine stayed frozen on the road, half hidden by the branches of a tree, watching. She began to pray, praying desperately that God would, just once, see things the way a human would see them.

It was, after all, God who had tangled these two lives so, against all odds of it. God was the one who'd given Parker his vision in France— that Jesus lived in all people—which led to his change of heart on the edge of town. God made Jordan and Parker, with their shared history of a gruesome war neither one would ever speak of again, such fast friends.

So their children became friends.

It was God who'd sent Isaiah home again when Angel was alone and grieving and most vulnerable to discovering what had lain secretly in her heart, plain for Geraldine to see in her anxious questions about Isaiah, plain for Parker to see when he talked and talked and talked to get Isaiah to go away to the service in his fear for both of them.

Thinking these things in the cool of a summer morning, Geraldine's lip trembled. For she knew God didn't always see things the way a woman might. That it might serve His greater purpose to kill these two beloved humans—or at least let them die; that might even be why they'd been born, to show the world or the town or somebody a thing that just couldn't be shown any other way.

The mother in her howled, prayed instead that Isaiah would have the strength to finish his work in Gideon before this blooming between them got them both killed.

— 31 —

October 24, 1944

Dear Isaiah,

I'm sitting at my kitchen table as I write this, the radio on with the war news. There's a lot of hope that maybe this'll all be over one day soon. Sometimes it seems like there's always been a war, that it'll never be over. And now, when I think of you being there in all the fighting, I get sick to my stomach and it feels like I can't hardly breathe.

Telegrams and phone calls are coming in way too much around here. 16 men killed, just from Gideon, this summer. Word is maybe 100,000 of our own men were killed, so many I can't even think about it. So many hearts broken. So many lives ended, just like that. I just don't know what God is thinking. I'm so mad sometimes I just want to have a knock down drag out fight. I want God to mail me a letter and tell me what this is all about.

I did cry about the animals, but your writing is so beautiful, Isaiah. Don't ever stop putting down those things. I can manage to hear whatever you need to say. It's you I'm crying over more—I'm so scared. I cried because it scared me so much to think of you out there, a big target for all those bullets. If God took you, too, with Solomon gone and my daddy going

[Never mailed]

October 26, 1944
Dear Isaiah,

You're breaking my heart with all your hungries. If I could send you sweet tea and baby limas, I'd do it, but I don't think they'd be much good by the time they got to you, so you'll have to make do with these pralines. Maybe you'll get them by Christmas. My daddy is sending peanuts and a fountain pen like you asked, and some other things he thought you might be able to use. In another package, I'll mail a couple more paperbacks I picked up for you. Whatever you can't carry, just give them away. I imagine you could use some distractions.

We're praying for you every day. I'll move it up to morning, noon and night. Between me and your mama, that should keep you bullet-proof.

I did cry about the animals and children and your description of the things you are experiencing. Your writing is so beautiful, Isaiah. Don't ever stop putting down those things. I can manage to hear whatever you need to say. I'm right here, listening.

They keep telling us to write cheerful letters to you all, upbeat and happy, and I will do that tomorrow, but today, I just don't feel real cheerful, and like you, sometimes I feel like I'll explode if I don't tell someone. My stubborn old daddy is the thing right now. He's got the cancer, but will he stop? No, works every day, just like always. He'll last the war out of sheer Texas stubbornness, just to see how it all comes out.

I do think he's got a lady friend somewhere about. Sometimes, he leaves after supper and I don't see him again till morning. Thinks he's fooling me by being there when I get up, but he isn't. I swear sometimes he thinks I'm blind or dumb or something.

And that made me laugh, so here are some cheerful things for you to think on. My garden gave me a big old crop this year, and right now, I'm looking at the prettiest dahlia bush you ever saw, just the color of sunrise. It was a real good flower year, though I couldn't for the life of me tell you why! Flowers are a mystery.

There are a lotta women in the fields this year. Your sister Tillie nearly beat your record picking cotton the other day. Said she's gonna do it before you get home. You wouldn't even know her, Isaiah. Nearly six feet tall, strong as you, and meanest eyes I ever saw. Your mama worries about her. I heard her telling Parker about it the other day, and he just laughed in that hoarse way he's got. "I wouldn't spend any time worrying over that girl," he said. "Not a minute. She'll be fine."

And he's right. There's nothing she can't do, but I reckon she's gonna have some trouble finding a man strong enough to keep her.

Reckon I ought get up and get the dishes done. You enjoy the pralines and the books and when you get home, I'll cook you catfish and beans and a gallon of sweet tea. You just get home safe. Keep your head down. It would break my daddy's heart not to see you grown into a man (and mine, too).

Your friend,

Angel

— 32 —

Angel closed the store for the day. There was no point to opening when everything was such a mess. Isaiah borrowed a truck to drive into the next county for supplies, grumbling that nobody in Gideon was gonna make a profit on the mess Edwin had made, not if he could help it.

The day was hot, the air thickening with summer. Angel walked to town, armed with her complaint, and marched into the sheriff's office.

He sat behind his big desk, sweating and red-faced, and when Angel came in, he was snapping at someone on the telephone. He acknowledged her presence with a wave, and she settled into a chair to wait.

It was his wife on the phone, evidently asking for something he wasn't willing to pay for. "Look here, Retta May, I got somebody in here needs to talk to me. I'm gonna have to cut you loose. We'll talk about it over lunch, all right?" He paused. "A pie sounds good, sugar. See you then."

Angel grinned as he hung up. "A pie for a sofa?"

"Yep." He cocked his head with a click of his tongue. "That woman." He chuckled. "She does make the best butterscotch pie in Texas."

"I'm sure she does."

"How you been, honey?" His watery blue eyes were kind.

"I've been all right, I guess. You?"

He shuffled a stack of papers into a neat stack on his already neat desk and picked up a pencil to slide back and forth between his fingers. "I sure miss your daddy," he said in a conversational tone that belied his alertness. "Don't suppose he left a passel of jokes behind for me?"

Angel smiled. "No. He was good at them, wasn't he?"

"Good man."

She shifted. "Sheriff, I came to tell you—"

"That your store got practically ripped to pieces last night."

"You know. "

He sucked in a load of air and blew it out through his lips. "It's all over town." He cleared his throat. "I'm already looking into it."

"You know as well as I do who did it."

"And you know that I can't arrest somebody without evidence." His voice was harsh. "You got evidence?"

She wanted to tell him that she'd seen it, had seen Edwin Walker and his cronies out there tearing up her store with her very own eyes. But Isaiah was right—that tree house had been a safe spot for a long time, and she aimed to keep it that way. "I think I do have evidence," she said. "Not much, but maybe it'll help."

"Let's hear it."

"I've got a pet blue jay. He was there last night and he scratched or pecked somebody pretty good."

He raised his eyebrows and nodded in resignation. "Thank you."

"It doesn't help, does it?"

"I'm sorry, Angel." His mouth was grim. "It doesn't help much, but you never know. I always need more than what I can get," he added, half to himself.

"Well," she said, standing up. "Thank you, anyway. I knew that—" She broke off and sighed. "I know you do the best you can."

"Angel."

She looked at him.

"You need to get the hell out that store. Ain't nobody going to bother you if you just move into town, get a job at the five and dime, maybe. They'd be lucky to have you, with all that experience."

"I'm working on it." But it suddenly struck her as completely unfair. "It means he wins, doesn't it?" She was fighting tears, and had to admit, at least to herself, that she was deeply frightened. But if she gave in now, it would be like spitting on her father's grave. "He's not going to get that store. At least I can make sure of that."

He shook his head. "Stubbornness runs in the family, don't it?"

"He's just not gonna push me around."

"No—maybe he'll just kill you instead."

She narrowed her eyes. "No, he won't. Mark my words, Sheriff." Smoothing her skirt, she stood and smiled politely. "Thank you for your time."

"Angel, girl—"

She didn't wait, holding her shoulders straight and proud as she walked out. Out in the open, her bravado melted. She paused in the shade on the sidewalk, her stomach a little weak as she tried to decide what to do next.

The morning bustle was in full swing. A blue pick-up drove by and pulled in front of the drugstore, and she saw Agnes Miller tugging surreptitiously on a slip as she pretended to window shop. Across the street, through the plate glass windows fronting the diner, she could see Joe Brown in his mechanic's overalls, eating a late breakfast with Douglas

Neally, the dry cleaner. Angel had gone to school with Milly Reading, the waitress, who came by with a pot of coffee to fill up Joe and Douglas's cups, trading jokes with them as she picked up an empty plate. Milly had been really pretty once, with loads of auburn hair and a slim figure. Four children and twenty-odd years of Texas sun had done a lot of damage. She was still slim enough—nobody worked on her feet like that and then went home to all those children and got fat all at once. Traces of prettiness lingered, but it had gone hard around the edges, her smile slipping right off her face like a rubber mask as soon as she hurried away from the table.

It made Angel feel vaguely sad. Didn't anything ever turn out the way you thought? Didn't *anybody* ever get what they wanted? She looked down the single main street of downtown upper Gideon with an almost oppressive sense of discouragement.

She had to get out of here.

Realizing she'd been standing there a long time, she roused herself and started walking without any real sense of where she was headed, but if she didn't move, everybody would soon be staring.

Aimlessly, she wandered down the sidewalk in the close, heavy air. Lucas Meyer approached with his head down, a circle of shiny dark scalp gleaming in a bald circle at his crown. He didn't speak, nor did Angel expect it, even though she had been waiting on him in her store for at least ten years.

The incident stopped her in her tracks.

Rules. Rules for what you wore and who you talked to, and how you talked to them. A rule that nobody had ever had to tell her made her walk aimlessly down the street, made her keep her eyes averted from Lucas Meyer—entirely for his sake, of course. If she spoke in defiance of the rules, it wouldn't be her who'd pay the price.

She thought of Isaiah, in the trees, his great ambitions turned to dust; thought of her mornings in the store with the women, their own pool of quiet before the world intruded, a pool of time that would now be lost no matter what she did.

She was suddenly so chokingly angry that she couldn't swallow. Just ahead was the feed store, and she acted without thinking, something cold and new making her smile as she headed straight for it, ducking into the dark, vast interior. The smell of hay and fertilizer filled her nose. Nearby somebody measured out nails into a bag.

"Why, Angel!" came a voice from behind her.

She turned and Mrs. Walker, limping slightly, hurried over and touched her arm.

Angel took a breath. There was no point being ugly to this simple and protected woman. "I've been real busy running the store," she said.

"Oh, I reckon that's a real big job. Edwin was just telling me how well you're doing with it, though."

So summoned, Edwin stepped from behind a pile of feed bags.

"Is that right?" Angel said. A long, fresh cut slashed through his eyebrow and into the puffy flesh of his eyelid. Below, on his cheek, was a series of tiny scratches. She cocked her head, unable to curb a triumphant lift of her chin or the slightly sarcastic tone of her voice as she exclaimed, "My goodness, Edwin, whatever happened to you?"

His eerie eyes flared hot and mean for the barest second. "Just a little altercation, sweetie. Nothing to concern yourself about." He gave her his dark smile. "What brings you to town today?"

"A little of this and little of that."

"Ah-uh." He drew a cigarette out of his pocket. A ghost of a smile played around his eyes as he tucked it into his lips. "What can we do for you today?"

Something in his voice made Angel think suddenly that it had been very very, very stupid of her to come in here like this. "I need some bone meal for my roses."

"You want that delivered?" His raspy voice promised more than bone meal.

"No, thank you."

"Gonna send your nigger over here to pick it up, are you?" He didn't bother shield his hatred. "I offered to fix that roof for free, why you let him do it, anyway?"

As if disturbed by this turn in the conversation, Mrs. Walker fluttered her hands and made an airy excuse to escape them. Angel stepped forward. "Because I don't want you anywhere around me, Edwin, and you know it. I'm sick to death of you doin' whatever you want, and I'm not afraid of you, you understand me? Stay away from my store and me."

Very slowly, he smiled, jeweled eyes glittering. "Or what, Angel?"

"I'll kill you." She delivered the words in a voice she didn't even recognize as her own, before she knew she would say them. It shocked her, but she meant it. Like she had never meant anything in her life.

"I'd love to see you try, sugar." He leaned in close. "Because if you don't kill me, and I'm hurting, I might finally forget I'm a gentleman where you're concerned. I might remember that you're nothing but a little scrap o' white trash and nobody in this county would give one little goddamn about what I do to you."

Angel stood her ground. "I'm not afraid of you anymore."

"S'that right," he said softly. "Well, I reckon the war is on, sugar. We'll see who wins it. "He spun on his heel, chuckling softly, as if there was no question at all about who the victor would be.

As Isaiah unloaded shingles and glass from the back of a pickup into the side yard of the Corey store, late afternoon sunlight slanted yellow through the trees. It fingered Angel's straight, fine hair, setting it ablaze as she helped him with the lighter bundles. He could see that she was preoccupied, and waited without speaking for her to reveal her thoughts.

When the last roll of roofing was propped against the side of the house, she crossed her arms on the edge of the truck and leaned in. "What do you think happened to Edwin?"

Isaiah frowned. "He's crazy, that's all."

"He was a sweet child. We used to be in the same Sunday school class and most of the time, he was a cherub. Happy." She chewed on her bottom lip, looking toward the river. "He was a mama's boy, too, crying to her whenever he got a little scratch on his knee. The other children used to tease him."

"'Raise up a child in the way he should go,'" Isaiah quoted, "'and when he is old he shall not depart from it.'"

"I guess."

He slammed the pick-up gate closed. "You have any luck with the sheriff?"

"He can't do much." She flashed him a grin, her pale green eyes glittering. "But Edwin's a sight."

"What?"

"Ebenezer tore him up. Practically took out his eye."

"Where'd you see Edwin?"

She shifted. "At the feed store."

"You went looking for him." It wasn't a question. When she didn't reply, he cursed softly. "You don't have the sense God gave a monkey."

Instead of protesting, Angel lifted her shoulders in admission. "It was my pride and my daddy's Irish temper that marched me in there." Her face clouded. "I was standing there before I knew it—and then what could I do? Turn tail and run?"

In his imagination, he saw it—Angel standing in the dark, cavernous store in her thin little dress, suddenly realizing how foolish she'd been. "Well, I don't know nothin' about pride," he said with a rueful smile.

She returned his smile, just as the sun sank an inch, sending an arrow of gold over her, like a spotlight. Isaiah remembered suddenly how she had felt in his arms this morning—slender and fragile and pliant. So right.

He swallowed, "Better get this truck back to Harold, now."

Before he climbed in the driver's seat, he hesitated. "Keep that gun by your bed tonight."

"I will." She looked a little forlorn somehow, standing there by herself against the big Texas sky. "Thank you for all your help, Isaiah."

He gave her a nod. "You're welcome." It took everything he had to climb in to the truck and pull out of the driveway, and even after he had returned the vehicle to Harold, and went home to eat supper with his mama, the picture of Angel standing alone in her yard stuck with him.

— 33 —

V-Mail
December 1944 (don't know the exact date anymore)

Somewhere in France

Dear Parker,

I been thinking so much about you and my own daddy while I'm out here in France. I think about y'all in the trenches. Must have been terrible, but I reckon I'm starting to understand what y'all saw here, too. How it changed you. As we move through the villages, the people bring us food and hard cider and call out welcome. L'Americanz! L'Americanz! Never felt so welcome in my life. A white man came right up to me and hugged me like I was his own child, kissed my cheeks, pushed a bottle in my hand. Vive L'American!

Never knew how much Jim Crow I was still carrying around until I stood straight up under those kisses. I reckon you might know what I mean. Got my daddy killed, I guess, knowing what I'm finding out, but as long as I stay out of Texas, I'll be all right.

One more thing. I been busted down to private again (and you know that hurt my heart, hard as I been working) but for a good cause—I'm infantry, now, combat ready. Guess they found out in Italy a black man could be a good solider. Orders came down from Eisenhower himself. No sense in telling the womenfolk, of course. Just between you and me. You take care now,

Isaiah High

V-Mail
December 1944

Dear Angel,

I got your package, you sweet thing, and all the men in the squad are now thinking you are the queen of the world. You just don't KNOW how bad we need socks. You see I'm writing with this fine fountain pen. Fine, fine Christmas present. Thank you.

Can't even <u>tell</u> you how cold it is. The Jerrys sure know how to deal with all this weather, but I ain't got the hang of it at all. I'm mainly thinking of days so hot the air shimmers. Remember how it used to be in the tree house sometimes? Like if you stepped out you could walk on that shimmer, way up in the middle of the treetops.

Different kind of forest here. Big pines and spruce, full of snow. If it wasn't for what we're doing, it'd be like a fairy tale. I can see Hansel and Gretel holding hands, walking to Grandma's house.

Now the Christmas rush is over, men here could use any number of things. Soluble coffee, if you can get hold of any, and whatever food you can send and more socks and mittens and salted peanuts. Not if it causes any hardship, of course.

Just heard had a letter from a friend in England who said Mrs. Wentworth got killed by a V-2 last August. Got through so many raids she never blinked an eye about sirens, and she gets it from one of those robot monsters. Don't seem fair. I sure will miss her.

Thanks for all the things you sent her, Angel. She was real good to me.

Your friend,

Isaiah

V-Mail
December (still) 1944,

Gotta be getting close to Christmas. Wish I could be in Texas eating my mama's roast turkey and macaroni and cheese, instead of freezing out here with cold toes. (No frostbite, tho—socks dry out pretty good if I take them off and put 'em next to me at night.)

Hell, Angel. This is hell. I wish everybody could just see one time what happens when a man steps on a mine.

Too cold to do this now.

(Next morning)

*It's morning now. Real early. Sky like cotton balls,
falling right down on top of the trees. Cold, but not so bad
as yesterday. It's snowing. Fella from New York say that's
why it's warmer. Has to be warmer for snow. Ain't that
something.*

*Wish I could tell you more about what I been seeing,
thinking, but the censors will just cut it out, so I'll save it
up for when I get home. I will tell you the battalion is
integrated now, and hasn't been near as much fuss over it
as you might imagine. How about that?*

*You'd like the snow. It slips down from nowhere, from
that big, heavy sky, so quiet, like a blanket. And it's true
about all the snow flakes being different. I think sometimes
they're like people, so different, even though there's so
many.*

*So quiet right now. Just the snow and me and this
piece of paper. I woke up cuz there was a rock in my
shoulder. Always a rock somewhere, no matter how you try
to brush the ground smooth before you go to sleep. Think
you'd get used to it, but you don't. Body keeps
remembering how it used to be to sleep in a soft place.*

*I just ate my last praline. Sucked on it till there was
nothing left but sticky fingers, and then I cleaned them up,
too. Been eating just one every now and again. Kept them
in my shirt pocket, shared a few with some people I know—
what few are left, anyway. Faces change so fast you don't
know who's gonna be there the next day. Keep wondering
how God picks which one to take when there's so many of
us out here, all jumbled up like a pile of firewood. How
can somebody right beside you . . .*

*Never mind. I liked the candy, girl. Don't know how
you got the sugar to make pralines, but you were a hero
the day they came. How's your daddy? Still poorly? You
tell him Isaiah said he gotta get well. I got a few words to
say to him. Him and his big ideas.*

*Naw, you just tell him I miss him, allright. You, too.
Keep up them prayers. We need all we can get.*

Love,

Isaiah

— 34 —

After dinner, Isaiah went outside to smoke, looking across the river. Crickets whistled in the undergrowth and a haze of gnats hung near a trumpet vine. Briefly, he considered getting his pole and going fishing, then rejected the idea. Too restless.

All day long, a ghost of Angel had been clinging to his body, an echo of her against him this morning, crying her eyes out. His heart had nearly broken when he'd come upon her, looking poor and broken in her old, thin robe, with sleep-mussed hair. Even then, when she was as ordinary as a glass of milk, she did something to him, just like she always had, as long as he could remember. In that minute, he just hadn't cared anymore about anything except letting her know that as long as he walked the earth, she had a friend.

In the darkness, he smoked and listened to the river swishing against the bank, and thought of her arms around his neck, slim and strong as rope. She'd clung so hard, so tight, that he bent his head and buried his face against her warm neck and sat down and rocked her. He should have done it sooner.

Because that very minute, with Angel curled up in his arms, his own sense of being constantly, eternally, forever solitary had evaporated. Angel had always been the only one. The only other human he could be himself with, the only person he couldn't stand to think of living forever without—although he had really tried, once upon a time, when Solomon had married her. He thought he'd written her to offer condolences.

An excuse, he saw now. He'd just wanted to hear from her, be in touch with her, remember that there was one person who knew him. He wanted to hear her voice in the words she put on the paper, wanted to think about her pretty laugh and sharp mind. Through the war, her letters sustained him.

Best friend. That's what he'd told her last night. You couldn't hate your best friend. And she was that, all right, his best friend in the world. But a man didn't want to do things to a friend that holding her for five minutes this morning had brought to his mind. A man didn't think about slipping the old, tired robe from the body of his friend, think of touching the fresh, supple skin below. A man didn't ache all day with hunger for a friend.

And God help him, he ached. No matter how busy he'd kept himself, no matter how often he made himself think of something else—songs or war or books—the ghost of her body clung to him.

A gunshot sounded in the still air. He leapt to attention. Another. It came from the direction of the Corey store, and for an instant, Isaiah was frozen in horror. Then came another shot, and the faint ping of metal. He smiled to himself. She was practicing. "Good girl," he said aloud and went inside to find a cache of bullets. He slipped them in his pocket and headed through the kitchen.

His mama called out in a tired voice from her bedroom, "Isaiah?"

"Yeah, Mama."

"You going somewhere?"

"Just down to the juke joint for a minute."

"Isaiah High."

He went to the doorway of her room. She was stretched out on her bed, a blue chenille spread beneath her, feet bare, ankles swollen. She looked tired. "Just gonna holler at Sam Reed," he lied. "Won't be but a minute."

She scowled. "What you need to do is come back to church with me. Everybody's been asking."

He drew the curtains over her window, picked up a pillow that had fallen on the floor. "Maybe one of these Sundays." He kissed her head. "You need anything?"

She waved a hand. "I'm fine, son. Don't you get in any trouble out there."

He grinned to himself. He'd been halfway around the world, waded across a hundred battlefields with bullets and mortar flying around his head, and his mama still wanted to warn him about the players down at the juke joint. "I'll be all right." He paused a moment more, feeling guilty. He'd find her some sweets tomorrow.

Walking over the bridge and down the road to the store, he called himself nine kinds of fool, but the minute he laid eyes on Angel, that nasty voice halted. She was in back of the store, still wearing the dress she had worn to town that morning. It was blue-bonnet blue, with little sprigs of white flowers all over it, buttons up the front and a lacey white collar. Her feet were bare. In her hand was the gun, which she aimed at a can set up on a tree stump near the river. As he gained the yard, she straightened, held up her arm and fired. The bullet hit its mark.

"Getting pretty good with that thing," Isaiah called. Angel glanced over her shoulder as she headed for the stump.

She waved, then picked up the can, put it back on the stump and walked back to Isaiah. "What brings you out tonight?"

He reached in his pocket and pulled out a handful of bullets. "I heard you," he said. "Figured you'd be needing some more ammunition."

"Just in time." She aimed and fired. This time she missed. "Obviously I need more practice."

"Can you load it?"

She gave him an impish grin and tucked a lock of hair behind her ear. "Yes, sir, I can." To illustrate, she flipped open the chamber and, taking bullets from the cradle of his palm, demonstrated how very efficiently she could load the gun.

It gave him a strange feeling to watch her fine-boned fingers handle the bullets and revolver with such confidence. When the gun was reloaded, she took aim and fired once more, her attention completely focused, her hand steady. She hit the can square center—and laughed with throaty delight.

He stood there in the gathering dusk, holding bullets as Angel practiced. She made him think of the women he'd seen in France, young women from little villages with rifles and ammunition belts wrapped around their sweaters, jaunty smiles on their mouths. They were good soldiers, quick and intuitive. A lot of them had died.

"Do you have a cigarette with you, Isaiah? I left mine inside."

"You're doing real good, Angel," he said, reaching in the pocket of his shirt for the pack of Chesterfields. She took the cigarette and bent her head to the match he struck for her before she answered.

"I got good reason." She inhaled. "I told him I'd kill him if he came near me again. When I got home I decided I oughta be able to back it up."

"It's not the same, firing a gun and killing a man, Angel—no matter how much you hate him."

She looked at him steadily. "It beats the alternatives, though, doesn't it?

He lifted his eyebrows in agreement. She practiced some more, cigarette dangling in her left hand while she fired with her right. Something about her was changing. Her step was firmer as she strode over the grass to prop up another can, and her arm swung comfortably at her side. She'd always been much stronger than her frail appearance would have led him to expect, and there was a grit about her that he forgot sometimes, but this change went deeper. The sweetness of attitude that made her seem so innocent was receding, replaced by something solid and knowing.

Isaiah liked it. He sat on the steps and watched her firing and smoked, grinning to himself.

"You better not be laughing at me, Isaiah High," she said as she returned.

"No, baby, I'm not laughing. I'm proud of you,"

For an instant, a flash of heat showed in her eyes and she glanced away, tossing her cigarette on the ground. With a glance at the rising dark, she said, "This'll be my last round, I guess."

He crossed his arms on his chest, the ache back where it had lived all day. He waited in silence as she emptied the chamber, waited as she pivoted and met his eyes. He waited out the powerful urge to touch her, run his fingers over her ears and the dip of her waist. It buzzed in his ears.

She looked away before he did and he saw her swallow.

Flustered, he took the cigarettes out of his pocket, but couldn't get hold of one with the shells in his hand. "Hold these things, Angel," he said gruffly. She crossed over to him and held out her hand. Darkness surrounded them. Crickets whirred in the grass.

As he gave her the bullets, he found himself trembling—trembling!—like he was ten and scared to walk past Edwin and his bullies in town. Then he tried to shake a cigarette from the pack, and dropped it on the ground, and both of them, probably aiming to dispel the tension, bent to retrieve it at the same instant. His forehead slammed her cheek, hard enough to knock her sideways, hard enough his hand flew up to the spot on his head automatically. At the same instant, they both made the same, swallowed noise of pain.

"Angel, girl, I'm so sorry," he said, reaching out for her arm to steady her. "You all right?"

"I'm fine—it was just a little bump." She let her hand drop from her face and a dark red mark showed on the pale skin.

Now he could smell her lily-of-the-valley talcum. Such an ordinary scent, he thought vaguely, but it always made him lose his train of thought. He moved his thumb on her arm, gently, just feeling the texture of her skin. Lost in a place without thought, he lifted his other hand to brush a lock of fine pale hair away from the bruised spot on her cheek. His fingertips skimmed her ear, and she didn't move away, looking up at him gravely. He heard her breath catch as he touched her cheek, traced the line of her jaw, pressed his big palm to the curve of her small face .

Time stopped. Dusk was so thick that only the pale gray stones under the trees were visible. A cool breeze blew in from the river. Isaiah, caught in some madness he couldn't halt, took one step closer, feeling the slight warmth of her legs through her dress. Her hair floated over the back of his hand as he moved his thumb on her chin, traced the edge of her eye. And still she simply looked up at him, her breath as airy and uncertain as his own.

She lifted a hand and touched his face in return, looked at his mouth. Said his name in a quiet whoosh, "Isaiah."

After twenty years of dreaming and wanting, never daring, Isaiah tucked his thumb beneath her chin, took the last step toward her, bent down.

And kissed her.

A soft noise came from her throat as she kissed him back, moving into him, pressing close. Her lips were full and giving, as ripe as grapes. He breathed it in, every detail—her soft cheek against the tip of his nose, the generosity of her movements, sliding closer, angling her head to accommodate him. Her body brushed against him, and her palms fell flat against his chest.

Only a sip, he promised himself, feeling something huge moving and growing in his chest. But she edged ever so slightly closer, and her lips parted and he pulled her closer, feeling her small breasts barely press into his chest, and the twilight no longer existed, or the world, or anything but the sense of whirling he felt as he kissed her, as their tongues tangled, met, curled—

When she broke away, violently and urgently, Isaiah was left dizzy and bewildered. Angel stumbled away, her hand pressed against her chest, and his first, pained thought was that he'd been wrong—she was disgusted at his touch.

And then he heard the sound of an engine passing on the road in front of the store, rumbling into the secret invisibility of the backyard. Reality returned, cold and bleak as a January moon.

He could dream all he wanted, fantasize if need be, take his lust to women who could ease the ache. What he could not do, not ever, was forget what could happen to Angel if he let himself move those dreams and visions and hungers into reality.

There was a glimmer of tears in Angel's eyes when she looked at him, a look full of sorrow and entreaty.

He spoke gruffly. "I'll be back early to get going on things around here."

And then, he forced himself to turn and walk away from her. He didn't dare look back this time.

The next few days passed in an almost supernatural state of quiet. Summer bloomed in the heat of the afternoons, afternoons that moved as slowly as high white clouds.

There was no sign of Edwin. The first night after uttering her challenge, Angel had not slept well, starting awake at every creak and snap. The next morning, she carried a blanket out to the tree house, just in case she needed it sometime, and after that, she slept all right again. Customers kept her busy, and she was grateful to them on two counts. She could no longer keep Paul, of course, and she missed him. And, as long as there were customers in the store, she didn't have to think of Isaiah.

Toward the end of the week, she knelt in her garden, pulling weeds. Isaiah was on the roof, working like a demon, as he had been all week. He hadn't lingered in the evenings, and Angel didn't ask him to stay—he was as scared as she was by the moment they'd shared in her back yard. He never met her eyes, never let their hands touch, never even asked for a glass of water. He just worked from morning till night, when he climbed down, visibly exhausted, and walked home. He seemed determined to finish the roof as quickly as possible—had even quit Mrs. Pierson's job to get it done. At the present rate, he'd be done in another day or two.

Then he would be gone.

Angel yanked a tangle of bindweed from between stalks of corn. The thought of Isaiah leaving made her feel hollow, almost breathless. No more hammering overhead as she fixed supper. No more quiet chats under cover of deep twilight, no more of the tales he shared of the faraway places he'd seen, the places that had given his voice its new cadence, his mind its new turns.

She straightened and brushed her hair from her face, pressing one hand against the small of her back. Isaiah clung to the edge of the roof, nailing shingles. He was shirtless beneath worn overalls, and the sun arced off the red-hued brown of his arms in waves. Muscles rippled in his forearm and back, tensing, releasing, tensing, and his well formed head glistened with a sheen of perspiration. All the outdoor work was turning the temples of his hair a glittery red and she knew he hated it.

The luxury of admiring him without observation was too rich to resist. A long stretch of leg braced against the ladder. He was strong as John Henry, and just as big. She had not really known until he'd stood next to her, holding her, just how much bigger he was than any man she'd ever known.

That kiss.

It lived in every turn of her joints, her toes and wrists, neck bones and hips. She called up the small deep sound that had come from his throat a hundred times a day, remembering.

Isaiah halted his hammering, wiped his brow with an arm and glanced over to where she knelt amid the young plants, under the dappled shadows of an elm. In the instant that his eyes caught hers, she could swear he knew what she was thinking—not only of that single, stolen kiss, but other pictures, too, visions of them tangled together, arms and legs and hands as well as lips. It made her belly twitch.

When he looked away, slamming the hammer hard against the roof—slam. Slam! slam!—Angel felt her cheeks flushed and she lowered her eyes to her task. When she reached for another weed, her hands trembled. The hammering did not resume as she had expected, but Angel kept her head bent, kept it bent even when Isaiah's worn boots showed in the corner of her vision, at the edge of the garden.

She leaned back on her heels, head bowed, waiting for him to speak. When the moment stretched, with him standing and Angel waiting, into a heavy, loaded thing as full as any noise, she finally raised her eyes. First to his hands, held loosely at his sides, those enormous, silk-skinned, elegant hands. Then to his collarbone. At last she looked at his face, to the deep and expressive eyes. There was sorrow there, sorrow and a hunger as deep as her own. "I got some chores to finish up for my mama. I'll come on back later."

Angel nodded. His step was heavy as it carried him away from her, but his head was still high, his shoulders square. As she watched him, she wanted to weep with frustration and loss—wanted to cry after him—*don't you see?*

But he did see. That was the trouble.

Rather than brood, which was really her first impulse, Angel left the weeding for another day, and went inside to cook. She turned on the radio for company and brought out pans and spoons and bowls. Cooking always made her feel better, and today was no exception.

By the time Isaiah returned, she'd made a feast—chicken and gravy and greens, a bowl of butter beans left from the day before, and a fat, juicy carrot cake bursting with pineapple.

For him, she finally admitted to herself. She stood at the back screen door as he climbed up the ladder without speaking her. Clouds hung heavy on the horizon and Angel knew there'd be rain within the hour. She could bide her time.

Taking the book of poetry he'd left her, she wandered out to the front porch to settle in and wait. In thirty minutes, the sky was darkening. She glanced up, smiled to herself, and kept reading.

When the rain started, she closed the book of poetry and went inside to check the food she'd left in the warm oven. The scent of paprika and nutmeg escaped on a wave of steam, and she pinched off a bit of crisp batter lying golden in the center of the pan. It was good.

Humming along with the radio, she filled glasses with ice and bits of mint and set the table. Outside, the rain and Isaiah's hammer warred over which could make the most noise. She checked the chicken once again, then grabbed a hat to cover her head and stepped out into the rain.

Isaiah still clung with ludicrous ferocity to the roof, rain pouring over his face and bare arms. "Isaiah High," she cried, "come down from there before you break your neck!"

"In a minute!" he called without looking at her, and reached in his pocket for a nail. The gesture was ill-timed. As he let go, his foot slipped, caught the guttering and knocked it loose. Desperately trying to right himself, he grabbed for the ladder and the edge of the roof, letting hammer and nails scatter. For an instant, he hovered, frozen against the nothingness of air and pouring rain—but the thrust was too far in motion to stop. The ladder, with Isaiah clinging mightily, toppled to the ground with a crash.

Angel cried out and jumped off the porch into the mud, running to his side. He lay still, his leg twisted in the ladder. One of the rungs had broken with the impact of his foot. His eyes were closed.

Rain streamed over her shoulders as she knelt next to him. "Isaiah!"

"I'm all right," he said gruffly.

Alive. Relief made her arms tremble. "Can you get up?"

He shook her arm away, "I'm fine. Go on and get out of this rain."

"Don't be so stubborn. Let me help you."

"No!" He turned to his side, dragging his leg out of the rungs, and pulled himself into a sitting position. The rain picked up, falling now in torrents that soaked them both. Shaking her head, she grabbed his arm. She had to shout to be heard. "Get up and let's get inside before we both catch our deaths."

This time he didn't argue. When he tried to stand up, he stumbled, grunting in pain before he could stop it. He swore, shaking off her hand.

"Come on," Angel said, moving close. "Throw your arm around my neck and I'll help you."

He did as he was told, limping heavily as they made their way to the back door. She got him settled in the kitchen and went to the bathroom for towels. When she returned, he'd taken off his boot and was staring at the swelling ankle with an expression of annoyance. "Hell," he said.

"Broken?" she asked.

"I don't think so. Sprained good, though."

"You're lucky it wasn't your neck, Isaiah." She rubbed a towel over her face. "What in the world possessed you to stay up there in the rain?"

"Hurry." Letting the ankle gently back down, he swore again. "Just cost myself a week, probably."

A trickle of blood showed at his crown, and Angel *tsked*. "You banged your head, too," she said, crossing the room to blot the cut with her towel. "You sure you're okay?"

"I'm fine, Angel," he said harshly. "Stop hovering."

Stung, she pulled back. "I'm going to change my clothes. You can go ahead and eat if you want."

"I ain't hungry."

"Suit yourself." Storming toward her room, she swallowed humiliation bitterly, telling herself that she was an idiot. Thinking of all the food, the set table, she sank down on her bed and pressed the soaked dress to her burning face. She was a fool.

By the time Angel came back to the kitchen, his ankle was swelling mightily, and he would never have admitted it, but it hurt. His head ached, too. Nasty fall.

Stupid.

She hadn't changed yet. Her hair hung in strings around her neck, making her look like a wet pup, and her dress was stuck to body. The lace of her slip showed through the fabric. She tossed a shirt at him.

"Put this on," she said. "Least you won't catch cold."

She was gone before he could thank her.

The kitchen was filled with the smell of chicken and beans and cake, the table set for two. Isaiah stared at it bleakly, the struggle within him raging once again. He'd done well all week avoiding her, keeping himself aloof, not letting one single stray thought to cross his mind.

But here in her kitchen the war was on again, and himself so hobbled he could barely walk—or, rain be damned, he'd be gone.

He needed to go, but even as he thought it, Angel came back wearing a clean dress, her hair combed away from her face. It was already drying, curling up a little at the edges.

She was not by a long stretch the prettiest woman he had ever seen. Lots of women like her in Ireland and Scotland—thin white skin and skinny arms. Ordinary, really. Oh, she had pretty eyes and a good mouth, but even those things didn't elevate her into anything close to a beauty. She was, if you looked at her, almost plain.

And yet, as she ignored him, opening the oven, taking out the platter of chicken, the bowl of gravy, he wanted her all the same, in a possessive way that had nothing to do with reality on any plane. As she slammed bowls down on the table, his stomach growled.

"Hope you don't mind," she said in a brittle voice, "if I go ahead and eat. I'm starving."

He shook his head. A stab of pain forced one eye closed.

"Good grief, Isaiah," she said, peering at him. "Don't you even feel that? You've got blood running down your face."

She pushed away from the table again and wet a towel with cold water at the sink, and with a look that dared him to stop her, she pressed the compress to his head. He winced.

"I'm sorry. It's deep. You probably need a stitch."

"I'll be all right."

"Yeah, you think you will." Her voice was brisk. "You always think you will. How come men always think they're made of iron?" She repositioned the compress, looked at him closely. "How do you really feel?"

He shifted, and his knee brushed the hem of her dress. He looked at the pattern, thin stripes in blue and pink and purple meeting in a cross hatch design every few inches.

How did he feel?

He felt that she was too close. The scent of her, plain unadorned Angel-skin, filled his head. The long stretch of her shin, bare and pale, filled his downcast eyes. The crook of her elbow hung near his jaw, and the faintest fan of her breath touched the bridge of his nose.

"Isaiah? Let me see your eyes. You can tell a concussion from the pupils."

It took a hundred years for his eyes to travel from her shin to her face, a long, unfocused journey over the terrain of her body. He let his eyes slide over her belly beneath the cinch of the elastic waist of her dress, over the small, free weight of her breasts, over her throat and plump lips to her eyes, peering at him in concern.

He knew she was too close. As he looked into the water-green irises with their tiny flecks of gray and blue and yellow, he felt the shift in events that tilted them, Angel and Isaiah, in a new direction.

Helpless, transfixed, he found himself lifting a hand to her waist. The cloth of her dress wrinkled under his fingers and he felt the fragile underpinning of hip bone. He moved his thumb over it.

In return, Angel settled a hand on his neck, her fingers curving around the column. He could feel every molecule of her palm. Her thumb traced the shape of his chin.

She whispered his name and the tilt of events pushed them closer still. He hung in the moment, hearing the heavy, rhythmic pounding of the rain on the roof echoing in his chest, and he thought of a thousand things as his hand moved on her waist. He thought of their forays into the trees and of the letters she'd written to him through the war, letters that had leant courage and comfort and hope.

Wordlessly, she moved a step closer and raised her hand to his face. Lightly, lightly she touched her fingers to his mouth. Isaiah fell forward with a soft groan to press his head against her, his forehead close to her diaphragm, his nose against her stomach, his arms tight around her body. The smell of her filled his mouth, his heart, the world, and he breathed it in as if it would save him. She made a soft noise and bent into him, gathering his head closer, her cheek against his hair.

For a long, long moment, they rested together like that. He no longer felt the ache in his head or ankle. It didn't matter that the world outside this room would curse him, that bloody Texas had hanged men for less.

"You know we can't do this," he said, but he felt himself exploring her back.

"I know," she whispered, but she touched his face, caressed his jaw, and he felt a tear land on his eyebrow. He raised his head, and saw that tears were streaming down her face. "Isaiah," she said, barely a whisper, and she opened both hands on his face, and as if in a dream, she bent to slowly, deliberately kiss his brow, each one of his eyelids, his nose.

"You are the only man I have ever loved my whole life." Holding his face in her small cold hands, she pressed her mouth into his, and Isaiah felt something splinter within him.

He pulled her down into his lap and tucked her hard into the crook of his arm and kissed her with all the heat and longing and deprivation he'd been feeling for a week. A year. A lifetime. Her mouth was plump and firm beneath his tongue, and her teeth nipped at his lips. She locked her arms around his head, her body twisting to press into him, their tongues meeting and feinting.

He threaded his fingers through the weightless strands of her hair, kissed her chin and bit her neck as she pushed her buttocks into his groin, rubbing against him in an ancient invitation. He covered her mouth and pushed up her skirts, running a hand over her thigh, sliding his fingers beneath her panties to her buttocks. She made a noise and wiggled against him, sucking on his lower lip.

"Sweet Jesus," he said, and raised his head, breathing hard. "I need to look at you."

She gravely looked at him, touched his forehead, rubbed a hand over his hair, his cheekbone, his mouth. Tenderly, he kissed a fingertip, pulled the tip into his mouth. Her nostrils flared.

"My Angel," he said, and reached for the buttons on the front of her dress. Paused and met her eyes. "Last chance."

She took his hand and pressed it around her small, taut breast. "I'm going to die if you don't touch me all over," she said, and there was hectic color on her throat.

His skin was electrified at the huskiness of her voice, and he unfastened the buttons one at a time, revealing a thin slip below. She caught her breath as he drew his fingertips over the bare skin, edged the lace covering the top of her chest, then slid over the rise of her breasts.

"Isaiah," she whispered, her hand on the back of his head. He bent and kissed her throat, tasting her skin. Her skin.

He had been waiting all of his life, *all of his life*, to make love with Angel Corey, and he didn't plan to hurry. He wanted to remember, for the *rest* of his life, what it was like.

So he calmed her when she panted. "Easy, baby," he said. "We got no place to be except right here. I want to remember. Sit up a little."

He gently slid the dress and then the ribbon straps of her slip away from her shoulders. A buzzing burned across the top of his head as her torso, pale and thin, was revealed, and he skimmed his hands over the delicate collarbone, her arms. She hunched a little as he touched her breasts, almost apologetically.

"I know there's not much there," she whispered, and it was true. Her breasts were not large, but they were as round as apples.

"You have no idea," he said raggedly, "how many times I thought about this." He traced the curves with his fingertips, touched each tip in turn, nipples that were not the soft rosy pink he'd always imagined, but ruddy and sturdy. He bent and tasted her. She clutched his shoulders, shivering, as he moved his mouth over the sloping terrain of a thousand night's imaginings. Every hair on his body was electrified, so that when she brushed her fingers over the nape of his neck, his hands prickled.

Remember, he told himself. *Remember this.*

Remember the silkiness of her thigh as he pushed up her skirts. Remember the taste of her flesh against his tongue, remember the restless way she moved against him. Remember finding the heat between her thighs, and the cry she let free, her hand grasping his wrist as if to push him away.

He said, "Trust me," and she let go, and he slid his finger inside, suckling her breast and she quivered.

For only a minute. "Not this time, not that way," she said, slamming her legs tight on his hands. She pushed herself upright and kissed him and Isaiah thought he would die. "Can you walk to my room?" she asked.

He rubbed his nose on her chin. "Oh, yeah."

So she stood up and collected her dress around her, modestly pulling it up over her breasts. She led the way to her bedroom. Isaiah hobbled behind her, and reached for the lamp. Yellow light flooded the room. It fell on the nape of her neck, the curve of her spine, the swell of her hips, and for one airless moment, he could not catch his breath both in fear and desire.

"God help us," he breathed, and reached for her.

Angel turned and wiggled out of her dress and slip, standing for a moment in her panties, and a shudder moved down her back at the look in his eye. He unfastened his overalls and let them fall, leaving his long legs bare. She moved toward him, and unbuttoned his shirt, one button and the next and the next, his hands on her shoulders, down her back. He bent to kiss her collarbone, her throat.

"My turn," she said, and pushed the shirt from his shoulders, leaving both of them only in underwear, and for a single, dizzy moment, Angel felt faint. She stepped up to him and pressed her breasts into his chest, touched his back, and felt his hands on her skin, all over her skin, and she said, "You don't know how many times I've thought of this. Sometimes, when I got a letter, I would put it under my pillow and it was almost as if you came to sleep with me."

"Believe me, I know," he said, a growl, and he captured her head, kissed her deep, and they tumbled backward to her small but adequate bed, and it was so much more, so much better than all the things she had imagined that she wanted to cry out with it. Their mouths, fitting, his slow, long way of kissing her, his hands on her skin. Her hands moving over his precious, precious flesh, his long back and muscled buttocks and powerful thighs. His engorged member pressing between her legs, and Angel hauling him closer with her legs until he gasped, "I need to be in you, Angel. In you."

They scraped away the last of their clothes. In the instant before their joining, Isaiah paused, his breath labored. She felt the hard heat of his thighs against her own, felt him nudging closer, and she hovered with him in the endless moment, waiting as he took her head in his hands. Light threw a halo over his hair.

He kissed her. "Since we were babies, Angel," he said hoarsely, "since we built that tree house, every day during the war, always, always, always I loved you." A tremor passed through him. "Don't close your eyes."

His dark eyes held hers as he slowly moved his hips. Angel took him in, hearing his breath leave him in a long, long sigh. "Now," he whispered, "now we really are one person. I'm you and you're me."

And as she stared into his eyes, the darkness softened until the true Isaiah was shining through. A swirling dizziness filled her, swelled through her mind and spilled into her limbs—the purest most beautiful sense of God she had ever known. Filled to bursting, she arched against him with a cry, and tears spilled from her eyes and she held him as close as she possibly could.

When Angel drifted up through sleep, she thought she was dreaming again, had dreamed all of it.

But slowly, her body awakened a bit at a time, to the length of Isaiah's thigh over her own, and the soft weight of his genitals pressed damply into the small of her back. His hand, so huge and warm and heavy, was spread open over her belly. His breath moved over her shoulder, and it was the most precious thing she could imagine.

Isaiah.

For a long time, she didn't move, didn't open her eyes, content to feel him so close, so protectively shielding her, even in sleep. Between them rose the earthy scent of sex, mingled with the scent of Isaiah himself, a smell like early morning forest and freshly turned earth and bruised grass. Sometimes, while he'd been away all those years, she'd catch a whiff of his particular blend of scents on the breeze, and loneliness would swamp her, swift and sudden and painful. Now, she kept her eyes closed, savoring it, savoring this time.

It was not yet dawn, but a blackbird whistled above them. Soon, the sun would rise to shatter the last of this precious, precious night. Soon, there would be travelers on the road, customers stopping in the store for coffee. One of them would be Isaiah's mother.

Angel felt unutterably altered, as if a sizzling field now surrounded her, one that radiated outward from the two of them curled in her bed, and would glow above their heads like neon, and stain the entire area around the store, so that anyone passing would know what had transpired.

A cool thrust of terror tore at her joy. She thought of what had been done to men in the forests around Gideon, thought of the brutal treatment Isaiah—and probably Angel along with him—would face if anyone found out about this.

Isaiah's hand moved on her stomach, moved to pull her to him as if he'd sensed her thoughts. He gathered her close, smoothing her hair, kissing her face, rocking her gently. "It's all right, baby."

Angel realized she was shaking, shaking all over, uncontrollably. She pressed more completely into his warmth, taking shelter against the broad wall of his chest, and the length of his legs. He murmured quietly, "It's all right, baby, you're safe, I've got you."

After a few minutes, she turned in his arms and buried her face against the sparse hair on his chest. He kissed her forehead, smoothed hair off her face. "We'll go away. Angel. There are places we can be together, where we can have a normal life. All you ever wanted to do was leave here, anyway. You're strong, baby. You'll be all right."

"You make me strong, Isaiah," and moved her hands on his smooth body. "I can do anything if you're with me."

"I'll be with you."

They moved together then, and Angel understood why she had always been so restless, what she had waited for, why Solomon's loving had left her so dissatisfied.

She'd been waiting for Isaiah.

She kissed him fervently. His big hands pulled her closer, he moved harder, and Angel breathed a prayer. *Thank you for bringing him home to me.*

And it seemed that she heard, far away, the sound of God laughing as Jordan High. The best sound, the richest sound, a sound of safekeeping.

— 35 —

May 1, 1945

Dear Angel,

After all these months in battle and all the death and misery I've seen, I didn't know anything could still shred my soul. But two days ago, we marched into Dachau, which is one of the death camps, and what I saw burned my faith right out of my soul. People so hungry you could see their whole skull, the cheekbones and the hollows for the eyes, and the bones at their wrists. Things I can't even stand to tell you, things I'd want to cover your ears if other people tried to tell you. I'm sick. Sick.

Probably shouldn't even mail this letter, but I'm gonna. I know you're worrying.

War is over now, though, so don't worry any more. Thanks for keeping me company.

Your friend,

Isaiah

June 2, 1945

Dear Isaiah,

We have heard some of the stories, and I have no words to try to make you feel better, and maybe there's nothing I could say anyway. I am so sorry for your sense of horror. You know, in your heart, that's not God, though. God doesn't live in evil and despair and loss. He lives in hope, in beauty, in courage and honor. All of which you have shown, so I know God lives in you, even if you don't want to live with God. It's okay. He's big enough for a crisis of faith. I'm not going to stop praying for you.

Your friend,

Angel

June 25, 1945

Dear Isaiah,

I'm worried about you. You haven't been writing to me or your mama or my daddy. Hope all is well.

Your friend,

Angel

July 21, 1945

Dear Angel,

It's terrible here. Terrible. Ya'll have heard the story by now. I got enough demobilization points to go home, but I'm gonna stay awhile in Europe. Mrs. Pierson wrote me about some family she got in Denmark and I'm gonna see for her is anybody left. I don't hold a lot of hope, but no harm in looking. Not like I spent any money the past year. There's time.

Tell your daddy I said hi, but that I ain't gonna live in Gideon when I get back. He'll be glad about that.

Isaiah

— 36 —

Dawn had not yet fully edged into the night when Isaiah left Angel with a last, lingering kiss, and headed home under cover of darkness. She had wrapped his ankle tightly and then he put on his boot and laced it up, as they'd done in combat many a time. She scrounged up a cane and he hobbled out the back door.

The river was too high from the storm the night before for him to cross the water so, despite the struggle, he walked the mile down to the bridge, hobbling along, and not minding in the least. His blood sang a chant, *Angel Angel Angel*. His arms carried the imprint of her small form curled up next to him all night. All night. He awakened to find her there, over and over, and every time it was like a miracle, and he would kiss her shoulder, her hair, cover her breasts with his hands, press his belly into her back.

She loved him.

He had known it on some level, but her tears had shattered him. Tears of longing, of release, tears of joy. She had put his letters under her pillow and thought of him lying next to her, just as he had imagined her a thousand times, a million.

She loved him.

He reached the bridge and hobbled across, making plans. They would go away, north or maybe west, where he'd heard there was plenty of work and no segregation. It would not, he knew, be an easy life for either of them, or for their children. Even without Jim Crow, theirs would be a union many would find tainted.

He had not been sure, before this, that Angel would have what it took to face that down. And yet, now as he ambled like a lovesick pup down the dirt road to his mama's house, he had no idea why. She was her father's daughter. She could stand the heat.

They would marry. They would have children. He wanted to weep with the joy of it, with the love of her, filling every rushing blood cell in his being, filling his heart, his mind, his soul. "Thank you, Jesus," he whispered, and for a little while, he could believe again.

As he passed the white frame church he'd been raised in, he paused. Church of God in Christ, the sign read, and he went inside, and stood before the altar, thinking of the churches he'd seen in his travels, the grand cathedrals, the bombed village churches.

"Get us outta here alive," he said, "and I'll do whatever you want. Hear?"

Geraldine was reading her bible on the porch when Isaiah came strolling down the road like he had not a care in the world. She shook her head as he came up the steps. "You been with that woman."

He waved a hand. "None of your business, Mama." With a grunt, he hobbled up the steps, and she saw there was a cut on his head.

"What'd you do to yourself?"

"No big thing. Fell off the ladder in that storm last night."

"Ahh-uh." Geraldine saw it all too clearly. Angel offering kindly ministrations. Isaiah falling under her spell. "Boy, you a fool. A fool."

He gave her a long look, full of bristling pride, and went inside.

Filled with anger and fear—yes, love—she followed him. "You think they won't kill you? They will. And that woman with you. Just givin' them an excuse to get rid o' you both."

"That woman," he said. "You mean Angel Corey, whose been tending to your needs every morning for the last fifteen years? That woman?"

Tears welled in her eyes, wretched and weak, and she swallowed hard. "I'd have given you up to the war, 'Saiah, and I'd have mourned you, but known you did what's right. Don't ask me to let you go like your daddy did. Don't ask it."

"Mama." He crossed the room and took her worn hands in his.

"It's time things changed," he said quietly. "People keep being quiet, we'll get somebody like Hitler in power and end up dead like all those Jews. You think a lynching's bad, you oughta see one of those camps—all those people dumped and starved and gassed. Children, Mama, so hungry they'd eat bugs, dying for some little piece of fruit I had in my pocket. All they people gone, nobody left." He pressed his thumbs to the fan of bones in her hand. "Not just time for me and Angel, but for all of us to have to have a different life. I can't go back to what I knew."

"Sounds good, Isaiah," she said, her voice hard and skeptical. "That's a real pretty speech. But you don't care about anything but having that woman. That's all. Rest of the world rot in hell long as you get what you want."

"Say her name, Mama. Use her name."

Geraldine yanked her hands away. "You don't care about anything as long as you have Angel Corey."

He bowed his head, pulled his lower lip into his mouth. Then he shook his head. "It shouldn't be so hard, Mama. It's not like she's a cat and I'm dog. You hear me?"

She stared at him, jaw hard.

"I ain't a preacher like my daddy was, or a crusader like Parker. I can't talk and make people act on their behalf." He smiled. "You got to have charisma if you gonna change the world. All I've ever wanted is to build things, and marry Angel."

Geraldine let him talk.

"Angel is my heart, Mama. She always has been," His eyes glowed, his features softened. "And she loves me."

Geraldine tore her hands from his. "How do you know that? How can you know? You wouldn't be the first black man to hang for the curiosity of a white woman, dabbling and tasting and then getting scared."

"You know better." He crossed the room to wash his face, putting his back to her.

Her words were low and hot. "You're a fool, Isaiah. Never thought, as long as I lived, that I'd see the day you'd let her get killed with you. And they just waitin' for a reason. And when they get her, the only blessing will be that you won't have long to live with it."

She turned and left him.

Geraldine considered passing by the store by this morning. But as she neared the worn wooden building with the brave morning glories giving it its only lick of color, she found she couldn't walk by.

As she came up the steps and pulled open the screen door, she smelled the heady scent of coffee hanging in the air. There were biscuits on the counter, and some jam she'd put up last summer.

Angel swept the floor, humming softly as she worked, *The Old Rugged Cross*. It pierced Geraldine's heart. She had loved this girl. When Jordan died, Angel had carried over the bridge a huge bouquet of wildflowers for her, walking by herself into Lower Gideon with her daddy's permission to deliver them. Then with an uncanny sense for such a young girl, she gave Geraldine a hug and said only, "I'm sorry."

Now, she thought fiercely, won't anyone defend her? But no one could.

She spoke. "Don't you think it's time to get out of here, Angel?"

Angel let go of a little startled cry, whirling. When she saw Geraldine, a bright flush brightened her cheeks. "Good morning, Miss Geraldine. Coffee's not quite done yet.

"I'm not here for coffee this morning." She leveled her gaze at the woman—no longer a girl, had not been a girl for a long time. Angel's skin was thin and pale, like a membrane, showing every little bump and scratch she got. A bruise lingered on her cheek from a few days before, but Geraldine had already seen that.

There were other things this morning, a reddened place on her jaw, a mark of hunger on her neck, lips over-full and a little bruised. And in her eyes, a glowing, living thing. As if Angel had finally donned the mantle of her womanhood. As if—the word came back to her—Angel was finally free. The lecture she had meant to deliver died on her lips.

Instead, very quietly, she said, "You have to go. Both of you."

Angel faced her, mouth sober. "I know." She swallowed. "I'm trying to find somebody to take the store, not even buy, just take it. Somebody who's gonna be fair and be able to stand up to the Walkers."

"Once you're gone, Angel, Edwin Walker won't give a hoot about this store anymore." She *tsked*. "And if you're dead, it isn't gonna matter who's got the store, now, is it?"

"No, ma'am. You're right about that."

At four, Angel gave up and closed the store, heading for town. She had made Isaiah promise not to walk today, to stay home and rest his ankle. After looking at it this morning, she really wondered if he'd chipped a bone in there or something. It was bad, no matter how brave he wanted to pretend to be.

She needed him strong.

As she walked, she noted the late afternoon sunlight and bluebonnets beginning to bloom in the fields. Birds and crickets, bees and flies filled the air with a busy buzzing noise. Beautiful, she thought, everything was so beautiful.

Because Isaiah was in every second of her day. That dimple lighting up his face, making him look so whimsical. His low groaning sounds of release against her mouth or throat. His laughter this morning.

She felt saturated with light. All those years of waiting, all those years of longing and denial. It was worth the struggles and the dark times and the eternal, restless longing for the things she had not dared name, all under a single umbrella.

Isaiah.

She knocked on Mrs. Pierson's big house. Her maid, Mrs. Reed, answered her knock. Her dark eyes met Angel's warily for a moment, then she stepped aside. "Mrs. Pierson's in the garden. Come on through here."

"That's all right. You go ahead with what you were doing. I'll find my way."

Mrs. Reed nodded. As Angel headed down the polished hallway, she said, "Miss Angel, I'm real sorry about your store."

"He hasn't won yet."

Mrs. Reed lifted her chin. Without a single word she managed to convey her opinion: *he will.* "I'll bring you a glass of sweet tea directly."

In the back yard, Mrs. Pierson was settled in one of the wicker chairs she favored, under the spreading boughs of the pecan tree. Gudren trimmed roses and daisies from the borders, laying them carefully in a basket by her knee. Seeing Angel, she waved. "I will be finished soon," she called. "It is wonderful to see you!"

"Take your time." Angel settled in the chair next to Mrs. Pierson, and took the older woman's hand. She seemed so much more fragile lately, Angel thought, suddenly alarmed. "Hello," she forced herself to say cheerfully.

"Angel." She smiled. "Isn't it a work day?"

"I knocked off a little early."

"I see." Mrs. Pierson moved her hands, captured one of Angel's fingers. "I have been worried about you, my dear."

"Whatever for? I'm fine."

"No. There is grumbling, Angel. From quarters that surprise me."

A slither of fear snaked through her throat. Edwin she could manage. He was, at least, a known enemy. "Like who?"

Mrs. Pierson turned her face toward Angel, her sightless eyes seeming to fix Angel where she stood. "Church people, who should know better."

"My church?"

"Yes."

"I already knew about them, too. Don't worry—the pastor is a good man. He'll keep them in line."

"Perhaps." Her rose-colored silk dress fluttered around her knees on a wisp of wind. "Perhaps he cannot."

She thought of her Sunday School class, and the pastor's angry sermon about loving your neighbor. The never-distant sense of fear flooded through her again. "I hate feeling so scared all the time," she said fiercely. "I'm just tired of it."

"Parker would be proud, Angel." Mrs. Pierson covered her hand gently. "Proud and afraid."

"I know." She plucked a leaf from the shrub nearby, watching Gudren clip flowers. "My daddy should have died three years ago. But he had to see how that war would come out. Had to.

"I hated," she continued, "to listen to all those radio reports of all the bombs. It was awful—I was so worried about Isaiah it almost made me sick. But Daddy had to listen every single day. Blow. By. Blow."

"Angel—"

"No, let me finish." She swallowed. "What was the point of all that fighting, all that dying, if nothing ever changes?" Emotion filled her throat, choking off her words, and she put the back of her wrist against her mouth.

Mrs. Pierson reached for her hand. "You love him very much, our Isaiah."

"Yes," she whispered. "I do. And I'm so afraid and—" She took a breath. "He was a good solider, you know that? I was so scared that he'd get blown up or shot or tortured." She sniffed. "I'm not making any sense, am I? Going in circles."

Mrs. Pierson put her arms around her. "Oh, but you are. I love you as my daughter, Angel Corey. And I am so proud of you. You've grown into a fine woman."

"We need to go away. Soon," Angel said. "Will you find someone to run my store?"

"Better yet," the old woman said, "you must let me purchase it for you. I will find someone to take care of my investment, and then you will have money of your own, which is always important."

"Oh, no, I couldn't—"

Gudren came over, putting her hand on Angel's arm. "Be wise, my friend. He loves you, but life can be capricious. He could die," she said simply.

Angel looked from old woman to young, women who had suffered unimaginable trials. "Yes, you're right," she said, and kissed Mrs. Pierson's hand. "Thank you. It is a generous offer, and I accept."

"The condition is that you must go within a day, or two at most. I can feel the danger."

"Yes," Angel said. "Of course."

"I will speak to my banker by phone this afternoon. Come see me in the morning." She touched Angel's face. "Now, you and Gudren should go to town and behave like the young girls neither of you could be. Drink chocolate sodas and read movie magazines."

Angel laughed. "That sounds wonderful."

"It makes you strong."

The two of them walked the few blocks into town, passing tidy frame houses ringed with hedges and thick lawns. A handsome Labrador looked up from the porch at one house, wagging his tail hopefully as they passed, then settled his head back on his paws when they didn't come up the walk to his place. Two little boys on bicycles raced by in the quiet street, headed for the river. An old woman, Mrs. Unwin, who'd been a teacher for thirty-five years before retiring, worked in her flower garden. A floppy straw hat covered her white hair, and she wore a pair of men's trousers to protect her knees. As the women passed, she waved a gloved hand merrily.

"That's the kind of old woman I want to be," Angel said.

"Because she's still working in her garden?"

Angel shrugged a little. "Not just that. I want to be strong and independent and enjoying myself. She's eighty years old, and doesn't give a hoot about anything anybody says about her." Angel grinned. "She used to wear the strangest hats to school all the time, with flowers or some wild scarf wrapped around them. It was wonderful."

"So perhaps we age in the pattern in which we live, no?"

"I suppose so."

"It seems a great blessing to grow old at all," Gudren said. "But should I gain that age, I would like, perhaps, to be calm."

"Yes. And wise," Angel added. She had a vision of Gudren at 80, elegant and patrician with a wreath of hair woven around her head. "I think you'll have many grandchildren by then."

She squeezed Angel's hand. "Perhaps."

They reached the main drag in town, called elsewhere Main Street, but here in Gideon, it was Drake, after one of the town's first mayors. There was a lot of foot traffic. The fabric store was bustling, and the barber shop. Usually Saturdays were the busy day, mostly no one came to town much except for then. The numbers out today served to emphasize Angel's outcast status.

A handful of people nodded and spoke—not everyone was out to get her, after all, she thought. But a majority walked by as if Angel were invisible, even some she'd known since youngest childhood. When Eula Hart passed by, her eyes carefully trained away, Angel almost stopped and stomped her foot over the sharpness of the rejection. Eula had made for Angel the prettiest, lacy dresses for Sunday School every year—had once brought her a doll with blond curls and a dress to match Angel's.

She lifted her chin.

By the time they reached the drugstore, she felt as if she'd been in a parade. Had it been like this the other day and she'd just been too wrapped up in her anger and fear to notice?

The druggist, Hubert Cox, was a tall man with gray hair that sprung around the bald spot on top of his head like a brush. He wore a white apron over his starched shirt, upon which he wiped his hands as Angel and Gudren came in. "Hello there, stranger!" he called, peering over his half-glasses.

Angel smiled in relief. "Hi, Mr. Cox. How are you?"

"I'm doing fine—and you look pretty as a sunrise, as usual."

"You old sweet talker. " Angel turned toward Gudren. "Have you met Mrs. Pierson's niece? This is Gudren Stroo."

"Howdy!" His bright gray eyes sparkled. "How do you like us so far?"

Gudren smiled, and as always the expression completely transformed her thin face below its cap of severe hair. "It is—er—very different."

"You got that right! " He laughed, "Wait a week or two and you'll see mosquitoes so big they can stand flat-footed and box a turkey."

Angel laughed. "I'd love to tell you he's exaggerating, but he isn't. Not by much, anyway."

"You ladies in the mood for something special, today?"

"As a matter of fact," Angel said, "I want a double chocolate soda. Gudren?"

"Strawberry, please."

"Coming right up. You two pretty young ladies go find yourself a seat and I'll fix you right up."

There were few customers in the long room. A mother with three children occupied one of the forward booths, and a knot of teenage girls hovered over the magazine rack. At one of the back tables sat a young colored man with a girl a little younger who learned forward to listen to his quietly murmured words. They had empty sundae glasses before them.

Gudren and Angel slid into a booth about midway down. "This is wonderful!" Gudren exclaimed. "He is a nice man."

Angel let her eyes flicker back to Mr. Cox and she frowned a little. "Yes. But I would have expected him to be one of the ones that didn't speak much, to tell you the truth."

"Why?"

"I don't know. He's always been pretty active in town politics and such—he was county treasurer and on the draft board—mainline." She shook her head. "I can't figure any of it out. I honestly didn't expect such a fuss over me keeping the store. When I found out people would—either because they think its unseemly for a white woman to be out there alone, or because they just plain think a woman oughta be doing something else—I had pretty much in mind who would be nice and who wouldn't. But I'm wrong a lot."

Gudren lifted her eyebrows. "Often, it is like that. We do not know who will be a friend and who will not until it is too late."

"I guess you probably know a little bit about that."

Mr. Cox delivered their sodas with a flourish, tall glasses nestled in tin holders. Whipped cream dusted with nuts was piled to an almost astonishing level above the glass. On Angel's was a circle of maraschino cherries. She laughed. "You remembered!"

"Oh, now, it hasn't been that long. You were still asking for extra cherries when you came in with Solomon."

"Thank you."

He winked. "You girls enjoy, now."

When he bustled way, Gudren asked, "You came here with your husband?"

"Sure. We came to movies and got sodas on Saturday nights when he had money." She sobered. "Everybody did the same thing." She drifted away, remembering a night she had come in with her daddy and they'd seen Isaiah walking with his girl Sally. Now she smiled, remembering him last night, so—

"Angel," Gudren said softly, touching her hand.

In surprise, she looked up. "I'm sorry, did you say something?"

"What is so different about you today?"

Angel flushed and stared down at her soda, feeling blood even at the tips of her ears.

"Oh!" Gudren laughed softly. She reached over the table to take Angel's hand. "You are so in love!" she said softly. "I am so happy. It is so good, Angel, so good I cannot tell you."

Blushing even more deeply, Angel opened her mouth to say something, and realized she had no idea what that might be. She closed it again.

"I did not mean to embarrass you." Gudren squeezed her fingers. "So many times I hoped for this."

"You did?"

Gudren glanced over her shoulder. The mother and her children were standing up, gathering small packages. Gudren sipped her soda, waiting for them to pass. When the bell rang over the door, signaling their departure, she leaned over the table and said very softly, "While I was healing, he came to sit with me. There was a beautiful garden on the hospital grounds, and it pleased me to be in the open with all those smells and sounds."

Angel could see it, imagining the nourishment it must have offered after so many trials.

"It was a long time before he spoke of his home. And when he did, it was only stories of you that he told." Again she looked around cautiously. "I did not understand the . . . trouble, then. But there was such a hungry sound when he said your name. I wanted for him what he most wished."

"Thank you," Angel said simply.

Gudren nodded, her eyes going deeply sober in an instant. "But now I say to you that you must never say his name in public, where anyone can see what I just saw. This place is strange to me, but even I know what will happen to you if you are not very, very careful."

Angel bowed her head. "I know." The heaviness of it all made her shoulders ache. After a minute, she picked up her spoon with determination. "We're supposed to be acting like young girls today. No more serious talk."

"O-*kay*." Gudren pulled forth the word like a prize, her eyes glinting.

After they finished their sodas, they lingered awhile, talking about new dresses they wanted, which styles they thought would work for them. On the way out, they stopped at the magazine racks. On one of the movie magazines was a picture of a young man. Gudren picked it up, grinning, "I had a beau who looked like him," she said. "He played duets with me and kissed my ears when my instructor wasn't looking."

Angel laughed. "He's handsome."

With an exaggerated shrug, Gudren put the magazine back. "They all were handsome," she said. "And in love with me." She shot a quick, amused glance at Angel. "But my great love was a man, not a silly boy: Mr. Vanzandt, my piano teacher. He was at least twenty-seven, and had the most soulful eyes I have ever seen."

They headed toward the door. "And?" Angel prompted.

"Oh, he was married to a very rich and beautiful woman, but I was sure that he secretly longed for me." She chuckled. "How vain we are at sixteen."

The door opened, forcing the women to step back in the crowded aisle. Angel saw who entered and her heart squeezed in sudden and painful fear. She took Gudren's arm. "Let's go," she whispered and made a move to go around the pair.

"Well, well, well," said the first, a ruddy-complexioned man of thirty. He wore the war-weary look so many men had these days, his face hard-carved, eyes troubled. "Angel Corey."

Angel forced herself to meet his eyes squarely. "Hello, Tom." Her voice sounded calm and steady, even faintly polite. "Jacob," she added, nodding at the thinner man next to him.

"The wife told me you been having a little trouble over at your store," Tom said, faintly mocking.

"Did she?" Angel returned. "Well, thank her for her concern."

Jacob stepped one foot forward, smiling. She found herself mesmerized by the yellow shimmer at the end of his eyelashes, and the pattern of freckles over his thin nose. "Too bad you ain't gonna keep it."

"Thank you for your concern," she repeated, and tugged Gudren's arm, moving toward the door, trying to get around them.

"Hold on, now, Angel. Aren't you gonna introduce your friend here?" Tom let a bold gaze travel over Gudren's slim frame. "Pretty skinny, but I reckon you'll fatten up, won't you, sugar?"

"Get out of the way, Tom. We have things to do."

"Yeah, I bet you do," he said, nudging Jacob. His eyes took on a speculative look as he shifted his gaze back to Gudren. "We heard what all you Jew girls did to get through the camps, didn't we, Jake."

Angel glanced at Gudren in alarm. The big black eyes were hot and snapping. She leaned close to Tom, and in a low, sexy voice, she uttered one of the filthiest insults Angel had ever heard.

For an instant, Angel was shocked. Then it took all she had to keep from laughing out of nervous reaction. There was no doubt at all that these two had been part of the vandalism at her store, that they were both mean as skunks before spending years and years getting meaner in war.

At the gathering thunder in Tom's face, Angel jerked hard on Gudren's arm. "Let's go."

But Jake pushed her, "Nobody told you to go yet. You still haven't properly introduced us."

From behind them came Mr. Cox's voice. "Tom and Jake, where the hell are your manners? Get outta that doorway right this minute. You wanna come in, come in, but don't stand there blocking the ladies' way."

"Ladies?" Tom echoed. But he stepped aside.

Angel pushed by them, the back of her neck rippling. Even out on the street, she didn't slow until her feet gained a path that led to the river. There, under the heavy shade of an oak tree, she shuddered and shook her limbs like she'd been covered in spider webs. "Ugh!"

Gudren said beside her, "Angel, I am sorry, I lost my temper—it was—"

"Don't apologize, please, Gudren."

"But I acted foolishly."

Angel gave her a wry glance. "Where did you learn to swear like that?"

With a grim twist of her mouth, Gudren said wearily, "You would be surprised at what I know. Much of it, I wish I could forget."

Angel met her eyes. "I'm sorry."

Neither of them spoke for long moments. Angel felt her fear slipping into the soothing sound of the river as it swished over rocks and eddied into pools. She took a long breath. "I'm so ashamed of them for calling you names like that. After everything that has happened, you would think . . ."

"I knew about America, Angel."

"What do you mean?"

Gudren pursed her lips, her gaze trained on the opposite bank of the river. "There was a woman with me, in the camps. She was a German Jew who escaped Europe on a ship that sailed to America." Gudren plucked a long stem of grass, her voice almost completely flat as she continued, "The ship was filled with Jews running away. A thousand or more. It sailed the length of North and South America. No one would let them in."

She repeated, "No one would let them in. So," she said with a bitter smile. "The ship came back to Europe."

The story left a hollow sensation in Angel's gut. "I do wonder where God was through all of this."

"God must have human hands, yes?"

"Yes." She sank down on the grass, and Gudren joined her. "Will you stay here, Gudren?"

"I thought I might," she said. "But I do not think so. I had hoped that we—my mother's sister and I—could go to Palestine together, but I think she will not live so much longer. So I will wait and then go alone."

The sudden thought that Mrs. Pierson, too, would be gone from Gideon gave Angel a thrust of sadness. It must have shown on her face, for Gudren reached over to cover her hand. "Will you come to supper before you go, you and Isaiah?"

"Maybe. I'll ask him." But disturbed, she looked back to the river, unable to shake the sense of impending threat Tom and Jake had lit within her.

Something was afoot.

— 37 —

September 10, 1945

Dear Isaiah,

I guess you aren't going to write any more letters to me. Haven't had one since July. I keep hoping I'll get another one, get your new address, but I haven' t got anything yet, so I asked Mrs. Pierson today what the address was where she was writing you.

It's a good thing, what you're doing for her. We've been hearing all the horrible stories, seeing all the pictures that are coming out of the war zone, all the wretched things the Nazis did. I can't even imagine how that hurt your heart, Isaiah. I'm so sorry. I don't hardly know what to say, it's been so long since your last letter maybe you don' t want to write any more. I understand that, but Isaiah, if you could come home just to see my daddy before he dies, it sure would be a good thing.

Your friend always,

Angel

PS He's really sick, Isaiah.

— 38 —

Exhausted from the long night and the week he'd spent working from sun up to sundown, Isaiah slept most of the day. It wasn't something he had intended to do, but his body took over when he settled on his bed to rest. He didn't awaken until late afternoon sunshine streamed through his window and in his face. For a long moment, he was disoriented. His head ached vaguely and his shoulder was sore, but he couldn't remember quite why. Had there been a battle?

No. Home. He was home.

He swung his feet off the bed and his left ankle shot a vicious protest through his leg into his hip. He'd fallen, twisted the damned ankle in the rungs and sprained it good. Rubbing his face, trying to clear the muzziness from his brain, he remembered the fall—slamming his shoulder, bumping his head—

Angel.

A fresh flood of love and heat washed through him as he remembered her plump mouth and fragile, strong body, the fury with she had met his lovemaking. And he remembered the strange, glowing light that had surrounded them in the darkness as they had joined, finally, after so many long years of denial.

Have mercy.

He had loved her a long time. In childhood he admired her will and sense of humor and lack of fear. In adolescence, her slim young body had been the focus of every raging man-thought he dreamed. No matter who slaked the edges, it was always Angel he wanted. As an adult, he thought he had learned to control himself and his unsuitable wishes; thought that he'd learned that nobody in this life got just what they wanted.

God, he loved her. So deeply, so completely, so mindlessly it was like a thing apart. It had only been a few hours since he'd left her and he was already so starved for her company that he could barely stand it.

The aching wish for her propelled him to his feet, and he made his way to the kitchen where his mama kept a rag drawer. The movements made him a little dizzy, and he had to practically drag the foot behind him. He collapsed on the chair near the drawer. There were no scissors there, or anywhere else he looked, so he tore long strips of ancient cotton sheets and wrapped the sausage-swollen ankle tightly. It helped.

He washed up and changed his clothes, and only then thought of his mother, who would soon be coming home to find him gone again. His conscience slammed him with a vision of her worn face and the worry it would show. Her eyes this morning had been filled with a terror Isaiah had never seen. She'd tried so hard to keep from showing it.

Wouldn't take long to fix her up some supper and leave it warming on the stove. Fighting the sense of urgency he felt to get to Angel, he fried potatoes with onions and bacon, and whipped up a stack of pancakes to leave in the oven. She'd always liked breakfast for supper and supper for breakfast—made her feel like a girl, she said. And it was the one thing she hadn't been able to enjoy when she cooked for her husband. *A man,* she used to say in a low voice supposedly imitating Isaiah's father, *got to have meat in the evenin'.*

As he baked flapjacks in a heavy skillet, it struck him that he'd always had a very strong, clear picture of his father. That was his mother's doing. She kept Jordan alive in Isaiah's heart by telling him over and over what his father had done, and how, and when, making of him almost a legend. He'd been a hero in France, fighting with a French battalion, then came home to battle for the poor and downtrodden in Gideon. He could shoot a deer right through the eyes at 400 paces and skin a catfish clean in about five seconds flat. She had loved him and kept his memory alive for his children with a thousand stories.

This morning had been the first time he'd ever heard even a hint of bitterness. "Talk," she said. "Lord he could talk."

When the supper was finished, he left the pan on the back of the stove and put a note on it that said only, *Don't worry, Mama.*

He headed out through the back door and toward the river, which had gone down considerably since this morning. Truth was, across the river to the Corey store was about a three or four minute trip and, aside from snakes and the odd flood season, it wasn't much of a crossing. Down the road and across the bridge was close to a mile.

The water loosened his bandage and he found himself limping hard on the opposite side of the bank, even with the help of the stick. As he reached the thicket of cottonwoods and pines that hid the store, the fogginess in his brain suddenly cleared.

What the hell was he doing?

I never thought I'd see the day you let them kill her. As the back of the Corey house and store came into view, he kicked something. A tin can, pierced with a bullet hole.

Where love had been shimmering through him, a harsh fury now burned—fury at himself. This was no game. Texas wasn't England or

France, where there might have been frowns him loving this woman—and most of those from his own countrymen, not the locals—but no danger to speak of.

This was bloody, bloody Texas. Where the dark forest was filled with the ghostly cries of those who had been punished with beatings and lynchings and worse, for real and imagined infractions of the careful class system that had been so grimly erected here. His daddy had been killed in this very forest. His own nearly-deadly beating had taken place here, and that one over Angel smiling at him. Just smiling. If Edwin Walker knew how much more Angel had now done, there would be no stopping his rage and violence, and this time, it wouldn't be Isaiah Edwin would punish.

There were things worse than dying.

His mind filling with brutal pictures, Isaiah paused, staring in despair at the worn shingles of the old store. *Have mercy.*

The door opened, and Ebenezer flew out, squawking out a litany of complaint and dire scolding. Isaiah stepped backward in to the trees, waiting for a glimpse of Angel before he took himself back across the river. The throaty sound of her laughter rang through the stillness, and she stepped outside on the back porch. Her dress was pale green with a white collar, the same dress she had worn the day she made pineapple upside down cake because she'd known he couldn't resist it. He remembered how hard he had fought that afternoon to keep his eyes from her mouth, from her legs, bare and slim beneath the dress.

The bird flew in the pitiful circles it could manage, chirping, and whistling and almost cackling with laughter, then flew right for Isaiah in the trees, shrieking out a greeting. Caught now—and hadn't he wanted to be caught?—Isaiah lifted his arm. With a tiny scratch of claws, Ebenezer landed and scooted up toward Isaiah's shoulder, nuzzling against his face like a cat. Isaiah laughed softly. "You funny thing."

Angel hadn't moved from the porch and, feeling absurdly shy, Isaiah finally had to look at her. Her hands were clasped in front of her, and her face was a mask of uncertainty.

But in her eyes was the same love he felt burning within himself, so deep a longing that a hundred years couldn't possibly quench it. Before he knew he would do it, he stepped forward, drawn by that expression. At the bottom of the steps he paused, giving her a faint, knowing smile. "Hey."

"Hey." In a calm voice, she said, "I have something for you inside."

"Is that right." He smiled, very slowly, and he limped up the steps to follow her inside. She closed the door behind him and turned to fling herself into his arms, standing on tiptoe to kiss him full on the mouth, her eyes glittering, her breasts and belly hard against him. Isaiah let go of the cane, hearing it clatter to the floor as he grabbed her closer to him, threading his fingers through her hair to hold her scalp so that he could fit their mouths together more tightly.

Drowning. He was drowning in joy.

Angel broke away and tugged him into her bedroom at the back of the house where they fell on the comfort of the bed, and there were no thoughts then, only mouths and hands and skin, only soft cries and fierce nips and the ancient rhythm of sex.

A long time later, Angel felt Isaiah shift away from her. "Don't go," she whispered.

"I'm not going anywhere, baby." He reached down to pull the sheet over them. He bent his head and kissed her neck before settling next to her again, propped on one elbow. When he grinned, the dimple in his left cheek gave him a boyish expression. "That was really something you had for me."

She stretched against him, rubbing her shoulder up against his chest like a cat. "I thought I just might fade away waiting to see you again. I didn't expect you tonight."

"I didn't expect to be here." He brushed her hair away from her face, eyes growing serious. "I stood out there in the trees thinking about all the things that could happen to you if Edwin finds out about this. It's dangerous, Angel. We should figure out how to get out of here, where to meet, and then just stay the hell away from each other until we get there."

"I know. I spoke with Mrs. Pierson this morning. She is going to take the store as an investment and find someone to work it."

"Good. Meantime, we just won't even talk."

"That scares me. What if we miss each other somehow?"

"We won't."

"All right. But let's not talk about it right now." She nuzzled her face in to his neck, smelling the familiar scent. "Not now."

"Look at me."

She sighed and fell back on the pillow.

"You can't run now into one of your books—and you got to be clear about what you want."

"You know what I want."

He shook his head, curling one hand around her face. "You have to tell me."

The light in the room was dim and smoky-colored. Angel tugged the sheet around her more closely. She shook her head. "You're still underestimating me, Isaiah High."

"Am I?" His face was sober, and more vulnerable than she had ever seen it, and suddenly she thought of him at six, reading to her on the front porch, so proud and pleased, doing it to impress her. "No matter what, it'll never be an easy life."

She touched his jaw, vast tenderness spreading over her ribs. "You want to make sure I know what I'm getting myself into, don't you? That I love you enough for that."

"You don't how ugly people can be."

She lifted her eyebrows, "What? Somebody might call me a name, or spit in my face or something? Somebody might threaten me or someone I love?" She pressed her lips together. "We'll be on the outside, never inside."

"Always," he rumbled, and traced the line of her collarbone. "Won't be easy to make friends, not for us, or—" He cleared his throat. "Any babies we have. D'you ever think of that?"

She thought of her dream, just before he came home, a beautiful girl child with black curls and chubby hands. The longing for that child slammed her so hard that she had to close her eyes, tears rushing up through her so fast she could stop them. In a cracked voice, she said, "Yes, I have."

He bent to her, pressed his head against hers. "Does it scare you?"

A thousand answers twisted around themselves. "Yes," she said. "And no. I wish it wasn't going to be like it is." She bit her lip and glanced outside to the falling twilight. "I used to get mad at my daddy sometimes, when I was a little older and nobody wanted to be friends with me because of him, where we lived, how outspoken he was about everything. I used to wonder why he couldn't just shut up for five minutes and let everybody think he was down here exploiting the colored folks like anybody else."

He laughed.

"I'm a naturally friendly person, Isaiah. I like to be with people and talk to them and know what's in their minds. It's always been a tiny bit hard to be always on the outside like I am."

"I see that." His hand moved on circles over her belly. "Go on."

"I wish it didn't matter." She touched his springy hair. "I wish there were all kinds of beautiful, all kinds of loving, room for everybody. I wish hate and bombs and Hitlers would just stop."

His hand was still. "But that ain't gonna happen."

"I know. It won't happen. And I'm going to love you until I die, no matter who likes us or our children or don't like us. So we might as well just make the best of it. Not like I don't know how to live on the outside."

He tugged her close. "There's a place for us. We'll just keep looking till we find it." His arms were tight around her, his big leg lassoing both of hers. "Are you gonna have some babies for me to hug and kiss?"

"As many as you want," she said softly, "but we better hurry up, cuz I'm not getting any younger."

"We just have to do more of this, then," he murmured and kissed her ear.

She giggled suddenly. "Oh, Isaiah, you know what my name's gonna be?" She collapsed against him, shaking with laughter. "Angel High!"

He laughed with her, then pulled himself upright. "Not until we can get out of here."

"It won't be long now, Isaiah. Somebody's bound to take this store, now they know I'm willing to just give it over."

He stood up, visibly wincing as his ankle took his weight. Tugging on his pants, he shook his head. "I don't think so, not with all that's gone on."

Reluctantly, Angel put her slip on. "Maybe you oughta go on to Dallas, wait for me there, and I'll join you as soon as I get things settled."

"Please," he protested. "I'm just gonna walk away and leave you here? That doesn't even make any sense, Angel. No sense. You shoulda had your behind outta here the first time Edwin smacked you. Maybe you should go on to Mrs. Pierson's tonight. I'll take you there."

She gave him a look. "You can't even walk across the room, Isaiah. How are you gonna see me over to Mrs. Pierson's?"

Isaiah sank down on the chair to put on his socks. A mulish expression crossed his brow.

"I'll be all right here tonight, go to Mrs. Pierson's in the morning. Everything will work out."

"That's what you always think, Angel, but it's just not always true. Life ain't a fairy tale, and even God can't help you if a man's crazy enough."

A terrible sorrow weighted his voice. So many things had been torn inside of him—war had torn him in ways not even the death of his daddy and the beating in the woods could do. It would take time for those places to knit, for his faith to come back—if it ever did.

Could even love heal that bitterness?

And yet, what were the odds that they would even be standing together like this, meeting each other's eyes in love and hope? She disappeared into her dress and shook her hair free. "God can do anything, Isaiah."

"I hope you're right."

"I'll get everything together tonight, say my goodbyes to the ladies in the morning." She held up a finger. "Wait, though. I want you to take something for me." She opened a drawer and took out the red tin where she'd kept his letters. "I saved every one. Take it with you."

"What are you afraid of?"

"Nothing. I just won't have room in my suitcase."

He tucked the tin close. "All right."

They walked to the back door, where Isaiah paused to kiss her tenderly. "That's going to have to last, Angel, for both of us. We can't be taking chances like this. You move to Mrs. Pierson's tomorrow and we'll figure out our plan from there."

"I promise." She grabbed his hand, lifted it to her lips, kissed the bend of his fingers. "I have never been happier, Isaiah. I mean that."

"Me, either, Angel. I mean it, too." Everything in him softened, and he lifted her fingers to his own lips. "I love you, Angel, that's a fact. I don't know if it's the best thing for either one of us, but I'm never going to leave you. Never, you hear me?"

"Yes."

"I had a cane here somewhere." He picked it up off the floor. "Keep that gun by you, Angel. Right by you."

"I will. Don't worry," She pushed his arm a little. "Get some rest." She watched his limping figure until it disappeared into the twilight and trees. As the dusty light swallowed him, a sudden sense of foreboding thudded in her belly and she wanted to call him back. Instead, she closed the door, shaking her head. *Just getting jumpy.*

A long hot bath and a cup of tea made her feel better. Ebenezer scratched at the window and she let him in, fed him and herself, and then gathered her things into two suitcases. There wasn't much she had to bring when it came down to it. Her clothes were mostly from before the war, all worn out and ragged. She had three good dresses, a few pairs of panties and slips, photos of her father and the store and a couple of books she had to keep.

Enough, she thought, finally headed to bed. Enough.

— 39 —

June 2, 1946

Dear Angel,

I'm writing this from my bedroom. Must be going on to midnight, and I'm not sleepy, because I'm on fire. Everything in me is lit up like Christmas, twinkling and blinking and dancing around. My little toe is tapping and my earlobes and my eyelashes feel lit up. I close my eyes and think of your mouth and my chest aches. I think of sleeping with you all night long and waking up in the morning and having coffee and I want to get up and dance. I never thought I'd feel this happy, and at the same time, it seems like this was coming for us since we were children. Remember when I brought that snakeskin to you, the night we read together? You were wearing a yellow dress with teeny polka dots on it. Someday, I'd like you have another dress like that.

I'm thinking tonight of our children and that makes me want to fly. Your babies. Mine. All of us sitting around some big table somewhere, having supper, day after day. That's not so glamorous, is it, but it sounds like a dream come true. Children, a home, you. And both of us following those old dreams however we can, maybe only in little ways. I can find some work with a builder. Maybe you can go to school. Maybe we both can, I don't know. I got money saved. A lot. Mrs. Pierson gave me more when I brought Gudren back, so we can figure something out.

I am just so happy, Angel. I want to write it all over the page. I love you, I love you, I love you, I love you, I love you, I love you, I love you, I love you, I love you, I love you, I love you. So many times in my letters I wanted to say something like that and I never could. When you wrote me that letter about the cake . . . .have mercy (ha ha). Someday I want you to read that letter out loud to me.

Now maybe I can go to sleep and get ready to start a new life tomorrow. With my baby. With you, my Angel.

Love,

Isaiah

— 40 —

Somewhere in the deepest part of the night, Angel awakened sharply, sitting bold upright in bed, her mouth dry with fear. She grabbed the gun automatically as she listened to the heavy silence, peering into the dark until dots danced in front of her eyes.

A noise blasted into the quiet—Ebenezer shrieking from the rooms in front of the house. A thud followed the eerie, warlike cry, and Angel realized vaguely he had thrown himself at the window or door. Quietly, she threw the covers from her and crept to the window of her room. Ebenezer cried out again, the sound unlike anything she'd ever heard him make before—almost a human scream.

Bloodcurdling.

From outside came the low sound of voices, and a rumbling chuckle she didn't recognize. Working sweaty fingers more tightly around the gun, she made sure it was cocked and moved soundlessly to the window to peer into the back yard.

Nothing. At least nothing she could see. A cloud filmed the half-moon and the flickering shadows of trees could have hidden a dozen men. She crept from her room into the hallway that led to the store, then slipped into her daddy's room, keeping her head low.

Here, the voices were clearer. She counted them: Tom and Jake, a voice she didn't know, and Edwin. Four. Moving stealthily in a way that was at odds with their previous crashing, crazy vandalism. This was like a mission.

Her heart was pounding so hard it interfered with her hearing and she took a moment to breathe in and out, trying to calm herself. Think clearly. What were they doing? Did she dare break for the woods out the back door?

Ebenezer shrieked again, and she glanced toward the sound. He'd follow her out and they'd know, she thought, grimly. Out the front, or out the back, but if she ran fast enough, she might be able to elude them long enough to get to the tree house.

One of the men shouted, "Ready!"

Angel ducked without really knowing why. She expected shotgun blasts or rocks through the windows. She didn't expect the roar that blew in from the front of the store, a sudden explosion—and then, the unmistakable scent of gasoline.

"Ebenezer," she whispered, jumping up to run toward the door. A blast of heat pushed her back almost instantly, and for one single, endless second, she stared in horror at the bright orange flames shooting up the walls, devouring the work of a lifetime.

If Ebenezer had been there, he was gone, sucked into the inferno.

Her heart cracked in two. *Baby!*

Sudden hammering blows sounded at the back door and Angel whirled back into her father's bedroom crouching behind the door, her throat dry, pulse racing. There had to be a way out of here.

Think, Angel.

Overhead, the flames began to lick over the roof, crackling and hissing like an evil serpent. *God, you're gonna have to deal with this one*, she prayed mindlessly. *Help me, help me, help me.*

Have courage.

Swallowing hard, she wiped her fingers, checked the gun again, and heard the back door give way, followed by footsteps and a cry. "Angel Corey!" Edwin bellowed. "You better come out here!"

She didn't know how he knew where her bedroom was, but she heard him in there, turning things over, swearing. "She ain't here again, goddamnit!"

Footfalls rattled along the hall way and the bathroom door slammed open, a closet opened, and they finally made their way toward her hiding place. As they approached, Angel ran across the room to the window, throwing it open, unmindful of the noise. She scrambled over the sill and fell to the ground outside, gun still in hand. As her bare feet hit the dirt, she started running. The sound of the flames was turning to a roar and she could hear shouts coming from inside, but she ran like hell, rounding the back of the house for the woods—

And slammed hard into a solid wall of man. Bobby Grover, the voice she hadn't placed. He grabbed her, and with a cry, Angel stomped on the arch of his food.

With a cry of surprise, he held her arm and backhanded her across the mouth. Angel tasted blood, but behind her, she could hear shouts.

They would kill her. Without hesitation, she lifted her hand and fired the pistol into Bobby Grover's soft gut.

He made a grunt of surprise then fell away from her. Angel felt his blood on her hand, but her adrenaline was so high that she nearly couldn't think.

A voice screamed in her mind—*run! Run!*

She tore through the trees, hearing shouts and a cat call behind her.

The fire roared high into the night sky, full of light and sound, like a celebration, an inferno.

She ran. Her feet, even leathery as they were, took a beating, tearing on hidden rocks and thorns and tree roots. Branches beat her face, caught her eyes and hair. She heard a sob and realized it was her own.

Behind her came the sound of other feet, following the sound of her own. Edwin cried, "Here I come, honey!"

He crashed through the trees behind her, and she could hear the others coming, too, making noise, crying out. Behind her, Edwin cackled, only a few feet away. "Here I come!" he shouted. He crashed through the trees behind her.

Angel could hear the others coming, too, making sounds of glee that sent an almost supernatural wave of horror washing through her.

Her foot caught in a tangle of vines, and she went flying. She felt it in slow motion, felt the earth rise up and then slam into her chin and breasts. The gun flew out of her hand, discharging as it landed. She coughed, the wind knocked out of her, and scrambled to her feet, wiping blood off her mouth. In the darkness, she kicked leaves and patted the earth frantically, trying to find the gun. Nothing. *"Please, please, please,"* she panted, like an animal, her voice coming in sobs.

Right behind her, she heard twigs snapping, feet crashing, and there was no time left. She sprang up and hurtled through the trees. A stitch caught her side and she stumbled, and scrambled again.

"I'm coming, honey! I know you're waiting!" Edwin cried, and it was close, so close.

Dear God.

His hand snagged her hair and Angel screamed. She swung her fists toward his face, catching the edge of his chin. He laughed. "Angel, I had no idea you were such a wildcat." She cried out, clawing for him, kicking, and he grabbed her close to him, her arms pinned against her sides. "I got her, boys." His hand was threaded painfully through her hair and he snapped her neck back, "Don't I, sugar? I got you now."

Angel stared at him and swallowed. Fear made her very cold.

"Isaiah!" There was such urgency in Geraldine's tone that Isaiah sprung awake, but not without a shaft of pain shooting through his eyes.

He groaned softly.

"'Saiah! Get up! The Corey place is on fire."

He bolted awake.

Have mercy. He struggled into his clothes, firing questions. "When you see it? How long? You hear anything else?"

"It woke me up just now." She pointed to the window. Above the trees shot brilliant orange flames. A sense of rage and helplessness flooded through him. Panic. "Where's your God now, Mama? Huh?"

Grabbing his mother's shotgun, he hobbled out the backyard. Already the bank was lined with the curious and horrified, who watched with sober eyes as the store burned and burned and burned—

He crashed through the river, cursing the weakness of his body—a body that had always stood up to the pressures he inflicted, could go the distance of any punishment, and now failed him with its slowness.

Thick, acrid smoke billowed through the trees, and he felt breathless with pain and fear. In spite of his curses, he couldn't stop the prayer that formed in his mind, "Oh, God—she loves you. Keep her safe. Keep her safe."

Have mercy.

He stumbled out of the water, and up the bank. But at the edge of the woods that circled the store, he stopped, heart plummeting. The worn wood burned with abandon, every single inch of it hellishly alight. Nothing in there had survived.

He staggered forward, pierced with grief, unmindful of the searing heat of the fire. He stared at the porch and the step where Angel had sat eating cake . . . where she had kissed him . . . where they had played as children.

As he stared, a plank of pine broke free and sailed outward, landing on what Isaiah had thought to be a pile of discarded clothes. The flames caught, showing instead the body of a man. Isaiah hurried forward.

Bobby Grover. Shot at close range by the look of the hole in his belly.

Good girl.

He whirled, headed for the woods, knowing Angel would have made for the tree house, her refuge. Now stealth would be his ally, not speed. If she was alive, he knew where to find her.

Moving slowly, looking through the smoke and night for something, anything, he crept along the path. The fire roared, drowning even the omniscient sound of the river. He pressed on, listening so hard he thought his ears might bleed.

Faintly came the sound of a voice—and with sick certainty, Isaiah knew where they were. A palpable, physical dread filled him, weighted his limbs and organs for a minute, paralyzing him beneath the trees. The horrors of war and Texas and all the imagined cruelty Edwin could conjure filled him.

Again the dread washed over him, solid as earth, but he had learned as a soldier in battle how to move against it, how to creep through the dark toward the sound of voices coming from the hollow. Arguing men's voices. His flesh rippled. Quietly, he moved, his bare feet making little sound in the undergrowth.

The night grew blacker as he moved deeper into the forest, away from the sound and light of the all-consuming fire. As the light faded, the dread he felt grew until he felt nearly smothered. He had to push and push against the almost supernatural sense of horror.

And in that terrible darkness, under the weight of his strangling fear for Angel, Isaiah had no choice but to pray. He used the words as he would any weapon at hand—prayed anything, recited words from verses learned in childhood, from songs, from the shouted, rising and falling words of preachers in the pulpit. As he crept through the woods, he chanted the old words as if they had power, like a spell.

In the hollow, a small fire burned. An ordinary campfire, yellow and cheery against the night. Isaiah hid himself and peered through the undergrowth, gun poised. He didn't see Angel immediately. Tom's back blocked her from view. A harsh, murmured argument was going on. Tom was disgusted with something Edwin had said.

Isaiah's dread evaporated. The soldier he was took control. He raised the shotgun and aimed at the burly back of the man in front of him. Tom moved suddenly, shifting a gun from his left hand to his right. Isaiah held off, waiting.

And there was Edwin, crouched on the far side of the fire, Angel gripped in his arms. Her face was streaked and filthy, her hair a tangle, and she wore only a nightgown that was torn and dirty. As Isaiah watched, she licked a bloody cut on her lip, and jerked away from Edwin, who pulled her back with a cackle.

The expression on Edwin's face renewed Isaiah's dread. The chuckle was edged with hysteria, and his strange eyes were wild and leaping. He lifted his gun toward Tom. "None o' this is yours, man," he said, his voice carrying clearly.

Isaiah sighted again, waiting for a clear shot. An instant later, Edwin loosened his hold to grab a bottle by his feet, and Isaiah fired, diving into the undergrowth for cover. Through a tangle of leaves, he saw Edwin spin sideways, taking the bullet too high.

Angel tore away from him, stumbling in the dirt, scrambling as Tom and Jake whirled, looking for the source of fire. Jake fired wildly into the undergrowth, as if there was a platoon in the woods. Tom bolted for the edge of the clearing, and Isaiah fired cleanly, catching him full in the chest. That one hadn't been too high, he thought as he ducked to his right through the trees, moving noiselessly as a snake. Another shot sailed wild over his head.

Angel screamed and Isaiah lifted his head to see Edwin, bloodied but still moving, grab her by the hair and head for the opposite side of the clearing.

Goddamn caveman. She kicked and scratched at him, even threw herself down on the ground, tumbling Edwin with her, but with a savage cry, he pulled himself and Angel back to their feet and crashed into the forest.

Isaiah heard Jake moving to his left. Angel's screams were abruptly silenced, and Isaiah jumped to his feet, struggling to chase the pair. He didn't break into the clearing, but moved laterally through the trees, keeping one ear cocked for Jake behind him.

He heard the shot whistling through the air before it hit him, hard and hot. He whirled and fired, but knew it was wild. Staggering, he pressed a hand to the wound in his side felt his blood running hot over his hand.

Oh, hell no.

From the other side of the clearing came Angel, shotgun in her hands. Blood stained her nightgown—Edwin's blood, Isaiah realized as he clutched his side, feeling his life pour through his fingers. Uttering a sound both primitive and savage, Angel leveled the shotgun at Jake and fired point blank. He fell, his face gone.

Isaiah fell to his knees and Angel whirled toward the sound, ready to fire again. She caught sight of Isaiah, and her face went lax for an instant.

The edges of his vision were going black, too fast, much too fast. The ground rose and smashed into him. "Aw, hell, Man," he muttered to God in weak protest. "Not here." Then Angel was beside him, weeping, clutching his shirt.

"Isaiah!" she cried. "Don't you dare die on me!"

"No, baby."

She stood up. Isaiah watched lazily, almost distractedly, noticing the fire shimmer in her hair, "All right, God," she said, and he heard a power in her call, even through her tears. "Enough. I *claim* this man, *this* man, as mine. You can't have him yet, you hear me?"

And it seemed to Isaiah as he slipped into lapping darkness that Angel seemed to grow and expand, seeming almost to glow, become light. He reached for her, touching her ankle.

So that's it, Isaiah thought, and fell into darkness.

"He's mine!" Angel cried, furious. Tears of anger flowed over her face, and she wanted to add an enticement, and bargain, swear she'd do some big thing in God's name, but held off. Bending down beside Isaiah, she pressed her hands to the leaking wound, and then remembered something from a movie. Grabbing handfuls of mud and leaves, she slapped the cool material on his body.

Panting, she begged, *please God. Please. Please.* She hardly knew what she was saying. The earth covered his wound and it seemed to stop bleeding, but Isaiah didn't stir. Wiping her face, feeling the grit of dirt and blood and heaven knew what else, she bent over him and put her forehead on his chest. The sound of his breath comforted her. She would run across the river for help. "Don't die, Isaiah. Please don't die."

"How come you love that nigger so much, Angel Corey?"

She bolted upright. Not three feet away, a shotgun in his hand, stood Edwin. Blood oozed from the wound high on his chest. His shirt was soaked with it. Gone was the wild hysteria. A grim, grieving sobriety replaced it, raw and all too human.

Sensing she needed to be calm, she stood up slowly, clutching the gun from Isaiah's hand, not even sure there were any bullets left in it. She held it loosely at her side. "I don't know, Edwin," she said honestly. "It would have been easier to love somebody else, but I always loved Isaiah. Can't even remember when I didn't."

He nodded, gravely, as if the motion gave him pain. "Shame, Angel." His voice was ragged and tired and bleak. "But I know how it is—that's how I always loved you."

Angel gripped the gun in her hand. She had shot the others in panic and a fierce need to survive. Edwin stood before her in a place of agonized recognition, his familiar face shadowed with the demons that had dogged him through his life. How could she kill him?

But she had to get help for Isaiah. "I don't want to kill you, Edwin, but I have to go."

"No." Angel lowered the revolver, but stayed close to Isaiah as Edwin stumbled forward, looking aimlessly around him as if he'd just noticed his surroundings. His face was ghastly white, his eyes too bright as he suddenly whirled, an edge of the insanity back now. "That man prayed like a preacher, you know it?"

Very gently, Angel asked, "Who did?"

But Edwin seemed not to hear. "He prayed and prayed, singing and hollering. Like to scare me half to death." He shook his head, eyes fixed on a spot at the edge of the fire. "'Praise God! Glory!'" he shouted in imitation, and Angel suddenly realized who he must be talking about. "Why'd he pray, Angel? Why'd he sing?"

"Jordan High sang?"

"Top of his voice. Never heard nothin' like it." He coughed suddenly, and blood came out of his mouth, and he looked surprised. He clasped a hand to the wound. His knees buckled. Angel glanced at Isaiah, lying still but breathing. She went to Edwin and put a hand on his shoulder. Her voice was very quiet. "Tell me."

He swallowed and looked down at his hands, covered now with his own blood. "He died. They did all kinds of things to him after, but he died before anybody touched him. From nothing." Tears welled up in Edwin's eyes and his lip trembled. His voice was ragged. "He looked right at me, Angel." He coughed and there was a bubbling sound in the wound.

She touched his hair. "Go on."

"Looked right at me," he repeated. "And he said, 'You are precious in my sight, and honored, and I love you.'" Edwin shuddered. "And then my daddy punched him, but he was already dead. Already dead." He grabbed her hand. "An' I'm gonna burn in hell. " He fell over.

Angel knelt and pulled her hand out of his grip. He stared sightlessly toward nothing, and Angel found she was weeping as she knelt again beside Isaiah. He was breathing evenly, and she kissed him. "Don't you dare die." Now that she could leave him safely, surrounded only by ghosts, she ran for the river, and splashed across to find help.

— 41 —

Isaiah was carried on a makeshift stretcher across the river and into his mother's house. Nothing would do that Angel had to be with him, and nothing anyone said could make her go, not to wash her face or change her bloody clothes. Geraldine brought a blanket to wrap around Angel's shivering body, and a cup of tea that sat at her elbow 'til it was cold. She clung to Isaiah's hand all night, praying, not caring what any one said.

Watching her, Geraldine was ashamed for flinging out her accusation to Isaiah, even though she hadn't meant it at the time. If Isaiah died, Geraldine expected Angel to lie down right beside him and go along.

And for most of the night, there was no doubt at all in Geraldine's mind that her son would not last the night. The bullet had gone clean through him, and though the wound had been cleaned and patched as well as possible, the blood that had been drained out of him would fill a small pond.

Toward morning, Angel started singing:

Praise God, from Whom all blessings flow;
Praise Him, all creatures here below;
Praise Him above, ye heavenly host;
Praise Father, Son, and Holy Ghost.

She sang it over and over and over, rocking back and forth in her shawl of blankets. Louder and stronger every time.

Geraldine was standing in the doorway when Isaiah opened his eyes and whispered, "Angel."

With a single, joyous cry, Angel sank to her knees by the bed and began to weep, raining kisses over Isaiah's hand. He smiled weakly and lifted his free hand to touch her head, sighing softly before he closed his eyes again in a more natural sleep.

When Angel awakened, she had no idea where she was—only that she was stiff and achy and grimy. It was Isaiah's hand that brought her around, finally, his big warm hand curled around her own, and his other, heavy on her hair.

She moved slowly, remembering, to look at him. Still sleeping, but sleeping right. Her throat clutched. "Thank you, God," she breathed. "Thank you, thank you, thank you."

The house was silent. Angel struggled to her feet. She need a bath, she thought vaguely, some clean clothes, something to eat. There was an empty clawing in her belly.

Wandering out into the kitchen, she found Geraldine at the table, reading her Bible in the quiet. At this simple sight of normal life, Angel swayed, the bitterness in her stomach roiling. Her hands trembled, and she must have made some sound because Geraldine looked up. Seeing Angel, she leapt to her feet and rounded the table. "Are you all right, Angel? You wouldn't let nobody see if you was hurt—or anything."

Her meaning was clear. "None of them did anything like that," she said dully and sank in to the chair Geraldine urged her into. She laughed without humor. "Edwin wouldn't let them."

At those words, the horrors came tumbling back into her mind from whatever place she'd shoved them away—and violent kaleidoscopic whirl, she saw them again. Saw Edwin with the gaping hole high in his chest, and Isaiah with his in his side, and Tom with no face and the flames exploding out of from the front of the store, killing Ebenezer and everything her daddy ever worked for.

"Ebenezer died," she said, then wildly looked at Geraldine, gripping her fingers. "I *killed* people," she whispered.

"Oh, Angel," Geraldine said, and she took her in her arms.

And against the cushiony bosom that had provided a pillow so often in her childhood, Angel wept—great, sobbing tears that washed clean the horror of the night. Geraldine murmured soothing words that meant everything and nothing, and cried right along with her.

When both of them were finished, Geraldine drew a hot bath in the tub in the kitchen and helped Angel into it, then left her alone to wash away the blood and grime, the sticky tears and smell of smoke in her hair. Clean at last, she put on a soft dress of Tillie's that hung almost to her ankles. She ate the food Geraldine put before her, then went back to Isaiah, curled up next to him, and slept.

Geraldine had to pretend that all was just as it had been. Once Angel was cared for, she put on her work shoes and marched over the bridge as she did every morning, even if it was a bit later than usual.

She had tried to prepare herself for the store, for what remained of it, anyway, but the sight of the smoking, blackened ruins made her feel instantly ill. A crowd of people milled around, the sheriff and his deputies among them. Geraldine spied Horace Walker by Edwin's truck, and Angel's aunt Georgia in her big car, looking half-terrified, half-gleeful. There wasn't a black face among them at all. Only white folks, here for gossip or work.

For a minute, Geraldine paused, breathless with a certain fear that all would be uncovered, and the two she had left safely back at home would somehow still lose. Then she narrowed her eyes and straightened her back.

No bodies would be found. When Angel had come splashing over the river, almost chillingly coherent about Isaiah and all the rest, there had been those who had taken shovels over the bridge, melting into the darkness to do a gruesome, ugly job, at great risk to themselves, for if anyone had come to investigate the fire that could almost certainly be seen in town, they would likely have paid with their lives.

But no one had come. The job was done. Today, Angel and Isaiah would be hidden, too. No trace of any of them would ever be found. It was the only way.

The sheriff spied her. With heavy steps, he approached. "I guess you saw the fire?"

She nodded.

"I reckon Angel's dead." His mouth twitched and he cleared his throat. "I know you cared about the Coreys, and I'm sorry."

Of all the things Geraldine had expected, this wasn't it. "Thank you, Sheriff." She bowed her head to hide her relief. "I'll go and talk with Mrs. Pierson, less you have already. She'll be making the arrangements, I'm sure."

He nodded, and for an instant, there was a sheen of tears in his eyes. "She came to me just a few days ago," he muttered. "Wish to hell I'd done . . ."

Geraldine nodded, then she turned away, passing the milling crowd, the resigned face of Horace Walker and the pinched one of Georgia. When her back was to the mess and crowd, she felt a smile she couldn't stop spreading wide over her face. There were hurdles yet, but sometimes, the Lord understood about humans.

Sometimes, yes, he cared about just a single pair.

— 42 —

September 22, 1946

Dear Mama,

I know you been sweating bullets, so I'm just writing to let you know we are safe. I'm fine, healing up so fast them doctors oughta write a paper about me. Angel fussed all the way, making me rest about three hours outta every four, so you know it's all right now.

She's so happy to be in England—we been to a couple of the castles around here and she lights up like a Christmas tree every time. The folks show you around just love her, cause she asks so many questions and makes them feel good. We've seen all kinds of things they don't usually show people. It's like they just take her on, even though Yanks are none too popular at the moment with all the problems there are here.

But the shortages and all don't bother me, nor Angel either, far as I can see. There's work for us both—Angel's working for a preacher, organizing his notes, and I have a place building as soon as I'm well enough. This ankle . . . .probably have arthritis in it. No real help for it, since it didn't heal right the first time. Angel puts all these packs on it at night—and much as I tease her, they really do help.

Anyway, I'm gonna go put this in the mail so you can get it quick as possible. Tell Aunt Muriel thanks again for risking her neck on our account. Hadn't been for her, I don't know what we'd have done. Now she gonna take these letters back and forth. Send her my love.

And speaking of love, today is my wedding day—just never thought such a thing could come true. I wish you could be here, Mama. I love you,

Your son, Isaiah

The chapel was built of ancient stone. In the crisp fall morning, the walls glowed topaz in reflection of the leaves tumbling by the handfuls to the earth on bursts of chilly wind. Angel had scouted it out for this moment, and as they stood before the chaplain, light streaming through stained glass windows, Isaiah thought it was the perfect backdrop for her. As she listened to the words of the ceremony, he couldn't take his eyes from her shining hair and bright eyes. The chaplain had to repeat twice, "Isaiah High, do you take this woman to be your lawfully wedded wife?"

His voice cracked as her dancing eyes lifted to his. "I do."

"Angel Corey, do you take this man to be your husband? Will you care for him in sickness and health, for richer and poorer, as long as you both shall live?"

Isaiah felt tears in his eyes and though he blinked hard, he couldn't hold them back. One fell from his eye and over his face as Angel smiled radiantly and said fervently, "I will."

It was all he could do to wait until the ceremony was over to gather her into his arms and kiss his wife. His wife.

Out in the blustery day, she squeezed his hand and grinned up at him. "I guess now that we're properly married, I can inform you that not only are you a husband, but you're finally gonna get one of those babies you like so much, too."

His mouth fell open. "You mean it? We're gonna have a baby?"

"Probably about February, I figure."

He grabbed her into a hug, laughing. A sudden flash of light hit his eyes and he blinked, looking for the source of the reflection. The focal window of the chapel was ablaze, a stained glass representation of the Shepherd. "Love One Another" was lettered below.

His grip loosened on Angel and as if drawn by some other worldly force, he found himself walking toward the window.

Love one another.

Love one another. He wasn't a man for religious visions, but at that moment, he came as close as he ever had—or ever would again. Love would halt the evils and angers and horrors. Enough love would heal it all.

Might take hundreds of years. Thousands. But in that golden fall day, with his new bride and his new child, Isaiah knew he'd been granted a miracle. "Thank you," he breathed, then turned to take Angel's hand. They walked back toward their flat, toward the dreams they had spun as children.

Toward life.

PART FOUR: DAWN

An angel, robed in spotless white,
Bent down and kissed the sleeping Night.
Night woke to blush; the sprite was gone.
Men saw the blush and called it Dawn.

—*Paul Laurence Dunbar*

— 43 —

Gideon, East Texas
2005

After her reading, Angel mingled with the Black And Whites, eating things she would rather have never tasted again in her life. Spam and beans had not been good to begin with.

But they meant well, and she loved their earnestness and wish to please. Imagine them meeting right here in the same spot where the drugstore had been where she and Gudren had enjoyed chocolate sodas so many years before! None of them could possibly understand how far they had come, what just the simple presence of them here, reading books and arguing like equals meant.

Her grandson Miles, twenty-five and absolutely perfect, approached her. "It's time to go." Under his breath, he said, "Do you know that girl? Johniqua?"

What he was really asking was if it was safe, if she was family. "What's her family name?"

"Younger."

Angel smiled. "I know her family. Let's ask her to come with us, shall we?"

"She is really beautiful."

Angel smiled.

There was already a crowd at the park, where a ceremonial stage had been erected before the white and Black granite memorial that still gleamed with brand-new sparkle, the copper and gold accents shining like comets.

As they got out of the car, Angel saw her family assembled in the front row, six children and assorted spouses, fourteen grandchildren, and two great-greats. One of the grands, five-year-old Nathan, leapt out of his seat at the sight of her and bolted across the grass. "Grandma!" He was her youngest's son's youngest son. He favored his mother with sharply angled African cheekbones and silky cocoa skin, but his hair was a wild apple and cinnamon tumble of loose curls, and it streaked out to gold in the sunshine. Angel's eyes showed up every now and again among them, but never as clearly as in this impish little devil child. She adored him.

She bent down and kissed him. "Hey, darlin'!"

"Can I sit by you, Grandma?"

"How about after while? I already promised your Aunt Rachel I'd sit with her."

"Okay!"

Readings took a lot out of her, and before she'd gone to the store, she'd stopped by the graveyard. Now she sank down next to her daughter, and let her hand over a bottle of water. "How are you doing, Mama?"

"We knew it would be a long day. I'm fine."

Other children and grandchildren came over to kiss her, everyone so proud, dressed up so tidily. Two teachers, a minister, an actor, a mother and a nurse among the children; a singer, a computer engineer, two soldiers, one doctor and who knew what else the grandchildren would be. She was proud of them for coming, some from a long way away, to help honor their grandfather, great-grandfather, and great-great-grandfather.

With joy, she accepted their hugs, kissing cheeks. "I love you," she said. "Thank you for coming so far, Adele. Laura, you've grown a foot since the summer! Maddy, you look wonderful. Thank you all. Thank you." They kissed her back, showed their new toys or rings. Later, there would be a reception for the whole family and she would have a chance to catch up with each and every one.

For now, a band in full military dress began to play, signaling the start of the ceremony. Angel took her place, and picked up her program. On her left, her daughter Rose squeezed her hand. "I'm so excited!" she whispered.

A man came across the grass, in his sixties, well-dressed and good-looking, with a spray of freckles over his nose. He looked familiar, but she had no idea who he was until he stopped in front of her and smiled. "Hello, Miss Angel," he said in a softly elegant voice. "I'm the mayor of Gideon, and I'd like to welcome you and your fine family."

"I'm happy to meet you," Angel said. "Mr. . . . ?"

"McCoy," he said, smiling. "Paul. Maylene McCoy's grandson. You used to babysit me."

"Paul!" she cried. She stood up, hugged him hard, and stood back to look at him. "Oh, my goodness! Look at you! The mayor!"

"I just wanted to say hello before we started. You look wonderful, and I hope we can talk some more later."

"Of course."

He lifted a hand and dashed toward the stage, moving with easy grace to the podium. He held up a hand and the band stopped. Paul said, "Hello, everybody. This is a day we have all been waiting for, and working hard for. We have a raft of people to thank and I'm going to get through that just as quick as I can, then we'll get to the business at hand." He ran through a long list of names—local business people, individual contributors, artists who made sketches, and the Black and White book club, which had raised over $27,000.

"Holy cow," Rachel said, clapping.

When they had finished, Paul said, "I am lucky enough to say I knew our next guest as a child. I had more than a small case of hero worship, I can tell you."

From the west side of the stage, from behind the memorial, came Isaiah. He climbed the stairs as Paul spoke, leaning only slightly on the cane he required more and more these days. Angel felt her throat catch at the emotion in his face.

Rachel took her hand. "Daddy looks so handsome!"

He did. He wore a suit, black, as befitted the occasion, and his shoulders were still straight and broad. He'd grown a bit of a belly over the years, but he liked to say it was so he could play Santa Claus for all the children. Or he blamed her cakes, depending.

"When I was four years old," Paul said, "all I ever wanted was to grow up and be Isaiah High. He came home from the war wearing a uniform, and he taught me to fish for cat, and let me hammer and nail and do all kinds of manly things. He was one of the first African American soldiers to see actual combat in World War II, and his unit was distinguished in battle. When he returned to England after snagging himself a wife—" Paul indicated Angel, and her children and grandchildren whooped "—the two attended divinity school together, where both were awarded degrees in 1953.

"That tells so little of the story, my friends, and you know it as well as I do—but there's no need to belabor the darkness of our past here in Gideon. We're here to celebrate the achievements of our World War II soldiers, all of them, in a manner that honors their achievements. So without further ado, I present to you Reverend Isaiah High, to christen the war memorial named for his father Jordan High, who was the first Medal of Honor winner in Gideon's history."

Angel took out a handkerchief. A big one, and even that was not enough. As Isaiah—handsome, dignified, loyal—took the stage, he was so overcome for a moment that he had to grip the sides of the podium tightly, his eyes downcast. The crowd settled, quieted. Isaiah raised his eyes and looked at Angel, across time and events and the flow of history. "My father," he said, "loved to read aloud. And he laughed just like God."

Angel pressed her lips together, remembering Jordan gathering them up in his lap in the stillness of a summer evening. Long ago.

And not. Looking at her aged husband through her own aged eyes, it seemed they were still somehow children, and those impassioned young adults afire with love for each other, and parents, and co-workers.

Love, she thought. Love is all you need.

She kissed her fingers and waved the love to him, and it leapt from her fingers into forever, to Isaiah, to Jordan, to the fine life they had lived together, to all the children—practically a nation of its own—they had borne.

Isaiah wound up the speech he had practiced with her. "What I know my father would wish, and all the medal of honor winners, and all the dead, buried here and lost too young, is that we would find another way." He raised two fingers. "As my grandson would say, Peace out.'"

The crowd stood and cheered.

Isaiah walked off the stage and directly to Angel's waiting embrace. "Peace out?" she echoed drily.

He laughed, and Angel laughed with him, and they went together into the hall to celebrate service. And joy. And love.

Visit Gideon, Texas Again In These Novels By Barbara Samuel

Excerpt from

In The Midnight Rain

Against the day of sorrow
Lay by some trifling thing
A smile, a kiss, a flower
For sweet remembering.

—*Georgia Douglas Johnson*

PROLOGUE

Sometimes, when the wind was just right, she could hear the blues.

Once the rainy winter passed into spring, she liked to sit on her porch late at night, held in a kind of wonder beneath the moon and tall pines. She rocked in a cane-bottomed chair, smelling the green and copper moisture coming off the water, and she listened, nodding in time as cicadas and crickets whistled their song to the night. From the dark trees sometimes came the whirring, nearly silent beat of wings, followed by a swallowed screech of death, a sound not everyone could hear, but she did. She heard everything.

What she liked best was hearing the blues. The music sailed down the channel made by the river, ghostly guitar and haunted harmonica, even the hint of a man's ragged voice. It came from Hopkins' juke joint, upriver a mile or two on the Louisiana side of the Sabine River, and spilled with yellow light and blue cigarette smoke into a forest as dark as sin, as warm as a lover's mouth. It floated toward her over the stillness hanging above the water. Sometimes she imagined they were playing it just for her.

She'd close her eyes and let that music creep under her skin, seep into her bones. She let a part of herself get up and dance while she rocked steady in her chair. Every so often, she let that ghost of herself sing along while she silently nodded her head to the beat. The slow, sexlike rhythm filled her with memories of a man's low, dark laughter and a baby's sweet cry; with the song of Sunday-morning church and the blaze of morning over the east Texas pines.

She rocked and danced, nodded and sang, and thought as long as she could die with the blues in her ears, everything would be all right.

—1—

The sky was overcast and threatening rain by the time Ellie Connor made it to Gideon at seven o'clock on a Thursday evening.

She was tired. Tired of driving. Tired of spinning the radio dial every forty miles—why did the preaching stations always seem to have the longest signal?—tired of the sight of white lines swooping under her tires.

She'd started out this morning at seven planning to arrive in Gideon by midafternoon in her unfashionable but generally reliable Buick. She'd had a cute little Toyota for a while, but her work often took her to small towns across America, and if there were problems on the road, she had discovered it was far better to drive American. Since she'd lost a gasket in the wilds of deepest Arkansas, this was the trip that proved the rule.

The gasket had delayed her arrival by three hours, but at last she took a right off the highway and drove through a small East Texas town that was closing itself down for the evening. She had to stop at a gas station to get directions to the house, but finally she turned onto a narrow road made almost claustrophobic by the thick trees that crept right up to its edge. It hadn't been paved in a lot of years, and Ellie counted her blessings—at least she didn't have to look at dotted lines anymore.

Something interfered with the radio, and she turned it off with a snap. "Almost there, darlin'," she said to her dog April, who sat in the seat next to her.

April lifted her nose to the opening in the window, blinking against the wind, or maybe in anticipation of finally escaping the car. Half husky and half border collie, the dog was good-natured, eternally patient, and very smart. Ellie reached over to rub her ears and came away with a handful of molting dog fur.

As the car rounded a bend in the road, the land opened up to show sky and fields. A break in the fast moving clouds overhead suddenly freed a single flame of sunlight, bright gold against the purpling canvas of sky. Treetops showed black against the gold, intricately lacy and detailed, and for a minute, Ellie forgot her weariness. She leaned over the steering wheel, feeling a stretch along her shoulders, and admired the sight. "Beautiful," she said aloud.

Ellie's grandmother would have said it was a finger of God. Of course, Geraldine Connor saw the finger of God in just about everything, but Ellie hoped it was a good omen.

April whined, pushing her nose hard against the crack in the window, and Ellie took pity and pushed the button to lower the passenger-side glass. April stuck her head out gleefully, letting her tongue loll in the wind, scenting only heaven-knew-what dog pleasures on that soft air. Handicapped by human olfactory senses, Ellie smelled only the first weeds of summer and the coppery hints of the Sabine River that ran somewhere beyond the dense trees.

The road bent, leaning into a wide, long curve that ended abruptly in an expanse of cleared land. And there, perched atop a rise, was the house, an imposing and boxy structure painted white. Around it spread wide, verdant grass, and beyond the lawn, a collection of long, serious-looking greenhouses. Trees met the property in a protective circle, giving it the feeling of a walled estate. Roses in a gypsy profusion of color lined the porch and drive.

Ellie smiled. It was a house with a name, naturally: Fox River, which she supposed was a play on the name of the owner, Laurence Reynard.

Dr. Reynard, in fact, though she didn't know what the doctorate was in. She knew little of him at all, apart from the E-mail letters she'd received and the notes he'd posted in a blues newsgroup. In those writings, he was by turns eccentric and brilliant. She suspected he drank.

She'd been corresponding with him for months about Gideon and Mabel Beauvais, a blues singer native to the town, a mysterious and romantic figure who was the subject of Ellie's latest biography. Ellie had had some reservations about accepting Reynard's offer to stay in his guest house while she completed her research, but the truth was, she did not travel without her dog, and it was sometimes more than a little difficult to find a rental that didn't charge an arm and a leg extra for her.

As she pulled into the half-circle drive, however, Ellie's reservations seeped back in. E-mail removed every gauge of character a body relied upon: you couldn't see the shifty eyes or the poor handwriting or restless gestures that warned of instability. And arriving in the soft gray twilight put her at a disadvantage. She'd deliberately planned to get here in daylight in case the situation didn't feel right, but that blown gasket had set her back too many hours. At the moment, she was too tired to care where she slept as long as her dog was in her room.

Pulling the emergency brake, she peered through the windshield at the wide veranda. Two men sat there, one white, one black. It hadn't occurred to her that Reynard might be black, though thinking of it now, she

realized it was perfectly possible. She gave the horn a soft toot—
something she hadn't done in years but that suddenly seemed right—and
the white guy dipped his chin in greeting.

Ellie stepped out of the car and simply stood there a minute, relieved
to change postures. The air smelled heavily of sweet magnolia and rose,
thick and dizzying, a scent so blatantly sensual that she felt it in her lungs,
on her skin. She breathed it in with pleasure as she approached the porch,
brushing her hands down the front of her khaki shorts, trying to smooth
the wrinkles out. "How you doing?" she said in greeting.

They both gave her a nod, but nobody jumped up to welcome her.
Ellie hesitated, wondering suddenly if she had the address wrong or
something.

A raggedy-looking mutt was not nearly as reserved as the men. It
jumped up and barked an urgent alert. Anxious to make a pit stop, April
started to follow Ellie out of the car, but Ellie said, "Stay," and with a little
whine, she did.

A low voice said, "Sasha, hush." The dog swallowed the last bark and
perched on the edge of the steps and waited for Ellie to come a little
closer. Its tail wagged its whole rear end.

Ellie resisted the urge to fiddle with her hair. It was mussed and wild
with humidity, but nothing short of a shower was going to fix it. She
settled for shoving her sunglasses on top of her head, which drew the
worst of it out of her face so she could at least see as she walked to the
bottom of the steps and looked at the men in the low gray light, trying to
decide if she had the right place.

The black man was the older of the pair, maybe in his mid-forties or
a little more. Judging by the length of his legs, propped on the porch
railing, he was tall, and his skin was the color of polished pecan. A neatly
trimmed goatee with a few betraying curls of white framed a serious
mouth. His eyes were large and still.

Ellie could imagine this face behind the notes Reynard had written.

But it was the other man who snared her attention. Darkness lay in
the hollows below slashes of cheekbone, and along the fine line of his jaw;
peered out from large eyes of a color impossible to determine in the low
light. Her mind catalogued other details, his bare feet and worn jeans, the
shadow of unshaved beard. His hair was thick and long, of indeterminate
color. A skinny white cat sat serenely at his ankle.

Ellie looked from one to the other. "I give up," she said. "Which of
you is Dr. Reynard?"

The white man rose with a half smile. Ellie had the faint sense that
she'd been tested, but also that she'd passed. "That would be me," he said.
"You must be Miz Connor." It was a bourbon voice, smoky and gold and

dangerous, and Ellie heard the unmistakable sound of money in the blurred Southern vowels. "We've been waiting for you."

Ellie took a breath against the sudden wish to stand straighter, toss her head, somehow be prettier. "You somehow don't look the way I pictured you, Dr. Reynard," she said mildly.

"Call me Blue. Nobody calls me anything but Blue around here." He inclined his head, and a wash of that thick, wavy hair touched his shoulder. "You're not what I was expecting, either, to tell you the truth."

"I'll tell if you will."

He paused, then gave her a slow grin, one that hid all the darkness and brought out the charm. "A woman named Ellie who writes biographies says middle-aged librarian to me." The grin said he knew she'd forgive him.

"Ditto," Ellie said. "A man who spends all his free time talking trash in blues newsgroups with a whisky at his elbow—I was thinking a Keith Richards lookalike. Middle-aged and worn out."

A surprised chuckle rolled out of him. "Dissipated, maybe," he said, lifting a finger. "Worn and ragged by hard living, definitely. But I don't spend all my time on the computer. Just nighttime."

The black man laughed softly. Ellie had forgotten he was there. Reynard gestured. "Miz Connor, this is Marcus Williams."

Ellie nodded politely. "How do you do?"

He answered, "Just fine, thank you," a Southernism she'd forgotten.

"Well," Reynard said, straightening, "can I get you something? I have some sweet tea, maybe some lemonade, and"—he held up his tumbler with a sideways grin—"good Kentucky bourbon."

"Much as I'd love to, I'm going to have to say no tonight. I'd just like to get settled." From the car came a deep, pointed bark. Ellie glanced over her shoulder. "And my dog urgently wants to get out."

"No need to make him suffer." He gestured. "Go on and let him out."

"She," Ellie corrected automatically, and hesitated. "You sure?"

"She won't cause any damage my own haven't at some time or another." April, as if overhearing the conversation, let loose another sharp alert. The mutt on the porch, unable to resist any longer, rushed down the steps and licked Ellie's fingers. Reynard grinned. "Let your dog out, sugar, before she busts."

"Thank you." Ellie hurried back to the car, the mutt at her heels, and opened the door. "Come on, sweetie." April leaped out and rushed to the grass to squat with an almost bashful look of relief on her face. To keep the mutt busy, Ellie rubbed her soft gold ears. "You're kind of cute."

From the porch, the black man snorted. "Ratdog."

Ellie smiled over her shoulder. "She must belong to you, then, Dr. Reynard."

"Marcus is a dog snob, that's all. Don't mind him." He whistled softly, and the mutt ran full tilt up the stairs, halting barely in time to avoid smashing into his knees. He bent down to give her that hearty pat men seemed to always bestow on dogs. As if to claim his attention, the skinny white cat circled around his ankles and Reynard stroked her back absently.

Watching, Ellie felt a little of the vague tension in her ease. He didn't appear to be unbalanced or particularly strange—it was probably safe enough. As if he noticed, Reynard straightened and eyed her, taking a swallow of the whisky in his hand. In the dusky stillness, ice clinked. "Now that your dog's all right, are you sure you don't want something to drink?"

His voice mesmerized her, that slow rolling depth, and it took a moment before she realized he'd asked her a question.

Which was answer enough in her mind. "No, thank you. Really."

"I'll get the key, then. If you want to drive on back down the road, I'll meet you over there." He pointed through the deepening gloom toward a path that seemed to lead to the greenhouses, which glowed a soft green against the twilight.

Ellie finally spied the small house set beneath a stand of live oak and loblolly pines. She clicked her tongue for her dog. "Nice to meet you," she said to Marcus.

"Good luck with your biography."

"He told you?"

"Mabel's our only claim to fame, so we're kind of proprietary."

Ellie smiled. "I promise to do my best."

"Can't ask no more than that, I reckon."

She whistled for April and got back in the car, only realizing as she drove that she was humming under her breath. "There's a red house over yonder . . . " and her mind was playing it, the Jimi Hendrix version, threaded with that smoky sex sound that had made him such a god among women.

She rolled her eyes at her subconscious, which had an annoying habit of coughing up the most embarrassing, corny soundtrack for her life— like flying into LAX and finding herself humming "LA International Airport"—and made herself stop before he heard her.

Blue. She glanced in the rearview mirror. She wished his name were Laurence.

As he cut through the open meadow between the house and the old slave quarters, converted in the twenties to a guest house, Blue told himself it was liquor making his skin feel hot. He'd worked hard in the sun all day, the warmest they'd had so far. Probably had a little sunburn. And the bourbon on an empty stomach had gone to his head.

But as Ellie stepped out of the car at the guest house, he found his attention snared again. She was not his usual type. He liked soft, shapely blondes. Women who wore gauzy sundresses you could see through just a little bit. Women with easy laughter and soft edges and no causes to champion. The less serious the better.

Bimbos, Marcus called them. Blue preferred to think of them as easy to get along with.

Either way, Ellie Connor did not fit the profile. Small and too thin, with angles instead of softness, khaki shorts instead of floaty skirts, and curly black hair that fell in her face instead of that swing of blonde he found so appealing. From her posts, he'd known she was strong and smart and knew her mind, an impression reinforced now by the set of her chin and the sharp, no-nonsense way she met their eyes back there. It wouldn't surprise him at all if she had a revolver in the glove box—she struck him as a woman who wouldn't leave much up to fate.

But even she had to struggle, trying to lift a big suitcase out of the trunk.

Blue stepped forward. "Let me get that for you."

"Thank you."

He grabbed it while she picked up some other things and followed him to the porch, waiting behind him silently as he unlocked the door. Inside, he flipped on the lamp by the desk. "This is it. Small, but comfortable."

She put a soft-sided case on the table. "It's beautiful," she said, and it sounded sincere.

"Thought you'd like it," Blue said, shoving hair out of his eyes. "I took the liberty of dragging out some of the material we talked about"—he pointed to a neat stack of books and files on the desk—"and had Lanie—she's my aunt, who lives with me—order some groceries to be delivered. She got most of the staples, coffee and milk and things, but if there's something you don't see, just holler. Nearest store is about five miles down the road, back the way you came."

For a moment, she just looked around her. In a lazy way, he zeroed in on that mouth again. She might not be his type in a lot of ways, but that was one hell of a mouth. Bee-stung, his mama would have said.

The light was better in here, and he could see the exotic cast to her features, a faint tilt to her eyes, high cheekbones; together with all that glossy black hair it made him think maybe Russian or East European.

"Ah!" she said suddenly, and moved across the room to the counter, putting her hands on a CD player. "Excellent. I carry a portable with me, but this is much better." She turned, and looked straight at him. "It's really very nice of you to offer your hospitality this way," she said, and a knowing glitter by her eyes. "Although I suspect you were drinking when you extended the invitation."

Blue winced. "Guilty." Not unusual of a late evening, which was when he generally signed on to the Internet, looking for a good argument. "How'd you know?"

"Your notes have a different tone. And you transpose letters."

He crossed his arms, smiling to cover his discomfort. "Here I thought I was being so sly, and all the time, I might as well have been hootin' in some club."

"Not exactly. It was really just a guess."

"Well, bourbon or not, I was sincere. The place is yours as long as you need it. I'm glad you're doing the biography. It's long overdue."

"And whatever the circumstances, I'm grateful. I really hate looking for a place to keep April, and I won't leave her in a kennel."

At the sound of her name, the dog swept her tail over the hardwood floor. "That speaks well of you, Miz Connor."

She looked at him, all calm sober eyes, and Blue looked back, and all the months of notes back and forth rose up between them. He'd liked her sharpness, a certain diffidence edged with wry humor. They'd stuck mainly to discussing the blues, but every so often, they'd go off on a sidetrack and he'd catch an intriguing glimpse of something more: a hint of anger, or maybe just passion, mixed in with the steadiness.

"It's really a shock to see how different you are from how I imagined you," he said impulsively.

Something flickered in her eyes, there and gone so fast he couldn't really place it, before she tucked her hands in her back pockets and turned her face away. A sliver of gold light from the lamp edged her jaw, and Blue found himself thinking he liked that clean line. She had very fine skin. It made him think of the petals of an orchid in one of the greenhouses. "Ditto," she said, and again raised her head and looked at him with that directness.

He wasn't used to women who looked so straight at him.

As if she thought better of it, she moved to the table and unzipped the soft-sided case, revealing dozens of CDs in their plastic cases, and scooped up a handful. It was a restless gesture, the kind of thing a person did to fill up an awkward moment, and Blue realized he ought to take the hint and leave her to settle in.

But a person's taste in music said more about them than they ever realized, and he couldn't resist peeking into the case. "What do you have here?" He pointed. "Mind if I look?"

"No. Of course not."

The CDs were piled in a jumble. "They have cases now that'll stack 'em up for you."

She made a rueful noise. "Yes, but they don't carry enough." She smiled at him, a quick bright flash. "I need my dog and my CDs to feel secure."

He lowered his head, oddly unsettled. He looked at the titles, wondering if he really wanted to know that much more about her, but he didn't stop sorting through them. Blues, of course. He *tsked* and took out a Lightnin' Hopkins recording, shaking his head.

She plucked it out of his hands. "You've made your feelings plain about the Delta style, Dr. Reynard. Unhand my classics."

He grinned. They'd had quite an argument about various styles. Blue didn't like the tinny sound of Delta, and she didn't care for jazz, which he considered just short of sacrilege. "Gonna have to turn you on to some good jazz, darlin'," he murmured, and bent back to the case.

Besides the blues, there was a huge variety. A little alternative rock and roll, some country he thought of as "story" songs, some classical. "Baroque, huh?" he said, pulling out a couple of cases from that period and flipping them over to look at the lists.

A flicker of surprise crossed her face. "You like it?"

"You sound surprised, sugar." He tossed the CDs back, the unsettled feeling growing along the back of his neck. "A man might say the same about you. Never saw you in the other music newsgroups."

"Do you visit others?"

"Some." That made him think about her comments on his drinking when he posted. Embarrassing. "Well," he said, straightening. "I guess I'll leave you alone. In the morning, I'll be glad to take you around town—show you where the library is, and introduce you to some of the folks who might have some stories to tell."

"You don't have to put yourself out, Dr. Reynard."

"Blue."

"Blue," she repeated. "I'm sure I can find my way around."

"I'm sure you can. But things'll go better if you let me take you." He lifted a shoulder. "It's a small town."

Still, she hesitated. Then, "All right. I'll see you in the morning."

"Don't let the bedbugs bite," he said. On the way out, he paused to scratch April's ear.

Out in the night, with lightning bugs winking all through the grass,

Blue stopped, feeling a little off-balance. He put a hand to his ribs and took in some air, then blew it out and shook his shoulders a little. In his mind's eye, he saw the bulging, soft-sided case and the big, well-trained dog. Security, she'd said. Music and a dog. Security for Miss Ellie Connor with the tough set of her shoulders and her head-on way of looking at him.

He shook his head. Probably just a case of the girls looking prettier at closing time. He needed some food, some sleep. But when he stepped back up on the porch, he said, "She's not just into the blues. She's got classical in there. And REM. Even some Reba McEntire."

Marcus nodded and wordlessly handed him a fresh glass of bourbon, an offering of solace.

Blue drank it down, taking refuge in the burn, then poured another and put the bottle down on the wooden floor of the porch. After a long space of time, filled only with the lowering depths of the night and the faint squeak of the porch swing, he rubbed his ribs again.

"Not one of your bimbos there, that's for sure," Marcus said.

"No, I don't think so."

"Hell of a mouth."

"Yep." Blue drank.

A dark, rolling laugh boomed into the quiet. "Oh, how the mighty do fall!"

"Not my type."

"Mmmm. I saw that." Marcus stood and put his glass on a wicker table. He pulled his keys out of his pocket. "I think I'll go curl up with my woman."

"Hell with you, Marcus."

Laughter was the only reply.

EXCERPT FROM

JEZEBEL'S BLUES

By Barbara Samuel

Prologue

It wasn't a big river. Mainly it ran sleepily and quietly through a sparsely populated stretch of farmland in east Texas. Fishermen angled for the catfish skimming its depths; young boys stripped and skinny-dipped in its pools; lovers picnicked on its banks.

Only a handful of old-timers remembered the old name for the sleepy river—a name murmured in hushed voices as stories were told of her power.

Jezebel.

Not the Jezebel River. Just Jezebel, a name reserved for women of lusty beauty and uncertain virtue. *Jezebel.*

There had only been one occasion in recent memory when Jezebel had awakened, like an aging courtesan, to remind those around her of the power she could wield. Only one life was lost that night, and as if placated by the sacrifice, Jezebel settled back into her sleep.

But the old-timers knew it was only a matter of time until she awakened once again to flash her eyes and spread her skirts.

Only a matter of time.

— 1 —

Not even hell could be so dark. His car headlights poked white fingers into the heavy rain, barely penetrating. The wiper blades sluiced the water away at a furious pace. It wasn't enough. Only square inches of the windshield were clear at any instant—as soon as the blades slogged away the rain, more fell to blur his vision once again.

He'd slowed to twenty on the back country road and was no longer intimately familiar with the twists of blacktop and the tiny bridges that spanned dozens of creeks. His fingers ached from gripping the steering wheel. He hunched as far forward in his seat as he could go, trying vainly to see.

Storm warnings had been broadcast on the radio, of course. But he'd grown up in these thick woods, amid the floods and endless early-summer rains. He knew the television and radio people were prone to exaggeration. It sold papers and commercial time.

The car slid on the road, its tires unable to keep a grip on the pavement. Eric swore as he fought for control. It made sense to ignore the news people, but he probably ought to have listened to the boy in grease-stained overalls at the gas station twenty miles back.

But there was his pride to consider. Nothing scared him like driving in the rain, in the dark. A night like this had once shattered his life, and he knew instinctively that he would be truly lost if he let the fear overtake him tonight.

Doggedly, he kept driving. A green sign with reflective white letters flashed in front of his lights. The words blurred before Eric could read them, but he knew what the sign said: Gideon, 5 miles. Almost there. With the back of his wrist, he wiped the sweat from his brow. For once in his life, he wished he'd paid attention—he'd have been a whole lot better off staying overnight in a motel in the last town. He sure as hell couldn't do much for his sister if he drowned out here.

His headlights picked out a wash of water pouring over a bridge just ahead. A new row of sweat beads broke out on his upper lip and he eased his foot from the accelerator. Sucking in his breath, he touched the brake. Easy, he told himself. His weakened fingers, slick with sweat, slid on the hard plastic steering wheel.

In spite of his care, the car hit the water with a hollow sounding *thunk*. *Easy now*. It wasn't the first creek he'd forded on this nightmarish trip. Every little trickle in the county was brimming over tonight.

But this one had more than bubbled over. Eric saw the nearby pond with which the stream had mated, and the offspring of their union looked like an inland sea. Through the side window of the car, he saw an unbroken span of water reflecting the oddly misplaced light of a farmer's barn.

The engine spluttered and coughed. Died. He slammed his good hand against the dash. When the car swayed under the force of the water that rose over its fenders, fear squeezed his belly hard. No time to brood.

He reached over the back of the seat, grabbing the heavy canvas backpack that held most of his earthly goods. Next to it was a guitar in a black case. He hesitated, fingers curled around the slim, plastic handle. A shiver of water shook the car.

He let go. It was no good to him anymore, anyway. It took a mighty heave to get the door open and then the water nearly knocked him down. Another flash of adrenaline sizzled over his nerves. Falling rain soaked his head and body in seconds. Shifting the backpack on his shoulders, he sloshed forward, head down. A big, broken tree branch swirled by him on the current.

Scared, man?

Damned right, he answered himself, putting one foot determinedly in front of the other. As he gained the other side of the bridge, the water gradually receded until it just covered the bottoms of his feet.

The little triumph pleased him. Only five miles to Gideon, to his sister, the only person in the world who mattered to him. And she needed him. It was bound to be easier to get to her on foot than in the car. So he ignored the beckoning lights of the farmhouse set back in the heavy trees and pushed onward into the thick, rainy darkness.

He trudged a mile. Two. He lost track. He crossed one stream, sloshing through water up to his knees, and when he got to the other side, he found the stream came with him, up to his ankles.

He thought about going back to the farmhouse, shook his head, and pushed on.

One foot in front of the other. Water obscured the road, making it hard to keep his bearings. He paused once to peer into the darkness, trying to mark familiar spots. There were none.

He reached into his backpack for a bottle of Jack Daniel's and slugged back a considerable mouthful. It warmed his chilled insides, calmed his racing heart. Thus fortified, he replaced the bottle, wiped water from his eyes and started out again. Not far now.

Celia Moon was making popcorn when the lights suddenly failed. For several hours she'd been trying to resist food—since the rains had set in several days ago, her main activity had been eating. But the pervasive thought of butter and salt and fluffy white corn had proved impossible to resist.

The sudden failure of the lights seemed like a scolding from on high—but not even heaven could make her quit now. There was enough heat left in the electric burner to finish the popping. The butter was already melted and the bowl was ready. If she had to sit alone in the gloomy darkness of the old farmhouse, reading by candlelight, at least she'd have some buttered popcorn to comfort herself with.

Working easily in the dark, she pulled the bowl over as the bubbling sound of exploding kernels slowed, then lifted the heavy pan from the stove and aimed as well as she could. There would doubtless be popcorn strewn all over the table in the morning, but since she lived alone, what did it really matter?

She did need a light to pour the butter. There were candles in a drawer by the sink and Celia lit one. A piney scent rose from the plump green candle and mixed with the smell of hot popcorn.

The whole elaborate ritual was designed to be a distraction from the endless pattering of the rain on the roof and windows. Endless. "A hurricane caught in a holding pattern over the Gulf," they had said on the news. Rain was forecast for tomorrow as well.

It was depressing. She'd been stuck inside the house for days, cleaning like a madwoman out of boredom when she should have been planting her first garden. A salad garden to start with, scallions and radishes and lettuce. Collards, maybe. Definitely popcorn. Her grandmother had always grown popcorn, sending big bags of it every fall to Celia in Brussels or Paris or Berlin, wherever her parents' travels had taken them.

A sudden, urgent pounding on the front door crashed into the rain-framed silence. Celia started, sending butter spilling over the whole table. She scowled at the mess. The knock sounded again, louder this time.

Who in the world would be out on such a night? She headed for the door, shaking her head, then realized she couldn't see anything without her candle and went back for it. The pounding rattled through the room again.

"I'm coming," she muttered under her breath. She grabbed a handful of popcorn as she picked up the candle, then ran lightly toward the door, her candle flame bobbing with her steps.

She flung open the door—and nearly flung it just as quickly closed. The man on the porch was soaking wet. No, not just soaking.

Dripping. Awash. Streams flowed from the pack on his shoulders and from his hair. A cut on his lip was bleeding profusely, and he was panting. "I—got—stranded," he managed to say, and stumbled forward, catching himself on the doorjamb.

Celia jumped back, alarmed. It was impossible to see much about him by the light of her single candle, but he was big. A stranger. He also smelled distinctly of whiskey.

He straightened and licked his lips. "I was trying to get to town, but that last creek nearly took me with it."

Celia hesitated a moment more—measuring the weight of the storm against the big man who obviously wanted shelter. His voice, ragged and hoarse, was definitely local, with a certain, unmistakable cadence that marked him as a native. She didn't think she'd ever seen him, but that didn't mean much. She'd only been in town a few months, and small as it was, Gideon played county seat to a lot of farms.

She stepped back. "My grandmother would never forgive me for turning away a stranger in trouble. Come on in."

The relief on his face, even in the dark, was unmistakable. "Much obliged. I won't be any trouble."

"Wet as you are, I'll be lucky if you don't die of pneumonia before morning." She sized him up, thinking quickly. "Stay right there. I'll get you something dry to put on."

"You don't have to do that," he protested.

"Don't be ridiculous." She headed for the back room, leaving the candle for him. He hovered near the door.

There wasn't much to choose from, but Celia found an old pair of overalls of her grandfather's and a shirt she was sure would be too small. Might not fit well, but it would be better than freezing to death.

The stranger still stood right by the door when she returned. A puddle had formed under his feet. His outer garment, a long vinyl poncho, had been shed, and the big pack rested against the wall.

The lights flashed on again, so suddenly they startled Celia. In the blazing, unexpected illumination, she stared at the man by the door. It was only by sheer force of will that she kept her mouth from dropping open. Men like this never walked into her quiet life. They crossed movie screens and album covers; they rode bucking horses in rodeos and raced cars in the Indy.

They didn't appear on her porch in rural Texas in the middle of a rainstorm.

His hair was black as sin and already curling around his neck and ears. The face was broad and dark, with high cheekbones and heavy brows over thick-lashed eyes. Amid all the masculine angles and jutting corners, his mouth was uncommon and compelling, even with a bloody cut obscuring it. The lower lip was full, sensual; the upper cut into an exquisite firm line.

There was only an instant for her to absorb the lines of his body, for the lights flashed off as quickly as they'd come on.

She laughed a little breathlessly, not quite sure whether the sound stemmed from excitement or fear. "Well, that was fast. I wonder if we're going to be treated to a light show."

"Somebody at the plant better get smart quick and turn everything off," he said, "or there's likely to be fires all over the county."

The man shivered and Celia hurriedly gave him the clothes. "I'll wait in the kitchen."

Standing there in the dark, nibbling popcorn from the bowl on the table, she wondered if she was completely insane. The world was not the same place her grandmother had lived in, although Celia supposed there had always been serial killers and rapists roaming the countryside. Computers had just made it simpler to track them down. The thought made her smile briefly.

The stranger's voice, with its odd edge of roughness, sounded directly behind her. "Jezebel's acting up tonight," he said.

"Jezebel?" Celia echoed, turning.

He'd brought the candle with him, and the light cast eerie shadows over the hollows of his face. She saw a grizzling of dark beard on his chin and top lip. It added an even more rakish appearance to his rugged face. Celia frowned at the blood on his mouth. "You're bleeding," she said, and reached into a drawer for a dishcloth.

Distractedly, he pressed the cloth to the cut, then lifted it and licked the spot experimentally. "I didn't even feel this," he commented.

Celia lifted the candle closer to his face, and understanding her intention, he lowered the dishrag. "You probably need a stitch or two," she said. "But it looks like you'll have to live without them until morning."

"I've lived through worse."

There was no boast in the words, just a simple statement of fact. Celia realized she was still standing next to him, the candle held aloft, peering at his face for clues to his nature like the heroine in a Gothic novel. She put the candle on the table. "Who's Jezebel?" she asked.

"The river. That's what the old-timers call her."

"Why?"

"Because," the man said, cocking his head a bit ironically, "she's as dangerous as a faithless and beautiful woman." He spied the popcorn and pointed. "You mind?"

"Help yourself." Celia ladled up a handful for herself. "Pretty sexist.

Why isn't she like a faithless man?"

A slow grin spread over his face. "Because no man alive can outsmart a wise and evil woman—and the old-timers knew it."

His voice, low and husky, acted like moonshine on her spine, easing the muscles all the way down. She straightened. "What makes you think she's acting up?"

"I've seen her do it." He glanced toward the window, as though the river was a banshee about to scream through the night. "Unless it stops raining right now, she's coming."

Celia frowned and crossed to the window. It was dark—inky dark. The pond in the hollow had crept up another four or five inches, and she thought she could see a fine film of water all over the saturated ground. "It's been flooding for weeks," she said. "Everyone says that happens every year."

"They like to forget about old Jezebel." He shifted. "Legends aside, this is a flood plain, and the river runs in cycles. She's gonna flood and you'd best be on high ground when she does."

"There's an attic here if I need it."

He scooped up another big handful of popcorn. "Is it stocked?"

She shrugged. "Sort of." She pursed her lips. "Do you think the river's going to overflow tonight?"

He wandered to the window, and as he stood next to her, looking out at the rain, Celia realized he was much, much larger than she. What if all this talk of a flood was just a way to get her up into the attic to ravish her or something? She crossed her arms over her chest, smelling whiskey and something deeper, a scent of hot nights that she tried to ignore. There was no law that said serial killers were ugly and hard to get along with. In fact, how did any of them get close to their victims unless they possessed a certain—well, animal magnetism that promised erotic rewards in return for trust?

But his voice was so very grim when he spoke again that Celia had no doubt that he was telling the truth. "She's coming," he said, the dread in his voice unmistakable.

Suddenly, from the depths of childhood came a memory. Celia had awakened thirsty and padded into the bathroom for a drink of water. On her way back to her room, she heard her father in his office, shouting into the phone. Curious and alarmed, she had paused by the door.

Her father had been a big man, as big as a grizzly, he liked to tell her. That night he hunched in the swivel chair by his desk, with his hair wild and his face buried in his hands. "What's wrong, Daddy?" Celia asked.

He turned in his chair and gestured for her to come sit in his lap. Then, because it had been his policy to tell Celia the truth, he said,

"There's a flood back in Texas and I can't get through to make sure Grandma's all right."

Celia didn't really understand anything else about the incident, but obviously, Grandma had been fine. She'd only died last year—in her sleep.

Thinking of it now, though, she realized the river had probably flooded then. "Okay," she said, taking a breath. "Jezebel's going to flood. Since you're here, you can help me lug things up to the attic." She crossed the room, taking the candle with her, and opened the oak cupboard by the sink.

"What happened to the old woman, Mrs. Moon, who used to live here?" the stranger asked as Celia took cans and boxes from the shelf.

"She died last year." Celia flashed him a grin out of proportion to his statement. Relief made her sigh. If he had known her grandmother, he wasn't likely to be a serial killer.

"Are you kin?"

"I'm her granddaughter. She left me the house."

He nodded, chewing popcorn. "What's your name, granddaughter?"

"Celia." She glanced at the nearly empty bowl. "You made short work of that popcorn. Are you hungry?"

"Celia Moon." His drawl and the ragged edge of his voice made her name sound beautiful. "I'm Eric Putman and I'm starving."

She tossed him a box of crackers and found the peanut butter. "That'll have to do for a little while." His name sounded vaguely familiar, but when she couldn't place it, she let it go. There weren't many names she hadn't heard on her grandmother's lips at one time or another. For a nice old woman, she'd been the world's champion gossip—not mean, for there was always an undercurrent of understanding in the way she told her stories, even when the preacher of the Methodist church fell in love with the choir director, who was then only seventeen, and ran off to Louisiana with her. "You must be from around here," Celia commented.

"Born and raised."

A harsh undernote told her he'd been glad to escape. A common attitude. She was the only one who'd run to Gideon instead of away. And the funny thing was, they were running to the very places she had left behind, places whose very names promised glamour. "You've been gone awhile," she said.

"Yep." He dropped the peanut butter and crackers into the box with the other food. "You have any other candles? I can get some blankets and stuff if you'll tell me where to look."

She dug in a drawer, and just as she was about to light the candle, a massive flash of lightning shimmered over the sky, a pale electric blue that seemed to hang for minutes in the darkness. On its heels came a crack of thunder so loud, it rattled the dishes.

As if a hole had been cut in the sky by the violent thunder, the noise of the rain suddenly doubled, then tripled. Celia gasped. "I didn't think it could rain any harder!" She went to the window and looked out, laughing lightly. "It looks like there's a thousand garden hoses going at once."

Eric grabbed the candle. "Where are those blankets?" His voice was gruff.

"Under the stairs." She pointed vaguely. Her attention was focused on the deluge. It excited her. A part of her wanted to run outside into that beating, pounding rain, just to feel it and taste it. Nature run amok, she thought. Humans were helpless in the face of it. A savage kind of joy raced through her at the thought.

"Come on, woman," Eric growled. "Won't take Jezebel long to flash her eyes now."

Of course, she probably wanted to *live* through whatever was coming. Time enough to observe the drama when everything was safely prepared.

Celia tried to ignore the ripple of excitement that passed through her at the thought of observing the drama with Eric Putman nearby.

Acknowledgments

This book was a very long time in gestation, as some books just seem to need. It was born one hot afternoon in St. Louis, when James Samuel, a black man in his seventies, began to tell me about his experiences in Italy in World War II. Until he told me, I had no idea that the United States fought Hitler with a segregated army. It seemed so astonishing, so hypocritical, I found myself inhaling every detail I could dig up about the subject. Ultimately, I found my story in the moment the American army became DE-segregated, at the Battle of the Bulge, a moment that led irrevocably to the desegregation of the South. Isaiah's story is only one possible journey—there are many thousands of others, and they are well worth reading. One book I found invaluable for tone and progress was Fighting in the Jim Crow Army, by Maggie M. Morehouse.

Many other people played a part in the gestation and writing. Sharon Lynn High Williams for early reads and encouragement, Barbara Keiler for another critical read later, and Deb Smith, my editor at BelleBooks, for believing in a romance novel like this one. I also want to thank my Samuel relatives, who were heavily in my thoughts as I wrote, especially James and Lurelean, whose stories helped flesh out my understanding of the south in the 30's and 40's. Their values of honor, truth, and hard work shaped my life and that of their grandchildren, my sons Ian and Miles. We would all be lesser humans without your influence.

Finally, thanks to my readers, who so willingly follow me wherever my imagination decides to go, from the middle ages to WWII to the current day. You have no idea how grateful I am for each one of you, and I love to hear from you. Please send me email at awriterafoot@gmail.com, or friend me on Facebook: facebook.com/BarbaraSamuelONeal.

About The Author

Barbara Samuel is a multiple award-winning author with more than 38 books to her credit in a variety of genres. She has written historical and contemporary romances, a number of fantasy novellas with the likes of Susan Wiggs, Jo Beverley and Mary Jo Putney. She now writes women's fiction about families, dogs, and food as Barbara O'Neal.

Her work has captured a plethora of awards, including six RITAs; the Colorado Center for the Book Award (twice); Favorite Book of the Year from Romance Writers of America, and the Library Journal's list of Best Genre Fiction of the year, among many others.

CPSIA information can be obtained at www.ICGtesting.com
Printed in the USA
LVOW050735010712

288345LV00004B/3/P